Beverley Farmer was born in Melbourne in 1941. A graduate of Melbourne University, she married a Greek migrant in 1965 and for some years lived in his village in Greece with his family. During this time she wrote her first book, *Alone* (1980). The short story collections *Milk* (1983) and *Home Time* (1985) draw upon her experience of Greece. Her more recent works are *A Body of Water* (1990), part fiction, part writer's notebook, and the novels *The Seal Woman* (1992) and *The House in the Light* (1995).

Also by Beverley Farmer

Alone
Milk
Home Time
Place of Birth
A Body of Water
The Seal Woman
The House in the Light

COLLECTED STORIES

BEVERLEY FARMER

University of Queensland Press

First published 1996 by University of Queensland Press
Box 42, St Lucia, Queensland 4067 Australia

Typeset by University of Queensland Press
Printed in Australia by McPherson's Printing Group

Distributed in the USA and Canada by
International Specialized Book Services, Inc.,
5804 N.E. Hassalo Street, Portland, Oregon 97213–3640

Cataloguing in Publication Data
National Library of Australia

ISBN 0 7022 2889 3

CONTENTS

GERONTISSA

It has been another cold sunny winter's afternoon, dripping dead leaves in sodden gutters.

I see myself move through the shifting darknesses in these rooms like an amber glow, *une lueur ambrée*, in Melbourne, of all places. City of my birth, city of the dispossessed. I drowse, in this as in other rooms, like one already dead: an aura among shabby furnishings. My various faces evolve in mirrors downy with dust. Nowadays, I see, I am embedded in a mask of wrinkles, sprouting a white whisker or two on the chin, blotched with brown stains and magenta clotted veins on nose and cheeks. Shadows well in the ripples round my eyeballs. Age has congealed on me like wax.

In the lamplit street the sun, to my dim eyes, is splashed with waves of darkening blood, pale and drowning in blood. *'Le soleil s'est noyé comme un oeil qui se fige.'* No, that's not it. *'Le soleil s'est noyé dans son sang qui se fige.'* A yellow eye, an egg-yolk, blood-botched. I used to know pages of Baudelaire by heart when I was a young girl, even before I went to Paris. I stole my father's copy from under the musty shoes in his wardrobe to transcribe poems from *Les Fleurs du Mal.* I had it in Venice after his death and must have lost it there. At dusk along the back canals lights splash and dwindle, lamps in the windows of decaying tenements are lapped with water. Far below me lie shaken images of windows, as if in sunken basements. *Les bâtiments engloutis.* On a fretted bridge the shape of a woman dressed in black stands gazing at me with amber eyes.

For many years I have walked about my city alone, robed in drab black, passing for an old woman long before I was. I repulsed the eyes of strangers in the streets. Now I am embedded once and for all in old flesh, and crowned with a white frizzle on a pink pate, I who wore diamonds and pearls. One jewel I have left: a necklace of perfect amber. 'To match your eyes,' the giver said. It hangs like a cord of dry honey about my wattles, my blue-tinged dewlaps. It was a string of worry beads originally, a *komboloï*, dappled and lucent and more precious to me than any metal. It is none of your business how I came by it. I wear it day and night. I intend to go to the grave in it, if my last wishes are respected as they should be.

I had many lovers, some rich; and two husbands. Now I have mirrors on every wall and never dust them. My eyes have in any case been blurring lately. In sunlight they look to me as deep as water, flecked with green and brown. When I sit out in the sun, my eyes make swollen drops of dew flash in the grass with iridescent spokes and webs. Once a shower of rain drenched the heavy curtain of dust and sun. A rainbow spanned the sky.

I often sit by my window like this in the late sun, sipping Turkish coffee. I have an ancient primus in my room, against the rules but I keep it hidden. It is copper, with a cylindrical brass tank for kerosene, and burns harshly with a sharp blue flame. Laboriously I stir the sugar and the thick soft coffee in a small brass pot, more, I grant you, for old time's sake than for its muddy taste. Picture me sitting by my crusted window pane, ancient and massive, gowned in black, a tiny *café turc* perched in my bulbous fingers. I am quite aware of my absurdity. I make a note of it. I have not reached conclusion.

Gerontion, yes. You knew. I knew a lot of poetry by heart when I was a girl. I might be his female counterpart, *Gerontissa*, let's say, though no philosopher. I was a sensualist. No contact was ever close enough. I lived in Greece for a while and learned to speak Greek well: I was married to a Greek. He was the first of the husbands that I started to tell you about before mirrors distracted me.

Panagiotis was dark all over, and covered with black hairs. He had singed eyes like those of the Christ in ikons. I married him on impulse soon after we met, in the grip of a lust from which we woke exhausted every morning, wrapped in the damp sheet, still enlaced. We lived in his mountain village of whitewashed houses with lichen on green slate roofs. When autumn came we ate walnuts and glossy roast chestnuts by the fire, and sipped raw new red wine like a flame in the glass. Hidden in the fog all day donkeys minced clattering down the cobbled street, saddle bags crammed with chestnuts, to the *kafeneion* and beyond. The *kafeneion* was on a platform overhanging a cliff, high above the glittering port and the gulf. Great trees shivering in mist, an icy spring. Women, decent women, sat in whitewashed kitchens gossiping and embroidering by the *somba,* the stove; they couldn't go to the *kafeneion* in those days. After church one Sunday I dressed up in my husband's second-best suit, sauntered in among the dour men playing *tavli,* and ordered an ouzo. A silly prank, it was greeted with outrage. In our shuttered bedroom with its gold-leaf ikon Panagiotis tore his clothes off me, beat and then raped me. The marriage ended soon after in a miscarriage. I wrote to Anne to meet me in, of all places, Lesbos. Bravado, yes, why not?

I had many many lovers in my time, Anne, my darling. I had my share of pleasure. I resigned myself to solitude only when my mirrors left me in no doubt that I was old and ugly, though hale — praise be to God, as they say — and hearty still. Only my eyes stayed young and clear, too clear.

Now I remember the sun's red eye. *Un oeil sanglant.* Yes.

Où camme un oeil sanglant qui palpite et qui bouge,
La lampe sur le jour fait une tache rouge.

That must be the morning poem, though. *Le Crépuscule du matin.* My father, who was a Parisian born, once met Guy de Maupassant. My father taught me French from childhood and filled my head with visions of cobbled streets by gaslight and trees turning to rust in the evening mist. There were aunts and uncles, first and second cousins, all over France. *'Oh, notre pauvre Paul! Et c'est toi sa fille, ma petite?'* And in Ravenna was his rich old Zia Livia in her splendour. Anne was a second cousin on his mother's side, Anne who always wore men's formal dress, and loved me, and drowned. How my mind wanders these winter nights.

At the darkening window I rim my eyes with kohl, as I have always done. I prepare a face, a sur-face, looming at me in the pane, black-rimmed heavy eyes and bright red withered lips over my bare gums. I know it is absurd. All is vanity. I do it for the girl under the wax mask. For her sake, too, I pour wine from the heavy flagon, shake it into a glass. I always loved dry golden wine. It sinks into my belly like cold fire, and may well be the death of me one day. There are crueller deaths. I expected to attain ease and amplitude in ripe old age, a benign calm to suffuse my last nights, as sunlight and wine do the days. I have attained only detachment. Solitude.

I find it harder to propel my tremulous masses through the grey streets these days. The landlady gets me my bread and milk, bless her. My ankles swell. My hands and feet are always frozen white. Ills and aches and pains assail me. Indignant at decay, I totter home of an evening clutching a heavy flagon under the cold red sky.

I spend a lot of time in the Botanical Gardens. I go by tram. Autumn and winter are best, when the leaves drip on the lily pads. I love spotted lantanas and the pods and wet bronze leaves of the Moreton Bay figs. On my bench under a moulting willow I sit in a black veil dipping my hooked fingers and nose into my *petit point* bag for bread scraps. Black swans with red-striped faces emerge splashing and lumber up on their webbed toes to snap at my fingers. I am an old beached sea-lion clutching crusts. I am the Bird Woman. Grey pigeons cling with tiny claws to my arms and knuckles. They have a gloss of green and magenta on their necks, and their throats press soft and warm on my blotched numb hands. One sidles up my shoulder to peer avidly at the jelly of my eyeball. I shake it away. Gulls squall and hunch. There are great flurries of birds and flashing water. *Puissance et délire.* Sun-sodden, I drowse.

Nets drying like leaves on a far sea wall. The pull and suck of waves rolling the grey stones at the water's edge. The late sun burns heavy on tiers of stone houses, on the crenellated castle walls. We swim slowly through the shaking sunlit images: on the green pebbles deep below, our shadows are outlined with bubbles of light.

As I watch in stupor Anne sinks slowly twisting and dwindling down to the sea floor, her black hair strung like seaweed about her silent gaping mouth.

I wake jolted with such anguish that I cannot move. Anne, my darling.

Molyvo, on Lesbos. A clifftop town of grey stone houses, crowned with a castle. I remember a cobbled arcade of cool stone and wisteria. Mornings on the balcony over the hazed blue gulf, with Turkish coffee and red felt peaches, liquid inside. Clay chimney pots and a white bell tower. A yard with white cylindrical fretty cheeses, *myzithra,* drying in the sun, and greasy wool in heaps, dun, white, black. A procession passes, bearded priests in black robes chanting, swinging smoke from censers; a *despotis* in embroidered silks bearing in a casket encrusted with gold-leaf the skull of the patron saint. A rooster and his hens at moonrise sprawled asleep on a stack of olive logs.

While I slept on in the shuttered heat one morning, Anne drowned in that clear sea. Fishermen thumped her, roped and sodden, out of the *kaïki* on to the stone sea wall. I cannot accept death.

We had eaten the night before in a *taverna,* on a high balcony hung with lamps and pots of basil. The far lights of fishing *kaïkia* flitted and slid on the black sea. A rowing boat below us lit a lantern in the shallows. The black image of a man with a spear stood in the prow. High above the clear stones of the sea bed it floated, trailing instead of a wake the throbbing reflection of the lantern. A waiter brought plump sardines and whitebait, wizened olives and peppered white cheese glazed with oil. We sat in silence and munched coarse yellow bread, sipped the cold island wine, picked grey flakes from the corpses of sardines. White beads of eyes and tiny clenched teeth. Lean cats twined glaring about our feet.

We were quarrelling, and she wept. I had been to bed with a neighbour, a fisherman. All right, so it was true, but it meant nothing! I stank of him. Fish, petrol, tobacco, sweat. I was a whore. I made her sick. She never wanted to see my face again.

She walked out, then. I sat on alone to finish my cheese and olives and all the wine, to the last drop. The rowing boat in its pool of light had drifted to the far stone ring of the harbour wall, where it lay like a fallen moon.

I turn on the table lamp and sit in its glow watching a tomato, its golden seeds spilling; a dish of brown beans; wine pure as glass.

Wine chills my mouth and throat. It calms my solitude. I munch cold glossy beans, a waxen lump of cheese, tomato slices, and sop chunks of yellow cornbread in the juice. Food is good, but wine is sunlight distilled. Wine is life.

I have been going through my papers these last days, rereading everything as I doze at my sunny window hour by hour, before I throw them away. I had kept letters, sheaves of poems copied in faded copperplate, Baudelaire, Yeats, Eliot, Rimbaud, Cavafy; old posed photographs and sketches; mementoes, dried flowers, cards; notes jotted in forgotten streets. These few pages are all that I intend to leave behind, as proof that there was more to me than cold flesh stiffening in black rags on a rented bed.

The dusty *odalisque* in oils hanging on the wall is mine. The landlady may have it, unless it scandalises her. A keepsake from my Paris days, *une femme lubrique.* Immersed in the paint, she is still long, sumptuous and shadowed, spread along the bed as if congealed, and stroked by tongues of candelight. At her throat, an amber necklace. She has a nest of dark hairs above her thighs; a green bottle and a candle by her side. She sips from a flute glass.

I pour another glass of floating wine.

Marcel is dead, who painted it: and here am I. There is no one left who can remember me. I think he had little talent, and he drank and took drugs. I found him waxen and gaunt on the bare mattress, blotched with cold vomit, urine, blood. I sponged and dressed him, washed his stale clothes and hung them round the room to dry, cadged bones and bruised vegetables for soup which I spoon-fed him. *Une Garde-malade paur l'amour de l'art.* In the end I left him, taking the painting with me.

My other husband, Tom, a journalist, brought me back to Melbourne just before war was declared forty years ago. Then there were teas and date scones by suburban firesides. Picnics in the tea-tree. I remember tram rides to the wooden Baths, and the flat red bay at sunset aglow with wet street lamps. Tom was shot in New Guinea. I have lived on and on. I have been many women in my time. There is much I could remember. But to what purpose?

An old man I often see trudging about alone has a look of my Tom about him. He has long gingery-white hair down to his wrinkled collar, a rough grey beard, slumped tweed shoulders, notebooks sprouting from his pockets. From time to time he scrawls in one. Passers-by stare. I scrawl notes, too, hobbling in the windy streets — was Melbourne always so windy? — my memory being frail now. I wonder what he writes, and where he lives. I figure to myself his rooms, his stove, his wash-troughs, his bed. I look at the lights of shaded lamps hanging in windows.

After the war I sailed back to Europe and the ruined opulence of remembered cities. *Le sombre Paris.* I worked when I had to, in hotels, eating houses, bars. Exiled in this sagging flesh, slowly I felt my heart stiffen and grow old and brittle, tired of the complexities of love. I embraced solitude.

I have forgotten when and why I came home to Melbourne, of all places; and to this house. I have lived in this one room for so long now that I am bounded by it as if by an old skin.

My long sash window faces the sun. A grey net hangs over it, and dusty cobwebs draped in a festoon. I have nailed a sugar bag across at shoulder height, since I leave the ceiling lamp on all day and half the night; but the top pane is always gold. *Une lueur dorée.* All my mirrors glint with it, mirroring me. My floor is glossy wood, with a worn square of carpet. My walls are papered with brown cabbage roses. I have a wash stand with a flowered water-jug; a table, an armchair, a sofa bed with a patchwork quilt. On the walls, a nude in a gilded frame, and many mirrors. A wardrobe with an oval mirror in its door holds my black rags, my copper primus and flagons of wine, my coffee, honey, bread, sugar. The landlady gets my groceries, bless her, and brings me hot soups in her speckled saucepan. A kindly soul, but garrulous.

The bathrooms and lavatories here are a long way down the passage. I have a china chamber pot with rosebuds on it. Taking pains not to wet my hoisted skirts and the carpet, I squat my buttocks on its cold rim. In the morning I must stagger through the dark echoes of the passage bearing at arm's length my rippling chamber pot. One night a week I take a precarious shower in the slimy bathtub, soaping my loins and my scant pate and the nest of rough hairs under each arm and between my legs. My knees shake. Warm streams of water splash down me, lap at my knobbled feet. I hasten to dry and swaddle myself again. I must not catch cold.

I sip the last of the wine: my mind is burning. Carefully, immersed in the mirror, I take off the black rags that drape me. The necklace glows on my livid bones and cords. I am humped and gnarled. The flesh that hangs off these bones looks like paint that has peeled in webs over cracked plaster. How many of us pliant women, embedded like bees in the amber of our mirrors, believed we must come to this? I turn out the lamps. In darkness, crawl between cold sheets.

I am tired of living.

BAPTISM

I held the kerosene lamp up to her face. At seventeen I was a shy and fearful young man. She looked like a slut to me, standing there on the sagging verandah, her black hair long and ragged, her face swollen and shiny, as if coated in oil. A coloured girl. Perhaps even Indian herself. I averted my eyes from her tight jeans and the heavy, dark-teated globes of her breasts in the red cheesecloth of her shirt. I suspected a practical joke, a prank to liven up a quiet Saturday night. Everyone in Sarina seemed to know that I lived like a monk in that decaying shack. St Simon the Stylite. I glanced past her at the dark trees, the far cane fields smouldering in a red glow. There was no sign of anyone. I have never enjoyed being made fun of, however, and my first impulse was to slam the door. As I hesitated she stepped back, wincing away from the lamp.

'Look, I'm sorry to bother you.' Her voice was deep, rather nasal. 'I saw your light on. Can I use your phone?'

'No, I am sorry —'

'Please! My car won't go. Just to ring up a garage.'

'I am sorry.' I lowered the lamp. 'There is no phone here.'

Her face crumpling, she turned away. I took a deep breath.

'What is wrong with your car?'

'No idea.' The lamp glinted on tears in her bloodshot eyes. 'It stopped, that's all, and it won't start.'

'I fix my motor bike myself. Maybe I can help.'

'It would have to happen now!'

'Where is the car?'

'Up there on the bend.'

'Would you like a cup of tea? You look tired out. And I'll see what I can do.'

She smiled then, in relief, perhaps, or in amusement. She might have preferred something stronger. But who can read a stranger's face? Anyway, she accepted gratefully enough.

I watched her stare around taking it all in, the wooden walls heavy with our shadows in the wavering golden light, the black window panes, the three unmade beds and, on the trestle table, my unwashed frying-pan and plate encrusted with the pungent brown rims of my curry dinner. A Madonna and Child and my family photograph pinned on one wall. Piles of books and papers waiting in the lamplight. A heap of black-skinned bananas furry with ants. Housekeeping had rather gone by the board. I had to spend every hour of every day of the August vacation studying for the exams if I was to have any chance of getting into the University. She said nothing, just chose a bed and slumped down with her eyes closed, sighing, her rough black head against the wall. I lit the primus and made the tea.

'How do you like your tea?'

'Milk and two sugars, thanks.'

The milk bottle was half full of a cheesy substance with a green pelt of mould.

'Ah, no milk. I am so sorry.'

'No worries. Just sugar, then. Thanks.'

She winced, sipping the hot tea. She had a scab on her full lower lip, like a baby's milk blister. One of her eyes was swollen, I saw, and ringed with a purple and yellow stain.

'I am sorry, this is none of my business, but I hope you have not been assaulted? Your eye —'

'Never you mind about my eye. I gave as good as I got. Better.'

Was she afraid I might use violence on her? I have always had difficulty knowing the right thing to say. I held my tongue, and we drank our tea in a silence broken only by the hissing of the lamp in its glass.

The moon had risen full and yellow by the time we walked up the dark track to look at her car, but neither of us had a torch, it turned out, and besides I was no expert. I regretted my rashness. With luck, she said, it was only out of petrol. She had filled it up at Rockhampton in the morning, but the petrol gauge was out of order. The sight of it was not reassuring: a crumpled, rusting blue Fiat with Victorian number plates on the gravel verge, sagging and mud-caked, packed to the roof with bags. In the back sat an animal the size of a grown labrador, with red glass eyes.

'It won't bite.'

It was a yellow plush elephant. I looked at her.

'Present for me kid? He's three.'

Absurdly, I looked around for him as she unlocked a door and crawled in to release the bonnet.

'He's at me sister's in Townsville. We haven't see each other for months. It's taken me a week to get this far.'

'On your own? From Victoria?'

'Yeah. Melbourne. And that's driving all day. I chuck the elephant in the front and bed down in the back seat at night. I'll be bloody glad when it's over.'

I stooped over the dark, dusty motor for a token look, but my head cast a shadow in the moonlight and it was obviously hopeless. A car surging past with headlights on full wrapped us in a cloud of dust and fumes. I slammed the bonnet down and shook my head.

'Oh, bugger.' With a despairing grimace. 'I'd dump it and hitch the rest of the way only I've got everything I own in the bloody thing.'

She was exhausted, it was late, and I was able to convince her that it was best left until the morning and that she should spend the night at the house. She locked up, hoisted a bag on her shoulder, refusing to let me carry it, and trudged at my side along the track. At least it would be nice, she said, to sleep under a roof again. I peeled a few of the best of the black bananas for her, and gave her the tin of golden syrup that was the only other food left in the house. She sat huddled on my bed, dipping each banana in the tin and curling a thick ribbon of golden syrup around it before she ate it.

'Want some?'

'No, thank you.'

'Well. My name's Claire. What's yours?'

'Simon. My Christian name.'

'Yeah.' She looked blank.

'I do not use my Indian name. Since I am a baptised Catholic.'

'Oh, are you Indian?'

'Yes, from Fiji.' Her eyebrows were fine and arched, drawn, I saw, with black pencil. 'People always seem to think I am Aboriginal.'

'Stiff shit.'

'I am an outcast here.'

She licked her fingers. I brought her a basin of cold water and she bent and splashed bright handfuls of water in her face, shuddering, and ran her wet hands through her hair.

'So why stay?'

'I am on a scholarship. I must not let the brothers down. And my family. I am the eldest of six.'

'How old are you?'

'Twenty-one.'

She put the basin on the table by the lamp and stood gazing into my face.

'You don't look it.'

'Yes, I am, really.'

'I'm twenty-five. I'm an older woman.'

I was too flustered to answer. She sat back grinning. Her teeth were beautiful, very square and white.

'There wouldn't be a cigarette anywhere, I suppose?'

'No one here is a smoker. Sorry.'

'Oh well.' She stretched and yawned. 'Tell me about yourself. Got a girlfriend have you, Si?'

I hastened to explain that two other Fijian students were sharing the house, although they were away that weekend, and that, although my mother was anxious for me to marry, actually I was planning on entering the priesthood. She made no comment.

'Are you a Catholic, Claire?' It was a Catholic name.

'Me? No. It's all a lot of bull I reckon, religion.'

She was struggling not to laugh.

'That is very funny, is it?'

'Oh, not that. It's just here's me shitting myself about you. It was that bloody big black bike out there on the verandah. Didn't see it round the side till after I'd knocked. Fuck! It's the thing from outer space, a monster ant or something. I thought I'd hit on the Hell's Angels.' She laughed, rubbing her eyes. 'What a day. I'm buggered.'

I wished she would not use bad language.

I smoothed the rumpled beds, apologising that I had no clean sheets. Never mind, she said, and wanted to know which one was mine. I showed her and she crawled in, dragged off her jeans and red shirt under the sheets, dropped them on the floor, sighed, and fell asleep. I spread the thin blanket over her. The nights could be cool there by the river.

I took out my books but it was harder than usual to concentrate on logarithms. The smell of kerosene and the smoky caramel of the burning canefields hung in the room. Moths thumped against the lamp and she lay submerged, still and yet seeming to move in the yellow light full of moving shadows. I must have fallen asleep at the table. I woke at daybreak with my head in my book and put out the lamp, coppery and faint in the grey of morning, and lay down to sleep on the next bed. When I next opened my eyes the sun lay over us in thick white rods.

I made some tea and sat down on the bed to drink it, watching her breathing face until at last her eyes opened.

'What are you staring at?'

'You looked Indian when you were asleep. You looked like one of my sisters.'

'Yeah? Which one?'

'Lalita.' I showed her in the photograph. 'Would you like some tea?'

'Love some. Me mum said me dad had a touch of the tar. That's Aboriginal to you. No Indian in me that I know of. I never set eyes on him meself, he shot through. Is she a nice sister? Lalita?'

'My favourite.'

'That's all right, then. What's your Indian name?'

I hesitated.

'Come on, you can tell me.'

'Shiva.' I said it on the spur of the moment, so as not to tell her my name.

'Shiva. Can I call you that? All right, I won't.' She yawned and stretched her brown arms, smiling up at me. 'That was the best sleep I've had for a week.'

'Good.' I brought her tea and, looking away, hastily gulped mine. 'Now I will look at your car.'

She gave me the keys from the pocket of her jeans. it was a burning day already sizzling with cicadas. Sweating, I checked the obvious things, the battery, the oil, spark plugs, terminals, radiator. I too hoped it was just petrol, and not something complicated that would waste precious hours arranging a tow and repairs on a Sunday. I would have milked my bike tank for her, but it was almost empty. My cheque was late again and I am frugal by nature. I went to the house to suggest that we ride into Sarina with a jerry-can, but to my intense relief she preferred not to come. Too bloody hot, she said.

'Get us something to eat while you're there, will you, Si?' She patted my arm. 'Golden syrup'll rot your teeth.'

My consternation must have been all too plain. 'My shout.' She thrust a twenty-dollar bill in my pocket despite my absurd protests. What choice did I have but to take it?

'And a packet of Marlboro,' she called after me.

I got her petrol, and some on account for me, and bought sliced bread, butter, cheese, tomatoes, ham, milk, two cans of Coca Cola, a packet of cigarettes and bananas at the milk bar, dim and quiet behind its sun blinds. As I went out I saw to my horror Father Michael's chubby black form toddle across the street, and I remember to this day the waves of guilt and shame as I bent to load the bike, as if I had not seen him, and thundered back down the shimmering asphalt. Sunday, and Mass had not even crossed my mind. I would have to confess.

With petrol in its tank the wretched Fiat started up with a bellow like a jet plane.

She came running from the house, overjoyed, calling out thank you, thank you, her breasts bouncing. Her hair was tied back with red ribbon. When she reached me she flung her arms round me and kissed me on the mouth.

I had never been kissed.

The house was cool and quiet, so dark that it took me a minute or two to see that she had tidied it and washed up and made all the beds. She shrugged and grinned at my thanks. I handed her the bag of food and her change. She grabbed the packet of cigarettes and lit one.

'Oh. Thank God.' She breathed out gusts of smoke.

'Are you moving to Townsville?'

'No. I'll go for a job on Hayman or somewhere, housemaid-waitress or whatever. Or cook on a prawn boat out of Darwin. Good money, they say.'

'What about your husband?'

'What husband's that?'

'Your little boy. Will you take him with you?'

'No. Let's get something straight, Saint Simon.' Smoke gushed from her flat nostrils. 'Since you're so bloody *concerned*. I put up with it for two years getting bashed every time the bastard got drunk.' She touched her purple eyelid. 'Benny's not his, see? Not his kid. I had to rush him to the hospital twice. Doctors aren't all fools. Betty can give him a good home and that's more than I can at the moment. And she bloody worships him.'

'I am so sorry!' I was appalled. Who was I to find fault? She had every right to be angry with me.

'Yeah. Easy for you to talk, isn't it.'

'You have suffered.' Tears filled my eyes. 'Forgive me.'

'I'll think about it.' Grinning, she stubbed out her cigarette and set about buttering bread and making sandwiches. 'Yeah. I miss him.'

Anything I said might be wrong. I nodded.

'He knows I'm his mum. Is there a shower here, by the way?'

'No, we wash in the river. Behind the trees at the back.'

'No crocodiles?'

'No!' I laughed. I was forgiven. 'There are lotuses.'

'As long as they don't eat people.'

'I will protect you!'

'You're on. Right then. A picnic and a bath sounds good.'

We sat on the river bank among the roots of dark trees and ate and drank everything. No one else came. Then she had a cigarette, undressed and slid naked into the river. Her hair afloat, she glowed in the heavy water, golden brown all over, her legs spindling into darkness and I remembered the lamplight and the shadows of the great moths. I watched her diving and splashing to the far side into the reflections of the trees and float there through sparkles, through thick rings of water, black and green.

'Come in, Si! Oh, come on! Oh, it's lovely.'

The water was icy at first, dark in the shade, almost opaque. Hair-like insects stilted over the glassy surface. She splashed me and challenged me to dive between her long, shimmering legs. A mirrored bird flapped over our heads and I thought of the holy dove, and I was horrified at myself. I was in every way out of my depth. In the green clumps on the far bank lotuses had opened their long petals, but she would not let me pick her one.

'Here is like home,' I said, swimming slowly at her side. 'Fiji. The river. Sugar cane. The sea.'

'Do you wish you were there?'

I did not.

As we waded out she caught me glancing at her dripping breasts and cupped them in her hands so that the dark nipples stood up.

'Want some?'

I giggled.

'Go on. Don't you like them?'

I stood gaping on the bank, my hands hiding my shame.

'You think I'm a slack, don't you?'

'No!' What a thing to say. 'I know you are not.'

'A black's a slack.'

'I am blacker than you.'

'What then?' She spread out her hands and her breasts quivered, released.

'I told you before.'

She stared.

'And I don't know how.' I gritted my teeth. 'I have never done — I have never —'

'Oh, is that all.' She reached for my hands and pressed them over her breasts. I could neither breathe nor look. 'Come on. Not here.'

We wrapped ourselves in towels and crept back hand in hand, not speaking. The dark house was stifling, the air hot to our cool skins. We lay down together on my bed and she kissed me with her soft tongue. Her mouth tasted of smoke. My heart was drumming madly. I clung to her in my terror and urgency. I was frantic to have her, and must have hurt her, at least in the beginning, but she led me calmly and steadily up to the last overwhelming moment.

When I finished, I remember, I sank my hot face into her wet black hair, which was warm on the pillow and smelled of the river water, and whimpered that now I could never be a priest. I had missed Mass and now there was this to confess as well. I foresaw myself in the confessional whispering, half-strangled with mortification. And yet I was proud too, burning with pride. We were lying with our arms and legs entangled, both of us hot and slippery, and I felt her clench and quiver with laughter at my words.

'Please. It is a serious matter to me.'

'You're a big baby. Si, that's all you are.'

And I did not mind at all. My face was mirrored in her smiling eyes.

She was on the road in no time. We got dressed in clean clothes and had a cup of tea first, tea with milk, to postpone her going, I suppose, since neither of us drank much. I pleaded with her to stay a few days, at least until the others came back, but she said no. I made her take my address and a silk scarf I had bought for Lalita. She got into the car, kissing me, promising to take care, yes, to have the car checked at the first garage, not to mention me there, to try to stop smoking, to write with her address when she was settled, to come back. I watched her drive away.

A brief postcard with a Townsville postmark came in a fortnight and I have it still.

MARINA

The last light flowed in and lapped around the baby asleep in the bassinette, fingers waving like stalks of seaweed. The ginger cat, waking, stretched and licked and came to rub its pelt against Marina's ankles. With her foot Marina tapped the crusted saucer of milk. Its bold yellow eyes fixed, the cat yowled and scratched at the linoleum. She shoved it out and slammed the door.

She thought, I'm afraid all the time. Of faces. Interiors, dreams. Voices. Pain. Dreams most of all.

In the shawl that Michali's mother had sent, with the blue bead sewn on it against the Evil Eye, the puffy head was haloed. Hairs tufted it. She touched the milk blisters on its lips, the red blotches on its forehead and eyelids, and watched it flinch under her shadow and grope with monkey paws. Her nipples stung. Her eyes burned with tears. This was all she had to show for the long pain and terror of giving birth; the ache of the stitches between her legs; the brown trickle of blood.

She could hear the baby's breathing and her own. The sun ebbed away. She sat waiting.

In one dream, she thought, a brittle glittering cockroach crawls out from under my thumbnail. Its eyes and wild feelers thrust against my fingers as I prod it back in. More cockroaches sprout from under each bitten fingernail. What do dreams mean?

A grey web was spun across the pane. A grey lair, a crouching spider. The brown sun pierced it. Clouds blew loose on the square wan sky. Paint peeled in grey hangnails from the spouting and the furrowed weatherboards. Hanging raindrops glittered, dripped down. A bird hooted.

Michali was needed at the pizza bar until just on midnight. He would lurch in drunk and say, Go to buggery the pair of you, you shit me. When she first started working there, he talked like that to his wife, Joss. On the sly he kissed Marina. He said he loved her.

A black blowfly was squatting on the baby's cheek. It came out of its nose, or its mouth, or its curled ear. Marina waved it into the air.

She had written to Michali's mother. It must have got to Greece by now, but it might take Michali's mother weeks to answer. If only she could come and help. Even little Eleni had been led off, red and baulking, to stay at the pizza bar with her aunt. It's my baby too, Daddy, why can't I stay and help Rina? Mamma, Marina thought, you can't come to Australia. I wish I never had. My own mother hates me. I must get to a good doctor. Michali doesn't believe me. I must find another doctor or something terrible will happen. I can't take the valium, it would get in my milk. I won't wean it, I want to feed it myself.

Dear Mamma, she had written. Michali's mother was *Mamma* now. Her own mother hated her.

Dear Mamma,
Please write soon. Do you mind that it's another granddaughter? I know Michali wanted a boy. He has taken Eleni to the shop because I just can't manage. I'm not working there any more. Eleni wants to be godmother, I suppose five is old enough. We're calling it Anna. People are saying we should call it Olga after my mother, but why should we? She wishes I was dead. She came to the hospital to look at the baby and went home without seeing me. A Greek nurse told me. We should have stayed in Greece. I told Michali.

I wish this one could have been called Eleni too, after you.

I have plenty of milk. Why does it vomit and cry so much, Mamma? Tell me what to do. I'm afraid to sleep, I have such terrible dreams. You'd know what they mean. Write to me soon, please write.

Your loving daughter-in-law,
Marina

I often dream that I am hiding behind the dark curtain in my parents' bedroom watching my mother go out. I advance to the pane. My mother outside is watching me, advancing on her own face printed in sunlight on the glass. Her golden mask obliterates mind. Mine. I watch her raise her black bag and bring it down, shattering the thick pane: glass splashes me.

Marina lay down on the bed, twisting her hair into a knot. The baby stirred and sucked in its sleep. Somewhere a clock struck seven.

At seven the first morning in Michali's village his mother burst in with green figs ripe to splitting, opened the hot shutters and perched on their bed to peel figs for her son and his *nyfi*. Don't come bursting in like that, Mamma, Michali said, if you want us to make you a grandson. When he laughed, pink seeds oozed from his mouth. The whitewashed house was hot and sour, full of grapes in baskets.

On burning afternoons Michali's mother bathed various grandchildren one by one, sitting Laki, Niki, Eleni in the brimming copper tub under the grapevine, soaping them and rinsing off the bubbles with her tin watering can.

Eleni still clung to Marina. In the cool of dusk Marina humped her round the village to buy icecreams at the petrol station. Voices called from a walled garden: *Ela, nyfi, na sas doume ligo.* Coffee with opal bubbles was brought under the shade of a pear tree, and conserves of tomato and quince like red glass. All the cows came joggling home in the dusty streets with swollen udders hitting their mud-caked legs. Their eyes watched as their muzzles plunged into buckets of water.

Was there a woman that Michali visited even then behind locked shutters? He said he was fishing in the river while they slept the afternoons away but he came back empty-handed mostly. I fell asleep, he said: they got away. There's this big old one I'm after and he knows it.

He was happy before the wedding and after. They all were. He was proud. Look at her, he said, she's all of eighteen (he was thirty). She speaks perfect English and Greek. He showed people photos of the pizza bar. It was years since he'd been home. Everyone soon found out that she was pregnant already and no one seemed to mind.

The nights when he was at the *kafeneion* with his old friends his mother sat crocheting the white shawl, her glasses low on her nose, and talked about Michali's boyhood. We should have stayed, Marina said into the dark air. I wanted to.

I told Michali. Find me a doctor who can help me.

She lit the wick afloat in a skin of oil on water at the base of the ikon, and the faces of the Panagia and the Child appeared behind its flame. Their eyes were heavy with sleep or sorrow. *Haire,* Maria. Marina crossed herself.

The priest at the wedding sprouted so much black hair that she thought the resonating cave of his mouth must be furred bushy black, but no, it was smooth; it was the colour of a sea urchin. For the first time in her life the smoke from the rings of candles and the incense filled her with nausea. Faces grinned. In the dome Christ Pantokrator stared. She swayed, numbly aware that she might faint, or vomit, or cry out. The glass of the chandelier splashed.

In another dream, Mamma, I have fed the baby thick porridge. I knew I shouldn't, oh I knew it wasn't right. Its nose and mouth ooze porridge and it chokes. I see its little tongue roll lolling out to its scabbed navel, roll out like a paper party whistle.

In the brown stillness Marina jumped up and grabbed her handbag. She bent over the breathing baby. It was so quiet. There was an hour or so before it should wake for the next feed. Michali had to work late. He was seeing another woman. His hands were clamped on a red dress. Tell me what to do. The baby's cheek was hot. *Panagia mou,* watch over my child.

Quickly she switched on the lamp by the bassinette and crept outside, locking the front door. On the verandah she wavered: in the front bedroom window her shadow covered the glass.

The corner milk bar was drenched in white light. Newspapers lay yellowing in heaps, *Neos Kosmos, Nea Ellada,* inside the plate-glass windows. In the back room a television set yelled and chuckled. Kyria Anna was behind the counter weighing out sweets for an old woman in a ginger coat.

'Kyria Anna, *kalispera,*' Marina blurted, 'I have to ring Greece. Can I use your phone? I've got the money.' She fumbled in her bag.

Kyria Anna flounced and shrugged, but she was too fond of Michali to say no outright to his wife. Marina sidled behind the counter, checked the number in the torn book and rang International Calls. She stuttered to the shrill operator, and hung up. There was only one telephone in Michali's village: his mother, called over the loudspeakers, would come running down the dusty road. Marina stood wringing her hands. The old woman smiled. A stench of urine rose from under her hairy coat. Sticks in loose stockings, an umbrella, grey straggles squashed under a beanie. Among her freckles and creases her bold yellow eyes peered.

The telephone rang.

'Hullo, Melbourne? Would you repeat your number, please. I'm sorry, the number you are calling is not answering.'

'Oh. Thank you,' Marina uttered. 'I might try later. Thank you.'

'Is anything the matter, Rina *mou*?' Kyria Anna's grey face glinted. She would report to Michali. The old woman chuckled, trudging out.

'No, no. I'm fine.' Marina's head throbbed. 'They must all be out in the fields.'

'Well, never mind. You can always have another try. Sit down and keep me company for a while.'

'Isn't Elly home?'

Daughters like Elly were never home. Kyria Anna sighed complacently. Ach, *aman*. The thought rose into Marina's mind that it was Elly with Michali the other day in the half-dark of the cobbled yard. The black hair, the body draped in red. Elly, of course. Pain and anger surged in her.

'Tired, Rina? You look tired. Let me get you a little coffee.'

'No, thank you. No. I can't stay.'

'*Ela*, Michali won't miss you for a minute or two.'

Kyria Anna knew very well when Michali worked late; they had been neighbours for years. Marina glared into her pouched old eyes.

'No, I'd better not. Isn't Elly in, Kyria Anna?'

'No, dear. She had to go for a fitting.'

Kyria Anna was an old hand. Marina peered around the cluttered walls for mirrors and darkened panes to reveal to her how she looked to Kyria Anna. A dupe, parading her anguish and disorder. Brown hair failing in wisps, damp patches over her nipples, a draggled skirt. Long eyes slit against dazzle and suspicion.

'I really must go straight home.'

'*Kala, kala*. Come back and try again.'

'No. It's no use.'

Marina watched herself turn and sidle out in multiple faint images on glass. Lamps glittered over the grey street.

In another dream I have hurtled from an ivied window and lie crumpled on the cobbles in my white dress. Poor dead lady, look here she comes walking in the park with us in her wedding dress. Going upstairs to our warm bed we look back sorrowfully. She sleeps in her smashed carcase. The window strikes eight. Dreams will drive me mad.

At St Kilda beach the boats were rocking on the ruffles of the bay. Seaweed lay over the rocks to dry like calfskins. Gulls mewed and splashed. The pier lamps sank deep: men were fishing under them, crouched to fumble with whitebait, their long lines dipped in the eddies of light. One wound in a line with a pewter fish hung on it. Eleni, running up and down here one night in summer: Rina and Daddy! Come here! I want you emergently!

What is it?

Look! That man's caught a fish.

Ssh. That's the sinker.

It is not. It's a fish. It's very little, isn't it? Are you going to eat that little fish?

It's a fair size for one a these, missy.

Why don't you throw it back?

Shadows hid Marina on the ribbed wood of the landing stage. The piles under the jetty were shaggy with weed and mussels. She stood on a mess of crunched whitebait, and shuddered. The bay was fringed with lights under the heavy sky. As she watched, a shape of lights split from the lights of Princes Pier and drifted, a ship drifted out to sea.

The moon was rising, smeared with smoke or cloud.

She wandered on to the black sand. She was waist-deep in the water, hobbled by her long skirt, shoes in one hand. The waves glittered around her, the sand crumbled away under her feet. The cold water stung between her legs.

I am riding pillion on a motor-bike over a bumpy metal bridge, carrying the baby piggy-back. It falls off into the river. I see it lying on its back deep inside the clear water. I plunge my arms in and lift it up, but its head topples off and floats away. What can I do? Mamma, tell me.

Marina heard that she was sobbing. Her mouth groped and gaped. She tugged her wedding ring over her knuckles and hurled it glittering out to sea.

She strode through the water and up the sand to the street. Through the archway a flight of steps led to the Upper Esplanade. A tram clanked overhead. Leaves and papers littered the black steps. Here was where Michali had pushed her against the wall out of the jagged glare of the streetlamp and kissed her for the first time. A married man. The heavy gold of the asphalt by night. The smell of the flat sea.

Elly was there all the time, of course, in the back room of the milk bar watching the television. Elly and Michali were both there, furtive and bold, sneering at her.

In the moonlit air hung a vague smell, a dimness, an omen of smoke. Shivering, Marina broke barefoot into a clumsy run. Her skirt clung as she went pelting and gasping down the hot streets to fling the door open on silence, on a glow of lamplight. The baby stretched in its sleep.

The wick had dowsed itself in water furred with black insects. She poured more oil in and relit it. The faces shimmered. *Haire*, Maria. The insects would be burnt.

I had a doll that had been my mother's, with a china head on a cotton body. Dolly's head came off on the footpath. My mother took Dolly away and slapped me. She hates me.

Marina pulled off her wet clothes and put on dry ones. Her nursing pads stuck, yellow-crusted with milk. There were napkins soaking in the outhouse. She sagged at the thought of washing them out in the concrete troughs under the bulb in its net of cobwebs.

Outside an owl hooted. In Greece owls were unlucky. Ominous birds. Village women refused to go outdoors at night when one was about. There had been one under the lamp at the crossroad near Michali's village, sitting with a golden gaze in the dust, ruffling away, if you came too close. A dowdy cat with wings, over the wheat fields.

Her cold feet clinging to the linoleum, she opened the

refrigerator: olives, hard-boiled eggs, tomatoes; slices of old *tiropita,* dried cheese in curls of pastry; a bottle of milk, cold and thick, not like her own blue milk warm in her breasts; wooden yellow apples. She ate everything with both hands.

The baby slept on and on, breathing deeply. It would stay awake the whole night now.

Michali, coming home drunk the other night, had found the baby awake, shrieking — Eleni hovering pale and anxious — and yelled that the place was a madhouse and stank of shit. He staggered to the toilet and hugged the bowl, his chin on the rim. Vomit burst into the water. She wiped his loose mouth and dragged him along to the separate room that he had slept in for the last two months driven out, he complained, by her thumping belly and her moaning when the cramps clutched her legs. She peeled off his sodden clothes and tucked him into bed. His breathing was slow, heavy. She flushed the toilet.

What the hell's wrong with you anyway, Rina? My brother's got three kids. His wife can help us out in the shop. Why not you?

His first wife, Joss, was smart and efficient, but she drove right off an overpass at the end of the West Gate Bridge. She had passed safely over the towers of factories, the still white tufts of steam torn from them, ships at berth, clouds hanging. In the dim mass of the city all the lamps were coming on. The sun glared on sheets of rainwater mirroring sky and clouds. Dazed, surging past, Joss had been crushed at full speed.

Michali had never loved Joss. He had often said so. It had only been a civil wedding. Her Greek was hopeless. Why had he married her? Because of Eleni? Marina had been ill with remorse for having wished Joss out of the way. The other day behind the crates of bottles Michali had been kissing someone, Elly. Marina had faded into the passage. It was Elly's turn now, Elly he entered with a groan and prodded and hammered. Elly could have him. They were both — they were bestial.

A whimper echoed in the lamplight. The baby began its squalling. Its napkin was soaked with mustardy excrement; pimples studded its buttocks. She dabbed methylated spirit on the rash, as the Sister had advised, while it screamed under her hands. She should bath it, but she shrank from its panic, its slithering body dripping soap. In her desperation she stepped back, tipping over the cat's saucer. Sour milk splashed her foot and lay curdled on the floor.

She picked up the baby, sat down, dragged her jumper up and shoved the bawling head at one tight nipple. It shrieked. Its frilled gums grinned.

'Stop it!' she shrieked back. 'What's wrong with you? *Stop it.*' She grasped the baby's feet in both hands and swung it with all her strength head-first against the wall. And again. And again.

Then it stopped its noise, hanging from her hands.

She cradled the head. Blood trickling from the nose was staining the cheeks so she wiped them and kissed them and held the lips to her nipple. With a sweet sting her milk let down. Ah, she sat back and the white spray fell quietly in the baby's face.

ISMINI

Behind its hooded verandah the house was deep in evening shadow. Ismini unlocked the front door, trudged through the green gloom to the kitchen and dumped her schoolbag on the plastic tablecloth among long slabs of late sun. A fly nodded, stroking its hinged legs.

With a wince she unwrapped the two slimy speckled translucent squids and rinsed them under the tap. Their beaks and torn eyes had to be prised out, then the fretted glassy backbones, the inksacs. She cut up the ornate tentacles and the sheaths of their bodies. She made a salad glowing green and red, put it with the *retsina* and the blubbery squid in the refrigerator, poured a glass of milk and sat down to her homework.

One morning on a hot wooden jetty her father had hauled a squid out of the flashing sea. Dripping, its bright mantle fading, it had shuddered and wheezed at her feet, blind in the white sun, as it died.

Oh, what is it, Baba?

Kalamari.

Mummy, Baba's caught a kamalari!

Oh yes, look. A squid.

In English it was a different creature.

'Write a pen-portrait of a person you know well. The subject's appearance, attitudes, way of life, character, should be covered. 250–500 words.'

She scribbled notes. My Grk grandmother. Yiayia Sophia. Will Mrs Brown object if the subject is dead? She won't know. Red eggs for Easter, the lamb on the iron spit, the awful offal soup. The brain broiled in the charred skull. Mother cat, kittens buried alive. Bad luck to kill a cat. Perpetual mourning.

A hard marker, Mrs Brown had said that Ismini was clever and should have no trouble getting a studentship to Teachers' College, if that was what she wanted. Mrs Brown had said after class that she might need Ismini to babysit on Saturday if her live-in girl was still ill. Oh yes, I'd love to, Mrs Brown.

The deep sun was making Ismini's face burn like a brass gong in the window pane, like the mask of Agamemnon, long-eyed, long-lipped. Her breasts lay round and heavy under her uniform. She fingered her warm hair.

Doan be hard on your Yiayia, Ismini *mou.* She give up everythink to come out here, look after us.

We didn't need her, Baba, did we?

We need her, you know that. She been like a mother to you.

She's always picking on me.

She just frighten. She tell your Theia she see your mother in you.

Oh does she? Good!

Baba once said Ismini could cook squid better than Mummy could, even better than Yiayia. These squids were fresh ones from the market especially for his birthday. Out of her pocket money she had bought real Greek *feta* cheese and the *retsina* and a carton of the Greek cigarettes he loved, Assos Filtro, supplied by Poppy's sister, an air hostess. In Greece, Baba said, they didn't celebrate birthdays. Mummy loved birthdays. If Mummy had been Greek and not Australian, who knew if she would have left home like that? Theia Frosso said no Greek woman would. Today there was no letter, no birthday card, in the box. Yet they had been one flesh.

She had run into Mummy the other day by chance in the Mall. She had stopped to chat, her own mother, grinning and tapping her foot on the hot tramlines, lighting a quick cigarette and blowing out smoke. She was really sorry to have to rush off like this.

I saw Mummy in town today, Baba.

Doan talk to me about that bitch.

'Ismini?' Theia Frosso was shrilling from outside. Ismini sighed. Theia Frosso, not her real aunt but Baba's second cousin, lived next door and felt responsible. The doors slammed. She strutted in, kissed Ismini and sank on to her usual chair.

'Ach! All alone, you poor gel, why you doan come an watch television with the kids, eh?'

'I haven't even started my homework, Theia.'

Ismini poured her the daily, the ritual, dose of sweet vermouth; caught a coil of her orange-peel preserve glowing and porous in the jar of heavy syrup and set it still in the spoon on a glass dish; poured iced water; mixed coffee for two in the red *briki.* It frothed and sputtered in the gas flame. She bit her lip.

'It boil out? Is nothing. *Yeia mas.*' Theia Frosso ate and drank and licked her lips. 'I tell you, your Baba, he a very lucky he hev a daughter like you look after him. A good little Greek housewive.'

'I'm not really Greek.'

'What you tokkink about? You Greek.'

Theia Frosso lit a cigarette and turned the coffee cups upside-down to read the future in the grounds. Yet Theia Frosso was *moderna:* she encased her flab in pantsuits, she dyed her hair red, she smoked cigarettes.

The telephone rang. 'Hullo?'

Theia Frosso was intent.

'Ismini? Hullo, love, it's me. Look, somethink's come up, I be home late. Sorry, eh? You doan mind, do you, love?'

'Well, how late will you be?'

'Dunno for sure. Doan wait up.'

'You won't be home for dinner?'

'Doan worry, I grab a *souvlaki.*'

'Baba, I got *kalamaria*!'

'Tomorrow. We hev them tomorrow. Sorry, love, I gotta go, I double-parked. Make sure you lock up, all right?'

'All right. *Yeia sou.*'

'Yeia.'

She slammed the phone down. Happy birthday, Baba.

'He hev gel fren.' Theia Frosso giggled, inspecting the brown ripples in Ismini's cup. 'You hev to expect. A taxi-driver meetink lotsa people. He still a quite yunk men, you know thet.'

'So what if he has?'

'He never tell you, *kale,* he be shame.'

'Why should he be?'

'Mamma? Eh, Mamma?' Theia Frosso's scrawny youngest was shrilling out over the grey fence. She rose sighing, her duty done at least, stubbed out her cigarette, planted more rubber kisses.

'Without me they carn do nothink. Sorry, I betta go. You come an hev dinner, eh? Why you wanna stay here all alone? No good for you.'

'Too much to do, Theia.'

Ismini rinsed the dishes. The sun had left the window in a bronze haze. She switched the sallow bulb on and sat down under it to write.

MY GREEK GRANDMOTHER

My Greek grandmother, Yiayia Sophia, was swathed in her widow's mourning clothes and headscarf until she died. Her mouth was folded over her toothless gums, her skin yellow and creased, her grey hair worn in two long pigtails even in bed. A wick floating in oil on water kept a flame sputtering all night in front of the ikon in her room.

She knew all the prayers. All through Lent she fasted until she could hardly stand, her candle shaking, outside the church at the Easter midnight service. There were fireworks hanging and flaring, and we all cracked our red eggs and ate them and nursed our candle flames all the way home for luck. Then we had to eat her magieritsa.

I remember her hoarding our hens' eggs for days beforehand and hard-boiling them on Holy Thursday in red dye. We polished them, still warm, with cloths dipped in oil. She baked plaited tsoureki *loaves. She made the* magieritsa, *the traditional soup of lamb offal, flushing out the lungs and entrails with the garden hose, screeching at the avid hens, stirring it all in the pot with onions and herbs like a witch at her cauldron.*

The lamb itself my father had skinned and impaled on an iron rod. Its red eye-sockets, its grinning teeth with the spit thrust out like an iron tongue. All Easter Sunday morning it was twisted and basted over the trench of coals, speckled with charred herbs, while it turned dark brown and neighbours and relatives danced to the record-player on the back lawn. When they split the skull for my grandmother, she offered me a forkful of the brains.

'Eat it, silly,' she cackled. 'God gave it to us.'

'Ugh, no! I don't want it.'

She shrugged, mumbling the grey jelly.

Our cat had kittens once. A lovely pure black cat, a witch-cat, she lay purring, slit-eyed, as they butted and squeaked at her pink teats. Our cat was necessary, as the hens attracted mice. Kittens weren't. One day the cat was crying and clawing at a damp patch of ground under the tomatoes. I dug up the corpses, their fur and tiny mouths and moonstone eyes all clogged with earth. I accused Yiayia.

'Don't be silly,' was all she said.

She is dead and buried herself now, in foreign earth. I saw her dying, her old mouth agape fighting for breath; and dead in her coffin at last, a yellow mask and folded lizard-claws. She was always too old to love me. I'm too old to hate her any more. (430 words)

At the funeral Baba had sobbed on Theia Fosso's shoulder. Mummy hadn't been there. Ismini shuddered. In her old sepia wedding picture nailed up beside the ikon, Yiayia had Ismini's face: everyone said so. Ismini had wanted to burn all the photos, but Baba made her put them back up in the hollow room. There was one of Mummy in Greece, on a plump donkey with her legs sticking stiffly out; Baba was there, and Yiayia, swathed even then, and a crowd of solemn children with shaved heads. Mummy looked happy.

The phone rang. Ismini's lip curled. So he was sorry, was he? Well, better late than never.

'Yes.'

'Hullo? That's you, Ismini, is it? Oh good.'

'Oh! Mrs Brown!'

When she had just finished the essay!

'I was hoping you'll still be free to baby-sit for us this Saturday. Have I left it too late?'

'Oh yes, I'd love to!'

'Oh good. The thing is, though, we'll be very late home. Will your parents let you stay the night?'

The wood-fire whispering, Ismini thought, flaring over the crammed bookshelves and the sofa bed in the bow window.

'Oh, yes!'

If Baba says no this time, then I'll leave home.

'You're sure? Oh good. I'll pick you up at seven on Saturday, then. Can you hear the bub bawling his head off? I'd better go. 'Bye, Ismini.'

The first time she stood for ten minutes on their front verandah, too nervous to knock. When she asked Mrs Brown what to do if the baby cried, the eight-year-old scoffed, but the two-year-old patted her knee: I'll help you, Minnie, he said. He always stops for me.

They sat round the fire while she read them Little Golden

Books; calling her Minnie Mouse, exploding with giggles, chanting Meany, Meany, when she said lights out at nine.

I'm eight. I don't have to go to sleep yet.

You do so. Mummy said. He does so have to, Minnie.

Shut up you.

It was a funny name though, a fancy classical name, a whim of her pompous old godfather's, when she should have been called Sophia after Yiayia. His wife had lapped Ismini in rosy withering flesh, pressing lips soft as a cocoon on her wincing cheeks. Once her parents split up, her godparents stopped visiting. Only her name was left of them.

If Baba said no, she couldn't stay the night, then she'd ring Mummy. No, don't be silly. The last time, a man had picked up the phone. Lyn, it's for you, he'd called.

Mummy, it's me. Can you come over just for a while? Baba's gone out. Can you, please?

Darling, no, sweet, you know I can't, I have to get up at five to go to work —

I want to talk to you!

Well go ahead, sweet, what's the matter?

Baba says I can't go to Poppy's birthday party.

Oh, lovey, I'm sorry. What a shame.

I'm sixteen! I'm not a child! The whole form's going. He won't let me go anywhere. Please, will you just ring and talk to him?

He wouldn't listen to me. You know that. God, I'm the last person —

I'm sorry. You're otherwise engaged, aren't you?

Ah, Ismini —

She'd cut Mummy off. Mummy hadn't tried to ring back. Baba had been right all along, of course: forget about your Mummy, Ismini *mou*, she doan want you. Sixteen, Ismini said aloud, is old enough to leave home legally. She wondered if Poppy would like to share a flat.

It was getting late. She trailed down the dark passage to her father's room. Its velvet curtains were the same, like sleek brown fur, and the painted-over fireplace in the wall, and in the wardrobe doors those long hazed mirrors that she and Mummy had always polished together. She had dressed up and posed in the dim mirrors. Baba slept alone now. When nightmares had woken her he had come and carried her in to sleep between their big warm bodies.

Mummy's old forgotten red nightdress lay hidden under sheets in the bottom drawer. Ismini undressed to slip it on: it fitted now. She stroked Red Ruby on her lips and cheeks, and rimmed her long eyes with kohl. She brushed out her hair. In the blurred gold of the mirror a dusty ghost looked back.

Once, black and faceless against a half-light from the passage, Mummy had stooped over her, dragged down her pants and crammed a suppository like an iron spit up her bottom. She had had to rush out to the toilet, her bowels surging and snorting. Poppy said sex hurt like that. Poppy was raped.

Room by room Ismini snapped on the lights and checked that all the doors and windows were locked. Yiayia's room of dead faces, the kitchen, laundry, bathroom, the musty sitting room, and her own room last.

She had been lying awake, trying to make sense of their jumbled shouts in the kitchen, when Mummy had come bursting in, sobbing and shuddering, and slammed the door. They clung together in the dark until at last Baba's yells and crashes petered out, daring only to whisper.

I'm leaving. This time I'm leaving.

What's happened?

He's insane. He's capable of anything. God, I hate that man!

But what about me?

I'll have to go into hiding. I'll find somewhere to live where he won't find me. Ring you at school.

I'm coming with you!

No, sweet, you can't. He won't let you go. He'd stop at nothing if I took you. He said so.

Mummy, don't go. Don't, please.

In the chill of daybreak they found him asleep with his head in his bloodstained arms on the kitchen table glittering with smashed glass. Mummy crept past with her suitcase. Ismini draped his jacket over his wet shoulders, switched off the light, and crawled back into bed.

Now Mummy got up before daybreak and stood waiting

among furled glittering lamps and skeletons of trees for the first golden tram to trundle up wrapped in fog like a caterpillar in a cocoon.

If I fail HSC, Ismini had remarked the other day, you can get me a job at the hotel with you.

Oh, you'll pass. Still want to be a teacher?

I don't know what I want.

In the kitchen Ismini lit the stump of her Easter candle and switched off the light to watch the little flame flap and tower. She thought of opening the *retsina.* No. Well, why not? She prised the cap off and filled a glass with the acrid wine. Happy birthday, Baba. She drank it in gulps, and ate all the salad, since it wouldn't keep, dipping chunks of bread in the juice, sucking the olive pits. Lovely ripe plums for later.

By candlelight her arms shone, and her breasts too, only half hidden in crimson silk.

You're so beautiful, he would say, sitting opposite, and she would smile mockingly over the rim of her glass at this dark tall grave man, a man who had lived, who had known sorrow. His name? What did it matter? He would bend to heap hot kisses on her hands.

Ah! But you're too innocent, my darling.

I'm so tired of innocence. Slowly, significantly.

God! Don't tempt me! And overcome by a wave of passion, crushing her fiercely in his arms, he would carry her limp and golden to her bed.

Ismini took a long swig and held her glass against the swelling candleflame. Light swung rocking all over her, the kitchen walls, the window panes. The luminous crimson plums sat glowing there. She bit one through its skin and its juice spurted.

Darling, she murmured out loud across the table. Oh, my darling.

MARIA'S GIRL

I had not heard from my sister Maria for thirty years when a short letter in Greek arrived from Melbourne announcing her death of a brain tumour. Dear Uncle Manoli, it said. Her daughter, Niki, hoped her letter would find us. As the only child, she felt that she should let the family know. The name of the village had been on her mother's papers. She and a friend would be in Greece in January on their way to London and could come and visit us, if that was all right.

'Not a man friend, Manoli?' my wife said.

'It says *filo*. Yes.' I peered down at the letter. So Maria had had a child. 'Write to her, Vasso, will you. Tell her to come.'

Vasso sniffed. She wrote that same night.

After the letter the dreams began. I have seen others die Maria's death, slowly, in silence. Cancer eats the brain alive like wasp maggots in a spider. Her body, like mine, must have sagged, aged, all its hair gone grey. Grey corrugations mat my skull. My face is like a withering potato with white slit eyes. Night after night I shamble, my head thumping, to gape in a mirror aglare with yellow light at a grey face and blood-streaked eyes. Yet Maria in the dreams is twenty-six years old as I last saw her. Souls may not grow old when bodies do. I have a vision of yellow, speckled hands folded in death.

She was three years older, but once we were grown, strangers often took us for twins. We lived here alone for a time, as close as twins. Our mother had died of pneumonia in the winter of '41. When our father was killed in the Civil War three years later I was still only sixteen. I carried my pistol everywhere. Relatives wanted to send us to the city, but we insisted we could manage. We treated each other, now I look back, with the tender respect of an engaged couple. Until the night of the fire.

Her guilt and shame forced her away. Not all at once, a gradual estrangement. As in a clear pane that crumbles before your eyes, the image beyond is lost in a mesh of white crystals.

When she left for Australia on the bride ship I went down to see her off, a gruff and grubby peasant jostled on the floodlit wharf with the city aunts and cousins. She was scarved and dressed in black, a widow already at twenty-six. Her eyes were wet. When my turn came to kiss her goodbye, she flinched. Neither of us ever wrote. Silence, for ever.

I watched the ship dwindle, flickering its golden lights.

Vasso must have noticed my dreams and wild awakenings, but we never discuss them, or much else these days but the goats and the firewood, the apple trees that need pruning, simple things. The violent years are behind us. Vasso has been a good wife and mother. She was always a cold woman, not like Maria, poor Vasso. If she has dreams of her own, she keeps them to herself. She is lonely now, I think. Each summer our sons arrive back in shiny cars from Munich and Zurich with their painted wives and little children. Each has named his eldest son and daughter after us. The children feed the hens and goats, chase fireflies on the river banks at nightfall, pick the fat, hairy mulberries, ride with me on the haycart. They cry when the time comes to leave. The little tragedies of children.

It is deep winter now. The river trickles, congealing, its banks heaped high with snow. The black trees could be wrought of ice and iron. Even at noon the whitewashed houses have lighted windows glowing under their crusted eaves, patching the snow with gold. The air is grey. In the yard our few white laying hens, almost invisible, jab at the frozen snow.

Niki is delighted with the snow.

Niki is just as I had imagined her, the image of Maria, the same age, and even dressed in black. The same golden skin and long, honey-coloured eyes and hair, banded hair glowing. How well I remember her, dressed for church, stooping low to iron the ends of her hair straight, the old flat-irons heating on the stove. She speaks good Greek in Maria's own voice. She is still wearing mourning for our sake, I think. It is our custom.

The whole village has exclaimed over the likeness, and made

much of her. Only Vasso is critical at times, but Vasso is not from here. She never knew Maria. They are going on to London soon, anyway, Niki and her young man. They make no secret of sleeping in one bed, and stay there half the bitter white morning. Her Bill is forgiven a lot, not being Greek. He is well-liked, in fact, tall and blond, with his stutter and his glasses, his few words of Greek, his way of wheedling the old folk to pose for his camera with their carts and looms. In the *kafeneion* he buys beers all round and tries to dance to the juke box. They have been invited everywhere, even to the school. They are both schoolteachers. They are hoping to find jobs in London and come back to us in summer.

Over coffee the other day I showed them my old photograph of Maria and me on old Marko the horse in the vegetable patch. There was our old apricot tree, and the sunflower beside it, as tall as a man.

'Mamma looked old, Theio. Older than you.'

'Well, she was three years older. But she was only twenty then. Our father had just died.'

'No, I mean now.'

Yet I know I look old for my age, though I am strong as rock.

'Fifty-six. That's not very old.'

'No. Poor Mamma.' After a while, handing it back, she said, 'Is that a sunflower? Mamma always had sunflowers in the garden.'

'It comes up every summer.' I wiped the pane and pointed out the spot where it will rear its shaggy golden head. The snow fumed in a dark wind. Icicles glinted on the barbed wire fence. On all my land I see, with an inner eye, golden seeds lying in wait.

Niki is shocked by our poverty, the relentless cold dour poverty of our village. In the house we heat only one room, the front one with the old black fuel stove that lives on apple wood. Vasso grills bread and chestnuts on the top, boils the lentils and beans and an occasional hen, heats the bathwater, bakes her famous *pita* in its black depths. Vasso and I sleep in that room, and she takes the young ones a *mangali* of hot embers at bedtime, and squabbles when they open the window a crack behind the shutters.

'You'll catch your deaths!'

They look warm enough to me under Vasso's wedding *flokati*, like two humped shaggy sheep, as she says goodnight and switches the light off. What a blessing that we have electricity now.

Niki hates the way the hens dart in if the door opens and flap up on to the kitchen table to peck at bread and leftovers. When she chases them they squawk and rush around, skidding on their splayed claws and dropping brown splodges. The lavatory is a problem too, a concrete hole at the back, sheltered by plastic superphosphate bags hooked on blackberry brambles. There are always splodges of brown around its sloping mouth. In summer she will hate it even more, when the blackberries bring the wasps and glittering flies buzz in the hole. During the snowstorm the other day I said to go and do it in the barn. We all do. The goats don't mind, and the soiled straw will go on the fields anyway. No, she would squat outside in the storm with a sheet of plastic over her.

The animals make up for a lot, I think. She loves them all. Our wild yellow cat pads behind her, yowling. She feeds the goats and strokes their hot white pelts and long ears while they stand smiling and spry, fixing her with their slit gold eyes. I'm fond of the goats myself. Maria loved them. How she mourned when they were taken in the Civil War.

I showed Niki the soot still on the barn walls and asked her if her mother had ever told her about the fire.

'No. You tell me, Theio.'

'Well, it was a long time ago.' I patted the hairy mudbricks. 'This was our house then, with rooms on top. The Partisans burnt it in the Civil War. But no one was hurt.'

The goats bowed and nudged me, the swollen pink bags swinging between their legs. Niki's long-lidded eyes betrayed disgust as I squatted to pump the teats with these knotty old hands of mine. My hands are like treeroots, at home only in the soil. She's no good at milking. You have to squeeze hard. Vasso has taught her to make cheese.

Baths are a problem in winter, too, even once a week. At first she wanted one every day, with the pipes frozen and gallons being heated on the stove. One afternoon soon after they arrived I tramped in from the barn, kicked off my boots, and, hearing a voice call in the warm room, naturally I flung the door open. The thought never occurred to me. It wasn't a Saturday. I'm getting hard of hearing now, besides.

She was stooping naked in the shallow copper pan that we all use for baths, her hair in a coil at her nape, running a shower of water from a saucepan over her long back. Her black clothes off, she glowed all over with the gold of ripened wheat.

'Maria!' I groaned.

But of course it was Niki who was crouching, turning away, shame and outrage in her eyes. My blood froze. I muttered an apology and slammed the door shut.

That night I dreamed of Maria as she stood naked in the smouldering barn. Out of her bright hair burst the great knuckly clusters of a brain tumour. She was weeping black tears silently.

New horrors were just beginning then, as the Germans withdrew. Our father and other village authorities — our father had been mayor when we were little — were taken at gunpoint, tied up, marched up the mountain and threatened with death if they refused to join the Resistance. Some who fell in their tracks were shot where they lay. My father was shot escaping. Others who came back safe told me. My father, who had fought beside that Partisan leader on the Albanian front, would not fight against Greeks. Next, our animals were taken. Burnings had begun at night in villages in the foothills.

That day, I remember, Partisans from the mountain had made speeches in broad daylight in the square and withdrawn as night fell, but no further than the vineyard slopes across the river. The village hummed with fear behind closed doors. Thank God, a shepherd crept home after dark and gave the warning. Five houses were to be burnt. Ours was one.

I rushed Maria, empty-handed, stumbling and splashing, to our Uncle Stathi's house. He was alone, having sent our aunt and cousins weeks before to Thessaloniki. A lame, grey man stroking a rifle. We barred the doors and shutters and huddled there like roosting hens by lamplight. Hours went by before we saw through the slats a red flame on the sky.

Our uncle growled and cursed, swallowing great swigs of his *tsipouro* and thrusting the bottle at me. That was what I needed to make a man of me, he said. Harsh and fiery, the *tsipouro* made my blood beat hard. Maria, swaying, exclaimed and wailed. I sat with my arm round her, and could not have uttered a word if my life had been at stake. I have never spilt human blood.

When he sank back in a stupor we covered him up warm and crept with the lamp to our cousins' room. We rolled ourselves in blankets on the divans there, but we could not have slept. Maria was still making a sad whimpering.

'Maria? It's all right.'

'What can we do now, Manoli?'

'It's only a house. I'll build another one.'

'I'm too afraid.'

I could only just see her face by the dimmed lamp.

'Manoli?' she whispered. 'Can I get in with you?'

I nodded. She lifted the blanket and slid in against me, her hands on my shoulders. Transfixed with shock, I burned and ached, clenched against her. She kissed me with her tongue tasting of tears, and put my hands on her soft breasts and the long, furry lips between her thighs. When I went into her she grasped me with folded legs. Never since have I felt such joy and pain and terror with any woman.

Afterwards we lay still. Her long eyes were closed, Her hair had come undone and scarved my throat with hot itching amber swathes.

'Let me go. Oh, my God! It's a great sin. Manoli, no.'

'You don't love me?'

'Ssh. Yes. But you mustn't ever tell. Swear.'

'I swear. Are you sorry?'

She kissed me and moved away, smoothing my blanket down.

'Are you? Maria?'

'I don't know.'

It was my first time. I wanted to tell her, but her back was turned.

At some time the lamp sizzled and went out. I remember half-waking. We woke together much later, and without disturbing Theio Stathi's snores we crept into the first blue light of day, trailing our white breaths, jumping as cocks crew. Our house was charred, smouldering. Beams protruded, black-blistered and gnawed. Shutters and window-panes lay smashed in the mud. I thought of unseen eyes following our backs through the hot doorway. A stench of kerosene. Our feet crunched on a black flood of wheat.

The old trunk with her wedding things in it had fallen through the burnt floor of the bedroom and lay burst open on a heap of ashes. With a cry she knelt and dragged out her ruined linens and sheets and hand-dyed woven blankets, the patient embroideries and laces of all her winters. She held up a singed cloth to show me. Black tears began to trickle down her face.

I hugged her then, both of us crouching as the darkness around us crackled and fumed. Wisps of flame still glowed here and there on black tufts of sacking. I found one of the crocks of water we always kept under there, wetted the cloth and wiped her face with it.

'Let me see you,' I muttered.

She shook her head, but did not resist as I took off her black clothes one by one until she stood there golden all over and I could touch her nipples and the curls of brown hair in her armpits and her groin that I had never seen before. Sudden voices and footsteps outside brought us to our senses. Frantically she pulled her clothes back on.

'Help me! Quick! Are my eyes red?'

She gave a sobbing laugh, and went out. Theio Stathi, haggard and vague, and all the family and neighbours had gathered in the yard, volubly indignant about the burning. They escorted us back with a chorus of commiserations. The sun came up and went down before they had all had their say. In the end it was decided that Maria must be sent out of harm's way to his sister-in-law the *modistra* in Athens, where she could learn dress-making and earn her living keeping house. I sat there, struck dumb with anguish and bitterness, and not once did she look my way.

We were never alone again. They arranged a marriage for her down there, a ship's cook of forty who loved her madly, they said. I never met the man. It was at short notice, at the height of the Civil War. I rented her share of the fields from her and sent her the money. I visited her once, on business. There were others there. Numbly I watched this polite stranger fumbling with coffee cups. They had no children. When her husband's ship was lost at sea in '49 I bought her share so she could take a dowry to Australia. And for years I thought about her every night.

The new house I built has walls of stone one metre thick. My shoulders will bear the scars of those stones to the grave. It is the bitterest thought to me that our sons will rush home and sell the house and land when we die.

Yesterday, as night drew in, we were sitting round the open stove in a firelight yellow as maize oil, eating the last wrinkled winter apples that Niki had roasted with honey. Bill sprawled, scribbling aerograms. Vasso was kneading a last *pita* for them. They are going in a day or two.

'It's been lovely, Theio. I'm glad I wrote.'

'Lucky you found the address. Where was it?'

'Oh, on her birth certificate,' she yawned. 'And she told me about her brother Manoli when she called my baby brother after you. She said you'd never leave here.'

I could only gape at that golden face.

'You didn't know? He only lived a few weeks. Something wrong with his heart. Mamma was shattered. She called the *papas* to come and baptise him with the neighbours as godparents. Emmanuel, that's right, isn't it? After you.' She grimaced. 'My father was furious. His father's name was Yannis. He kept saying, "What right had you? What bloody right?" '

I poked sparks in the glowing apple wood.

'Were they happy together?'

'Sometimes.' She shrugged.

Last night, when I saw Maria, shreds of dead flesh hung from her, black shreds, and her black clothes. Her mouth gaped in silent shrieks. 'Manoli! Manoli!' Nothing I can say can comfort her. Throwing off the covers I stumbled shuddering outside into a black silence. The sky was hung with icicles and a white sickle moon. On the snow the shadows of trees lay in nets. A far wolf howled. Safe and warm, a goat whimpered in her sleep. My shaft of urine, glittering, pitted the white crust. Soon the thaw will set in. Heavy work brings heavy sleep. She has promised to come back to us in summer, Maria's girl has.

She will see the sunflower.

THE HAREM

When Bell was nine the SEC transferred her father from Melbourne to Wangalla for nine months. In no time he was sick and tired of living in a room at Doolan's pub. He sent Bell and her mother scrawled postcards full of loneliness. For the school holidays he found them a cheap house near the station, and they could have the run of it but for Mr Grey's own front room where he kept himself to himself. Bell sneaked in for a look. His double bed was a smelly bundle of grey sheets and blankets. Morning sunshine burned in fluff all over his oiled floor and the dusty mirror over his dressing table.

Mr Grey owned the house opposite too, where the Harem lived. He owned the woodyard next door, its stacks of red-furred wood guarded by a savage dog. It said so on the gate. He owned half of Grey Bros iceworks; sometimes they met him on hot afternoons, chipping out shimmering blocks and carrying them wrapped in sacking on his shoulder into the shaded houses, while his horse stamped. Mr Grey was a widower and childless, and ought to have been well off but for his drinking problem. Bell thought he was old, but her mother said no, but he'd let himself go. Mr Grey was affable in the evenings and surly before noon. His little wrinkled eyes had veins, and when he yawned he showed yellow pegs of teeth. He spent most afternoons in the pub and even ate there. He shambled in about seven, banging doors, and sometimes crashed and swore, and sometimes sang snatches of 'Knees up, Mother Brown' or 'Oh, you beautiful doll'.

The yard at Mr Grey's was shaded by a red-leafed tree dripping with little red plums sweet and yellow inside and warm when the sun was in them. A tame bird lived behind the tree. A curlew, Mr Grey said. It squatted in the dust or minced around and cocked its gold eyes. Once Mr Grey caught Bell throwing plums at it to make it hop and bridle.

'Know what happens to kids ut do that, do yer?' he growled. 'Bird gets in at night. Pecks their eyes out and swallers um.'

All night in the dark it hovered. A weird cry, a scimitar beak. Her mother insisted on fresh air. Every night once her light was off Bell leapt up and latched her windows.

Down the lane from the house there was a long footbridge over the railway lines, and the Spirit of Progress surged under it gushing great clouds and hooting. The wheels pumped, grinding, glittering. The high blue engine whooped. Every morning Bell rushed to the bridge for the Spirit to wrap her in hot white billows.

Once as she tore out she saw that the woodshed gate was open, the red dog bounding up, barking, slavering. She propped, but he only wanted to prance and bow and lick her hands. The Spirit shrieked. Bell and the dog took off and reached the bridge in good time. When the train had slid away they sauntered back together.

'If yer gunna take Rover out,' Mr Grey warned, 'watch out yer bring um back. Worth a packet, that dorg is.'

After that whenever the dog saw Bell he bowed and whined, a slobbery wood-chip in his teeth for her to throw. At Spirit time he jumped at the gate with his tail whipping. She called him Red, not Rover. Red was covered in such tight curls he looked as if June had permed him with her lotions and pins.

June lived with Mr and Mrs Peterson and their daughter Kate in the Harem. Mr Malone the grocer called it that. Met the Harem yet? He winked at Bell's mother but she seemed not to notice.

'Mum, what's a harem?'

'Oh, a sort of Arab family.'

June was tall and heavy, with curly red hair — hennaed, Bell's mother said — as glossy as plum-skins. Advertisements in shop windows said that Miss June Smith did hairdressing in your own home by appointment. Bell's mother said June looked fast, and she was, pedalling along from head to head on a glittering bicycle with netted wheels. Women waited for her with their hair lank and wet in kitchens soaked in the waxen light of hot sun behind holland blinds. Often three or four women would wait in the kitchen of one of them, who laid on tea with buns, or scones, or fruitcake. The teapots wore their best knitted cosies. June's bicycle was parked on all the best Wangalla verandahs. Sometimes it was leaning on the hot brick wall of Doolan's for all the world to see.

When Bell's mother first had her hair done, she hadn't met the other SEC wives, so no one else was there until Mr Grey slouched in. June laughed and smoked and told long jokes, and ate more than her share of the buttered Boston bun at afternoon tea time. When she had gone, Mr Grey wiped crumbs off his whiskers, sighed, and muttered, 'Fine figure of a woman. They say she's got a temper, but. Stands to reason, eh? Hair like that.'

Bell's mother sniffed.

'I reckon it's a blasted waste,' Mr Grey droned on.

Bell and her mother met Mrs Peterson at the grocer's. She had a toothy grin and long hair coiled in a dun roll on the bone of her nape. She was so homesick for the Old Country. Here the neighbours were so standoffish, weren't they? Do call me Mary, she said. Bell's mother said to call her Judith. Well now, how would Judith's little girl like to come over and play with her Kate? Kate wasn't much older really, only eleven, and so awfully lonely, poor child.

Sullenly dressed up in frills and strap shoes Bell was sent over to play.

Kate was tall and slim with a white face and straight black hair. Bell was tubby and pink, her hair butter-coloured. Kate was allowed to be barefoot, and dressed all in black. She had bitten her scarlet nails. Her eyes when they met Bell's were long and scowling, unsmiling. With her light on in bright daylight she showed Bell her treasures, her jewels, her greasepaints. She was going to be an actress. She let Bell try on in the dressing table mirror her Arabian brass bangles — so they *were* Arabs — and the strings of green and gold glass beads she spent her time threading. She showed Bell fuzzy photos of her relatives back home, then they sat on her bed to read her Enid Blyton books, stealing glances at each other in the yellow glare of the lamp.

When Kate said 'grass' it rhymed with 'mass'. She said 'somethink' and 'anythink', and called lemonade 'pop'. Later Bell's mother was annoyed when she said things Kate's way: don't copy poor speech, Annabel, please.

Bell was asked to stay to dinner, and ran across to ask her mother, who said yes. With the door open, the Peterson's kitchen table only just fitted in between the stove and the ice chest. Mr Peterson squeezed in on one side between Mrs Peterson and June, and Bell and Kate sat opposite. The light bulb was on a cord and swilled shadows over them with every gust of the northerly. The tablecloth of pages from the *Age* lifted, flapped. They had a sweetish red stew with lumps of meat and soft potatoes, and drank 'shandies' of beer and lemonade mixed. They all called the lemonade 'pop'. A rare treat for Bell, it was spoilt by the beer. The grown-ups had just beer. Their breaths smelled like the hot buffets of air when the bar doors opened at Doolan's. Bell's parents never touched liquor.

'Coom on, Mary. Drink oop, loov.' Mr Peterson cuddled Mrs Peterson, winking at Bell. But Mrs Peterson only shook her drooping head.

After the stew Bell thought she should say thank you for the lovely dinner and go home, but Mrs Peterson gave them all peaches and spotty apples from the ice chest. They peeled them on to their dinner plates. June, showing Bell how to cut her apple through its equator to make a star-apple, dropped it and splashed stew on Bell's dress. June peeled her own apple all in one piece and tossed the peel over her shoulder to see who she would marry. Mrs Peterson's bony nose turned red. You couldn't make out any letters in the coils of apple peel. June and Mr Peterson lit cigarettes and blew smoke.

'Cheer oop, Mary, for the loov of Mike,' Mr Peterson boomed. 'Ah'll open anoother bottle. Put a bit of life into the blooming proceedings.'

'I'm making coffee, Bob,' was all Mrs Peterson said, putting the jug on. Their coffee wasn't boiled in a saucepan with grounds on top, but mixed with syrup from a long black bottle with a picture on the label of a turbanned Arab. At home Bell was only allowed a drop of tea or coffee in her milk. She and Kate filled their coffee with sugar. Not even Kate was taking any notice of Bell. They were all shiny with sweat.

After the coffee Mr Peterson and June left the table hand in hand and shut themselves in a bedroom. Mrs Peterson sighed and boiled the jug again for the dishes. Bell helped scrape plates. Footsteps shambling down the back path startled them all. 'The boogie man,' breathed Kate in Bell's ear. But with a cough Mr Grey's shabby head was thrust into the lamplight. He said no thanks to coffee. He'd just dropped in to pass the time of day. He'd better be off home, thanks, Mary.

When Bell asked Kate in her room what her father and June were doing, Kate said that if she didn't know at her age, thut was too bud, wasn't it? She shrugged.

'Bob looves them both. Me moom and June.'

'Oh.'

'He likes me best. He said so.'

'Oh, really?' was all Bell's mother had to say to that when she heard.

That was another interesting thing: Kate's father would only answer to 'Bob', not 'Father' or 'Dud'. He wore a bristly brown moustache and once belted Kate with his razor strop, and worked as a foreman at the cannery.

'Mum, can we buy that Arab coffee?'

'No, we can't.'

'But it's lovely!'

'They had no business to give a child coffee. You've got sauce on your dress.'

'June did it. It's stew.'

'Don't answer back.'

'Mum, what's a four man?'

Her parents decided that if she was asked again she was to say thank you, but her tea would be ready at home, and then come straight home. Because we say so, they said when she asked why. But she could still go over and play. She kept quiet about the shandies.

Kate came over the next morning to see if Bell could go for a swim in the river with them. Mr Grey said he'd be in that: too right he would. 'Well, well, well. Here's K-K-K-Katy,' sang Bell's father jovially, and Kate said, 'My name's Kate.' Bell's mother said definitely not, what with snags and currents and tiger snakes in the river. Bell's mother and father were awful. Kate was, too. They all were.

That was the Sunday the roast leg of lamb got blown as it waited on the table for the vegetables to cook. Her mother said the flies had got to it, but Bell could only see little white threads in rows, like specks of fat. Her mother said she wasn't to tell a soul, did she hear, and ran over to the Harem to borrow some meat. Bell and Dad read the Sydney Sunday papers. The hot darkness by the one fire stove was full of the sweaty smell of the roast. A long time later her mother came back with a tin of Spam, and served it cold with the vegetables. Bell sulked and said it was a blasted waste, but she had to eat Spam or starve, while in the woodyard Red tore and gulped the grey leg and lay dreaming afterwards with the bone in his paws. The treacly dripping had to be poured into a hole in the garden, not back into its hole in the speckled wax in the dripping-basin.

Bell's mother told Dad that she had found poor Mary alone and in such a state that she had had to stay and calm her down. They sent Bell out to play while she told him all about it.

'Oh. But there's nothing to *do*.'

'Go on, sticky-beak,' grinned Dad.

There were some very hot days that week. For hours Bell lay and read in nothing but bathing togs on the cool linoleum in the kitchen. She was allowed to spray herself with the hose in the yard, squinting through rainbows and sheets of wet light, water pounding her. Tawny butterflies shook their wings. She swung ropes of glittering water under the tree, where the dry lawn glowed all over with soft plums. Her mother spent one whole afternoon boiling and bottling jam, some for them and some for Mr Grey. At teatime she sighed, saying how in Melbourne they could have just hopped on a bus and been at the beach in no time. She and Dad quarrelled that night in their hot room beyond the wall. Things were scurrying on top of Bell's ceiling. Her mother was always hoping to high heaven it was nothing worse than possums.

At the window the curlew wailed.

Bell was sent over to the Harem with a jar of plum jam. In her yellow room Kate made her shut her eyes. 'Now open them,' Kate said. She had a solid glass egg. When Bell cupped it in her hands like a chicken it was cold and glowed, a heavy drop of stony water, magnifying her palms. Through it she could see all the bulging golden room. A rainbow light lay deep inside. The egg caught lamplight and sunlight and nursed them like seeds.

'It's crystal,' Kate whispered. 'Bob gave it to me. It's valuable. I can tell fortunes in it. I can read minds.'

Bell peered again.

'No, it only works for me.'

'How does it work?'

'Never you mind.'

She swore Bell to secrecy. Even so, she hid the egg away and wouldn't say where, or even let Bell have another little look, however much she begged and wheedled.

For a week Bell clung to Kate's side. Every afternoon they walked Red along the river banks or behind the ice cart for chips of ice to suck. Kate showed Bell her school with its empty yard of asphalt and yellow tussocks. Bell showed Kate Mr Grey's curlew. Kate threw plums and one hit it. She wouldn't talk about the crystal egg.

At last, alone in Kate's room while Kate went to the WC, Bell gave in to temptation. Evening was falling from a hot sky the colour of apricots. In Kate's golden room Bell dared to kneel and go rummaging. But as she grasped it, hard and icy in a singlet in the bottom drawer of the dressing table, Kate's face appeared. It glared down at her in the lit mirror.

'Put it down, you thief!' Kate hissed.

Bell, sick with shock, turned to face Kate's white face. Had Kate read her mind? They were both shaking, both in pyjamas and slippers, as were the grown-ups, it was so hot, out in the kitchen playing a rowdy game of cards with Mr Grey.

'I only wanted a look!'

'Oh did you now? Well, joost for thut, you're never going to see it again. I've a good mind to tell Bob on you.'

'No, Kate, please!'

'He'll belt you till you bleed.'

'I wasn't going to take it! Why *can't* I have a look? Aren't I your friend?'

'No. You're not. Go home, Sneak.'

Bell stared and burned.

'Go on. Before I change me mind. Tell your moom you're a thief. Tell her I'm not her babysitter.'

Shaken with sobs, Bell ran home. No one saw. She latched her windows and got straight into bed to hide in her hot pillow. She pretended to be asleep when her mother looked in, opened a window and switched off the light. Bell latched it again. The slow night passed. Over breakfast the next day she told about the shandies and so was banned from the Harem forever. She brought up her breakfast though, and had to go back to bed. Her mother and father brought her cool drinks, and food that she couldn't face; they read to her, sponged her, took her temperature and worried all day whether to call the doctor. By teatime she felt a lot better. She had scrambled eggs and slept for fourteen hours.

Next morning Kate was out on the footpath with scrawny Cynthia Malone, the grocer's daughter, drawing with chalks, so Bell had to make herself go out for the Spirit, with Red for company, prancing. They whispered and giggled behind her back. Afterwards they were still there having snail races, prodding the frothed brown shells and barracking. Cynthia's baby brother that she was supposed to be minding picked one up and ate it.

The gas heater blew up that afternoon. No one could have a bath. Bell's mother cried. She said it was the last straw. Then she said that the last matinee of the panto at the Tivoli was next Saturday, so they could still see it if Bell wanted to, but only if they went home a week early. Bell was overjoyed. She wanted to go home very badly. Even though it would mean leaving Dad and Red. So that was all settled.

June came over after tea to give Bell's mother's hair a quick trim. She was in a hurry and took puffs of her cigarette as she snipped.

'No time for a coopa, thanks, dear,' she said. 'No rest for the wicked.'

'June?' Bell said. 'Can Kate really read minds with her crystal egg?'

'Not now, Bell, June's busy.'

'What's thut, Bell? Did Kate tell you she had a crystal egg?'

'She *showed* me. It's beautiful.'

'Well, well. And where does she keep it?'

'In her bottom drawer in a singlet. It's valuable.'

'I'm sure it is. I'd like to see it.'

'Oh, she won't show you. It's a secret.'

'Oh, I think she will.'

June's face was dark, her crimson lips thin and tight. Bell kept quiet, then.

Over the road that night the lights were still on late, all the lights, and there were shouts and doors slammed. Bell was up way past her bedtime helping her mother with the ironing that she'd put off till then in the cool of the night. Dad looked up from his crossword.

'Sounds like the Sheik's got a war on his hands. Might just pop over and help him out. Even up the odds, eh?'

'It's no laughing matter, Alan. It's a disgrace.'

'Who do you back to win? I'll have two bob on June.' He winked. 'Or one? One Bob on June.'

'Oh, Alan, really. That poor little girl, that's all I can say. What hope has she got?'

'Why's Kate a poor little girl?'

'Never you mind. Off you go now, lovey, it's high time you were in bed.'

'Oh, Mu-um.'

Bell lay awake for ages with her door half-open in the dark, listening to squeals and scamperings above; bird cries outside; silence from the Harem. Her parents' light and Mr Grey's were yellow stripes under their doors.

In the morning the Harem was still silent behind its blinds until, just before the Spirit was due, the front gate slammed. June was out there alone, holding a suitcase and wheeling her bicycle. Her eyes and hair were hidden by her black-veiled hat, but her plummy lips were tight, her head high for the benefit of starers in the gardens and front windows. As she faltered in the dazing sun, Mr Grey appeared in pyjamas in his doorway, padded to the front door, and opened it. Then June came striding over.

'Well, here I am, Tom Grey,' she said. 'If you still want me.'

'Too right I do,' he said, white under his whiskers. So in she came and snibbed the gate, propped up her bicycle, handed her suitcase to Mr Grey still sagging in the doorway in his fluffed pyjamas, and kissed him. Bell and her mother stood by open-mouthed as Mr Grey and June, hand in hand, shut themselves in his bedroom.

Bell hung around as long as she could, until the Spirit hooted: there were only a few mornings left. That was the golden day they had sandwiches and cordial on a bank of the river where ruffled branches hung their shadows looping in brown water. Red capered then snoozed. Her mother let her take snaps with the Box Brownie, and asked if she was sorry to go and if she'd miss Kate. When Bell said she'd never really liked Kate, her mother nodded, and left it at that.

At teatime they went out for a fish-and-chip tea at the Bridge Cafe, for the first time ever, to give the lovebirds a go.

'How's that for calling a bloke's bluff, eh?' Dad couldn't get over it. 'Well, he's bitten off more than *he* can chew. What a woman!'

'Can I ask June for a ride on her bike?'

'No, you can't. Don't talk with your mouth full.'

'Must've really done her block to walk out,' Dad went on. 'What set her off, I wonder? That's redheads for you.'

'It's dyed.'

Dad went on about how the blokes at work would be all agog, especially the ones that drank at Doolan's and had seen it coming. Her mother's answers were in such long words, Bell lost the thread, watching how the white bubbles heaved in a milkshake when you blew down the straw. Her father paid the bill and slipped some pennies in Bell's pocket. They all strolled home arm in arm the long way as the sky turned green and stars showed.

The next few days were a flurry of washing and pegging out wrung sheets and shirts that flapped like yacht sails on the lines; packing suitcases; having goodbye cups of tea in waxy kitchens.

Bell and her mother were booked on the Spirit, and Dad was moving back to Doolan's pub. The bicycle stayed proudly on the verandah, but June and Mr Grey never seemed to be in. No one saw Kate or her parents at all, but Mr Grey told Dad that Bob and Kate were moving to Sydney and Mrs Peterson was on her way back to the Old Country. He wrote down Bell's Melbourne address for the wedding invitation.

The day before they went Bell said goodbye to all the house and the yard, the glowing shaggy plum tree stripped of its plums, the ruffled curlew, and poor sad Red who sensed it and whined, thrusting his rough head into her hands. In the house she visited every corner, remembering moments. No one was home. Her heart thumping, she pushed open the door of Mr Grey's front room. His bed was flat now. Silver brushes and combs and bottles of green-gold scent stood on lace on his dressing table. The mirror, burning, reflected Bell's joy and amazement. There at last was the crystal egg. It was glowing with inner fire among the ornaments.

THE ALBATROSS

When, in the last period on a sunlit autumn afternoon, Madame swung her broad shoulders around from the blackboard and asked me coyly to stay behind after school, the rest of 5A craned and raised their eyebrows or sniggered into inky palms. I was Madame's pet, top of the form in French, *sa petite* Rose. I shrugged, grimaced, mantled with red under my pimples but assuming nonchalance, copying verbs down.

The bell went and they all crowded out. I sat there alone, steam furring my glasses, while Madame cleaned the board down with long, ungainly swipes. In the slanting sunlight the chalk dust floated. My desk top was varnished amber, engraved with old initials, the wood around the inkwell blotched black.

Madame had liquid brown intolerably mild eyes, heifer eyes. She had clear skin, coarse-grained and as innocent of make-up as any of ours, and about her large head was curled a coronet of greying plaits. She exuded foreignness. We called her Madame, prouncing it 'madam' because *madame* sounded too, too affected. All the same we were proud of having a real French teacher: although she was Polish, she had lived in Paris before she came out to Australia, and studied at the Sorbonne. We had even heard that she was a Resistance heroine decorated for valour in both Poland and France. Yet in class we all teased her and misbehaved, puppies nipping at her thick heels, secure in her helplessness to punish us. We looked on in sorrow and amusement as tears swilled in her merciful eyes.

Smiling demurely, Madame approached me with that clumsy saunter of hers. Some 5A stragglers on the way past the open doorway grinned in behind her back. The desk creaked as she eased herself down, the yellow poetry book clasped with one plump finger in the place. I shrank from her burly body and the ordeal to come by poetry book.

'Ecoutez, ma petite. Listen to zis.'

She read me '*Harmonie du soir*'. My first Baudelaire poem. Over its majestic slow syllables her heavy voice shook, and her ringed hands, tinged yellow with nicotine. Some of the girls were sure the Gestapo had tortured her. A quarter of 5A were Jewish migrants who knew about the SS and the Gestapo. They gathered at recess times to share the latest news of the war in Israel; this was in 1956. Some had brothers already over there fighting, and talked of soon joining them. I peered to see if Madame had fingernails. Did fingernails grow back? I had no idea.

'*Lisez, maintenant.*'

I read it aloud as best I could, striving for a good accent, a tone of recitation both elevated and sombre, striving — *hypocrite lectrice* — for feeling. I felt her moist gaze. She went over the hard words and explained with a dramatic shudder that the poem was once thought an outrageous blasphemy. She made sure I saw the sun drowning in its congealing blood. Flowers censed the evening air, the violin quivered like an afflicted heart. '*Un coeur tendre,*' she insisted. 'A tender heart.' Her eyes probed mine. I smothered an urge to explode in wild snorts and brays. She talked on about Sin and the *Poète maudit*, under a dark curse. She read it again. Massive, tobacco-tainted, wheezing with emotion, she leaned back with a sigh at last.

'*Eh bien, ma petite.* Now I sink you 'ave understood.'

Dismissed, I ran to my locker. Everyone was long gone. Beyond the windows of the cold corridor, the lake was full of mist and cloud, milkily lucent. Tawny leaves spun in bright dust all the way to the tram stop.

Shut in my room by lamplight, the bed covers around my shoulders, I read it aloud again to a Ravel quartet on the radio. To my parents' amusement I had taken lately to huddling alone in my room full of music. The words of the poem sounded resonant, hieratic, stately and golden. In my mind's eye rose a sombre figure, a dark tormented face, a poet in love with sonority, splendour, decay.

That autumn of my sixteenth year discoveries were ripening in me day by day. I thought my heart would burst open like a fig. Ravel, by then, and Turina, and Tchaikovsky; *Under Milk Wood;* the poems of D.H. Lawrence; and now Baudelaire, noble and sinister, a dark god. I had begun the slow deciphering of *Madame Bovary*, an improper book redeemed, Madame said, by a limpid style and a bad end. I had been to hear chamber music in a gallery of Russian ikons, the gravely resonating violins, viola, cello, with their flaring female haunches varnished amber and glowing in the half dark. In class one day Madame had watched me copying out that sad Verlaine poem full of autumn and soulful violins. 'Verlaine? *Pas mal,*' she had shrugged. Why couldn't she leave me alone?

The next week she kept me back in the grey classroom curtained with rain, and read me '*L'Albatros*'. The *Poète*, she said, is identifying with the albatross, *gauche et veule* — you know *veule*, Rose? — *comique et laid,* comical, ugly, this gigantic bird stumbling on the deck, its wings like oars. The crew torment him and jeer. He cannot take off again into the sky. Tears, intolerable tears, glowed in her eyes. Was she identifying with the albatross? My flesh crawled. This was grotesque. She was reproaching me. It wasn't fair, when I was no naughtier than anyone else! I could hardly wait to be released.

As we stood up she shyly handed me a thick typescript: fairy tales for children that she had written in Polish and hoped to have published. Would I correct the English for her? As if I would have dared. She had not had a child of her own, she said. I read them that night by the bed lamp, her sad, ethereal, gossamer stories. In one, a moonbeam imprisoned itself in a stone for love, as a living sacrifice, and so the first moonstone was born. I had never heard of moonstones at the time, and thought they were a fancy of hers, milky, lucent, embedded in filigrees of silver like willows by moonlight. Before I ever saw one I was prepared to love moonstones.

Full of bashful praise, I gave the typescript back unmarked, and she asked me to her place for tea on Saturday.

Well, this is an honour, Rosie, said my mother. I wanted to wear school uniform, but she sent me off in full armour of brassiere, suspender belt and nylons under my cousin June's outgrown grey suit. In my armpits the reek of depilatory cream was not quite swamped by the sharp sweetness of eau de cologne. I had spent all morning scraping the dried cream and hairs off the stubble with my nails and dropping the little pills of debris on a newspaper spread over my bed. For years I had been short-sighted, and even through thick glasses the world was fuzzy and glowed. My eyes got worse, my lenses thicker, year by year. An article in the *Women's Weekly* or *Woman's Day* or *Woman* had inspired me to varnish the frames with crimson nail polish to match my glittering nails, my caked lipstick and acne blotches studded with pustules and floured like a scone.

'You look really nice, dear. Quite grown up.'

I dragged on last year's coat of shrill Ming blue and my patent leather court shoes to shuffle to the tram stop, head bent, glaring sidelong at any passers-by who dared to look. On the glossy amber seat of the tram, jolted windblown along, I saw nothing, sunk in trepidation.

Fallen leaves filled the gutters in Madame's street. Street lamps flickered on, red on the red sky. The door with her number in brass stood in cold shadow. I knocked. It opened on to dark stairs and at the top a golden room, a red-barred radiator, lace curtains and cloths.

Madame welcomed me and took my coat. I shook hands with Monsieur and with *Madame sa mère.* For some reason it embarrassed me to see that Monsieur was a handsome man. Madame's mother was frail and bent, crowned with white braids, her voice a cricket's chirrup in her knotted throat. Her hand felt like dry bones in a glove of skin, and webbed skin shrouded her cheekbones. Proudly she came tottering to the little table with the tea set and a sliced brown cake with no icing, steaming and spicy.

'My muzzer has made us her honey cake in your honour.'

They were all beaming at me. I had come empty-handed. I had not even thought of flowers.

'She said you have a French name. *Rose.*'

'Well, it's Rosemary really.'

'Rose Marie. And you know the meaning?'

'Rose! plus Mary, I suppose.'

'*Pas du tout. C'est la rosée marine.*' She raised her eyebrows.

'Oh, dew, is it?' I faltered. 'Sea dew?'

'*C'est ça*. From Latin, of course: *ros maris*. Dew of the sea.'

Even heavily sugared the tea smelled sour. All my life I had hated tea. It was one of my chores to empty the teapot down the gully trap after meals and swill away the rank leaves. I munched honey cake and gulped my tea, then a second cup, blowing to cool it until the wrinkles rolled across its surface.

When the table was cleared they had treasures to show me, from Montmartre and the quai d'Orsay, the Quartier Latin. Yellow gargoyles copied from the great stone ones on Notre-Dame. *Bouqins* garnered from green barrows along the Seine, in another life. The old books had a smell of earth, an autumnal smell of leaf-mould in their yellow, mottled pages. I wondered what Madame made of our sedately fenced houses and gardens after Warsaw and Paris, after the fires of war. With what dreams had she sailed into Melbourne?

Dew of the sea. I had always loved golden things and whatever glows with a bright fuzz, like sun in the down on white skin or on peaches; on moths and striped bees; in eyelashes that shade the deep iris with rushes. The defect in my vision, perhaps. In any case, they were all three coated with dim gold, their heads bent over aging books and gargoyles. Shadows lay soft as moths in the hollows of them. From time to time they laid on each other's shoulder a lamplit hand.

On and on I blundered in lame French. Once or twice my stomach growled. My suspender belt was crushing my belly, my taut bladder. It was beyond me to ask such an intimate question as where the toilet was. Weren't they ever going to start cooking tea? Of course Continentals ate late. How late? On Saturday nights at our place we had an early tea of fish and chips, all golden in the oily newspaper. I stole a glance at my watch. Ten to eight. I would miss the concert broadcast. Worse, I risked disgracing myself and offending Madame, too stuffed with honey cake as I was by now to eat a thing more. Unless — could she possibly have meant *afternoon* tea? Was it time to go? A fountain of heat washed through me and my face boiled: what if they were only waiting for me to go? How — what to say? My bristly armpits stung. I writhed as hot buffets of sweat and depilatory cream and the sickening cologne filled my nostrils.

At eight Monsieur gave up and withdrew with courtly apologies for wanting to listen in to the symphony concert. From behind the door came trickles and swells of resinous music and then the whimper of a violin solo. The old lady's head drooped, soft as a coiled white cat. Madame sat smoking in the lamplight. When at last I found the nerve to lurch to my stiff feet, we were all galvanised into inane grins and nods, gushes and reassurances, handshakes, waves and merry yells in the doorway. *Au revoir! Au revoir, ma petite!*

The tramlines stretched back long and glinting. I could not go home yet and bare my humiliation to my mother's sharp eyes, my father sunk in silence, my empty room. I clopped and shuffled through fallen leaves down the broad streets and along the canal, turbid and sleek, coiling and uncoiling into the bay. No one was in sight. Quickly I hopped over the sea wall to spread the blue wings of my coat and squat like a hen: hot urine poured, hissed out of me, the aching hoard of hours, steaming, rank with tea. Above the grey sand moved the dome of the stars. I sat and watched the moon float up from the sea floor of city lights and lie hanging, milk-white in a net of clouds.

And I thought of the albatross.

I wondered through what trials Madame had had to come, and I would have to come. I thought with loathing of the gauche and shallow, sniggering schoolgirl who had cringed at her side while she gave up her free time to read Baudelaire aloud patiently, over and over. How could I face her in class now? I was hot with remorse and shame.

Worst of all was the thought that Madame could not have seen, in the heart of the pimply gawk shifting on her hams in that golden room, intolerable knowledge planted there and thrusting, uncurling, like a watered beanshoot.

INHERITANCE

Here I sit in your armchair shrouded in shadows of grey lace; my glass of red wine glows on the sill; the garden is starlit beyond the mirroring pane.

Again and again you were taken to the hospital and came back determined not to die. My father each time grey with terror that you soon must. Your mind, half-dead since your stroke, stumbled on among twisted words and phrases, hostilities, old affections, shards of memory. Some querulous love left for your garden and for my little girl, Claire, whom you kept calling Paula. Splutters of anger or distress when anything was out of place or time. My father in his closed room tinkered with clocks and radios, played scraps of Bach on his piano, studied the stars by telescope. He died years ago and is charred bones now.

Up at the hospital they said that this time you would die. You'd given up. Why?

You used to ask me to promise not to look at your dead body. 'That's not how I want you to remember me, Paula,' you said. You didn't look at your own mother, who died young. 'What remains is only the husk,' you said, 'the soul being ascended unto the Father.' We went with Auntie May one cold afternoon to put lilies on your mother's grave, cold white folded lilies. I crept among the staring statues in bony drapery. The cypress trees had seeds like snails on their black fronds.

'Promise you'll have me cremated,' you said.

The first time you didn't want me to know that something serious was wrong. I was in the middle of examinations at university and must not be put off my stride. But Auntie May rang me in college.

'Paula, if they won't tell you the truth I will,' she shouted. 'It's *cancer.* Your mother might die under the knife. *Yes.* You ask your father.'

Cancer was what I had always most feared for you. You

smoked such a lot. You rolled your own. Godgies, I called them. (You loved my baby talk.) Pipes and lipsticks and lollipops were all godgies, and the little stalks that boys could pee through, but not my father's bicycle pump which was the hogfig. Daddy hated your godgies too. You lit the first, convulsed with deep coughs, at daybreak. I delayed opening my bedroom door and letting in the smoky breath of the rest of the house. In winter on the way to school — streetlamps still gold, a grey light spreading — I watched in disgust as white smoke poured out of me.

In the holidays when we went to the city for lunch and a show I wouldn't sit in a smoking compartment and flounced on my own to a non-smoker. Perched on a green seat by a shuddering double window I watched bridges and factories trundle beyond my dusty shadow. On the city platform you were waiting, breathing smoke through an angry smile.

At ten, on some dull visit, leafing by lamplight through old magazines while you grown-ups played cards, I read that cigarettes caused lung cancer. I tore the page out. 'Oh, what rubbish,' you said. Tearful and urgent, waiting on the comer that frosty night for a brown bus home: 'Mummy,' I whimpered. 'Please, please stop. You'll get cancer and die. Daddy, you tell her.'

'It's your mother's own business, Paula. Just keep quiet.'

You never got lung cancer. Eight years ago after your stroke the doctors made you stop smoking. My father and I weren't mean. We kept quiet.

When I rang from college, my father denied that it was cancer you had.

'You know what your Auntie May's like, lovey. Always got the wind up about something,' he soothed. 'Mum's got to go in for a minor op, that's all. A fissure of the anus. Now you do your best. We're proud of our girl.'

But it was cancer of the bowel. You survived the colostomy and learned to fasten plastic bags to the new hole cut in your belly. You've had to do it for nearly twenty years. You were both cool after that with Auntie May, for having interfered. But my results weren't bad.

By then I was deep in first love and that was all that mattered.

He was married. I never told you. He behaved like a gentleman and paid for the abortion. In all that summer of muggy heat and secrecy I only wrote you a letter or two. I'm sorry.

When that was over I hitchhiked down to see you in your bedroom that Dad had moved out of by then. In the hot noon darkness crowded with old furniture you lay asleep, tangled in bedclothes, your lamp still on. Your mouth gulped, grimaced, when I stepped inside.

'Hullo, Mum.'

'Paula! Is that you?'

Tears, glowing, trickled down your furrowed throat.

'Are you all right, Mum?'

'Paula!' Your voice blurting in the pillow. 'Why didn't you ever come?'

Later, after your shower, you called me into the bathroom to show me by its furred yellow light: I had never seen you naked. You hesitated, frail and shaking, your knees slack; then took the towel away. Your eyes rolled up in appeal. From hip to hip your belly grinned at me with crooked lips. On one side, your new anus, a puckered bud, a hole. Your nipples lolled, pink eyeballs staring down. Under the belly's sag nestled the shaggy grey chin of your groin.

'Is it still sore?'

'Not too bad.'

'It doesn't look too bad.'

You smiled at last, and I kissed you Your wet suede cheek.

At Claire's age, at seven or so, I remember reproaching you for looking so flabby, wrinkled and sick. Why don't you look pretty like other mothers? I persisted. You were close on fifty, no longer pretty, but loved. The grocer sold you more butter, the butcher more meat, than you ever had coupons; old ladies poking in their dry flower beds straightened stiff backs and held you up with gossip; neighbours were in and out all day for coffee. The tram conductors on our way to the second-hand bookstore told you their life stories. One whole summer in the hot twilight before bedtime you read me and my playmates *Alice in Wonderland* from my faded green copy that smelled, still smells, of autumn leaves.

Daddy read me music in bed. Scales, crotchets and quavers. FACE and Every Good Boy Deserves Food. We hummed the first bars of sonatas he was going to teach me. But I had no ear, and disappointed him.

Waking in terror of cages and shadows and furtive rustlings I would call out to you. It was always he who came, he the lighter sleeper. 'Mu-um, my leg's got cramps.' His knee joints crackling at every step down the dark passage. He would switch on my dazing light and sit rubbing my calves, wryly yawning.

'Not better yet?' he would sigh.

'No. Daddy, can I come into your bed?'

'No, lovey. Back to sleep now.'

'But I'll dream about the hospital!'

'No, you won't.'

'Will you leave the light on?'

'All right. The passage light. Night night, Snooks.'

He would kiss my cheek and stalk crackling back to the dark room you two slept in. Snoring in counterpoint.

I was always dreaming about the hospital. This great terror of hospitals, all my life. At five I spent six weeks in one with scarlet fever. You dressed me in my best brown jumper and skirt and Daddy took me there in a taxi. A nurse bathed me in phenol. The children's ward was long, cold, dim. Its balcony had a high wire fence that I clambered up one day for a dare. I was caught, punished with isolation; the nurse had short red hair and an angry contempt that stunned me. You rang the matron daily. No visitors were allowed for fear of infection. The fenced ward was our prison. Often I overshot the bedpan and rubbed the sheet for hours after, to dry it; the white cage of my bed jiggling, tinkling. I could see one skylight with stars behind it turn blue, grey, gold each morning. Nurses sponged us and replaited our plaits tightly. When Daddy came for me at last, I refused to speak. My brown jumper and skirt were brought out folded. I had given up hope of ever seeing them or home again. It was a sunny day. A stiff wind blowing.

As he aged and in retirement became remote — brittle, silent —

his nights were more disturbed and the crackling of his joints woke me several times a night as he crept outside but by then I never called.

My knee joints crackle too. I take after him. Daddy's girl. We were skinny, to your plump. Daddy's little skinnamalink. He dinked me on the bar of his bicycle to vacant lots where in other summers circuses had appeared overnight, soiled elephants shambled, and we climbed up into the golden skeletons of the new houses. He lifted me high into our gumtree to pick off its crouched caterpillars. He built bonfires like haystacks and lit Catherine wheels warily. He held my cheeks in rough palms to direct my gaze at planets and constellations. Four trees waved giant hushed shadows over skyfuls of stars.

You weigh five stone now.

On that last day, when you trotted in right on time with his morning tea, he lay flung half-off the bed in an attitude of terror, his grey eyes wide; heart pills all over the sunny floorboards. I was two hours getting here. An aged, sorrowful child, you sat numbly for hours by the window; scurried to pack away his clothes; on the telephone mumbled over and over broken self-reproaches, despair. You had squabbled over breakfast. He had trudged back to bed in a sulk. Feeling sick, he said.

'Mum, you couldn't have known.'

'Should have. Should. Oh yes. Oh.'

Once his clothes were packed off to the Brotherhood, the piano and telescope sold, you asked me to find you a flat near ours in the city. I looked around on my days off: it had to be a ground-floor flat because of your heart. There was nothing suitable. After a couple of months you said you'd changed your mind, you weren't helpless, thanks all the same. You'd stay put.

I wish I was one of those women who give up their lives to care for the old and sick.

You always hoped I'd want to be a nurse when I grew up. When I got out of hospital you had made me a nurse costume. When I was twelve you talked me into spending Saturday afternoons helping at the hospital with friends from school. The patients were old, paralysed, incontinent, blind, abandoned. We folded linen and peeled potatoes. We hacked off the green shells of pumpkins, polished and grooved, with orange seeds and rags of flesh hanging in their wombs. One afternoon the nurses asked me to feed a young blind man his custard. It was a privilege: nicknamed Freddie, he was their favourite. In my awkwardness I let hot custard trickle down Freddie's neck and puddle in his pillow as he lay smiling up. Tears spilled from his white eyes. Frantic, I mopped his raspy throat and chin. I was too ashamed to ever go back. He kept asking after me, my friends reported. 'Oh, Paula,' you said. Shaking your grey head. 'You are heartless.'

We were down here just last Sunday. Whimpering, you bared your sore, swollen ankles. 'Oh don't want. Turn into a vegetable.' Your veined eyes round as you faltered, saying that. You spent most of the day in bed and refused to eat. On Tuesday the Meals on Wheels man found you lying on the kitchen floor and called the ambulance. The matron rang me at work.

'Can you come down? Doctor says her heart's grossly enlarged. She's very weak.'

'She'll be all right, though, won't she?'

'Well, we can't say. Come down if possible. She's asked for you.'

You'd asked for me.

I took time off and drove down with Claire to the little bush hospital. A day of midwinter spring, with the lamps lit all afternoon along the shore. Kookaburras and magpies in the shabby gumtrees in the grounds. From your window, late sun glazing the hollow sea. Woodsmoke from chimneys in the hills, towering.

When you had your stroke a few days before Claire was born, we had been estranged for months: my child would have no father. I lumbered in to visit you in the city hospital, kissed your cheek and flopped gasping in a chair with my offering of daffodils. You could hardly move. Slowly your stiff mouth drooled words.

'What, Mum?'

'You. Go. Now.'

'What did you say?'

'Want. You. Go. Now.'

I flung the gaudy flowers down and went.

Last Sunday Claire found some of your old photographs. She brought one in to show us, the one of you and Auntie May smiling on a staircase. Two little sepia girls with frilly dresses and bows in their hair.

'Have you still got that dress, Mummy? Please can I have it?'

'No, that was Granma's dress.'

'But you've got it on!'

'No, that's not me. That's Granma. When she was your age.'

'Oh. Have you still got it, Granma?'

You smiled, shaking your head. That was all. Later I found the photo in the rubbish bin. I took it out, stained and creased, when you weren't looking.

A while ago I played all the tapes that Dad had made, mostly of broadcasts of organ recitals. His beloved fugues wheezed, thumped and groaned. In the middle of a slow passage I heard him sigh. I played it again. There it was, his deep sigh, embedded in the music.

I told you about it. Would you like to hear it? I'd play it for you. You shook your shaggy head. Were your eyes blank, or hostile? You would have loved to hear his voice, wouldn't you? You would have.

You turned your head away.

This time I brought red tulips propped in a carafe on the locker like five sunlit glasses of red wine. They are opening unseen beside you now, showing their yellow throats. Inside each are six rods of black velvet like the legs of an upturned insect; and a three-pronged tongue, its colour lost in the glow.

Your mottled hand crawled to huddle in mine, a dry claw for all these years plump again now with the same fluid that was welling in your ankles. In your lungs.

'Sorry dear. Accident. Shower.'

'You fell in the shower?'

'No, no.' Shaking your angry matted head. 'Accident. Bowel. Mess in bathtub.'

'Oh, Mum, that's nothing! I'll clean it up!'

'Disgusted.'

'Of course not. You couldn't help it. Don't be silly!'

You rolled your filmed eyes up to gaze at me.

'Thank you. For coming.'

'I'll be back tonight. Now you get some sleep.'

I kissed your hollow cheek. Your cropped grey hair sodden, fetid, all on end. You nodded and twisted to watch me go back to Claire, anxiously on tiptoe in the doorway. We waved to your mute face watching. Watching us go.

I dropped Claire at the Smiths' to play and came back alone to sit here drinking as night fell. The wine was dark as blood by lamplight. Remembering.

I drove back alone in visiting hours. I was too late. Your body, wracked as if in childbirth, was heaving up off the bed with every gasp; your mouth a mute howl; your eyes bulging blood-stained. I called you. Nothing. No hope now, the doctor said. Did you know I was there? When I was holding your swollen hand, could you feel my hand? You'd asked for me. Did you want me to go now? I'd always promised not to look. I crept away.

What should I have done?

I picked Claire up. Fast asleep by their fire, she hardly stirred when I carried her to the car and then to bed. 'Read me *Alice*,' she mumbled, but fell asleep again.

I sat up gulping wine. Your wracked grimace accused me. So weak, how had you found such strength, such anguish, to fight for each breath, each heartbeat, one by one? I sat slobbering with shame and dread until the telephone rang and the doctor murmured that my mother had passed away, and suggested an undertaker. So it was over, you had cast your loose old skin: it lay there stiffening in warm sheets. Nurses will sponge you now and stop up all your openings — the warped anus, too, in your seamed belly. You used to apologise to new nurses for it. At home you flinched as wind purred out, escaping the taut bag; with strained composure visitors would ignore the sudden smell.

Stars roof your luminous garden. The trees are still. Empty snail shells, small brown skulls, litter the flower beds and the frosty grass. A blue glow covers the fuchsia with its dangling bells, the japonica's red paper petals, the studded daphne. Pale lilies are coiled around their dusty rods. Soon your dry wisteria vine will hang out its frilled mauve pods in bunches.

In one of the grey snapshots by the bedlamp in your room you and Dad walk elated hand in hand past the pillars and steps of the GPO, just married at forty at the start of the War. In the other you grin squinting into the sun on the verandah, your only baby, bald and glum cuddled in tentative white-downed arms. My lifetime ago.

The shower taps are smudged with brown. You told me. The soap as well. Splatters here and there blotch the grey enamel of the tub. With rubber gloves on I scrub away the hard brown spots, pour boiling water over and wrap gloves, soap and steel wool in newspaper before I ram them in the bin.

Stooped here in splashing yellow water, sludge oozing from your hole and between the puffed fingers that tried to hold it back, did you decide to die?

Rust is tarnishing the steam-furred mirror. I am shiny under the dusty globe, my lips black from the wine. The dim skin of my eyes is bruised, wilted. My bones are yellow ridges. Hollows lie dark along my jaw and throat.

Claire's tread thumps down the passage. In the mirror her sleepy face that was mine once. Her warm hair all on end.

'Granma just died, darling one,' I say.

'Won't we ever see her again?'

'No. She wouldn't like us to.'

'Does she look horrible?'

I shake my head. She leans frowning in the doorway.

'This is our house now, isn't it?'

'Yes.'

'Are we coming to live down here?'

'Maybe in summer.'

'Where's Granma's soul now?'

'I don't know.'

'Not here!' she shrieks.

'No. Not here.'

'With Granpa's?'

'Nobody knows.'

'Can I come into your bed? And leave the light on?'
'All right. The passage light.'
She comes and presses her hot face against me.
'Mummy,' she whimpers. 'Don't *you* die.'

DARLING ODILE

On the way from Sydney to Tahiti I stood for hours every day at the ship's rail and gazed into the wake: Tahiti, the Island of Love. Whales, under their mirroring roof of waves, the tossed balloon of the green sun, must be shrilling, wallowing, coupling. I tried to see dolphins and flying fish. At night, hot in a daze of red Algerian wine, I watched the mast point creaking to this star and that, while under the lifeboats red cigarettes glowed, faded, glowed like far lighthouses. A ukulele twanged and voices sang.

I had brought a sleeping bag but Hamid, the Madagascan cabin 'boy' — Hamid was fifty if a day — said not to think of sleeping on Tahitian beaches, whatever I might be used to back home. No, he said, let me find somewhere safe for you, *chérie*.

Before lunch all the last week Hamid, cringing in the dark behind bulkheads, had beckoned me into a cabin where he had glasses and ice ready, a bottle of aniseed *pastis*, and *casse-croûtes* of crusty flute bread with camembert and frills of sweet pink ham. He knew my lunch in fourth class would be stale and greasy, inedible: he wheedled or stole his treats from the larder chef. He was the first black man I'd ever met.

While I nibbled and made conversation he sat taut and trembling. Then right there on the hot bunk he pounced and spread me out and lay on me wriggling until with one sharp squeal he subsided like a clockwork monkey. The first time I thought he was having a heart attack; that's what a sheltered life I'd led. He stained my dress. I kept all my clothes on — a silken summer dress was all — and clutched his curly grey head to stop him kissing me. He hissed. His wild eyes were red-threaded, his teeth furred green.

Through the port-hole came splashes and the squalls of birds.

By then — I would turn twenty in Tahiti — I felt that my formal education was complete. The day after my final exams I sold my textbooks to buy silk dresses. It was time for my *éducation sentimentale.* In theory, I knew what to expect. I had liberated views for those days — 1960 — and read widely. In practice I was a virgin; indignant young men had even called me frigid. (Was it true? Masturbation was a word in Freud to me.) But I had read *The Second Sex* from cover to cover in the original French. I had read Colette. I dreamed of becoming one of Colette's *grandes nonchalantes*, a *chère artiste*, a Léa. I wanted my defloration to be a slow and sensual, transcendant rite of passage. Where else but Tahiti, which was not only French, but Polynesian (I had read Margaret Mead)? I would be taught *le plaisir, l'amour, l'amour libre — libre* because untainted, there, by commerce or by force — in the tawny arms of a tropical man.

I was lucky. Tahiti would have remained nothing but a Gauguin daydream but for my mother's new lover, a bookmaker just widowed, who adored her. It was bliss and orchids every day, and champagne, French champagne, always there like a green cannon in its misty silver ice-bucket. 'This is the lap of luxury, Rosie,' she sighed. As a graduation present she offered me a fur, but I wanted a sea voyage.

'But darling, not on your own?'

'Mum, I've hitch-hiked all over Australia on my own.'

'But why Tahiti?'

'I can practise my French. Do some skin-diving. Please.'

'I don't know. I don't understand my own daughter. All this gadding around. I was a married woman at your age. Look at all the girls in your year that are married already or at least engaged. You've got an Arts degree, so what? You've still got a lot to learn. You're a worry to me, Rosie.'

'Oh, Mum, come on. It'll broaden my mind.'

'Well, I don't know.'

A few days out of Santo a telegram came from my mother: I had passed my final exams. NOW WHAT? she had added. That night I drank too much of the crude Algerian claret and sat on the rolling deck in a fever. Now what, indeed? Adventures on these high seas? A teaching job in Sydney? But first, Tahiti!

Là, tout n'est qu'ordre et beauté,
Luxe, calme et volupté.

That's a strange word, *volupté*. So is defloration, because it isn't like a flower at all, this female hole we have. Perhaps like a brown-fringed sea-anemone with a wet red mouth. Or a velveted clam. When the ship left, my mother gave me one long-stemmed rosebud that looked like withering before it could bloom. I held it to the tap in the cabin basin and pressed its red mouth open. Swollen red drops glowed on it as it stretched out sipping like a crimson snake. When my pubic hair first grew I stooped and peered with a torch and mirror at the coral frills of those lips ringed with whiskers. It is like a heart, its red folds and chambers. The membranes open like the petals of my rose, but shielded, husked with fur.

At our last lunch before Papeete Hamid grabbed my hand and offered to set me up in his apartment in Paris in the Arab quarter. Was this *love*? But Paris! There would be weird drumming African music in the grey air, and the smell of baking bread and coffee; on the sky, those grey trees I had seen in so many films, scribbling themselves in the slow river, fading in mist. Rows of lights glistening in the boulevards. He'd be at sea a lot. Regretfully, I turned him down. Why did I? I might have been better off, who knows?

He didn't seem to hold it against me, anyway.

After all the passengers had disembarked and been through customs he sneaked me back on board and into the cabin. Gaudy girls in *pareu* dresses were sitting there, sipping *pastis* or ruby-red grenadine with ice. They were prostitutes of course — what other girls would Hamid know in Papeete? — with bodies like egg-loaves just out of the oven and tasselled black hair with a tongued hibiscus flower pinned in it.

I was taken aback at first. Prostitutes, here? Then I felt proud that Hamid believed that I was so enlightened I could chat with a pack of whores and never turn a hair.

'Hamid, *chéri*,' cooed one. 'She is *sensass*, your little *Australienne*. What are you worried about? I'll take care of her myself.'

Sensass was slang for *sensationelle*. Good. I wanted her to like me. She was fat and half-Chinese, paler, cooler than the others. Her eyes were the black enamel of a goldfish's under fine faint eyebrows. Her doll's mouth cooed broken French. Her name was Odile.

On the quay she waited smiling while I said goodbye to Hamid. I let him kiss my neck. Don't cry, Hamid, *chéri*, I murmured. I'll write to you. I promise. He pressed a wad of Pacific francs into my hand, as I had known he would, and he wouldn't let me give them back. I licked the tears from his poor red eyes while he whimpered in my arms like a puppy.

In the streets of Papeete women sat on the footpaths plaiting green baskets. At one end of the quay a replica of the *Bounty* was moored, looking too small to be real, as corpses and waxworks do. Her blurred spars and shrouds were winter trees twigged with yards on which her dusty sails were scrolled. At night she sat in a pool of oily light. MGM was making another *Bounty* movie. American extras with long hair swaggered along arm-in-arm with *vahines*, or slouched with them sipping beer in waterfront bars while Tahitian men glowered. Marlon Brando was said to be at large in this bar or that. All the footpaths said in long chalk letters: MGM GO HOME.

Odile took me to stay with her at her aunt's, in a big household full of women, children, ducks and black piglets with one ambling sow. It was one of a cluster of thatched and plaited *fares* with electric light but no glass in the windows, their hibiscus hedges draped with washing, on the outskirts of Papeete near a river and a black beach.

Those first long indolent days were filled with a hot, a golden light. We had nothing to talk about. We lay on sand that was the black ash of volcanoes, long plumes of palm shadow stroking us, and wrapped in *pareus* swam and wallowed in the still lagoon, twisting among bubbles, her gold body and mine still white undulating side by side. Fish slipped by, mailed and supple, trailing their silky fins. In the sunlit shallows they breathed dappled water.

'Rosie, you'll get burnt.'

'Will you put more oil on me?'

Her hands stroked the scented oil, *monoï*, on me, then mine on her.

Sometimes we fell asleep, waking with a hot headache, cross and surly. One afternoon a hot wind blew and the sand fluttered with the sound a wood-fire makes, burning us. Once a burly *vahine* waded thigh-deep with a net heavy with fish. Cats sat waiting at the waterline. The sky at sundown tightened and cooled on the sea like the skin on hot milk.

In the last orange light we had showers in the bathhouse with the ducks. We dressed up and brushed out our hair, songs on the radio, French and Tahitian. Odile taught me to dance the *tamure.* By the lamp at the window she put on mascara, white eyeshadow, lipstick. Arm-in-arm we strolled into Papeete, to this or that waterfront bar, Quinn's, Le Col Bleu, Bar Léa.

Once Hamid's money ran low, Odile was amazed, then scornful, that I refused all offers from men: not in the name of virtue, but of *amour,* of *volupté.* She was offended that my refusals pushed my supposed asking price up to five times hers. A white girl, a *vahine popaa,* was a novelty in the bars back in those days.

'Rosie, why not? After Hamid, he looks good.'

'After Hamid, who wouldn't?'

'*Et alors*?'

'*Non.*'

We both shrugged and pouted. I was not going to admit to virginity. Besides, I didn't like their attitude: that gross and condescending, sly black sailor plying me with wine punches, that silky Chinese millionaire, that rowdy Bounty extra. She soothed and cajoled my rejects, taking them in turn to a room she rented overlooking the quay. Most nights I walked home the long way alone.

Barefoot on the soft dust of the road I breathed the night's hot breath of jasmine and nectar under the stars. The hibiscus flowers were all curled up, all tightly folded. Strangers sauntered past talking, singing, plucking a ukulele: *bonne nuit, vahine popaa,* smiling at me. Sudden downpours of warm rain sent us all scattering with shouts and laughter to break off banana leaves for umbrellas. Afterwards the rain had washed a sweetness of strange flowers into the starry silence. Those flowers open only at night, Odile said once, pointing up, and then they wither at daybreak. No, that can't be true, I said. It's too beautiful. *Si, si!* She swore it was.

The first night that she came home at dawn I had lain awake all night, afraid. What was that pattering across the lino? Oh, a spider, Odile shrugged. Or a little mouse. She sighed, lying down beside me on the *pareu* bedcover, a Gauguin blue-and-yellow on the double bed her aunt had honoured us with. She was translucent as butter, so fat, so smooth, carved out of pale jade, my golden Odile. Her great breasts swung, blossom-tipped.

'I have borne a child,' she said. 'You can tell by my nipples, of course.'

Could I have? I wondered how.

'He is nearly two. My mother is raising him. They live on Bora Bora, where I grew up. Willy is his name.' She had a sad smile.

'Were you in love, Odile *chérie*.'

We girls in the bars called the whole world *chéri, chérie*.

'Love? No. Not with that one. No.' She looked sidelong, those glossy eyes of hers narrowed. 'But now I am in love.'

'Mmm? Tell me about him.'

'He is American. In the Navy, the Seventh Fleet, I think it is. They were here on a visit last month. He lives in Hawaii.'

'Is he in love with you?'

She shrugged, and again that smile.

'Well, what's his name? Is he good-looking?'

'Yes, of course. *Sensass*. His name is Stéphane.' She took a letter from a mother-of-pearl jewel box by the bed.

'Oh, a letter! What does it say?'

'It is in English.'

Darling Odile,
Got your photo today, gorgeous. It goes everywhere I do. Wow, am I missing you! I can't get to sleep these nights thinking about how hot and wild you got me. We sure did have ourselves some good times! Honest to God, no woman ever made me feel the way you do in my whole life. What wouldn't I give to be sinking my you know what into that hot little Chinese pussy of yours this minute!!! I'm saving up real hard for your fare over here, honey, so don't you let me down now. Soon, soon, soon. I'm going to grab hold of you and eat you all UP! Write me, OK? French, Tahitian, Chinese, what the hell, so long as you write me, OK? The photo smells like your hair. Baby, words fail me.

Here's looking at you, kid.
Steve.

'I think he loves you,' I said.

'Ah, *oui*? What does it say?'

'Oh, you poor darling!'

I translated it. Tears of happiness rimmed her eyes with light. Mangoes when ripe have just that glow of red in their golden cheeks as Odile had. The sun was striking through the banana trees: I ran my fingers along her sumptuous breast and flank as daylight brimmed about us in the room.

'Sleep well, *ma pauvre petite* Odile,' I whispered.

But she lay stirring, sighing, for a long time.

Most mornings, while Odile slept in, I wandered round the market. There fish as tall as men hung from hooks by their horny lips, their huge silver eyes soaked in blood. I bought red and yellow bananas, and scented mangoes, and grapefruits with skins like pitted green balloons. Pale green flesh glowed in them. We always ate lunch at one long table with Odile's relatives: fruit and breadfruit, avocadoes from the tree, taro, raw fish. I learnt to make the raw fish, tuna or bonito, soaked in lime juice and coconut milk. Odile's aunt would never hear of my paying board, so I gave money to Odile to pass on to her.

At night if we were hungry we bought fried food from trolleys on wheels or ate *maa Tinito*, Chinese rice and red beans, in family restaurants with four or five tables, a basin on the wall, and one stand-up *cabinet* for everybody in the yard beyond the kitchen. Money was short.

That afternoon was stormy, not beach weather, so when Odile woke we went early to Quinn's. Sleepy girls drifted in from time to time and sat around gossiping, writing letters, lazily sipping beer. The band was rehearsing for the floorshow: the drums, the steel guitars, ukuleles, a hoarse baritone. The tables had a nap of golden dust. Between storms wet sunlight probed thickly through any gap into the languorous red glow cast by the stage lamps. Their crimson gloss coated all our hot skins.

I wrote postcards to my mother and to Hamid. I saw Odile's lip curl. Then we wrote Steve a letter in English. Odile dictated, and I embellished.

'Steve darling, I miss you too.'

Steve darling,
I can't forget you. I remember everything about you, everything we did. It scares me to think we might never meet again. Tell me we will.

'I shut my eyes and keep remembering how you made love to me. I dream that you're here beside me.'

I shut my eyes and keep remembering how it feels when you're inside me. I stroke you all over in my dreams, thinking you're here beside me.

'When they're lying on me I shut my eyes and think of you. You're the only one I love.'

When they're lying on me I shut my eyes and think, oh, Steve, Steve. You're the only one I love.

'I want to be with you. I'll come when I can. You know I will. Trust me.'

I want to be with you. I'll come when I can, and we'll make a new life away from Papeete. You know I'll come. Trust me. My Australian friend Rosie is writing this for me.

'I love you, Stéphane, no, put Steve. Your Odile.'

I love you, Steve.
Your Odile.

The days that followed were too hot to go trudging to the beach. After calling at the Poste Restante we walked to the river instead. Beyond the ford of pebbles there was a deep pool where we floated helpless as watermelons in the churning, froth, our *pareus* billowing. We landed in the shallows, thrown together, our bare skins grazed. Once a snake lashed on the pebbles as I lay gasping, no, a thick grey eel, then flickered away. Shadows arched in the water. We were green-lit there like Gauguin's strange white horse stooped to sip the coiled surfaces of water.

Once the whole family came with food in banana leaves. We all splashed and dived, giggling. I heard Odile's cousin, a sleek boy whose voice was breaking, ask her something about me: I heard 'Rosie'. She replied in Tahitian, grinning scornfully, and finished with a jeering laugh. Then she saw my face. Ah, *te voici*, Rosie, where were you? She took my hand and waded to the bank to plait out of leaves a crown for me and another for her, and pressed them on to our dripping hair.

Was Odile not to be trusted? I dismissed the thought.

On my twentieth birthday there was a letter for Odile from Steve at last at the Bureau de Poste, and a letter and a cheque for me from my mother, with best regards from the bookmaker. 'Wishing you many happies, pet,' she had scribbled. 'How's my free spirit? Not too free, I hope! Thank your Odile from me, won't you, for looking after my girl. Be seeing you soon. Don't do anything I wouldn't do!' Of course, I hadn't written much about Odile in my postcards home, as she'd only worry. We cashed the cheque at the Banque de l'Indochine and went to Quinn's, where I wrote Odile a translation of Steve's letter.

Darling Odile,
Just a short note to say I love you. You are just the sweetest juiciest woman I ever saw. You are. I'm sending you a little something by registered mail: wear it for me, baby. I mean, all the time. You promised. Write me again real soon, another letter like that. I can't wait. I can't get to sleep for thinking about you. I just want you like crazy the whole damn time.

Mad about you, kid.
Steve.

P.S. Dear friend Rosie, thanks a million and keep up the good work huh?

There was a photo, too, of a grinning, heavy, broad-shouldered man, Polynesian dark brown, wearing a crown of leaves on a blue beach with coconut palms.

'What's he sending you, *chérie*?'

'The ring, I suppose.'

'The *ring*!'

I bought us a prawn dinner to celebrate, and later back at Quinn's we ordered French champagne. Odile was wildly dancing, laughing everywhere. Half-stifled in the crush, the smoke, I sat numb in an icy, foaming dizziness of champagne. A hot, fuzzy yellow light floated among the tables: in the aisles men of all races were crammed to watch the floorshow, Ruita on the red stage dancing the *tamure* to thudding drumbeats. I felt a nudge on my bare shoulder and, glancing, saw a man's black trouser-legs. Absurd to object. I sipped more icy foam. He rubbed gently at first, then harder and harder, until I heard a sigh above my head. My shoulder felt briefly damp when he moved away.

A group of Tahitian men from behind me, surging across, grabbed a table nearby: I wondered which of them it had been. One stared back at me with burning eyes. You? I thought. Are you thinking you've defiled me, using me? I tossed my head. You haven't.

The way home was long, dark, cool. My dazed head cleared. I watched the moon set, paddling in sand and the frills of waves among the many-breasted coconut palms, tripping in the starlight over coconut husks and the outriggers of canoes. A man with a ukulele fell into silent step beside me.

'*Bonsoir.*'

'*Bonsoir, monsieur.*'

'You like Tahiti, *vahine papaa*?'

'Oh yes, I love it.'

He was Tahitian, very tall, smiling with broken teeth.

'You are *Américaine*?'

'*Australienne.*'

He hummed a song, walking close, strumming his ukulele. The way home wound past hibiscus hedges, the *fares* here and there beyond them still glowing gold. At a bend in the sandy path suddenly his arm came tight round my shoulders. He dragged me stumbling through swordgrass to a banana grove. His ukulele fell with a cry.

'Stop it!' I gasped, clawing him. 'No! No! Don't!'

'*Je veux de toi.*'

'*Non! Je veux pas!*'

'*Je veux de toi.*'

He shoved me down in the rough grass, lifted my silk dress and wrenched my thighs apart. I felt him bore between my dry soft lips. His palm clamped down on my nose and mouth. Struggling, kicking, frantic for breath, I scratched and bit. He grunted, riding me the harder for it: he lunged and rasped inside me. Then his hand lifted. He shuddered, and lay limp on me.

When he got up three more men were waiting.

'Oh, please,' I begged him. 'Don't let them.'

He put his arms round their shoulders, muttering in Tahitian, but they scoffed and pushed him to one side. The others watched, smoking, as one by one each man unzipped and lay on me, pushed his cock inside and thrust briefly. I shut my eyes. I was bruised all over, soggy and aching inside. None of them was brutal, and one who took too long was reproached by the others.

I opened my eyes: it was Odile's sleek cousin. He was hissing, wet-faced. *E hoa,* moaned the others; get a move on, friend.

When it was over the three left me alone again with the first man. He knelt beside me, lifting my head, intent.

'*Ça va*? You're all right?'

I nodded. Then he did it to me again, riding my white body gently, his mouth — not his hand — over my mouth. He squelched in blood and semen, moving inside me. When he finished he straightened my dress and patted my torn, gritty hair.

'Go home, *vahine popaa. Va vite. Vite.*'

He slapped me on the rump, picked up his ukulele and went.

I cried, staggering home in the starlight, not daring to go and wash in the river or the sea. The tears boiled over in my eyes against my will. My teeth clenched on a child's whimpers and wails in the face of loss, injustice. No one saw me creep to the bathhouse or to bed. I told no one. They may have found out, I suppose. Odile may have known all along. There were no more late nights at Quinn's after that, no more night walks. I stayed in the *fare,* reading by lamplight, until I slept.

So much for my defloration. As for *plaisir, volupté*: they were lies in books.

In the shadows of our black beach I wrote one more letter for Odile. I did my best for her, though my heart wasn't in it any more. I mistrusted her now.

> *Steve darling, darling Steve,*
> *I want to be with you so much, it's hard to wait not knowing when we can be together again. I think of you all the time. I think of how your hands stroke and hold me, and the look in your eyes then. I'm the same all over, but you're all different colours, brown, russet, yellow, black. I want to kiss you all over everywhere. I kiss that mole near your left nipple, and the one on your thigh. Then — guess where! I kiss the freckles on your nose and cheeks. Do you like that? And of course I'll wear your little something when it comes. I said I would, didn't I? Chéri, je t'aime.*
>
> *Your Odile.*
>
> *P.S. This is Rosie signing off and wishing you two all the best, Steve baby. Sounds like you're real hot stuff! Rosie.*
> *P.P.S. I'm blonde.*

In a day or two my ship docked.

I'd been only vaguely aware of the date and the passage of time until suddenly there she was: not the one I came on but a sister ship, throbbing and glittering at the quay, loading copra. I packed my bag and said my goodbyes. We had one last day, on a white beach. Marlon Brando was there with cavorting *vahines*. I didn't swim. I was bleeding. I wasn't pregnant. I could see the ship's doctor for VD tests. Coated with sand we ate slices of yellow watermelon. The slanted black eyes that were its seeds shone in its pale flesh.

I watched Odile rolling in the sea. Sometimes in the cold rough river, when her legs had tumbled apart, I had seen the hairy blossom between them glistening. That, and her lips, and her nipples, were the only red on her. She was the same all over. How had she been broken in? How had she borne it? Could she honestly love a man? The memory was sour in me of thrusts and shudders, and poor Hamid's soft squeals. Men are at women's mercy then, the strongest men: wise women made the most of it. My mother did. I should have asked Odile to teach me her trade. A whore, she knew love's bitter mystery. Odile *chérie,* I should have said, before it was too late: teach me what I have to know. Teach me pleasure.

In the chatter of the crowd by the gangway Odile hung a mother-of-pearl heart on a chain round my neck and hugged me, sobbing and sniffling. I knew I'd never see her again. I went on board and waved to her. The ship's strung lights lay spindling in the water. A band was playing. In the distance the *Bounty* was a ghost ship. Long before we sailed Odile had gone. She was at Quinn's.

Jostled, I watched the quay drift away, and the lights of Papeete, and Tahiti's black towers of mountains hung with clouds. Thrown garlands of white flowers tossed in the wake. Stars floated. Eels were weaving in their dark caverns. I would sleep on deck to the twanging of ukuleles. Steve and Odile, I thought, the brown and the golden: soon you'll be heaving and coupling like the whales, the long sun aslant over you.

SNOWFALL

Wednesday

That afternoon, while writing at the desk in the bedroom, Matthew had gone out silently, which he did at times; and come back with two long red roses in cellophane, and that was new. Now he was writing a letter to his wife, care of her sister in London because she had flown over there, who knew why. The house in Australia was empty. What was he feeling? He had lit a cigarette; smoke was drifting in the light of his lamp and I heard his first gasp of breath and long exhalation. His mind was on Margaret. I, sitting a room away at my double lamps, altered a line drawing on paper over which the twin shadows of my hand moved, and wondered about the roses. If it was to mark the reconciliation, now that I was staying after all, the quarrel was two days ago. It hardly made sense. We had made up and there was no call for roses as far as I knew. My window panes, closed fast, were dark blue, cold; a crack in one glittered like a dagger. Wasps had nestled in its shaggy corners.

These two windows which faced east were the only ones in the apartment to attract the wasps. They battered and crawled inside the panes, and when the lamps were on one or two always came bumbling in hesitant orbits to squat on my paper and rasp across it. Their long ringed bellies would jerk. They had yellow legs, these American wasps, and slim wings of celluloid, of stained glass. They were dying of cold. I had been stung as a child and I hated them. I slapped them down with folded newspapers and they lay where they fell. A dead wasp might still sting for all I knew, if you were to touch the sting.

Matthew's window was above the street and caught the last heavy sun in its dust. Standing at it he swung round as I brought the coffee, and said in a low voice: 'Sandra — Margaret's here.'

6 pm

He has taken Margaret to the Napoli 'for a drink'. I am having some cold yellow wine, American wine, and watching the blue evening draw in by lamplight: very stunned and shocked, shaking, and so must write laboriously or not at all.

When I looked out after them they were indistinct, strolling through drifts of leaves. The streetlamps flickered on. He has left her overnight bag just inside our door. She refused to come in, he muttered, so he'd take her to the Napoli for a drink. He put on a jacket and slammed our heavy door.

The roses are black by lamplight. Every step echoes. Two months today of living together, three weeks back home in Australia and six in the States. A year ago we hadn't even met, less than a year. It's hard to be a loving couple, out of our place and time, with me in my fortieth year and he six years older, both set in old ways. No one really knows us as a couple, ourselves included. Distances lie between us: silences.

Hope. Response. Contact. Possession.

In the bedroom I lit the cinnamon candle. Mirrored in its tawny pool was a bud on a black stalk. Fumes of cinnamon swayed. I swilled the pool around and made high waves and watermarks on the luminous wax. A vault formed, all ribs and ripples. A wasp, sidling, lurched into the flame and carefully I put the candle back on the mantelpiece beside the roses and the lighted lamp.

8 pm
Her bag is over by the door and I've still never set eyes on her. There is a possibility implicit in that, that she might sleep here. Would I be asked to go to a hotel? That would mean packing in front of Margaret!

At nine, if he's not back, I'll eat. Then pack.

Are they still at the Napoli? What are they saying? I should walk in on them there, confront them and make a scene, sit with them, insist on making my presence felt. Margaret would. Why wait meekly here?

Walk into the panelled lamplit warmth, buy a cappuccino sprinkled with cinnamon in a silver holder, pause and look round to give them a good look before I go airily up to their table. Is this seat free? May I sit down? Maybe we should talk. Or: Hullo, you must be Margaret. I think we should talk. Or: Well, you have given us a surprise! (Turning) Hasn't she, darling?

She could carry it off better, I dare say. What would he do? He might dismiss me in cold blood. Not now, Sandra, please. Leave us alone. And how to parry that? Margaret, if so dismissed, would give a scornful laugh and sit down, and cross her silken legs. I would gape and cringe. Or would they just get up and leave without a word?

Melodrama.

As I sat alone by the deep light that my lamp cast, one of the heavy wasps, circling, settled on my hair and became entangled. Its lunges and its rasp and buzz about my ear drove me frantic. Sobbing, I rushed to the bathroom to brush it out and stamp on it. Wasps were sliding all over my tall windows, their feelers flickering. Their tiger bodies droned. The first snowfall had been forecast. All the streets were deep in the buttery leaves of elms: white of snow, falling as leaves fell, on all that gold.

9.30 pm

Until today I have walked through the campus oblivious, incandescent with love and amazement. Arnaut Daniel in a tongue of fire, a sheath of invisible flame; the burnt air wavered at my edges. In love and down and out in America. If this is America, this college town of autumn trees and Gothic towers; slate roofs and mullions on bright bare windows; attics and quadrangles. The Old World in the New, its ancient stones and ivies proudly replicated, groined cloisters, vaults and spires set with jewelled glass and unmarked by time, by war. The College library is a cathedral whose naves reverberate: whiskered all over with ivy, and all of fifty years old. I have filled notebooks with sketches of towers and faces. A town set so wilfully in a borrowed past should be the perfect haven for lovers like us.

At ten o'clock I mixed an omelette flowing and frilling in the black pan, and ate it doggedly with bitter rye bread and more cold wine, and tart red-stained winter grapes. At ten-thirty I started packing. Ten minutes later he walked in.

'What's happening? Where were you?'

'At the Napoli.'

'All this time!'

'What time is it?'

'Nearly eleven! Is anything wrong back home?'

He shook his tired head.

'Then why is she here?'

'On impulse, she said. The cheap fares —'

'The cheap fares!'

'Well, London to New York is down to $175 return, it seems. Incredible. She wanted to see me while she was over on this side of the world.'

'How long is she here for?'

'Two days. Leaving on Friday.'

'What if she doesn't?'

'She has to. With those cheap fares it means you —'

'Yes, but —'

'Look, we can talk later. The taxi's waiting. She's in it. We just came to get her bag. I've got her a room at the Old Vienna. Be back in an hour.'

He picked up the bag and was gone.

It was just on one when the key turned in the door. I had given up hope. He found me sobbing in the bed, and undressed and lay holding me.

'You've packed.'

'I thought you'd decided to stay with her.'

'I said I'd come back.'

'It's one o'clock. I thought I'd better go. Before I was asked to.'

'No. If you'd said you'd leave if I went out to her this afternoon, I wouldn't have gone.'

'How can you *say* that?'

'No, I don't know what I'm saying. I'm so tired.'

'What will happen tomorrow?'

'Well, she says because she only has two days I should spend them entirely with her.'

'Yes, I see.'

'You won't mind, will you?'

I gasped. 'Well, it's only fair, I suppose. When she's come all this way.'

'We're meeting at the Library steps at twelve. I'll show her round, take her to Macy's, we'll have dinner, all that — I don't know. What will you do?'

'Some sketching. I don't know — take in a movie?'

'God, Sandy.' He screwed his face up. 'Is it true what the man says? That any fool can handle a crisis?'

'No.' I smiled back. It was a joke but where was the punchline? 'And don't try to get round me.'

He sighed, falling asleep with the lamp on.

What would I do? It was a good question. Will you try to stop her, he was thinking: intrude on us, or quarrel or fight back? He should have known me better than to wonder. I admired what

Margaret was doing. Her rash courage, her ruthlessness, took my breath away. She, I imagined, knew exactly who she was and what was due to her. She was never disconcerted to see herself approach in mirrors, in plate glass. I, evasive, often failed to meet the eyes reflected.

Steam hissed, clanking, in the radiators. He lay sprawled. The hair on his chest and belly met in a dark line in the shape of a feather and cast tangled shadows. Winter ivy on a stone tower.

2 am
I remember a long winter evening in my room at home, in another country, another life, two months ago when we lay side by side watching the wind tear the gum tree, toss it against the pane until it was a shadow on the swollen red of the inner city night sky. We drew the curtains and switched on the reading lamp. On the ceiling its light burned red, reflected from the bed cover. We were half-white, half-scarlet.

Thursday

Well before twelve the next day, having had a coffee or two and strolled through leafy quadrangles talking about *Middlemarch,* we were confronted on the Green by a breathless little woman who blocked our way. 'It's Margaret,' he said in a low voice and he dropped my hand. At that I began to shake all over.

She stood waiting with a rigid smile, her blue eyes bright with fury and hurt.

'Margie.'

'Hullo, Matt.' Her voice jittered. Then a beat before she turned to me. 'I'm Margaret. Matt's wife.' A longer beat. 'Now I can tell my daughter I've seen you.'

'Would you like some coffee?'

'No, I just came to talk to Matt.'

I nodded, I kissed him, on the cheek, and walked jerkily away without a backward look. I doubt if either of them watched me go.

A crouched black man in a soft hat did. He jerked and chuckled on the other side of the street, snapping yellow fingers. 'Sho' like to take yo' knickers down, white baby,' he called across.

In a day of wandering through the town I had not caught sight of them. Now I saw gold trees doubled in panes, and trees in small quadrangles still heavy with their unshed leaves. At sundown a thin moon rose and beside it a glittering point slowly wrote a trail down the sky. No sign of snow. Specks of mica sparkled among the leaves on the footpaths. I sat on a bench sketching. The black children shyly feeding squirrels on the lawn had pigtails and ribbons erect on their furrowed scalps. The squirrels begged, alert, like mice but for the silver-rimmed tails that followed them up tree trunks. Old men, their tortoise eyes bent down, moved on as the sun left their benches. The trail of the skywriter, ravelled and fuzzed, blew loosely away.

Soon it was dark. Branched chandeliers shone in a restaurant window, and candles in brackets on its wall. Lamps burned in towers of square glass or pointed stone. Headlights eyed my back in all the narrow streets. The white streetlights around the Green were hooped with red fairy lights. A crowned black tower, dimly lace-lit, began to boom and trill with bells like a music-box above the growl of slow cars.

The Napoli was on my way in any case. I went in for a sandwich and wine, looking in the thronged rooms for Matthew and Margaret, and sat at a table by the windows, watching the leaves twitch and fall. Lights went on one by one in the ivied college opposite. It was warm and noisy in the Napoli, the air dense with the smell of pizza and clove cigarettes, music and talk and I drank until my head burned.

When I stumbled out, in a clear sky of stars a scatter of snow came floating down, stars blowing loose. They stung for a moment and turned to water. 'O Tannenbaum,' I hummed under my breath. The scatter soon stopped, leaving the night still and black until I came to a lamp at an arched gate where a madrigal group, their scarves and hair white-flocked, stood singing something limpid and Elizabethan. They smiled when I stopped to listen. Mist and warbles came floating from their mouths.

This was a world I had no place in. He was not home. I switched on all the lamps and sat and cried.

Margaret,
The questions that brought you here none of us can answer. Why would he leave you for me? Why would he stay with me? How long can it last?

He said you had accepted the situation. I thought we had these months of his study leave in America to ourselves, away from those who had claims on us at home: you, of course, and Anne and my own daughter. Out of reach, no phone even. Now here you are, without warning. Were you afraid he might give you the slip if he knew in advance, or that I'd intercept a telegram or a letter? There was no need to be.

Are we any the wiser for having met face to face, you and I? Until now I was another unscrupulous other woman luring a married man into the toils of adultery. Where he's been before, but the fact remains. You were a name: Margaret. And an impediment: Matt's wife. I never put pressure on him as some other women do. I never rang him at home, only to hang up if the wrong one answered. I never said he had to choose between us, or hinted that he should leave you, or carried on when it was time for him to get dressed and go home to you.

He has no right, is that why you're here? When you've always been a good and faithful wife to him. How much can a new affair count against your twenty-odd years together and your onslaughts of grief and reproach? Don't tell me you're here to rescue *him!*

Who will he sleep with tonight? Does it make any difference in the long run?

I'll keep this after all. I won't leave it for you at the front desk at the Old Vienna or phone or waylay you in the street. You can jump to your own conclusions.

Sandra

He came in early, well before ten, his face grey, and slumped on the bed. I switched on the reading lamp and made coffee. Their dinner at the restaurant — The Napoli? No, the Green Room, why? — began happily. Then a quarrel broke out. He spoke slowly with long halts. How? Why? No, it was impossible to say, that would only compound the treachery.

At last he looked up.

'Thank you for being home.'

'Oh darling! When do you have to meet her tomorrow?'

'Twelve again. She's leaving at three on the Limousine for Kennedy. I said I had people to see in the morning. I can't take this, Sandra.'

'What if she comes here?'

'No, she won't. She called it "your love nest". It was all the honeymooners, in their love nest. She hates you, by the way. A lot of venom there. She kept asking about your past. How long you've been divorced, and why, and who got custody of Jenny and so on. She blames this whole thing on you.'

'How clever of her.'

'She said, "I'll always mean more to you than she does. I'm your wife, the mother of your child, does she think you can just throw half your life into the wastepaper basket? Is she passing herself off as your wife over here? Does she think she's the first cab off the rank?" "No," I said, "but I never left home for the others." '

'Thanks. What else?'

He hesitated, holding my eyes. 'She said: "That's not true, for a start." '

'No?'

'When Annie was little there was one other —'

'No, hang on — stick to today.'

'Well. She wanted to know how long it had been going on before I left home. I said most of this year. "Our marriage hadn't broken up as far as I knew," she said. "We weren't unhappy. You never gave any sign. You kept saying you loved me the day you left. Why did you do it?" '

'And you said?'

' "Margaret, yes, I loved you. Of course, I love you. I always will." '

' "Then what," she said, "are you doing in America with Sandra?" '

'That's a hard one. And you said?'

'What could I say?'

'You love her.'

'Of *course* I do.'

'Well, then.'

'No, I came back here, didn't I? I'm still here.'

'Try to sleep,' I said. 'You don't look well at all.'

'I was desperate to get home,' he muttered and lit a cigarette. 'Not to get back to you, so much, just desperate to make it back. I thought I was going to fall down in the street.'

I went to make more coffee. When I brought it in he was asleep. The moon shone through one of my windows, high and thin, wavering in the old glass as if in water. The heat was on full. The burnt wasp was stuck fast in the brown wax under the candle wick. The roses, flabby now, drooped on their brown napes.

1 am
He has fallen asleep with the reading lamp on. His face is blank. Faces tell us nothing. Thin caps cover the recessed round eyes fringed with fine hairs. Underneath his eyes are green, jade green and flecked. Fleshy beaks arch over our nostrils. The folded flesh of lips is creased, grooved. The downy surface, the veins and freckles and moles of human skin we can know with certainty. Nothing more.

'The past is a bucket of ashes,' Carl Sandburg wrote.

So is the present.

Friday

I woke early and sat by my lamp as the night turned blue and slowly the gables and trees were outlined then filled with faded light. He slept on. I tried to read, to draw, to write to Jenny. My lamp made an orange stain on the white walls and sheets of paper.

Over breakfast we had little to say and were careful not to touch. With the coffee poured, he went to the front room to get the ashtray from the window sill, leant out and spoke softly, and came back.

'Who was it?' I said, knowing very well.

'It's Margaret. She's out there.'

'Oh God, what! She —'

'Look, we'll talk later.'

'No! She can't do this!'

'She's been out there an hour or more, she said, standing waiting in the cold for the blind to go up.'

'Imagining us in bed. How pathetic! Picketing the love nest!'

He shot me a look of sudden cold disgust.

'Put yourself in her place, Sandra.'

'Ha! That's a classic.'

He had his coat half on, shrugging, and was on the way out. Hidden in the orange shadows of the room I could see them standing shivering in the street with Mr Kane, the landlord. If I'd called her to come in when I had the chance, what would she have done? I watched until they were out of sight.

There was no sign of the snow. It was as if I had dreamt it.

I had a long shower, washed my hair and untangled it at the mirror in the sun, watching steam rise from my head in a slow breath. I washed up the breakfast dishes. The bubbles in the sink quivered. The undersides of hundreds of taps are mirrored there, and on top of every bubble a peering face was swirling in opal, rimmed in froth.

I took the washing to the laundrette. Here was a refuge of sorts. I liked the drooling of old hit songs on the radio, the drumming of machines, black people sitting in silent pairs in the smoky heat. A black baby in a pusher was crying, refusing consolation. In the dryer Matthew's shirts spread out and swooped, rose, toppled forward, over and over again. Margaret had always laundered them before. She knew them all by heart.

Home with my warm bag of shirts I made a new start on my letter.

Dear Jenny,
How are you, sweet? How's university? I might be back sooner than I thought, I'm afraid. M's wife turned up here on Tuesday — we thought she was in London — and they are horribly distressing each other. She's leaving (I hope!) this afternoon — at least, I thought she was in London.

Of the three of us, only I am afraid to act. The implacable consequences of action alarm me. I shrink from it. Compunction impedes me. So events follow their courses taking no account of me.

M has to stay at least another month. I think he would prefer me to leave but can't quite bring himself to the point. So it looks as if you were right to doubt.

Wasps were whining, slithering on the panes. One circled my head and landed, its striped belly twitching, on the letter. I slammed a folded newspaper on it and swept it off. The floor-boards under the windows were littered with crushed wasps, black feelers awry, rolled up in fluff as if in a cocoon.

And a scrap of paper.

S —
I love you. That's all that matters.
— M

The blood beating in my head and the words melting. Oh, when had he written this? My darling! But I soon came to my senses: it dated from the other day, how could I forget? — the day of the quarrel. So it was old and meant nothing. I screwed it up and threw it out the window, his window, where it rolled among red leaves beside the stoop. Mr Kane, busy raking, tottered to pick it up. Above his loose pullover stuck with straws of grass he had a ruff of white hair growing across his shoulders. He smoothed the note on his chest with one hand and studied it, peered up at the window scratching his crazed nape and finally — no answer there — crumpled the note and dropped it in the leaves.

Once he was out of sight I hurried down to get it. A squirrel on the fence fixed one black eye on me in mad resentment. He whirled and stood erect, both beseeching hands folded on his belly. His muzzle twitched. He darted away in fits, looking back, and the silver spray of his tail bounced up and down.

The sky had become a deep funnel of wind, damp and white. A cold smell of snow.

At four he came in.

'Are you all right? Has she gone?'

'Yes. She's gone.'

'Was it very rough?'

'Not too bad.'

'Really?'

'Not as bad as I feared. Not like yesterday.'

Silence.

'So you had a nice day? Well, that's good, then.'

'I wouldn't call it nice. No.'

Silence. He lay down then, his back to me, and slept.

Jenny, I can't go on. It's all over. I'll post this as it is. I wish I had died before this could happen.

Love,
Mum

When he woke it was after seven. There being no food in the house, he suggested the Napoli.

Snow had begun to fall, must have been falling for hours, heavy and slow, whirling around the white streetlamps. Fir branches were caked white, drooping in the gardens; the elms with their last gold leaves were a fine white skin; lawns and parked cars and rooftops were thick-fleeced, and the streets glimmered, torn by wet tyre-tracks. In a sudden wild mood we went tramping through it, slithering everywhere. Students outside the Napoli were hurling snowballs. One hit him. His hair was white-flocked.

We sat in a dim booth with our glasses of wine.

'Tell me what's happened.'

'Well.' He sighed, breathing out smoke. 'She'd been out there since daybreak. Couldn't sleep. She was afraid she was having a breakdown. Said some wild stuff about killing herself. We went for a coffee but she was sobbing uncontrollably and couldn't get it down. It was so terrifying I insisted on ringing Annie from the coin phone. I had some mad idea of getting her to fly over. But by the time I put the call through she was quite calm. She talked to Annie as if nothing — of course she, Annie, was stunned. She thought the call was from London. God only knows what time it was at home.'

'And did you make any plans?'

'She said I had until Christmas. "You can't stay in Dreamland for ever," she said. "This is October. That should be time to straighten yourself out. Get back to reality." '

'But we were lovers in Australia as well.'

'Yes, she asked how long. She said Annie's still very hostile. "You won't win her over," were her words. "She won't forgive this. She'll refuse to meet Sandra." '

'Matthew, she's a grown-up woman. She knows these things happen.'

'Yes, but you don't expect' — he was frowning — 'when it's your own parents —'

'I suppose not. It's a lot to ask. Can you get your research over by Christmas?'

'No, no. The idea is — she would — well, the original idea —'

'Oh, I get it. She'd come here.'

'That's —'

'Out I go and in she comes, that's the idea.'

There was a silence. He broke it with a little sigh. 'Old Kane was out the front first thing.'

'Yes, I saw.'

'He thought she was a suspicious character.' He had a fixed sour half-smile on his face. 'Hanging around in the snow. Asked if she was looking for someone. She said, "No, thanks, I'm just waiting for my husband. Oh, here he is." '

'Well, he knew we weren't married.'

'It made his day. You should have seen the look! He says it won't last.'

'He does?'

'The snow. The *snow*, for God's sake! He says it's too early for snow. More wine?'

'I'll get it.'

I spilled the icy wine on my hands, carrying the glasses back.

'Matthew,' I said, and clamped my wet hands on his, 'you have a lot to lose by leaving home. In your own interest, shouldn't you consider going back? Margaret's given you your chance. You've talked things over these last three days. Mightn't you have reached a deeper level of understanding? You could try again.'

He stared at me.

'That's very generous of you,' he said at last. 'I admire you for that. Thank you for making it easy. Yes, you know, I think I must. She's won, you see.'

My blood shrank into my skin. I said, 'She stopped at nothing, did she?'

'I said to her, "You know, I think you're stronger than I am," and you know what *she* said? "I'll let you into a secret. I always have been." '

'That's not all.'

'No.'

'I could have fought her,' I said.

'That's what I mean.'

'Making it easy. I could have tried to stop it. Made scenes, said you had to choose once and for all, had it out with her. *She* would have. I felt sorry for you both. All that anguish. And so I end up the loser.'

'Sandy, don't cry, darling. I'm sorry.'

'Will you still be able to see me?'

He shook his head. In the yellow haze the jukebox cleared its throat and began to croon 'I did it my way'. He caught my eye, grinned and shook his head more ruefully still. 'Damn song,' he said.

We drank a lot more as time went on and the Napoli filled up, a yellow raft of smoke drifting under the lamps. Every now and then the heavy door swung open and let in buffets of snowy air and students who brushed and stamped off the snow in the entrance way and crowded the aisles. Against the racket we harked back to our early days, holding hands for dear life, and renewed our vows. When it came to having to lip-read we staggered out into the black and white frozen night to eat, at some extravagant restaurant on the Green, soft-shelled crabs fried whole and intact in flour. They sat on the lettuce like pale brown spiders, white-fleshed and alert under the knife. Their excrement in the fretty chambers of the shell had set and looked like scrambled eggs. We drank tart green French wine in a green bottle. A crowd came in for supper and a loud band started up, all jollity and bounce. We danced the slow dances.

Outside, snow lay everywhere on trees and roofs and footpaths. Flakes were still falling, lifting on the icy wind that stirred the leaves in flurries. Arms tight around each other, wet feet sliding, we made our way along the silent streets, stopping breathless for a long kiss from time to time, and stripped shivering with the lamp on while the air sizzled like a wasp around us and the steam pipes choked and clanked, and we lay down to couple as joyfully as if nothing had happened and no disengagement had so much as begun.

MELPO

When I married Magda, Jimmy is thinking, all our family danced. We roasted kids and lambs in our whitewashed oven outside. We drank ouzo and new wine by the demijohn. The whole village was there. My mother had cooked everything. Cheese pies the size of cartwheels, meatballs, *pilafia* … In spring she picked nettles and dandelions and stewed them with rice, for Lent. In autumn she brewed thick jams from our apples and figs and windfall apricots. Tubs of yoghurt and curd cheese sat wrapped all day in blankets by our stove. On feast days an aged hen seethed, tawny and plump, in the pot. Until the Germans came, and then the Civil War.

The day I married Magda, my mother led the line of dancers holding the handkerchief, making her leaps and turns barefoot on the earth of our yard, by the light of kerosene lamps.

When our family planted out tobacco seedlings in the dry fields a long cart-ride from the village, we started at daybreak and rested in the heat of the afternoon under the oak trees at the spring. We ate hard bread, and cheese and olives, and drank spring water. Once when I was small I picked up a tortoise where it lumbered among pale clods of earth. It hissed, spurting hot urine on my hands. I dropped it, then picked it up again. *Mi*, Dimitraki! my old aunts shrieked in their black scarves. Melpo! E, Melpo! But my mother lay there with earthen feet, in shade as cold and thick as the spring water, fast asleep. My mother. Melpo …

'Now your mother wants to meet me,' Kerry is saying. 'Why now?'

Kerry looks taut, as if angry, Jimmy thinks; but she is only disconcerted. Flecked with brown, her pale face is blushing. A green glow off the water, wavering up, lights her bronze hair.

'Darling, she didn't say.'

'Well, why do you think she does?'

'She said so.'

'Yes, but why?'

'She didn't say.'

Jimmy, balancing his rod on the warm concrete of the pier, lies back, his head in Kerry's lap, his heavy eyes closed against the falling sun, the swathed still sea.

'You know she wouldn't hear of it before.'

'She asked me your name again and said, "Dimitri, you sure you want to marry this woman? Really marry, in our church?" '

'And what did you say?'

'Kerry.'

'Oh yes.'

'And yes, Mamma, really marry.'

'What have you told her about me?'

'Nothing much. Red hair, I said. Australian, not Greek. Divorced, with one son called Ben. A teacher of maths at the same school where I teach Greek and —'

'Did you say anything about the baby?'

'No. Not yet.'

'Well, I'm not showing yet.'

'No.' He hesitates. 'Eleni and Voula have not told her either. I asked them.'

'They *know*?'

'Well, yes. I told *them*, they're my sisters. They said they'd guessed, anyway.'

'Oh, come on.'

'Yes. When they met you at the dance. They like to think they can always tell. They are pleased. A daddy at forty-five, they keep saying. Better late than never. They like you. How about after school on Thursday? Is that all right? Nothing formal. Just in and out.'

'All right.'

'You're blushing.'

'I'm nervous.'

'Try out your Greek on her.'

'I hope you're joking.'

'Me? I never joke.'

'You said she speaks English!'

'She does. She even makes us look words up for her. She hardly ever speaks Greek now, strangely enough. But very broken English. Nothing like mine. Mine is not bad, after only twenty years here. Would you not agree?'

'For a quiet life, why not?'

Shafts of sunlight are throbbing through the water as outspread fingers do, in fan-shapes.

'She wants to meet you now,' he sighs, 'because she is dying.'

'Oh! You've told her!'

'She wanted to know. I think she knew, anyway. Don't be shocked when you see her. She is wasting away, and her mind wanders. I wish you could have known her when she was young. Her life has been — *martyrio. Martyrio*, you know?'

'Martyrdom?'

'Yes. Martyrdom.'

'Because of the War?'

'Oh, yes, the War. Many things. The War was the worst. I was only about eight then. My sisters were too little to help. Our baby brother was sick. We were evacuated from our village. My father was a prisoner. Can you imagine it? His mother, my Yiayia Eleni, minded the little ones. I sold cigarettes, razor blades, *koulouria* — those rolls like quoits with sesame? — on the streets all day. My mother did cleaning, sewing, washing for rich women, to feed us all. But we were starving.'

'Can you remember so far back?'

'Of course. Everything. One night I remember my mother was mending by the kerosene lamp in the warehouse we were living in, in Thessaloniki. My grandmother put her hand on her shoulder.

' "Melpo," she said. "It is time you thought of yourself."

'My mother lifted her red eyes but said nothing.

' "You are young. Your whole life is ahead of you. And what about your children?"

' "Mamma," my mother answered. "Don't say this."

' "It is what I would do. He is my own son, my only son. But it is what you will have to do sooner or later. He will manage somehow, he is a man. Think of yourself as a widow, Melpo. The war will go on for years. You are still beautiful. There are good men who will help you. It is not a sin. You have no money, no home, no food. I mean what I am saying."

' "No. Your son believes in me and I have always deserved it. I always will."

'Yiayia shook her scarved head and said nothing more. Her eyelids were wet. My mother went on sewing. My baby brother cried out and I rocked and hushed him back to sleep. When I looked back, my mother was still and sagging over her work, so Yiayia took it away and laid her down to sleep and pulled the flour sack over her. She saw me watching, and hugged me.

' "*Aman, paidaki mou,*" she wailed, but quietly. "You must be the man of the family now."

' "I know, Yiayia," I said. "I am already." '

He lies still. Kerry bends over and kisses his brown forehead. 'I'm nervous,' she says again. Her long soft breasts nudge his ears. He feels her shiver. The gold spokes of sun have gone out of the water, leaving it black.

'Don't be.'

'Have we known each other long enough? Can we be sure? Long enough to get married?'

'Well, let me see. How long is it?'

'Ten months. No, eleven.'

'Is it eleven months?' He smiles. 'That sounds enough.'

'What will your mother think?'

'That we should wait. But I don't want to. You don't, do you?'

'No. She might like me, you never know.'

'Yes. Don't be too hard on her, will you, if she is rude? And by the way, better don't wear pants.'

'Pardon?'

'Pants. Trousers? Overalls? "Womans should wear only dresses." '

'Oh God!'

'It is her old age.'

'I don't have a dress. Or a skirt. I don't *own* one.'

'Oh. Well, never mind. Don't look like that. No, listen.' He sits up, agitated. 'Forget I said it. She can hardly see now. Glaucoma.'

'What flowers does she like?'

'Oh, anything.'

'Roses?'

'Yes. Fine.'

'Oh God! I hope we come through this!'

'Darling, of course we will.'

'Do you love me?'

'Yes, of course. *Kouragio*!'

She grins back at him, pushing her fingers through the shaggy grey curls at his temples. Shadow lies all over the bay and the far city. High above, a gull hangs and sways, silent, its red legs folded, still deeply sunlit.

Eleni and Voula, exchanging looks, have served Kerry iced water, a dish of tough green figs in syrup, a glass of Marsala, then Turkish coffee. They have exclaimed over her roses and argued amiably about vases. Flustered, Kerry waits, avoiding Jimmy's eyes. She feels gruff and uncouth, awkward. A bell rings three times in another room. '*Pane*, Dimitri,' Eleni hisses. Jimmy bounds away. Kerry grins blindly at the sisters.

When he comes back and leads her to his mother's room, hot behind brown blinds and stinking of disinfectant, she misses the old woman at first among the jumbled laces and tapestries, the grey and golden faces under glass: a skull on a lace pillow, mottled, and tufted with white down. Only her thick eyes move, red-rimmed, loose in their pleated lids.

'Dimitri?' The voice a hoarse chirrup. 'This is Keri?'

'Kerry, yes. I'm glad to meet you, Mrs Yannakopoulou.'

'Good. Thank you for the roses.' Rumpled already, they sag in dim porcelain, mirrored. '*Keri* is candle in our language. *Keri* is wox.'

'Wax, Mamma.'

'Yairs. Wox for candle. Dimitri, *agori mou*, put the lamp, I carn see Keri. Now leave us alone. We tok woman to woman.'

The door closes. Yellow folds of her cheeks move. She is slowly smiling.

'*Katse*, Keri, siddown.' Kerry sits in the cane armchair by the bed. 'My daughters they tell me about you.'

'They're very nice.'

'Yairs. They like you. They say good thinks about you. She hev a good heart, this *filenada* of Dzimmy, they say. She love him too much. She good mother for her little boy. Where your husband is, Keri?'

'My ex-husband. In Queensland, as far as I know. We aren't in touch.'

'Why he leave you? He hev another womans?'

'I don't know. He's been gone years.'

'You doan know?'

'No, Mrs Yannakopoulou.'

'You were very yunk.'

'Twenty-two. My son is nine.'

'How old you say?'

'Nine. *Ennea.*'

'Ach! You speak Greek!'

'I'm learning.'

'Yairs. Is very hard lenguage. How old you are, Keri?'

'Thirty.'

'Thirty. Yairs. You too old to learn Greek.'

'Oh, I'll manage. *Echo kouragio.*'

'Kouragio! Ah bravo.' A giggle shakes the bedcovers. 'Good. You will need *thet,* if you love Dimitri. He is quiet man. Mysterious. Always he joke. You will need to be stronk. You are, yairs. Not *oraia,* that doesun mutter. How you say?'

'*Oraia*? Beautiful. I know I'm not.'

'Better not. You not uckly. Too *oraia* no good. They fall in love with they own faces. They mek the men jealoust.' A smile bares the wires around her loose eyeteeth. 'Lonk time now Dimitri tellink me: this woman, this Keri, Mamma, I want you to meet her. Keri? I say. Her name Kyriaki? No, he say, she Australian woman, she not Greek. Not Greek, Dimitri? I doan want to meet her. But he keep saying please, Mamma. Orright, I say. If you thinkink to merry her, orright. Because now I hev not lonk time to live.'

'Oh, Mrs Yannakopoulou —'

'Orright. Is not secret. Everybody know.' Her hand clamps Kerry's arm. 'And before I go on my lonk, my eternity trip, I want to see my boy heppy. That is all I want now. My boy to be heppy.'

'Yes, well —'

'You are also mother. You hev a mother heart. You want what is best for your boy. You do anythink for him?'

'Yes, but —'

'You good woman. Good-heart woman. You hev *kouragio.* So mek me one favour. For *my* boy.'

'What?'

'Tell Dimitri you woan merry him. You love him. Orright. I understend love. Love him. Look after him. Live with him, orright. *Aman.* Doan merry him.'

Kerry pulls her arm away. The lamp casts a wet light on the ravelled cheeks and throat.

'So I'm not good enough.'

'You *good.* I doan say thet. But divorce woman. Not for Dimitri, no. Not for merry.

'But he's divorced!'

'Doesun mutter. Is different. She *putana,* thet woman. He love her too much, but she go with our neighbour, our enemy. Is shame for all our femily. We come to Australia for new life. Is not Dimitri fault.'

'Yes, I know. He told me.'

'Hwat he tell you?'

'It was twenty *years* ago.'

'His heart *break.* Some children they find them one night together in the pear orchard: Magda with our enemy. They mother tell me. Dimitri was away. When Magda come home, I tok to her, I tell her I know, all the village know. I cry for my poor son. He will kill you, I say. She cry, she scream. She say she waitink baby. I say we want no *bastardo* in our femily. I pack all her *proika.* I say, go and never come back. When he come home, *I* tell Dimitri.'

The scaled eyes close, wet-rimmed. Kerry sighs.

'He told me about it. My divorce wasn't my fault either. And I don't play around.'

'For Dimitri next time should be only *parthena.* Veergin.'

'Isn't that up to Dimitri?'

'Is up to *you* now. You know thet, Keri. You can say no. Say *wait.*'

'And then what?'

'I know Greek girls of good femilies —'

'No. You tried that before. He told me. He wasn't interested, was he? Why arrange a marriage these days? I love Jimmy. We want to get married fairly soon. I'm going to have a baby. Jimmy's baby.'

'Hwat? You waitink baby?'

'Yes.'

'Hwen?'

'August.'

'August. I understend now.'

'So you see —'

'You should be *shame*!'

'Ashamed of a baby? Why, what's wrong with it? We aren't living in the Dark Ages. Jimmy's very happy. He likes kids. Ben adores him. He'll be a good father.'

'I understend now why he want to merry you. *Apo filotimo!* For honour. Because you trick him.'

'No. That isn't true.'

'You know hwat womans can do if they doan want baby. You know.'

'I *do* want the baby. So does he. You have no right —'

'I hev the right of mother. The right of mother who will die soon! My only livink son! Doan break my heart!'

Kerry, her face hot, pats the writhing yellow hands and stands up.

'I'd better go, Mrs Yannakopoulou. I'm sorry.'

'Wait! Listen to me: I hev money. Yes, I hev. They doan know nothink. Inside the bed.' She claws at the mattress. 'Gold pounds! Hwere they are? Take them. Hev the baby. Leave Dimitri alone. Hwere they are?'

'No, thanks.' Kerry pulls a wry face. 'I'm sorry about all this. And I was hoping you'd like me.'

The old woman is moaning. Her eyes and mouth clamp shut, and she starts shaking. Kerry shuts the door softly on the dense lamplight and goes on tiptoe to the kitchen. It is full of shrill chatter. Saucepans hiss, bouncing their lids, gushing sunlit steam. All over the table sprawl glowing red and green peppers ready to be stuffed. Jimmy, Eleni, Voula, and three children, all suddenly silent, stare with identical eyes like dates; stare up in alarm.

'Someone better go to her. Quickly.'

The sisters hurry off.

'Darling, what's wrong? What happened?'

'Ask your mother. Can you take me home?'

'Of course. Just let's wait till she —'

'It's all right, I'll get a tram. Will you come round later, though, please?'

'Yes, of course. Unless she —'

'Look, if it's all off, fair enough. But you're not to punish me. I *wasn't* hard on her.'

'Oh, Kerry, punish? Why would it be all off?'

The children are gazing open-mouthed.

'She'll tell you.'

'You tell me.'

Kerry shakes her head, reddening.

'You are punishing *me*! Why are you angry?'

'Oh, later!'

The bell tings three times. Jimmy bounds down the passage.

'Mamma?' His voice breaks. 'Mamma?'

'Leave me alone, all of you. And you, go with your *putana.* Leave me alone.' She struggles to turn to the shadowed wall. *'To fos. Kleis' to fos.'*

He turns off the lamp and ushers his sisters out, though they linger, he knows, whispering behind the door.

'She had to go home.'

'Good!'

'Min klais, Mammaka.' He smooths her sodden hair. 'No, don't cry. Don't cry. No. No.'

'Give me a tablet. No, this ones. Water.' He slips his arm behind her knobbled back as she gulps, flinching. 'Ach. *Pikra einai.* Bitter.'

'Tell me what happened.'

But she is silent. He picks up the photograph on her dresser. It is one of the last photographs of his father. The old man is sitting in the doorway, feeding Eleni's two little daughters spoonfuls of bread-and-milk. They coaxed him in baby talk for *paparitsa.* It was his *paparitsa,* not theirs. It was all he could eat by then. A white hen is tiptoeing past them. Wheat was heaped in the long room that year, a great trickling tawny mountain; the barn was too full already of barley and sesame. The best harvest since the War, his father said. Bravo, Dimitri. None of them has seen the hen yet. In the light at the door they are like three shadow puppets on a screen. He alone looks frayed, dim, melting in the air. His death is near. He regrets, Dimitri thinks, that I have had no children. No grandchild of my sowing, no grandson to bear his name. Still, he is smiling.

In the photograph the bread-and-milk bowl is white. In fact it was butter yellow and, catching the light, glowed in his father's hands like a harvest moon.

'Mamma?' he says softly.

'*Nai.*'

'Tell me what happened.'

'She can tell you.'

'*Ela. Pes mou.*'

'This Keri. She hev not the right name. She not wox. Wox? She stone. Iron.'

'Why?'

'You want *her*? Hwat for? She not yunk. Not *oraia*. Not Greek. Not rich. For *proika* she hev hwat? A boy. A big boy. She zmok.'

'No.' He grins. 'She doesn't.'

'Australian womans they all zmok. Puff poof. Puff poof.'

'Kerry doesn't.'

'Dimitraki, listen to me. I know you like I know my hend. You my son. You doan love Keri.' She hesitates, then dares: 'Not like you love Magda.'

'Leave Magda out of it.'

'Thet time I save you.'

'Magda is gone. I was too young then. Forget Magda. I love Kerry now.'

'She waitink baby.'

'Yes.'

'Why you doan tok? You should be tell me this, not Keri. Is too big shock.' She sighs. 'If is your baby.'

'It is.'

'How you know? She maybe trick you. Australian womans —'

'Mamma, I know.'

'*How* you know? Divorce woman!'

'Mamma, I love Kerry. I trust Kerry. I need Kerry. All right?'

'*Thet* is how?' He is silent. 'You engry?'

'No.'

'Yes. You engry with me.'

'No. You will see in August if it is or not.'

'*Aman*. Dimitri,' she moans.

'Enough, Mamma, now.'

'Orright, enough. Enough. Merry her, then. I am too tired for fight. Do hwat you want. But you wronk, you know?'

He waits.

'I hope so she hev a boy. For the name, your Baba name. Is good for his name to live. August, *aman*! You think I livink thet long, to see your little boy?'

'Mamma, you will.' He squeezes her hand. 'My little girl, maybe. My little Melpo.'

'*Ochi.* If is girl, I doan want the name Melpo.'

'Kerry does.'

'Tell Keri if is girl, she must not call her Melpo.'

'You tell her. Next time she comes.'

'I *never* see her again.'

'Ah, Mammaka.'

'No. Sometime you askink *too* much.'

'You know,' he sighs, 'that if I have a girl, I will call her Melpo.'

'I doan want you to!'

'You do so.'

'*Aman*. Dimitri *mou*. Put me *rodostamo*.'

He tips red rosewater into his palm and sits stroking it over her cheeks and forehead and whimpering throat, the thin loose spotted skin of her forearms.

'Her heart is stone.'

'No. She is strong. Like you, she has had to be.'

'She will control your life, you want thet?'

'I *think* I can get used to it.'

'Well. I done my best. I hope so you woan be sorry, you know?'

'Thank you, Mamma.'

He bends and kisses her ruffled cheek. Her eyes close. '*Ela pio konda,*' she whispers. 'Closer. I have gold pounds inside the bed. Your Aunt Sophia's. Ach, if I had them in the War! The baby died from hunger. Take them, *paidi mou*. Doan tell the girls. Take them for your baby.'

'*Aman*, Mamma. You and your gold pounds. You gave them to Magda. You drove her away. And I forgave you. Remember?'

'For your good. For honour.'

But only after years, Mamma, he thinks. Bitter years.

'Sleep,' he says.

'I carn. I pain too much. Go and tell Eleni to come. Bring a clean sheet, tell her. When she goes, come back. Sit with me.'

'Can I do anything?'

'Nothink. Maybe Keri waitink you?'

'She will understand.'

'No. Go to her. When I was yunk, I was stronk. My God. Remember? And *oraia* also.'

'I know. There was not a woman like you in all Makedonia. You had a spirit like fire.'

'Hold my hend, Dimitri.'

One day when you are not tired, Mamma, he thinks, I must ask you: do you remember the storm, that last summer in the village, before the War when I was five? You sat on the porch in this cane armchair suckling Eleni. The rain was a grey wall. Hens shot past us slithering in the brown mud. The clouds were slashed by lightning and by spokes of sunlight. Afterwards I led the horse out, fighting to hold his head down, but he tore at the grapevine, splashing rain in clusters on us all. White-eyed, his dark silver hide shivering, he munched vine leaves. I was angry. You laughed so much, Eleni lost your nipple, and kicked and wailed. Then I laughed too.

Remember how we stood in the river thigh-deep, slipping on bronze rocks. You taught me to catch little fish in my hands. We threaded them on the green stalks of water plants.

SALLY'S BIRTHDAY

The pub the same as ever, good old pub. The same rippled green glass in its diamond windows, the hot bread reek of beer, and nests of smoke fuzzing the thick lamps day and night. Lamplight on the rough glass flickers like glowing leaves. No trees out there, though. Warehouses, and a few shops, factories. The faces under the lamps are red, shiny with sweat. No one is staring at him. Here it's live and let live. He smacks his glass down.

'Another beer, Mike.'

'Fair go, matey. Where's the fire?'

'Daughter's birthday today. Celebrating. Go on, have a heart.'

'Want to get me into trouble, do you?'

'Come and sit here, dear. Have one with me. Two pots, Mike.'

A roll-necked redhead further along the bar is beaming and nodding, waggling a fat hand with rings on. He moves down. The barman shrugs.

'Go for your lives.'

'Oh, thanks, Mike. Keep the change.'

'Well, thank you, missus. Cheers. Daughter's birthday today.'

'Is it, love? Well, now. How old's your daughter?'

Good question.

'Twenty-one. She's twenty-one today.'

'Well, here's wishing your daugher very many happies. What's her name, darling?'

'Sally.' He sucks a long cold draught. 'Sally.'

'Happy birthday to Sally. Sally Kelly with a rope round her neck.'

'Sally Jones.'

The woman wipes froth off her chin. She sighs and sips more.

'Haven't seen her for donkeys' years. Not since the old Yallourn days. She was going on seven.'

'How come, dear?'

'Her mother took off with her. We'd had a bad blue. Ended up here in Melbourne. She had a sister here. I didn't know where they were. Got a postcard one day. No address. Just "Meet us at the coffee lounge at five on March the tenth. Sally wants to see you." '

'That's today.'

'Sally's birthday, see.'

'Oh yes, Sally's birthday. Well, here's to Sally. Married again, did you, dear?'

'Me? Shit no. Once is enough.'

'Go on. You never know.'

'I bloody know.'

'Ah,' she sighs again. 'Ah well.' There are tears in her eyes. 'That's life, isn't it? That's life for you.'

He was waiting in the coffee lounge by half past four, though she'd said five in her postcard. By the window so he could see them coming, Jan with Sally, on her seventh birthday. He was afraid that Sally might not know him. His own face looked strange to him gazing in the plate glass, blue-lit; all the other faces that came and went further inside were gold, in a haze of steam, ribboned with smoke. Six o'clock. He had his presents and the cake wrapped on the seat beside him, and a big blonde sleeping doll in cellophane that the girls in the canteen had put in for. It was the right coffee lounge. The one she'd worked in, they always went there.

The street became dark, and his face too turned dim gold. He was on his fifth coffee. It rained, and stopped raining, and started again. Seven o'clock. Cars sprayed veils of rain under the street-lamps. Strangers splashed past. The lamps in the coffee lounge hung behind his head, huge luminous orange balls, juggled and frozen there.

It was the right coffee lounge.

At eight o'clock he got up and without a glance at the things on the seat he walked out.

'Do you have a good cognac? Courvoisier? A Napoleon brandy?'

'No, miss, sorry. Nothing like that.'

She is tall, sleekly dressed in black velvet. Her hair is in short black curls like an astrakhan cap. Green eyes slope upward in her white face. Sally in that last photo had her hair like that. Green eyes, too. The image of Sally.

'Come on. Give young lady whatever she's after. Hear me?' They all stare in the bottle shop as he leans over the counter. 'Go ahead, mate. Give lady what she wants.' But they ignore him.

'This is the only brandy I got in stock, miss.'

'Oh, well, that'll do, thanks.' She sighs, pays for it and hugging the bottle in its brown bag steps into the street. Headlights glow over her.

'Miss, mind if I ask your name?'

'Yes, I do, actually.'

'Got a good reason.'

People are looking. She hesitates.

'Please. I got a good reason. For asking.'

She stares as he shivers in front of her, wringing his wet hairy hands.

'Marian,' she says. She hurries across with the green light.

Marian? Not Sally? Not Sally?

Following her at a cunning distance, he loses her long black shape again and again in dimly lamplit streets, but sees her at last open a wooden door with stained-glass tulips in it. Beyond a tiled verandah and low fence and gate. He knocks. His words tangle, explaining to the hostile round blur of her face. Sally, it's your dad. Your old dad. Sally! He sees her go watery, then dark, dark, and falls at her feet in a dead faint.

A white dog, long and supple as a fawn, breathing and licking in front of a log fire, looks up grinning.

I feel crook. Sally. Where are you? Sally, I feel crook.

The dog pants. No other sound. He sleeps.

He dreams he is looking for Sally in a wild green sea. He rises and sinks in terror. At last he sees her in the distance, a little girl crouched in a snowy plain lost in an immense grey twilight. Cold falls through the air. She is burning matches to set fire to her body. Luminous flames batter against her. Dying away they leave a heap of ashes in a hole of sodden yellow grass. The wind swerves and roars. There is nothing in any direction but barren snow.

When he wakes again he is snotty with tears. He keeps his eyes shut. He assumes this is another morning in Pedro's room Good old Pedro the Dago, his best mate all those years up north, ever since Groote Eylandt. Quiet as a mouse, the old Pedro, sitting in corners with his guitar, until he got hold of some grog, then he'd go wild and fire shots in the air, chuck empties at anything that moved, and howl and scream and swear. Listen to who's talking. All right, but I draw the line at shooting, mate. Well, he could always have a kip on the camp bed at Pedro's, and bugger the landlady. On one wall there is a long lady in charcoal, twice life-size, and from time to time Pedro has added hairs in pencil, and moles, and tattoos. Squatting in front of her. She has huge tits and hips. Her name Conchita, Pedro said. She a big whore, mate. You can call her Connie. She was there when Pedro took the room, part of the furniture, but he's done a lot to her since. Pedro has never said who Conchita was. He himself has never mentioned Jan. He looks up now with a shy grin for Pedro, but this is not Pedro's room. Pedro? he croaks. He could have sworn. But he is too exhausted to insist.

A long white dog lying with its head on its paws looks up, yawns, and wanders back to the fire. There is no lamp, only this golden ebb and flow of rustling light. In the warmth of it his clothes stink, sour and musty. He is embarrassed by his singlet and shirt stiff with sweat, and the lumber jacket, its seams ripped now, borrowed from Pedro three weeks ago. Never needed this much clobber up north, Pedro, eh. His shoes are battered and grey. So, when he checks it in the round mirror over the fireplace, is his face. The grey bristles of his hair and whiskers are clumped around scabs.

The dog sniffs him. Good dog. Good boy.

On the mantelpiece a bottle of dark green glass sits with a candle in its mouth. CHAMPAGNE COGNAC, he spells out. The glass is dim, like fragments found on beaches, their sharp glitter worn and blinded by years in sea water. He picks it up. Trickles of wax like white roots cling round it. He gives it a shake, and wax falls in the fire. He peers into it against the firelight. Not a drop.

'Are you feeling better?'

Never laid eyes on this one in his life.

'Er, yeah. Thanks a lot. Er.'

'Would you like a cup of coffee? No? Tea?'

'Er, well, tea'd be beaut, thanks, miss.'

'Milk? Sugar?'

'No milk. Two sugar. Thanks. Er, miss? How come I —'

Baffled, he waves his shabby arms.

'You passed out on my doorstep.'

'Shit, did I? Jeeze. I'm sorry about that. Makes you the Good Samaritan, eh.'

She grins back, shrugs, and disappears. He remembers a pub with lamps in the afternoon. It is already night, though, at these firelit windows. In the pub some fat old redhead bought him a beer. A birthday. Whose, hers? That bit about the Good Samaritan was a bloody inspiration. Made quite an impression, knowing something from the Bible. More than just some old derro. Hidden depths. Course, it helps a lot to have a way with people. I always did have a way with people. They always want to look after me. The sheilas especially. All except Jan, the bitch. Funny that. Like that waitress in where was it? Gympie. Wanted to get married. I love you, Larry. Love you, love you so much. Oh God. Don't ever leave me, Larry. Oh darling.

'Here's your tea.'

Lovely voice this one's got. Like Pedro's guitar.

'Oh, ta, miss.'

He stirs it and sips, burning his cracked lips. She is kneeling to stroke her dog. He pats it. It looks sidelong at him. On its bent haunches the white hide is crisp as a calf's.

'Nice dog you got there. What's his name?'

'Bianca. It's a she.'

'Big, isn't she?'

'She's only a baby yet. What's your name?'

'Told you, didn't I?'

'No. I don't think so.'

'Larry Jones.' He stares across the dog at her dark curling hair. Now he remembers. He knows who she is.

'Mine's Marian.'

'That's funny,' he says. 'Marian. What's your mum's name?'

'Sylvie.'

'Sylvie, eh? That's funny.'

'She's French.'

'No. No. You look like someone.'

'Do I?'

'You look like my daughter. The spitting image of her.'

'Really? What's her name?'

'Sally.' He leans forward. 'I bet it's your birthday today.'

'No. Why?'

'It's Sally's.' He blows on the tea and sips some. 'It's her twenty-first.'

'Oh, really? Is she having a party?'

'I wouldn't know. They say she's dead.'

'What!'

That's what they reckon. Inform, I should say. That's how you find out these things, see. Like when the wife got her divorce and got married again. Letter from the lawyer bloke. Dear Mr Jones, we have been instructed by our client, Mrs Janet Thompson, to inform you that blah blah.'

'How did she die?'

'Drowned. Down Apollo Bay way. Kennett River. Ever been there? Last summer.'

'Oh, how terrible! I'm sorry.'

'I hadn't seen her for a long time. I mean fourteen years is a bloody long time. If it's true, my Sally's been dead for months.' He stares into the flowing red and gold of the splintered logs. 'If it's not, I'd know her. If I see her again, I'll know her.'

We have been instructed by our client, Mrs Janet Thompson, to inform you that your daughter, Sarah Margaret Thompson, drowned on 17 February this year while swimming in heavy surf at Kennett River, Victoria. Miss Thompson's body was recovered, but all attempts to revive her were unsuccessful. A funeral service for Miss Thompson was held at the Memorial Park Crematorium, Altona, on 21 February. May we extend our deepest sympathy to you in your loss.

That's how it went, something like that. He glances up from the fire. She is staring at him. As if she's seen a ghost. Maybe she has.

'They changed her name,' he explains, 'soon as her mum got married again. To a respectable bloke. It was me Sally wanted to live with. Steal me, Daddy! she says. We'll run away and live together, you and me. No fear, I says. Want your dad to end up in jail? I been sorry ever since. Let her down, see. Her dad never let her down before. Deserved to lose her, eh. And I done time inside anyway. I was inside when the letter came. Only got out last month. Tell you what. It's not that bad. Life goes on.'

'Why would they make up a story like that?'

'If you knew her mum,' he snorted, 'you wouldn't ask.'

'You can check with the Registrar of Births, Deaths and Marriages.'

'Oh, I will, don't worry. They can't keep me in the dark forever.'

A great joy has begun to burn in him. He sucks the last cold drop of tea and puts his cup down. Clumsily. It falls and rolls on the saucer, spilling sandy sugar. She stands up.

'Are you feeling better?'

'Bit better now, thanks, love.'

'Could you eat something?'

'No. No. Couldn't keep it down.'

'You're sure you'll be all right?'

'Bit of a snooze and I'll be right as rain. If that's all right, miss. If I'm not in the way.'

'Well. All right then. I'll leave you to it.'

'Wait on.' She is letting him stay! He feels in his torn pockets. 'Got a photo here. Last one she sent. Used to write to me now and then. Send photos. They always caught up with me sooner or later. Somewhere up north.'

It has cracked and faded: a glossy print of a smiling schoolgirl with crinkled dark hair. It is inscribed on the back. *From Sally, with love to my Dad. X 0*

He waits as she looks intently as if into a mirror.

'So what if they changed her name,' he says, taking his time. 'Sally'll still know I'm her real Dad.'

* *

At Cowes that last summer, the time they were boarding at a guest house, Sally came fishing off the pier at daybreak. She made such a song and dance about it that he took her. He woke her at five. They walked hand in hand down streets still sunken in cool darkness, their footsteps chiming against the black plate glass. Wisps of cloud turned pink, then gold. He cast again and again, catching nothing. A seal looping in the green water below gazed as she knelt calling. Daddy, look. It likes me. Catch it for me.

Oh Sally love.

Flames in glass flutter and breathe. The dog whines, nosing at its singed hide, it is so close to the fire. There is a rug over him now: he jumps up with a cry, then sits down slowly, dizzy, sick. Take it easy now. Where the fuck? Oh, Sally's place. Lie down and listen to voices muttering. Whose?

Somewhere in another room, her voice and a bloke's. One, then the other. Her voice a slow guitar, then the bloke's threatening, it sounds like, annoyed, but finally laughing, convinced, or distracted. Now both are silent. He lies in a sweat. Bloke's not going to mind if her old dad stays the night, is he? Don't say Sally's married. All these years and it seems only yesterday.

By the time the lawyer's letter caught up with him it was July or August and if it was true she'd long been incinerated by then. Her hair, her white flesh burned. Shards of bone left, bones and ash. Ashen bones. A lock of hair she had sent him, all that was left, he had gone and lost God only knew where, once when he was drunk and disorderly and woke with a blank mind in Fannie Bay. His last letter came back from the lawyer's: *Sally love, this is a view of Ayers Rock. I promise I'll come down south and see you soon as I can. Your loving Dad. X O*

His bladder will burst. Where's the bloody john? He creeps unsteadily through the firelight with the slender dog smiling and nudging him through the archway where she had appeared, hadn't she? Yes, with the tea. A throbbing pale refrigerator, a dark grey sink. The deep house lying in wait. He huddles over the sink, groping through layers of clothes. The piss splashes and rebounds in a loud spray. He struggles with a tap. Too tight.

Oh Jesus Christ.

Still in the paper bag, her bottle of brandy that she was buying when he saw her: sitting there on the table. And if that's not Fate, I don't know what is. Grabbing it, he stumbles back to the firelight. Slumps on the couch. Pulls the rug up over his thudding head. At long last he manages to twist the cork out and have one long hot swig. Happy birthday, Sally. And another.

The door slamming startles him awake. A car starts up. Headlights, sweeping over the pane through thin curtains, flash over the room. The fire is dying. Sally? he croaks.

'Oh! Are you all right?'

'Sally. Come here a minute. Want a word with you.'

'It's Marian.'

'Don't give a fuck! You can call yourself Cinderella! Anyone can change their fucking name!'

She snaps the light on and gasps at the sight of him wildly grinning up, the bottle in its soggy bag clutched to his chest.

'Have some.'

'No, thank you.'

'Celebrating. You never told me you were married.'

'I'm divorced.'

'Oh. Who's the bloke, then?'

'He's a friend of mine.'

'Don't give me that. It's your dad here, remember? And I've seen it all. Friend going to marry you, is he?'

'It's not really your business.'

'Turn light off.'

'He's coming back.'

'Turn fucking light off!'

Soft darkness covers the room. His stung eyes can open.

'What's time?'

'Half past twelve.'

'Divorced, eh? She's done a good job. Here's to your mother.' He has a sip. 'Friend going to marry you, is he, Sally?'

'He's married.'

'I see. Well, well. Gone home to his wife.'

'Can I get you anything? You look terrible.'

He lifts the bottle for another swig, but this burning in his belly will be the death of him. He groans.

'No. Want to talk.'

'Let me just get —'

'Sit down!'

She squats to stir the embers in the grate, and is outlined with fire. The dog whimpers, its long head laid in her lap.

'Don't hold yourself cheap.'

She nods.

'Hear me? Don't hold yourself cheap.'

She nods, her back still turned.

'Any bloke'll have a bit if you rub his nose in it. Hop in for his chop. Too right. Be a fool not to. Then you're the whore for letting him. See? Your mother might have got away with it. Your mother was a rotten lying whore. She'll burn in hell for it. You're not like that, are you, Sally?'

She stands looking down at him.

'You've turned out a very lovely young woman. Man can be proud of you.'

That gets a smile out of her.

'Voice like a guitar.'

'Oh, come on!'

'No bloke's going to think he can treat my daughter like a whore. I'll soon piss the bastard off.'

She laughs. He joins in with a joyous cackle.

'That's the way. That's my girl. Piss him off, eh? Get me a drink of water, will you, love? Feel a bit crook.'

She hurries through the archway. The light snaps on. He wasn't too harsh, was he? A dad's got a duty, like it or not. Then he hears her sniff and gasp. He remembers. With a moan he remembers groping in the dark. Pissing in her bloody sink. Oh Jesus Christ. A torrent of water gushes in the sink. Stronger hands than me. He squeezes his eyes shut and huddles down. Oh God, Sally, he rehearses silently, I'm real crook, love. I'm dying, Sally.

'Here's your water.'

'Ah.' He gulps some. 'Thanks, love. I'm crook, Sally.'

'Where do you live? They'll be worried about you.'

'Got this mate in Punt Road. Pedro. Pedro the Dago. What his mates call him.'

'That's miles away. This is Carlton.'

'Carlton, eh?'

'Can I give him a ring to come and get you?'

'Not on the phone, love. He won't worry, though. Shit no. He's prob'ly gone fishing.' A quick sip of the water, a grin. 'Hey, remember that last holiday at Cowes? Trooping through those tunnels in the tea-tree, remember? The sand was like fire. We could hear the sea a mile off, and cicadas. We went fishing. I was teaching you to swim, Sally.'

She stands up. His eyes are sore. He shuts them.

'What did you say?'

'I was teaching you to swim.'

'Where in Punt Road?' Her voice is far-off, and tense. 'Will I ring a taxi for you?'

She is holding the front door open.

'Hold your horses. What's going on?'

'I'm sorry. I must ask you to go now.'

'What do you mean, you're sorry? Kicking me out?'

'Please, just go.'

'What did I do?'

'Never mind.'

'We got to have a talk! It's important!'

'No, I'm sorry.'

'What do you mean, sorry?'

'I'm sorry, but you have to go.'

'Well I like that. Middle of the fucking night. My own fucking daughter. If I'm not disappointed in you!'

'Come on, please.'

'Just a minute.' He is on his weaving feet. He peers at her. 'Hang on. Give us a good look. You look like Sally all right. But I don't think you *are*.'

He only waves the bottle to emphasise the outrage of it, but she recoils and shrieks. The white dog cringes.

'Get *out*!'

As he wavers, intent on remonstrating, she gives him a wild

push that sends him staggering, gaping, out on to the verandah. The door slams. Lights flash on in all her windows. Silence.

'Sorry won't mend it,' he grumbles. Whore.

He hugs the bottle in the bag, wandering down a street filled with flurries of light. Lamps and housefronts and footpaths shimmer as if behind flawed glass or in the shaken air above a fire. Then there is the moon, sitting full and golden on the roof of the brewery. It is still there when he blinks. A fiery blur.

Across the glinting tramlines, if only he can make it, is the old pub.

With caution he starts out, eyeing his shadow on the wet bitumen, lights flaring under his feet, across tram rails and then more rails. Make it. You can make it. Rails surge round his feet. Cars slide past and daze him. It is too small for a pub. It has a tower, seats, diamond windows. A sign. He spells out LADIES.

Propped against its dank wall he fumbles at the bottle, but it slithers out of his hands and cracks with a fat splash at his feet. He sinks down, scrabbling in wet paper and broken moonlit glass. He sucks salt blood and brandy off his fingers. Glass stings his lip. Tears spill down his face, through his nose, out of his jagged mouth.

Oh Sally love I'm sorry.

In his dream he is rising again, bobbing and stumbling, stunned, deafened, hurtled, out of a shaggy uproar of green waves. He is carrying to safety his lost, his only daughter. Cicadas rasp. Her eyes open and smile at him. He lays her down gently on the sand.

WOMAN IN A MIRROR

She had a painting that Peter had given her. In it a blue-headed fish lay alive or dead on a wooden table in a stone room lit by one white-washed archway. Dark waves towered beyond it. Inside in the calm, there was a jug of wine or water beside the fish, a knife and fork, a goblet, one twisted chair, and a cold glow off the sea.

'Because you love the sea,' he had said. He had loved mountains.

'He who does not enjoy solitude will not love freedom,' Schopenhauer wrote. She had printed that under the painting.

But must he who loves freedom enjoy solitude?

Behind her the sun beat in gold slats through the blinds. The child stirred, still asleep. He was flushed. Bubbles of sweat gleamed on him. His hair was damp. He lay naked, white and sturdy, a big boy for three, very calm, very self-contained. Peter's boy, but not like him. When he woke, they could go to the beach. It was hot for April.

She took her dress off and watched the woman in the mirror stroke oil on herself. She was long and flexible, but thin. Her breasts drooped over her ribs. How they had swelled, white with milk and netted with thick veins, while she was feeding the child. Only to shrink and hang down, little drab pouches. Silver tracks were left on them, and inside her loose thighs too, and on her belly, there in the centre where it had bulged until her navel turned inside out, quaking when the child moved inside. Like crushed velvet, David said it was. Peter had never seen it. Peter, who for years had known her perfectly; who had not lived even to see the child born, but had died on a mountain road in Yugoslavia.

The Adriatic there was a sea stiller than any other, as still as the sky. Grey islands floated in it. A fisherman in his boat on the shingle showed them a fluted pink shellfish that glowed like an ear in the sun, like a red candle when the wax has dripped. When

Peter asked what it was, the man croaked a word, and laughed when they tried to say it. 'Let's have a swim,' she said, walking into the water and stooping to dabble her hand in it: her feet glowed, huge on the pebbles. 'Before we tackle the mountains.'

They were a white wall in the east.

'No time,' said Peter. 'We'll be lucky if the road's still open now past Titograd.'

A broad woman had come crunching down the shingle with fish, a whole bunch of brown fish hooked by their bony lips, shimmering.

'Fish! She thinks we want to buy fish!'

'Well, we don't. When would we cook it? Look, if the passes are closed, we're going to have to backtrack up the whole Dalmatian coast in any case. If not, we'll be swimming and eating fish in Greece tomorrow.'

The fisherman and his wife exchanged a look. The woman bent with a groan to dip her bunch of fish in the sea and swung them up high, nodding: see, fresh. Water fell flashing from them.

'It's so warm, though! So still and clear.'

'Fish,' said the woman suddenly. They all laughed. But Peter was impatient. Wasn't she the one who hated taking risks? So they shook hands with the couple and drove on east into the mountains.

Now she sat with her legs apart to see the fur and the red ridges it enveloped, crinkled like a small hen's comb. Hidden in the warm hollows inside was a gristly knob, her cervix, with the thread of the IUD emerging. Tomorrow all the quiet women in the stuffy waiting room at the Hospital would go in one by one and lie back with their bent knees apart. The doctors' hands in glittering rustling plastic would palp their soft red masses. Some of them would have cancer.

'Cancer of the cervix? That's impossible!' she had protested the first time. 'I'm only thirty-five! Why? Is it the IUD?'

Could death and decay be growing where the child grew, so soon after?

The doctor was patient. No, it wasn't the IUD. It probably wasn't cancer. She had had two tests now, though, and abnormal cells had been found both times. At the Women's Hospital they would do definitive tests. 'Make the appointment today,' he said. 'There'll be a long wait. These things can be left too late, you know. Don't put it off.'

'You fool,' she said to the face in the bright mirror. 'You coward. You were the sensible one. You never took risks.'

She had let months go by.

If she dared to ring David, he might be some comfort. David? she could say. It's me. Can you come over? I know, but sneak out for a little while. Please, it's important. They think I have cancer. Yes.

No. Impossible. She had never rung him. She had never even looked up his number. It was understood that she would never ring him. His wife would suspect. And she could never tell him this. He would hate to think of her diseased, doomed, monstrously invaded in there. He would never want her again. Once or twice a fortnight he came to stroke her and cling, and turn her over at the end so that she was any woman, and then bore between her thighs, barred with sunlight. She loved him a little. He was afraid she might.

She put on her blue bathers, glossy and pale as the sea. The child sighed. 'Hey, wake up,' she whispered. He was beautiful, crossly moving in his sleep his sturdy white arms and legs on the damp patch of his sweat. She kissed his cheek. 'Wake up, come on.'

I have a strong white body, she thought, still free of pain, streaked with silver and sunlight. The child, the sea, freedom and solitude. And more time. Please.

More time.

On the tramline a long sheath of grey dust and twigs was trying to move. The child picked it up. A casemoth. From the little cap a blind brown and orange snake-like head nodded out. She helped the child find a ledge on the grey palm bole where it would be safe, and it groped around there, wagging heavily, the velvet neck of its case wrinkling with the strain like an elderly wrestler's.

'Will the casemoss die, Mummy?'

'No, not now.'

They wandered across to the beach. The sand was deep gold, pitted with shadow. The child paddled, naked in rings of water, looking for shells. Afloat all around him, the gulls stared. She tied up her hair and waded into the cold clear sea and swam off, splitting the yellow sky, turning and drifting. Angrily he called her back. There were deep shells to get for him. She was mirrored; stooping over the sea, a woman of glass shimmering, blurring her own image with slow drops of water. As she swam back he flung splashes at her and stumbled away laughing.

They sat on the towel and admired her shells and his. He put the best ones in her bag. She had oranges in it. She peeled one and pulled its striped segments apart. In that late light they shone, crescents striped inside like ice or quartz, and beaded: warm and very sweet, ripe autumn oranges. She split another one and they ate it.

Chilled, she changed awkwardly out of her wet bathers under her dress and the towel, then pulled on the child's shorts for him. 'The pier, Mummy': he was dragging at her hand. Now a flow of deep light was all over the sky and the drawn skin of the bay. Palms moved against it, black as rooster tails, flourished, then still. A woman with long straight grey hair sat perched beyond them, busily painting.

'My tutor always did say never to try a sunset,' she called across cheerily, 'but how could I resist this? I'll make him eat his words!'

As the sky dimmed and a pale moon rose, she sighed and stood back. The child asked to see. The woman showed them shyly and turned to pack up. Her sky and sea were streaks of orange, vermilion, chrome yellow; the pier and the boats, all the hulls and strung masts, black; and there they were too, the child and she, drooping beside a bollard, her hair and her hands spread out.

'Who's them?'

'That's us.'

'You don't look like that, Mummy.'

'Ssh. I like it very much,' she said, smiling at the woman's smile.

The child went to make friends with a man fishing. Left alone, she watched a domed jellyfish come lolling into the green water under the pier. It was not aware of her, of boats and a pier, of the city's faint towers of light swaying over it. Were there beings just as unknowably watching her as she watched the jellyfish, with a vague detached goodwill? It would have been a comfort to believe there were.

Once she had been shown a painting in which reflected lights on a river leaped and faded in the black sky. 'The river runs through Zagreb,' the owner explained. 'The lights are dead souls. There were massacres that winter of the War. The artist fled. Corpses and chunks of ice choked the river.'

We drove through Zagreb, she thought. A grim stone city. Was there a river? She couldn't remember one.

White and orange lights were lit all around the edges of the bay.

It was near Zagreb, wasn't it, that Peter pulled up at a farm and asked a little boy to fill our water-can? There was a Jack-and-Jill well in their farmyard. When he brought the water he got an orange for it, a huge red Cretan orange, and looked amazed. His little sister stared. His face red, he sidled away, his orange safe behind his back. The little girl wailed. Their mother leaned out of a window shrilling, but he pretended not to hear. 'Milan! Milan! *Milan*!'

Milan smiled at us. A gold frieze of corncobs was hanging under their eaves. Snow in the mud, melting.

There could be a soul bursting up out of the bay that minute. There, that bubble of hurled light. How could you ever know? Like a shooting star, or lightning. People did drown in the bay, and lie sodden in the dark, hung in shrouds of seaweed. Fish grazed on them. One day they tumbled on to the beach at high tide and were found.

The soul itself might be only a metaphor. An image, a hope.

Do I have a soul, Mummy? She could imagine the child asking. Not yet, but in a few years. I don't know, sweet, she would answer. Nobody really knows. You *should* know, he would frown. Tell me. Yes or no? He hated uncertainty, He was like that. So had his father been.

'Mummy, I'm cold.'

On the way back the child went to the palm bole to visit his casemoth. It was gone. In the spurts of light from a failing streetlamp he found it at last on the tramline, crushed, its grey fuzz oozing thick orange-and-brown. He bent over it in disbelief, and his face crumpled and turned red. Tears splashed from his eyes.

'Look! Casemoss *died*!'

'Oh, yes, look. Oh, poor thing.'

'It's *died*! So you're a *liar*!'

She bought him an ice cream. It consoled him.

The brandy burned in her mouth and throat. She sniffed its hot breath over the rim. Glossy as honey, it cast its heavy light over her fingers.

Time was slower in solitude. There was the steady rise and fall of the sun, then the night. Time was *andante*.

The child lay warmly asleep at last.

Everything deteriorates, she thought. Nothing lasts. Flesh, and love, memories, relationships, the will to live. Love also is an act of will. David doesn't love me. He has stopped loving his wife. Does she love him? I'm not allowed to know her name. Did I love Peter? It's nearly four years ago. Love too might be a metaphor.

We went to Mount Buffalo for our honeymoon. We walked to the Horn, the summit, in the sun, picking brown flowers. We nibbled raisins and oranges that spurted sour juice in our eyes. Crows croaked among the boulders. A dark thunderstorm struck. We ran to shelter in a hut sewn with cobwebs. Later we lay naked on a ledge of the Horn out of sight of the day trippers in cars. Far below us the trees were blue as mountains, and crows floated. Peter staggered laughing at the edge of the abyss until I screamed. In the flat grey of nightfall we walked down to the hut, drinking from a glassy trickle over dark rocks. We had a bright campfire and slept folded together on a bracken bed.

Later we camped on mountains in Greece, those grey-skinned mountains. We camped among silver olive trees and on river banks under the plane trees, in the sand and the brown leaves and the golden fur of their crushed seed balls. In crumbling fortresses sheep bells woke us. We slept on tideless pebble beaches and watched each morning as the sun erupted out of the yellow gulf. We drove to Italy, France, Germany, Austria. Yugoslavia.

The brandy stung her dry throat.

The road up from Titograd was narrow, pot-holed; a wreath at every bend marked a death. On a crest it was blocked by a heap of refrozen snow and as we skidded over it a timber lorry met us roaring round the white curve. Our car glided under the lorry, crumpling slowly. My head hit the dashboard. In amazement and rage, my head dripping, I heard our engine then the lorry's stop.

Peter was hanging over the steering wheel.

People had scurried from the buried farmhouses. Women helped me limp in. They made me coffee in a dark stuffy room, wrapped me in rugs and forced bristly grey gloves and socks on my hands and feet. They brought fried eggs and pickled cabbage, and thick glassy slivovitz. I drank that, but left the food. Curving my hands over my belly I showed them there was a baby. They made a compassionate whimpering as I lay curled on a sofa by the smoking stove. I woke with a sting, an ache, in my soggy head. It was bandaged. My hair was full of dry blood. A girl was there then who spoke English: Nada, her name was. Nada put her arm round me and told me that Peter had died. The sallow women cried drearily, plucking at their drab sweaty rags.

She sipped the burning brandy.

After her return she had written to Nada; after the formalities and the long flight; after the funeral. She had sent little presents. In return Nada had sent her cards that she had painted for the tourist trade. Snow, cottages by the road with golden windows and smoke coiling, icicles hung from their eaves. No wreaths where the road curved. No soul flung up in a shower of light out of all that snow.

Peter was reckless. He was happy-go-lucky. 'Hullo, you two happy-go-lucky young people,' a neighbour used to call as they went past. She never had been. She was the sensible one.

On the other side of the world, in the southern winter, the baby was safely born. She named him Peter Milan.

She took a last gulp of brandy and undressed. By lamplight white hairs at her temples glistened. Her eyes were bruised, but they always had been, all her life. Her teeth were patched and yellow-tinged. Rubbing oil on her legs these days, she could see the fine skin with its blue net of veins move, a milky plastic casing, over her shin bones. All over her the flesh was beginning to loosen like an old dress. Her elbows were sharp sockets, folded in shrivelled skin.

In his sleep the child chuckled.

'You fool,' she said to her yellow face, 'why did you put off going? How could you? Who will look after him if you die now?'

She laid her head beside his. His breath fluttered against her. She stroked his warm white arm downed with silver hair. He rolled into her arms.

Someone will, she thought. My treasure, my darling. My beautiful boy. Someone will look after you.

A PAWPAW ALL THE WAY FROM QUEENSLAND

The newspaper with its yellow splashes of pawpaw and broken glass was still spread out all over the lino. She folded it into the bin somehow and made real coffee in the saucepan, trundling from the sink to the gas stove, leaning out over the arms of the wheelchair. She spilt some, straining the dark grounds, and sipped the rest luxuriously. She wasn't allowed to use the stove. Still, rules were made to be broken and in this case it was after midnight and Alan still wasn't home. He was ashamed. You've been a good son to me, she wanted to say to him. You, not Billy. You've looked after me. I know it's been heavy going. It doesn't matter. Forget it.

I always liked a rainy night, she thought. I was always one to go skimming over bright puddles, the raindrops throbbing down on the taut black veil of my umbrella, rolling and glowing there. Cars slid by in their lamplit steam. Jessie, good God, woman! You smell like a wet spaniel, Jack always said. I roasted my legs by the fireside while he made coffee and poured us a whisky. Poor Jack, the whisky killed him. Six years ago already. Yes, I was fifty-eight last birthday. He being an older man, retirement's the killer. The whisky on top of the diabetes, and then his heart. It's my turn now.

At about nine o'clock when Alan walked out the rain was so heavy the windows looked as if they had shattered into crystals. Later the drizzle set in. A grey skin of mist grew on the closed panes. These days she felt unsafe with a window open, as if she might float out. She kept inside by a radiator with two red bars and a fan heater that breathed warmth: together they were almost a fire. From room to room she wheeled herself, lamp to lamp. She always had at least two burning day and night, the stooped, white-cowled reading lamp, Alan's really, and her mother's porcelain one with the red silk shade that glowed in the polish of the sideboard like a pagoda on a lake. A street lamp flickered on the front windows. The glass doors of the sitting-room always held some light, red, white or gold. Within the sphere of this or that lamp hour after hour her hands made shadows on her empty skirts and on the pages of the book in her lap. Not that she read any more. She remembered as much as she wanted to of her books. Besides, drops or no drops, her eyes were bad. The same with the television Alan rented. She made a show of watching for his sake, while her mind wandered. Nothing on it could hold her interest for five minutes together. Alan would read to me once in a while, she thought, if I asked. He's hard to talk to. A man of few words. Worse since his marriage broke up. And what he *did* say ...! Well, he flew off the handle and no wonder.

My poor sad boy, she said aloud. Come home soon. It doesn't matter. How can I make you see?

Her back ached. She sighed. No use getting upset about the aches and pains. Bodies are like cats and dogs, they have a will of their own. They get slow and stiff, cranky. Think of old Smoky at the end. Pamper them, humour them, do what you like, the day will come when they turn on you. Make messes. Get sick and die and break your heart. Smoky, so fat and sulky, the way he kept rubbing his plushy old head on my legs with this creaky little meow, meow, he knew — what would he make of me these days? He'd take my having no legs as a personal insult. I think I've wet myself, she thought, but never mind. It's warm. Bodies are like the Irishman's dog, one word from me and he does what he likes. Cuddling Jack one night when his manhood had let him down, I told him about the Irishman's dog. You make fun of me, woman, he snarled, and you'll live to regret it. Oh, a morose man. Alan's the image of him. Oldest sons are. Those three years made all the difference. Look at Billy. Nothing throws Billy. He behaved so badly today. He goaded Alan. That's why Alan turned on me and said. Said what he said.

A ring at the door at six o'clock, she remembered, and who should be there but Billy and Wendy, back from two weeks hitchhiking up the coast to Queensland, panting and dusty, all laughter, hugs and kisses. No sooner in the door than Billy was dragging clothes and towels out of his rucksack. He peeled a football, orange-gold and blotchy, out of a tangle of singlets and rolled it over to her chair.

'Good heavens,' she gasped, leaning over to peer, 'whatever's this?'

'A pawpaw, of course!'

'What?'

When she meant why. He bent and picked it up. 'Beauty, eh? It better be,' he crowed. 'We've humped it all the way from Queensland.'

'They sell them in Melbourne,' Alan said.

'This is the real thing, but. Picked ripe from the sun. Have a smell, Mum.'

She put on a great show of delight, made him bend down for a big kiss and thanked him for bothering. Billy, do you or don't you know I'm hanging on by a thread? she wanted to say. First the legs and now the kidneys, how long can I go on dragging this out? I want to do away with myself. No use saying, and she just smiled while Billy, of course, had to set about cutting the thing that very minute. Wash it first, she said. It must have been years since she tasted pawpaw. It was all for her, Billy said, knowing how fond of it she was. Nonsense, she insisted, look at the size of it! They would all have a share. So he sliced it in four, scooped out the glossy round seeds that lay in rows on their beds of flesh like spawn, gunmetal grey — how I used to love crunching those seeds that tasted of capers, of peppercorns! she suddenly remembered — and sprinkled each shell with lemon and sugar. No sugar for me, she said weakly, and at that he grabbed hers, rinsed it under the tap and tried again with plain lemon juice. She ate what she could. It had a bitter aftertaste, or it was the tablets she was on. The blotch on the skin was slimy and had a fur on the outside. She said how delicious, of course, rolling her eyes for him like when they were little after one of her treats. Billy and Wendy gobbled and chattered on about Queensland. They made coffee. All this time Alan had not moved.

'Hey, eat up, Al,' said Billy. 'What's the matter?'

'No, thanks.'

'Come on!'

'Thanks, I don't happen to like pawpaw.'

'Don't know till you've tried it, do you?'

'I have. Tastes like cold boiled pumpkin to me.'

'Oh! It does not! Does it, Mum?'

'It's lovely, dear.'

Billy was watching her eagerly. Foolishly, she couldn't move, transfixed with sadness, and why she didn't know but tears were dribbling down her nose. Billy, ever helpful, grabbed the spoon from her hand. 'Open wide,' he said. He dug out a bright yellow chunk and crammed it between her shuddering gums.

'She doesn't want it. You can see that,' Alan said.

'She's my mother too, you know.'

'So help look after her why don't you?'

'I wish I could.'

'Oh yes, *you're* married. I forgot. Sorry.'

'I happen to put in a sixty-hour week.'

'Oh right. In between hitchhiking.'

'That's you all over,' Billy said. 'God. Always the martyr. Saint Alan.'

Alan walked out of the room. 'God,' Billy spat after him.

'Good heavens, aren't you *brown*, you two! Come here and let me see. You're *burnt*! Better watch out you don't peel!' She was babbling anything she could think of to fill the silence. 'Did you get as far as Townsville? I was born there, you know, dear.' Grinning at Wendy who grinned tremulously back. 'My happiest, earliest memories. I met Billy's father there. We sailed back on our honeymoon on the old *Kanimbla*.' That got them chattering on and on. They had no money left. What was the point of a sixty-hour week at that rate? They seemed to think they could carry on like this for ever. Why get married then? Because they had to, of course, why else: or he thought they did. A boy of nineteen. Well, he's twenty-one now and off my hands. The lamplight dazed her and her eyes kept closing, but at last they were packing up the rucksacks, looking up train times, calling out taut goodbyes to Alan, who didn't answer. He came back in after they had gone. His wedge of pawpaw was still glistening on the table.

'Where do you want this?'

'In the fridge, I suppose, thanks, lovey.'

'Can't you eat it and be done with it?'

'Oh dear.' She was too tired for this. 'I couldn't. Tomorrow.'

'It won't keep.'

'Oh, we can't just throw it out, can we? Not when they carried it back all the way from Queensland?'

'It was off. They got it cheap. You'll end up with the runs before you know it.'

'I'll end up before you know it anyway,' she said, and heard with a pang of shame — and alarm too — the quaver of injury in her voice. Self-pity. Alan had spread a newspaper on the lino to wrap the peels and the coffee grounds. Now he slammed the bowl of pawpaw face down so hard that it smashed. He sat on his heels glaring up in defiance, livid, her jealous little Alan of a thousand tantrums. 'Oh, Alan, dear,' she sighed, smiling.

'Oh Alan dear,' he simpered. He stood over the wheelchair, head down and snarling in her face. 'What does that bloody well mean, "Oh Alan dear"?'

'Oh, don't.' She closed her eyes.

'Don't what? God damn you to hell, bitch,' he shouted then. 'What are you waiting for? Die and be done with it. Is that what you want? What the fuck's stopping you?'

Before she could say a word he had dashed out and slammed the front door. Rain was falling in a white rush round the street lamp. There was no sign of him. She had drawn all the curtains and sat among her warm lamps for ages. She rolled up closer to the mantel clock. Could that be right, half past two? She must have dozed off. The fan heater fluttered her empty skirt. Where was he? He never stayed out all night. So dreary, this long grey rain.

Perhaps, it occurred to her, he was home all the time. He might have found her in here asleep and still been angry enough to leave her be and go straight to bed. Alan, she called out softly. Alan, and then thought better of it. He needed the sleep. Carefully she rolled down the passage and turned the handle of his door. No, his bed was made, more or less, the covers pulled up in lumps and wrinkles, still empty.

Surly Alan with his black moods, she thought, and rowdy

greedy silly Billy, how I loved them once! They're heavy weather the pair of them, now they're grown men. Alan who's clammed up since his wife walked out and can't stand self-pity. No, that's his preserve. And Billy who was the ant's pants, he got well and truly caught, a false alarm, the oldest trick in the book and he falls for it. If you ask me, she really is expecting now, though, which should bring him down to earth with a thud. No, as men they were a disappointment, only real when she caught a glimpse of their childhood selves. Did they feel the same? Most likely. Who's the old bag, then? The cripple with the goggle-eyed face under a tangle of veins, her, leaking into her chair? Not me, not the real Jessie. Some old baglady has got in under the skin of the real Jessie, the buxom and bustling younger Jessie who loved her little boys. I take myself by surprise, she thought, at the sight of these stumps of thighs and my arms as the Sister sponges them, the flesh loose and yellow on the bone like overcooked chicken. When did it happen? Time was thin and vague now, the after as lost and out of reach as the long before. It might be the tablets. All the months when ulcers ate at the grey flesh of her legs and she sat up night after night clenched all over to keep so much as a whimper from waking Alan — even these times were washing away. Dozing off, she was this and that other Jessie, young Jessies with long legs. Which only went to show that the truth still hadn't sunk in after all this time, not into every fibre of her being, that the helpless old bag of bruised and aching flesh here, in and out of hospital, gangrened and lopped and gangrened and lopped all over again, was the real and last, one and only Jessie. While it lasted.

She wheeled over to the window and rubbed a space in its cold mist. Was he down on the beach? On the day he moved back in, when he spent hours trying to tell her his marriage was a failure and could he come home — for hours that day he kept her hobbling up and down on the beach in just such a soft rain, the grey waves slowly beating, pitted. Their faces were wet. Raindrops glowed in his hair. Her legs were so bad he had to prop her up. In fact she had the artificial leg by then. When was the first operation? — she was on one leg. The dry sand was hopeless so he kept to the firm sand, the wave line, higher and higher, so that now and then a cold, fine cloth of water would be thrown up as they went, and go flattening and frilling around their shoes. He never even noticed.

He only got married because Billy was. That's all, deep down. Spite. They're as bad as each other, it's just that it takes them differently. Neither boy can face facts. Alan goes into his shell and as for Billy, look at him — Billy's all glitter. Night was falling by the time we struggled home, she remembered, for coffee and pancakes. By way of consolation. Oh, Alan, dear, always coming home for consolation! We had a whisky, just like the old days, which I shouldn't have, I know, but life isn't worth living if you can't break a rule when needs must. We had our guzzle of whisky in the lamplight and at last we could hug, and laugh and cry. None of that now. I still had the one leg. My one wet foot I could feel, the wash of the water and sand between my toes. I'm not allowed to cook any more. Or laugh, or cry.

Oh, Alan, dear! A cup of coffee would be nice. They bring me Meals on Wheels, bless their hearts, and Alan dishes me up his little treats of a night. I can't complain. Even oysters he bought me the other day as a surprise, shiny and grey on their crinkled half-shells, my favourite food. I'd forgotten how delicious. It's all soft foods since my upper plate broke. I used to like cooking. Banana pancakes, that was Alan's favourite. The boys had pancake races. Let's see who can eat the most. Usually Billy won: not that he was that keen on them, which is Billy all over. Me in the kitchen, not knowing till too late. We had pancake picnics in the tea tree along the foreshore of a summer night. Fed the seagulls. I stare out at a seagull now as if the beach was a world away.

How ironic life can be, she thought. No longer caring if she slept or not, she had saved up more than enough tablets to bring on an easy death. *Easeful* death: that was in some poem. Alan would never know. The Sister or Doctor Smith might, but even so they would never let on. But now that Alan had said *that*! He'd blame himself. He'd have this hanging over him for the rest of his life. *Die and be done with it*. How could she take them after that, no matter how desperate she was, even if he wanted — which he didn't. She shook her head. You're getting morbid, my lass, she thought. You'll go in good time. You and your tablets. Wait for nature. Because in a few hours, when the first bird woke with a hoarse chirrup at the window, wouldn't she feel ashamed to show a poorer spirit than birds and snails and avid unfolding green plants? Another day. Snooze and roll about the house, be sponged and dressed and fed and jabbed and dosed again.

She trundled into the dark kitchen. A blown leaf — a mouse? — rustled across the lino. She leaned over the sink to fill the saucepan, measured ground coffee into it and, carefully tucking up her sleeves, lit the gas ring. The coffee frothed up. She strained and sipped it black and strong. Woman, you don't boil coffee! Jack, shouting. You'll ruin it! Poor Jack. At least with the heart you go quicker. She smiled. Oh, the fireside nights and Jack, far gone in whisky. All gone now. It'll be morning soon. Oh, Alan, look, I understand. How can I make it better?

Pancakes! she thought. And when he comes in — Look, I can say. Alan, look what we've got for breakfast — pancakes!

She crouched rummaging in the cupboards for flour. In the white glare of the fridge she found an egg and half a bottle of milk. No banana in the house. We get the giant pawpaw lugged home in person and yes, we have no bananas. Well, then, lemon and sugar. No lemon: it all went on the pawpaw. Never mind, jam will do. Hugging the bowl, she mixed and beat, mixed and beat. Flour settled on her lap and sleeves and in her coffee, which she gulped down. The batter should be left to stand. No time for that. She had a feeling he would walk in any minute. She had better be quick or her surprise would be spoilt. *Look, Alan:* smiling, she pulled out the black iron frying pan, rubbed a butter paper over it and relit the gas. A curl of smoke soon rose from the pan. With a tea towel she grasped the hot handle and raised the bowl to pour some batter down into the middle. Her hand shook and, afraid it would spill, she jerked both hands sharply up to save it. The little crown of flames, catching at the tea towel, sprang roaring up her sleeve. Flames glared into her eyes, clawing her, and she beat at them with seared hands. Flames tore her other sleeve. There where she sat, her hair and her hanging skirt flared. Fire covered her.

MILK

I was nine when my father first took me to Greece for a summer. He came from a northern village. There were, as he had promised, animals everywhere. And my grandparents did love me. Yiayia, my grandmother, read me stories and spoiled me. My grandfather, Pappou, was deaf, so we didn't talk much. But he took me everywhere. My cousins, the other grandchildren, all lived in the city and were only visiting. Sometimes they were nice, sometimes they teased me. They picked fights. They sulked.

'Niko's our boy,' Yiayia said. 'He's flown thousands of miles just to be with us. So don't be mean.' They groaned. 'You all have mothers,' she added. 'Niko hasn't. His died when he was three.'

When they'd gone home it was better. As well as feeding the animals we did heavy work in the fields, Pappou and I. I helped load bales of lucerne and hay on the cart, and lay the pipes for watering, and hoe the tobacco. My father helped too. I wanted us to stay for ever, but he said no.

My father and I took Pappou to the market town and bought him a cow with a calf. Whatever we and the calf couldn't drink, Yiayia could make into cheese or yoghurt, or sell. Not many people in the village had a cow then, though there were goats and sheep with pink bags of milk between their legs. Our cow, all hide and bones, had an udder so huge that she looked, Yiayia said, as if she was perched on a barrel. She was put in the barn next to the house with her calf and Pappou's old horse. I helped with the milking. We let the calf suck first, to start the milk flowing. When we hauled him away, the calf propped and pranced and the cow gazed round in dismay, both of them mooing. After the milking we set the calf free to finish off. Once in his rush he knocked Pappou over in a pile of wet black dung. I shrieked with joy. Pappou sat there and cursed me.

'Niko! Niko?' Yiayia was furious. I blushed and said sorry to

Pappou. He was looking sheepishly at me. Niko was his name too, of course. I was named after him. Who did she mean? Bemused, we looked at her. She laughed and shook her head.

Yiayia asked me to hang up the curd cheeses at night in their white cloths, high up on a pole near the grapevine that shaded the porch, so that cats and dogs couldn't snatch them. I wished I didn't have to. Up there near the porch lamp beetles rattled against me as I tied knots. Cobwebs clung. The whey dripped in my eyes and down my arms.

'Good boy,' Yiayia said. 'That's fine. Up there nothing will get them. Not even the wolf.'

The wolf. My cousins had told me horror stories about a wolf: a *lykanthropos,* a werewolf that they said lived in the village.

'Is there one here, Yiayia?'

'Lots. Ooooh.' She made a howl and laughed up at me, her eyes lost in yellow wrinkles. 'Not in summer, silly. There are in winter.'

'Why?'

'Why? It snows here, that's why. They get hungry.'

'Where are they now?'

'Up on the mountain. And there they'll stay till you've gone home, so you can get down now.'

I slipped down. The mountain hunched grey beyond the river, the lights of its villages twinkling and fading like fireflies.

'Have you ever seen one, Yiayia?'

'One or two. There was one last winter as big as the calf. It was full moon like now, but on snow, so I saw it clearly through the window. The men went after it with guns. You'd have shot it for us, eh, cowboy?' She said it in English, *kaouboyee.* 'It'll be back.'

'Did it kill anything?'

'It couldn't get in. The foxes were worse. It only came for the donkeys.'

'But it couldn't get in.'

'They were outside, though. On the hill over the river. They were tied.'

'In the snow?'

'Yes, poor things.'

'Why?'

'What use is a donkey in winter? There's no room, no feed. They say it's cheaper to buy a new one in spring.'

'So they feed the old ones to the wolf?'

Yiayia shook her head. That meant yes. No was when she tossed her head back, frowned and said tsk.

'They didn't have to tie them,' I whispered.

'Yes, they did, or they'd have come home.'

I gazed in horror.

'If you aren't your father all over again!' she said. 'Here in winter there's nothing all round but snow and ice. People die too.'

'I'd go and untie them!'

'God love you,' she said. 'They'd die anyway.'

'I'd feed them!'

But she'd gone in. Layers of mist were floating blue and silver over the rooftops. I shivered. The porch lamp blinked. Cobwebs full of beetles hung from it. The muddy cups of swallows' nests were empty of birds. Dogs barked. It seemed to me that the night had a chill already.

A fat donkey jiggled past. The rider, her face turned away from our house, was Kyria Tassoula.

Kyria Tassoula never spoke to my grandmother. It was some old quarrel, my father said. Women and their quarrels. Her house was just over the road. Some of the family would say hullo as I went past, but as if it embarrassed them to, so I mumbled and scuffled on. Their boy Stelio liked me.

One afternoon, too hot to sleep — we all slept after lunch — I found an old woman in the kitchen with Yiayia eating yoghurt. She hobbled over to me, peering hard, and patted my cheek. Her breath was sour. Like all the old women, except Yiayia, she was wrinkled, toothless, all wrapped in black. They were talking, but it wasn't Greek. I ate some yoghurt and watched them. Yiayia dressed in colours and left her white hair uncovered in a bun bright as a snowball in sunlight. Only close up her red cheeks were cracked with lines. She smelled of rosewater.

She told me later that that was Stelio's grandmother, his

father's mother. She sometimes came over in secret and if she wasn't well enough they kept in touch through a neighbour. She was Kyria Tassoula's mother-in-law, but she hated her too. She was glad I was friends with Stelio.

I wasn't really. Stelio, though bigger and older — nearly fourteen — had played soccer by the river some evenings with me and my cousins. Once, seeing that I was fascinated by the fireflies, he chased and caught me one. In the red ridges of his palm it glowed weakly, a little battered grub.

'What is it in English?' he grinned. He was a greasy boy, always grinning, heavy yet loose and light-footed.

'Firefly.'

'Fyah flyee. Fyah flyee.'

He walked home with us, so I had to keep the firefly. From the corner he lagged behind. Frightened of his stepmother, my cousins whispered. Kyria Tassoula, she beats him, and she beats his father too, and one day you'll have a stepmother, too, Niko. I hoped not.

There were always night noises. Cats fought on rooftops, roosters crowed at the moon, donkeys burst out in sudden sobs and groans. Tractors roared past from daybreak, then the early bus. When, that night, frantic yells and snorts woke me I thought, I hoped, it was just a donkey. I thought of the *lykanthropos*. My father ran to open the shutters. The screaming blasted in then, loud, agonised.

'What is it, Dad?'

'I don't know.'

Yiayia and Pappou were on the porch staring over at the yard of Stelio's house, where torches glowed and thrust agile shadows among men and thistles.

'It's all right,' Pappou said. 'It's only a donkey. Tassoula's donkey. *Gennaei.*'

Laying an egg. I knew that word. But Stelio's stepmother's donkey wasn't. It was shrieking with pain.

'Oh my God!' my father said. 'Can't they do something?'

'Tsk. Not now. It's finished. Listen to it.'

Lights went on in house after house. Dogs barked.

'If they bring a *haïvan-doktor*?'

'Tsk. Too late.'

I clutched my father's arm.

'Oh God. Why don't they shoot it?'

'Them?' Yiayia grinned. 'You don't think they'd waste a bullet? Slit its throat maybe. That's more like it.'

'Sssh, Sevasti,' Pappou said.

'It's my bet she poisoned it.'

'Sssh.' Pappou took her inside and turned out the lights. My father locked our shutters. In the dark I crawled into bed with him and he made room, one arm tightly round me. The screams and sobs were quieter after a while.

'She's getting better, Dad,' I said. 'Isn't she?'

'Yes,' he said. 'Go to sleep.'

'What was wrong with her?'

'It's over now. Sleep.'

The bed smelled of my father, as he smelled when we were in Greece. Of sweat and dust and hay.

In the morning, helping Yiayia to search the barn for eggs, I found out the truth. The donkey had not got better. It was gone. At first light it was carted to the hill.

'*Pethane, totes*?' It died, then? I still wasn't sure.

'*Psofise*, little one,' she said. 'Not *pethane*.'

'*Psofise?*'

'*Petbane* is for when people die.'

'What if you say *psofise* when people die?'

'No, you mustn't, it's an insult.'

'Then it's an insult for animals too.'

'Don't be silly,' she said. 'People are more than animals. People have souls.'

'Well I'm saying *pethane*.'

'Tsk.'

I had to see for myself. I sauntered past their yard and just glanced in. The tall thistles were all trampled and torn up. There in the midst of them stood the grey donkey. *Den pethane*, I said aloud, it didn't die, so there. It trotted to me, breathing hoarsely, and pushed its gazing head through the barbed wire. It came up to my middle. At last I understood. It was a baby, a newborn *gaïdouraki.* I rushed home and told her.

'I think it's hungry,' I added.

It was sure to be. It had stayed by the mother's corpse all night and sucked it. My skin prickled.

'Will the wolf eat the mother, Yiayia?'

The wolf or something else. Weren't they all God's creatures?

'Yiayia, can I please feed the *gaïdouraki?* There's plenty of milk!'

It was too small. It was best to forget it.

'With a baby bottle, please, Yiayia, I know how!'

No, it was a waste of time. It wasn't ours. Stelio's stepmother would stop me. The whole village would laugh at us both. But she gave in and wearily found me an old bottle with a teat and handed it to me to fill with warm milk.

The *gaïdouraki* stumbled to me with little sobs and wheezes. I held his head. At first his lips fumbled, then they clamped on the teat. As he gulped I stroked his fluffy back with the dark cross on it. His eyes watched, river-brown eyes lined with black. I patted his rough nose.

'What are you up to, Niko?'

Stelio was always there before you saw him.

'It's hungry, isn't it? What's its name?'

'Hasn't got one, silly.'

'What'll we call it?' I asked him. It was their donkey.

'I know!' He grinned. 'Fyah Flyee.'

'Firefly. All right.' I liked it. Stelio laughed. When the bottle was empty I climbed out. Through the wires Firefly nudged me, panting. I looked back. Stelio waved.

On the next market day Pappou and my father went on the bus but I stayed home to feed Firefly. Preparing his bottles — he was becoming insatiable — I chattered on to Yiayia, though as usual she wasn't listening. She often wasn't happy. She had been very quiet all that day. As I turned to go she put her hand on my shoulder.

'Wait. Are you going over there?'

I just looked at her.

'Well, look, do something for me, eh? Will you, Niko? Stelio's grandmother's sick in bed. Take her this yoghurt.'

'Yiayia, I *can't*. I've never been to the house. I go to the yard not the —'

'Stelio's your friend,' she said. 'His stepmother went on the bus, I saw her. I can't go, you know that. Come on, Niko, you do it for a donkey, won't you do it for a poor sick old woman? Niko, please.'

I left the bowl with its embroidered cloth over it on a fence post while I fed Firefly, and Stelio found it.

'What's this, Niko?'

'Oh. It's for your grandmother.'

'What's in it?'

'Yoghurt.'

'What?' He had a look. 'Yoghurt for my grandmother?'

'She's sick, isn't she?'

'She's sick, so what? We've got food.'

'Oh.' What would Yiayia say?

'You idiot, take it home. What next? Ha ha.' His voice when he laughed was a yodel. 'See if Firefly wants it.' Firefly poked his head between my legs and Stelio doubled up. 'See! He thinks that you're his mother. Ha ha ha! You are now, aren't you, Niko?'

I hoped Yiayia would give up then, but no. She would take the yoghurt herself, but I had to come and carry it. She ignored my whining protests. Stelio gaped when he saw who had knocked, but he led us in politely and left us there. It was hot in the dark inner room, its windows and shutters all locked. There was a bad smell. Yiayia kissed the head lying above a tangle of dim sheets. 'Sophia,' she murmured. I heard an answering croak, but I understood nothing of what they said. When Yiayia said '*Yiaourti*,' I stepped forward with it.

'*Ligo*,' the voice struggled. A little. '*Ligo*, Sevasti.'

Yiayia went to look for a spoon. I hurried after her. She stopped short. Kyria Tassoula stood there, Stelio behind her.

'You?' she said to Yiayia. 'You sneak in here when I'm out, do you?' Then she saw the bowl. 'And what's that?'

'Yoghurt,' I whispered. 'For Stelio's grandmother.'

'*What*?' Kyria Tassoula grabbed it, strode into the bedroom with it and hurled all the yoghurt on the bare floor. It splashed in lumps like vomit.

'You old fool!' she said. 'You beg food from her, do you? Now eat it.' She swung round to us. 'You think no one else can make yoghurt?'

'*Fonissa*,' hissed Yiayia. I didn't know that word.

'Get out. You and your brat.' She gave me the bowl. 'Mad old women.' She smiled. 'Do you find each other by the smell?' Stelio's laughter whooped.

Yiayia said nothing on the way home. She locked all the doors and shut herself in her bedroom. No one was home. I sat in the silence praying that my father would come soon. In the end I made coffee, thick and sweet, I knew how, and took it in to her. She drank it. She was crying. My father and Pappou, when at last the bus came back, sent me to hang up the cheeses while she told them. When I'd finished, Yiayia was whimpering into my father's shoulder. Pappou sat grey and stiff.

'Tassoula came home in the bread van,' he was saying.

'When I was little,' Yiayia said, as if she hadn't heard, 'I thought she was a princess. Sophia's clothes! Her braided hair! In church the priest couldn't think straight.' Her yellow lips shook. 'You should see her now. I've kissed corpses with more life in them.'

Kissed corpses. My own grandmother.

'She says Tassoula's poisoning her,' Yiayia said, 'and she won't eat or drink. *Fonissa einai*, she said.'

'Since when?' asked my father.

'Since the night the donkey died.'

'What!'

'She said it was a sign.'

'Mamma, you know that's nonsense,' my father said. 'She's sick, she's dying of cancer, haven't they told her?'

Cancer was a word I knew. *Karkino*. My mother had died of that. It was something inside you that ate you, not like a worm, like a giant wart. You couldn't catch it from anyone who had it. You died slowly.

'Is hungry sick, *paidi mou*?' Yiayia's lips stretched in a yellow grin. 'Is hunger a cancer? Is it? That's what she's dying of.'

'Mamma, she has cancer. The doctor told me.'

'Tassoula wants her dead, that's all I know.' She looked at Pappou, who looked down.

'Mamma, if she won't eat —'

'She would have eaten the yoghurt.'

The house over the road had a horror in it now. Not during the day, just as the cemetery had none then, but lay there sunny and green beside the gravel road that led to our tobacco fields, its stone crosses crowded by thistles with mauve flowers and the singing of furred brown bees. After dark came the horror. Rattling home in the cart I could never look at the cemetery, and to shut my eyes was worse. I gazed ahead at Marko, Pappou's horse. I saw nothing but Marko's bouncing rump and the swung black hair of his mane and tail. We turned at the church, its storks' nest sprawled on the tower. Then past Stelio's house with a clatter. I looked away. At last, our own bright porch.

That night I was in the fetid room again. An indistinct shape in the bed mewed words I didn't know. Yiayia sobbed. Kyria Tassoula leapt into the darkness. Pale yoghurt splashed. I begged for the light to stay on. My father said no, it would bring every mosquito in the village. So he let me come into bed with him and talk till I felt better.

I asked him what *fonissa* meant. I thought it might be something like *lykanthropos*. Kyria Tassoula had pointed eyeteeth and, in my dream, gold eyes.

'A *fonissa*,' he said, 'is a woman who kills someone. A murderess.' He hesitated. 'Your Yiayia was very angry when she said that, Nick. She didn't mean it, you know.' I didn't answer. 'You mustn't talk to people about it. All right?'

'Yes.' He turned over. 'Dad? Did my mother — smell like that?'

'*What*?'

'That old lady smells — dirty.'

'Oh no. God, no. Your mother was in hospital. The nurses took good care of her. Jesus Christ.'

'Why doesn't Stelio's grandmother go to hospital?'

'Well, only people who might get better go to hospital here. If they're too sick they come home. She's lived in that house for fifty years. She'd be frightened anywhere else.'

'She's frightened of Kyria Tassoula.'

'No, no. She doesn't like her, that's all.' I said nothing. 'She gave you a fright, I know. She has a bad temper. But that doesn't make her a *fonissa.*'

'Yiayia said —'

'I know. But Tassoula does her best. Most people do, Nick. That's what I think.'

'Yiayia doesn't think she has cancer, does she?'

'You can't change an old mind. It's no use trying. So go to sleep, Nick, will you? It's three o'clock.'

Yiayia gave up. The next couple of days she woke late, and in the afternoon heat when we went to bed she lay crying. My father prepared meals. The dirty washing rose out of its basket like dough. Yiayia wouldn't help with the milking, but sat inside while Pappou clashed buckets and cursed. She groaned, the second day when he brought the milk in, that milk was more a burden than a blessing. Pappou hurled it, bucket and all, through the kitchen window. We had none to drink. I gave Firefly water. When we came in from the fields that evening we found her in the last red light from the window, peeling potato after potato into a pan of water. Again, nothing was cooking. On the table at her elbow a hen flounced and jabbed at crumbs. Yiayia's cheeks were wet. Pappou and my father bent over her.

I found Firefly gasping with hunger, grieving.

'Yiayia!' I burst in, frantic. 'There must be some milk somewhere!'

'Are you thirsty, little one?' she droned.

'For the *gaïdouraki,* Yiayia.'

'Ach. You and your *gaïdouraki.*'

'Please, Yiayia.'

'Come on, Nick, don't bother Yiayia,' my father said in English.

'The *gaïdouraki,*' Yiayia muttered. 'Why should I feed their *gaïdouraki*?'

'It's starving,' I said in English, and burst into sobs. 'And it's bloody not fair!'

'Nick, that's enough!'

Pappou, plodding in for a bucket, looked at me.

'What's wrong with our boy, eh?' he said.

'*Aman!* That *gaïdouraki,*' Yiayia snapped. '*People* can starve there and no one will lift a finger.'

'You want some milk, is that it?' I shook my head. 'Come and help and I'll give you some.' He patted my shoulder and bent over Yiayia, but I heard. '*Ela,* don't be hard on the boy, Sevasti *mou.* He's going soon.'

I stared at my father.

'Are we going soon?'

'Of course. You know we are.'

'When?'

'The day after tomorrow.'

'*No!*'

'Yes, we have to, Nick.'

In the barn I was not much use, but Pappou gave me the milk. I asked if he needed a donkey. No, he had a horse. He slapped its rump. He had no room, no feed, no use for a donkey. He said he was sorry. He was, I saw.

It was dark in the yard by then. Stelio was chasing Firefly with whoops and cracks of a whip. I said hullo. He stopped short with a giggle.

'Fyah Flyee. Here's mummy with your milky.'

He went on, though, cornering Firefly at last and trying to mount and ride him. When at last I had a chance to give him the bottles, he gobbled them and pressed hot and shaking against me.

'He loves his mummy,' Stelio sneered. 'Did you miss me yesterday, Niko?'

I shook my head and grinned back at his oily face.

'Know something, Niko?'

'What?'

'Your grandmother's mad. Everyone knows that.'

'Do they.'

'You know what else?'

'What?'

'If my father sees you here again he'll shoot you.'

That was a lie too. They didn't waste bullets. Besides his stepmother beat them both. I wished I could watch.

'You're going home this week, I hear. Poor Fyah Flyee.' He pulled up one long soft ear and crouched to yell. 'You hear that? Your mummy's going home.'

'Will *you* look after him, Stelio?' I wheedled, but sick, hopeless. 'Look, he likes you.' Firefly cringed.

'Me? *I'm* not a donkey's mother.'

I picked up the bottles. He was still hungry. Would I dare come back with more? Stelio's chant followed me home.

'Niko's Fyah Flyee's mother. Niko's a donkey's mother. Eh, Niko?'

He saw me turn by the porch lamp.

'Niko, *tha psofisei, xereis*?'

Niko, he'll die, you know? I knew.

'I'll eat him alive! I'm a *lykanthropos*. Ooooh!' He laughed, howling. I went straight to bed.

The next day, our last, Stelio's grandmother died. Her corpse would stay at home until the funeral, my father said. If I met any of the family I was to shake hands and say sadly, '*Zoï se sas*,' long life to you. But I kept well away. Yiayia, her face like iron, sat on the porch watching a file of old people shuffle into Stelio's house. Finally she went herself. No one spoke to her or tried to stop her, she told Pappou. Who would have dared? I wondered if she kissed the corpse. She came back remote and eerie, a listless stranger, even her cheeks pale, and her white bun loose in wisps. She sighed, pouring me milk.

'It's my fault,' she murmured. 'I meant well. Am I to blame? But no one was a better friend to Sophia than I was.'

'They wouldn't let you help her.'

'Even so.'

'Yiayia.' I clutched the bottle and in spite of myself I said it. '*To gaïdouraki mou tha pethanei*.'

'Ach, little one, yes.' She hugged me. 'Yes. *Tha psofisei*, poor thing. Ach, Niko *mou*.'

'Yiati tha pethanei, Yiayia? *Yiati*?' Why? But my last hope, gone.

'What can we do? It has to be so. We all have to die. We die, and donkeys die, even wolves die.' Tears shone in her eyes. 'Your own mother died, on the far side of the world. Do you think I didn't nearly go mad when they told me?' She had a smile. Not, as I saw, an easy smile. 'But you're a big strong brave boy now.'

For the last time I brought water in buckets to the cow, the calf and the horse. I hung the cheeses high among the cobwebs. I fed Firefly five times, the last time at night, a hard cold night with stars. I didn't see Stelio again. Candlelight moved behind their shutters. A dog howled. The mountain crouched black, spangled, a new moon above it.

We stayed up late after the bags were packed and we'd had dinner and drunk our milk and honey. My father and grandparents talked for so long, I woke in bed with my father at dawn before I knew I'd slept. We had coffee, all of us yellow and rumpled under the lightbulb, trying to hurry, but when we carried our bags to the bus stop the porch lamp was a blotch on the wall and the morning hot and white. Firefly's head was bowed through the wires. He moaned when he saw me coming. Even after we turned the corner I could hear.

When the bus came Yiayia, in tears, kissed us goodbye. Pappou hugged her.

'They'll be back, they'll be back,' he said. 'Won't you, Niko.'

'Tsk,' I said. I jerked my head back. No. But they just smiled.

AT THE AIRPORT

Her son clatters into the airport building, impatient to go. She gloats over him, his wheaten hair, his eyes the same colour of dark honey that his father's are, his sturdy long body and legs. He is eight and she will not see him again for three months. Again he is going with his father, who used to be her husband, to spend the winter, the Greek summer, in his grandparents' village. He will write to her.

> *Dear Mum haw ar you goad you shod come one day it is relly fun we have watafites and jamp off the hen house. Grand Dad is all ways snoring i can not go to sleep! Zzzz I wish we cod stay here. love from me and Dad and Grand Mum and Grand Dad and the rest off the famaly XXXX XXXXXX PAUL*

He will send photographs of himself with his grandparents, who were fond of their foreign daughter-in-law. She will see him grinning into the sun in villages and on beaches that she will never go to again. As time passes they are becoming like the house she keeps dreaming of, which has never existed, she is sure, yet which she recognises when she goes there.

She will miss him. He will not really miss her. They no longer live together and haven't for four years. He stays at her flat on weekends and school holidays. For all this, her ex-husband blames her. Her mother, who is dead, blamed her. Her son, more than anyone else, blames her.

Her ex-husband, flustered and tired, waits in line to check in his luggage. The girl he lives with now fills in his immigration cards for him. To give the couple time alone, her son and she go to the cafeteria. On the way they buy a doll for a new baby cousin in Greece whose godfather her son is going to be. She herself will never see this baby girl. Photographs will show him taking a wet and oily naked baby from the bearded priest, just as six years ago he was taken, splashing and furious. She buys a coffee, and a trifle for him. She asks for a taste. He gives her spoon for spoon of it, sandy, soaked with wine.

'I thought you liked trifle?' She is disappointed.

'Oh yes, I do.'

'But you've given me half?'

'Well, you like it too. Don't you?'

His smile is sad. He is sorry for her, because he is going and she is not.

They are stopping over in Bangkok. She remembers her son at two on his father's shoulders at a rainy temple in Bangkok, a flounced and gilded temple full of a statue of the Buddha. A cat lapped a puddle in which grey pigeons and the gold robes of monks were reflected, fluttering. He climbed down to stroke the crouched cat.

She remembers him that year on the shoulders of an uncle emerging from the dark vault of a mulberry grove into the noon heat. He munched, stained with juice. His hands made crimson prints on his uncle's bald dome. They washed each other at a tap in the yard. His white hair trickled. Seeing her, he opened his arms and leaped into hers. He was glossy, cold-skinned. '*Moura,*' he said. Mulberries.

That was the year he was baptised in the font of the village church. He was given his Greek name, his grandfather's: Pavlo. And Greek nationality.

After drinks at the bar and hasty kisses and farewells they are gone. She is left with Vanessa, who lives with them now but has never gone with them, not yet. She and Vanessa go back together to sit in the bar beside a window through which they can see all the plane. It is late taking off. She is sipping riesling and Vanessa vermouth. They are not alike in any way. Even the man each of them has loved in her time is not the same man. She looks in the pane at the sleek eyes and hair of this younger woman warmly nestled, looking out. No sadness is showing. She .sees herself, looking no less calm. Their glances, meeting, jump away.

The plane taxies and turns. They stand to watch it hurl itself up. Then they take polite leave of each other.

She pays her parking fee at the gate and drives on to the freeway. Planes in the foggy air blink their lights and rise and sink. There is a dim full moon. It will shrink and fill again three times before his father brings him back. He must, he has made promises. No self-pity, she thinks, having worked hard to keep her composure, the outward sign of dignity, intact. It is her crust, her shell. Her carapace. Loss and the fear of loss assail her.

'Daddy wants us to go and live in Greece now,' she remembers him saying a while ago. 'But you can come too.'

'I couldn't go and live in Greece, Paulie.'

'You used to.'

'Ages ago. I don't belong there now.'

'Why not?'

'I just don't.'

'*I* do.'

'Yes, I know.'

'I'm Greek.'

'Half-Greek.'

'No. I'm Greek.'

'Well, I'm not.'

'You can speak Greek.'

'That's not enough.' She hugged him. 'You belong here too.'

'There's better, Mum.'

'Why?'

'Well, *there's* a family.'

In the next two months she is patient. She goes to her job in a coffee shop and then to classes. She hands in work on time. She sleeps late. She walks along the winter beaches. On the grey sand she finds mussel shells, feathers, dulled glass. She sees a yacht trail close in to shore. Its heavy sails move cloud-coloured, the late sun in them. Out past the shore water shadowed by this or that drift of wind, a red ship hangs in midair.

She remembers their summer beaches. She dwells on the time when he was four, only four, and they were in Greece for the last time together. She blew up his yellow floaties on his arms, took his hand and swam with him in tow far out into the deep water where a yacht was anchored. Puffing, they clung to a buoy rope that threw bubbles of water in a chain on the surface of the sea. Scared and proud, they waved to his father and the rest of the family, those dots on the sand, aunts and uncles and cousins. The yacht tilted creaking overhead. On the sea, as if in thick glass, its mast wobbled among clouds. They glided back hand in hand. Used to waters where sharks might be, she had never dared swim out so far before. Here there were none. They passed, mother and son, above mauve skeins of jellyfish suspended where the water darkened, but not one touched them. Bubbles had clustered, she saw, on the fine silver hairs on his back, on his brown legs and arms and on hers.

She often dreams of this swim now. It was a month after it, back home in the early spring, that she left home. Her son was asleep. When he woke he thought Mummy was playing hidey. He laughed, looking in wardrobes. Then his father told him. 'Your Mummy's sick in hospital,' he said. Her son told her all this much later. 'Well, what I should say?' his father shouted at her. 'You walk out, you want I say that?'

She found a flat in South Melbourne, two hours' drive from their town, and a job in a hotel. 'I thought you'd be a good mother,' was what her mother said. 'You were at first.'

Her son's black kitten, black but for the circles of gold round his eyes, sits and nibbles one paw. He has been entrusted to her while her son is away. He is used to her now. He falls asleep on her lamb's fleece, stretched on his back. When he wakes the bell at his throat will tell her so. At night she sits and studies. A cowled white lamp peers over her shoulder at the shadow of her hand writing. The kitten wakes — chink — and gazes. He eats crouching, his sharp little shoulders almost bald. She lets him out during the day, but is anxious. At night he must use the litter box. He prowls in it and flips the granules over the carpet obsessively. Nothing must happen to him while he is at her place. Growth, of course, must. He is becoming a stolid cat. Will her son still love him? Will her son come back?

On her balcony she listens to a slow sonata, a hollow clarinet, watching a sunset douse its cold flames in the bay. The bridge has its gold lights on. The moon, when it rises, is nearly full again. The moon she sees tonight shone a few hours ago over her son. Does he ever think of her? Remember me, she says. Miss me. I miss you.

The pot of basil they gave her for her balcony before they left is still there, but black and dry. Basil dies in winter. Her balcony faces the sea wind. The lane opposite is always full of dark rainwater. The sunset shows in it. Night fills it with lamps.

'It's breaking your mother's heart,' a neighbour reproved her when she first left. It was true, in a way. Her mother's little clockwork voice was always on the phone.

'I've talked to a lawyer,' it piped. 'Act fast, she says. The longer you delay the more weight it gives to the status quo.'

'Delay — what?'

'You have to *apply* for interim custody. You can't wait till the divorce.'

'Oh, Mum, no, I can't contest custody.'

'What do you mean? He's not going to hand you the child on a platter. He'll fight you for him.'

'He talked about that before I left. Even if I won he wouldn't let me get away with it. He'd kidnap him and go home. He would.'

'There are laws —'

'Constantly being broken. You know that.'

'Well, try, at least. What's got into you?'

'That'd turn him completely against me.'

'So *what*?'

'Mum, as things are, he lets me see Paul. And he lets *you* see Paul. He's sorry for us.'

'Why should anyone be sorry for you? You've brought it on yourself. Where did I go wrong? A real mother would go to hell and back to keep her child!'

She writes to Paul about his kitten and the football and the village. She knows it amazes him that she knows the village. He forgets that she went there before he was born and then twice with him when he was little. With an incredulous grin he looks at slides of her in the village with his family, when he comes to visit, as if she was there by some magic. She knows how he feels.

She takes out the old projector and looks at the slides again. She gets photographs from him in the mail and studies them. She gets a letter.

> *Dear Mum haw ar you i am very well evry day we go to the beche, evry after noon the weves have gron hiarh and hiarh and moore hiarh and hiarh. i went very deep on tuesday. how is my cat. there is a kitten here its names psipsina. i was bitten by a wosp on the neck twis i was pritending i was drackula. any way love from me and evry body XXXXXXXXXX PAUL*

He used to ask her why. Why don't you love my Dad? Why did you leave us? (Why didn't you wake me? Take me?) Won't you ever come back? Why not? Will you always be my mother?

He would understand one day, she used to answer: it was a long story. She doesn't ever want to show him wounds or admit to the rage and spite that caused them. Nor, she thinks, does his father. They both cringe under their son's accusing gaze. They have stopped accusing each other, and now make what amends they can. They trust each other to behave well. It was not always so.

What matters after all is that there came, in their anger and terror and despair, a point of silence one night in which she went to her sleeping child, kissed his cheek, picked up her suitcase. Left. This is what counts. Might it have been otherwise? Yes. No. Whatever happened before it belongs to one life, which is over. What comes after is another. In dreams, what is meshes with what was and what might have been; as in dreams she goes to a remembered house which does not exist. What might have been cannot be.

Since Vanessa moved in, he has stopped asking questions.

She brought him to stay at her new flat and took him to the Zoo. Politely they gazed at the animals, especially the sandy, sleepy lions. He rode on the train and on a white pony. On the spiral slide he made her go up with him the first time and clung to her as they spun down; then he went up alone again and again while she waited to catch him at the bottom. They had hamburgers and milkshakes. Then he had to go to the toilet. The Men's, he insisted. She promised to wait but after a while she called out that she was just going to the Women's: wait, she said. When she came out he was not there. She stood in the smelly shade until a man looked in and told her there was no little boy inside. She rushed over to the lions, then to the slide, the ponies, the train, the toilets again. A microphone blared. Reception! she thought and hurtled along crowded paths. There he was, red-faced. He turned his back.

'A lady brought him in. He said his Mummy went home!' the woman at Reception accused. 'Of course I said Mummies don't do that, but he was that positive! "Why ever would she?" I said and he said, "I don't know." '

'I was only in the toilet,' she explained.

'You were not!'

'I was. I called out.'

'You did *not*!'

'Darling, I *did*! You just didn't hear.'

'No, you never! You did not call out! Oh, why didn't you?'

She tried to hug him and wipe his eyes. Sobbing, he pushed her. But he walked beside her out into the sun.

'Remember our long swim?' she asked as they watched lions.

'In Greece?'

'Yes. Remember?'

'No,' he muttered.

One afternoon the cat doesn't come back in. She wanders, calling, along streets filled with cars and darkness. The lamps twitch on. The pairs of gold eyes that she stalks and chases all belong to strange cats. His cat must be lost. The wind tugs and hurls cold sea-spray. She blunders through puddles.

At home in the lamplight she can't concentrate on work. She can't finish her letter to her son. A child is wailing in the flat next door. Mamma. Ma-amma. Every half hour she goes to the door and calls the cat.

Once as her son stepped out of her car after a visit with her, he saw his kitten playing on the road. He called, but the kitten lifted his tail and danced away. 'If I catch him I'll kill him!' Her son's face was dark red. 'He knows he's not allowed out! I'll kill him!'

'Oh, Paulie,' she said.

'I will. I mean it. I'll flush him down the toilet!'

'He'll come back,' she said.

He just looked at her.

Before she goes to bed she opens the door a last time and calls out. Suddenly the cat is there, flattened against the wall in the wind, thin and black as his shadow. He struts in and prowls, purring, and folds himself on the lamb's fleece.

After the divorce, when her ex-husband took her son home to Greece, her mother would not be consoled. Paul was gone, her only grandchild. He was as good as gone before that. But now his father would never bring him back.

'Mum, he will.'

'What makes you think so?'

'He just will.' Compassion, she thought. Respect for the tacit bargain: you keep him, but *here.* Even mercy, for the defeated opponent. 'His business, for one thing.'

'Why did you have to go and marry a Greek?'

'Oh, come on. You always liked him.'

'Can't you work something out?'

'No.'

'I can't get over it. How could you do it?'

'I had to.'

'It wasn't that bad.'

'It *was.* I was spending days staring at one comer in one room. The sun never came in. Everything was grey. Shadows moved, that was all. Nothing mattered, not even the child, and he was so persistent. When footsteps came near me, I banged my head on the window frame until it bled or they went away.'

'You should have seen a doctor.'

'A doctor! When my *life* —'

'A doctor, yes. Depression can be treated, you know.'

'I've come alive since I left.'

' "I, I, I." When you realise how selfish you've been all along, and how *weak,* when you finally think of the *child* —'

'It's best for him not to be fought over.'

'You *hope.* Oh, the easy way out, as per usual. You're a callous and self-centred woman. I'm ashamed you're my daughter.'

'You make better chips than Vanessa,' her son told her on a visit a few months ago.

'That's good. Who's Vanessa?'

'A lady. She lives at our place. She's got this dog. Its name's Roly. Guess why.'

'Short for Roland?'

'No. Because it's always rolling! Mum, if my Dad marries Vanessa, will Roly be in my family?'

'I suppose. Vanessa. She's not Greek, is she?'

'No. She comes from Sydney.'

'Has she been to Greece, do you know?'

'Yes. She loves it. She'd like to live there, she says. Could she take Roly?'

'I don't know. Maybe. Is he friendly?'

'Oh, yes. You make the best chips I've ever aten.'

'Eaten.'

'Eaten.'

They did come back from Greece that first time, and the next. Her son loved her mother just the same after the divorce, and she spoiled him. Now, two years since her death, he often mentions Granma, his voice hushed and sorrowful. He remembers her best cooking dinner when they visited, ladling gravy, hovering over a frizzled chicken. He knows he will die one day. He buries dead birds and crickets, and saves moths from his cat.

One morning in September she has a good dream. She is at the house she is always dreaming of. It has a deep verandah of sagging boards that looks on to muddy grass and bare trees. A window burns with light. As the sun sets she strolls in and opens a door of gold wood that she has never opened in any previous dream. She knows the moment before she looks that her son will be in there. He is asleep, his cat at his feet. He wakes and looks up, smiling.

She lies awake breathless with joy in her rented bed. She wishes she could tell her mother this dream. Some time, she hopes, her mother will be behind a door, in one of the bright rooms in this house.

Dear Mum how ar you we ar coming back 15 september. its at 4 oclock in the morning. pleas meet us at the airport. i wont you to. XXXXXXXXXX *PAUL*

She rings the number Vanessa has given her, but is told that Vanessa is up in Sydney because her mother is sick. So Vanessa won't be at the airport. On the night she wakes to the alarm with a sour headache at three, crams the cat into his basket and drives through the dark under all the faint lamps of the city. The airport building, full of light, is crowded already. Voices boom, echoing. The plane has landed. After an hour passengers start bursting through the door with luggage trolleys. Her eyes are crusted, dazed. They will keep watering. Her ex-husband and her son push through last of all. Her ex-husband looks smaller, gaunt and grey. But her son! So big, so brown! She is full of exclamations and this delights him. He thinks she is crying, though she says no. They all talk at once and wish aloud for coffee, but there is nowhere open, so they go out to the car-park. She has forgotten where she left her car. In the cold wind and half-light they all wander over the painted asphalt, looking. Her son sees it first. He wraps himself in his sullen cat. The sun comes up, a gong on the rim of the sky.

'Glad you're back?' She hugs Paulie.

'Yes, if you are.'

'I am. I'm very glad.' To her ex-husband she says in Greek, 'There are times when —' She can't speak. 'Life —' she tries again.

'Oh, life. Life. Well, yes.' He smiles wanly.

The trees toss and swill the gold light. Their eyes glitter with it.

SNAKE

We are not told anywhere, are we, that winters in the Garden of Eden were not cold? The olive and the lemon ripen in winter and it could not be Paradise without them. Lemon and olive, sour and bitter, my mother would say: they suit you, Manya. Mamma misjudges me.

I think as winter comes, why huddle here in three warm rooms? Why not go to Athens, say, and see Aunt Sophia? My dear old Aunt Sophia. Walk up to the Acropolis again. Order coffee and sit and watch the hollow city brim with a violet glow, and the lights and stars shine out. Sit on the cold stones of the theatre, high above its golden statuary, where I saw Euripides performed, Aeschylus. Or even go to Crete. It's sunny there. But I feel anxious away from here now.

Three years ago I went away. Mamma and I went to the village in Macedonia when her sister Vasso died. As always when the ferry casts off in the crescent harbour of Mytilene I felt lost, speechless with dread. The Thessaloniki ferry passes between Turkey and Molyvo in the strait. I see Molyvo in the distance, its blue citadel. I never rest — those weeks in the frozen village, my God! — until we pass it again. So I might stay and see my olives through the press instead.

Aunt Vasso's own sons hadn't come down from Germany. Uncle Manoli, a dour man at any time, hardly spoke. After the funeral we were snowbound for silent weeks. I remember the full cheese-cloths hung high on black branches of the grapevine over his front door, their icicles of whey pointed down like teats. A wolf off the mountains howled at night. We cooked what we found: macaroni, rice, icy potatoes and onions, eggs, my aunt's tomato paste and preserved pig from a crock deep in snow on the window sill. There was milk. We made cheese day by day and stored it in its crock in brine, weighed down with flat river stones. At night — from three o'clock, I remember, it was night —

Mamma and I huddled by the sooty *somba* roaring with apple wood until we succumbed in the stuffy dim yellow room to stupor and sleep. My uncle kept a horse and goats in the barn. An Arctic winter of darkness they lived through, shivering and crusted with excrement. He came home to milk the goats — we boiled the milk — and then sat in the *kafeneion*, glowing with ouzo, silent. The river froze. I had been there before, but in summer. Thank God I need never go again.

I keep busy all day in the garden, and at night I read. I paint a little and my work sells in town. It is not dull, just peaceful, in Paradise. And our green Lesbos is not like other islands. Lesbos was rich in art and poetry when Athens was a village and Thessaloniki still under the sea. They are as natural to Lesbos as her olive trees are, and we who love them are not thought eccentric here.

Still, I am thought eccentric. I am over forty and have never married. Mamma has stopped her wailing over me and her tireless matchmaking. No man would have me now. Even Mitso the Idiot, who tried to rape me at a wedding once, would scowl and snarl at the thought now. As a girl I had no money, only beauty. That has gone. My dowry was my olive trees and the garden. Lemon trees grow here, pear and quince and apricot, peach and almond. We have red hens and a vegetable patch. This little house too would have become mine on my marriage, though my mother was left nothing else, as that is the custom here. Then my daughter's in her turn. I think Mamma would be upset if I did marry. Not because of the house — she would stay here, of course — but because we make a good couple, she and I, whatever she says. We get on.

The first few times we saw Louka and my cousin Dimitra in company Mamma worried, sighed, watched to see how I was taking it. I have never told her the whole story. She guesses that, perhaps. Perhaps she even forgets now that I was engaged to Louka. She forgets my daughter. She fusses over them when they visit. She spoils their boys with sweets. It gives me no pleasure to see Louka. No pain either.

I was twenty when Louka came back from his army service to

work in his father's restaurant in Molyvo. I was staying with my cousins there — Dimitra was still a schoolgirl — in their stone house at the base of the Genoese fortress, the citadel on the hilltop. In the whitewashed sun of the chapel next door striped cats lay sleeping. We could see from three windows the stone arm of the port curled round its fishing boats.

Louka had always flirted. Now he came to the house so often, and singled me out so persistently and so respectfully, that we knew he was serious. His mother called on my aunt to discuss the match. My cousins were thrilled. My aunt asked me what I thought. Yes, I said. The priest in his gold brocade came. We exchanged rings and were engaged.

It's hard to believe now what a passion I had for Louka.

He was beautiful, though, I remember, his hair so heavy and black when he let it grow, and his athlete's body dark brown and golden. After the rush in the restaurant he would sit with the tourists joking in scraps of their languages and put on music to teach them to dance the *sirto,* the *tsamiko.* The *zeïmbekiko* he danced by himself, his head sunk between his shoulders like a sated tomcat. He glanced at the women. Enthralled with Louka, they all clapped in time. There was ouzo, but most drank wine, yellow *retsina* from the barrel with its faint rankness of urine, of salt: as if the men treading it, unwilling to stop, let urine and sweat slip down their thighs into the must.

On still nights I could hear the *bouzoukia.* I lay awake. When the music stopped, the restaurant was closed and Louka would come and whisper at my shutters. Shutters in Molyvo are solid, not slatted. I was a good girl, and shy. I wouldn't open them. *'Den m'agapas?'* he would growl, his voice thick.

'You know I love you.'

'Then let me see you.'

'I mustn't. I can't.'

'Come on, Manya, open the shutters, I just want to see you, just for a moment. Manya!'

'No. Go home, please. Louka, *please.* They'll *hear.*'

Some of those nights — or mornings, by then — he must have had Valerie with him.

* *

She was not a typical tourist. Not one of the Europeans who descend in hordes to loll on the pebble beach oiling their bones or hire donkeys and ride giggling across the headland to bathe naked at the sandy beach and the hot spring. She was staying with some Australians who lived all the year round in Molyvo. But she looked like them. She smoked and drank and slept with men. She was tall and brown with lank yellow hair and a cat's pale eyes. Her nose and shoulders were thin, red under the freckles. What would a man like Louka want with her? So when friends warned me, I scoffed. Laughing, I accused Louka, but in fun. He tried to laugh.

'Don't look so guilty,' I teased.

Shifting and shuffling, he lit another cigarette and pleaded not guilty. I said I would call witnesses. I laughed as I scored this point but Louka leapt up.

'All right then,' he said. 'So it's true. So what?'

'You're in love with *her*?'

'Valerie? Don't be stupid.'

'Then — *why*?'

'Look.' *He* would not look. He breathed smoke in and coughed. 'I'm in love with you. You know I am. These others, they're whores.' These? How many? 'They won't leave a man alone. I'm only flesh and blood, Manya, for God's sake!'

'But if you loved me you couldn't —'

'Don't be such a baby!' He thrust his face close. To kiss me, I thought, and drew back. But no, it was twisted with feelings I could not read, of hatred, of desperation.

'*Afti me gamaei.*' She — makes love to me (so to speak). He bared his teeth to say it. Then he walked out.

I found Valerie sipping her morning coffee alone by the balustrade of a *kafeneion*, her eyes half-closed against the dazzle of the strait. She had no idea who I was. I sat at her table. 'Manya,' I said, pointing to myself.

'*Ego* Valerie,' she smiled.

'Louka,' I said, showing my gold ring and not smiling. She frowned. Her nose had peeled and her brows and lashes were white like a cat's whiskers. She had a pocket dictionary. She looked in it and asked in broken Greek if I was Louka's wife. Not yet, I said, we were engaged, and found the word for her. She looked wise.

'Hmmm. *To paliopaido*,' she grinned. The bad boy. She shivered and picked up her towel. '*Thalassa*, Manya?' she said. '*Ela, pame?*' She really thought I'd go to the beach with her. She shrugged, grinned and flapped away down the steps. I was too amazed at the cheek of her to smack her face. I had expected to.

Louka, grown fat and bald, deceives Dimitra with tourists in summer — more deftly now, I hope — and with other men's wives in winter. Everyone knows. She will never leave him, though, nor he her. There are children, two boys: the elder a solemn bookworm, the younger a darling, a sparkling boy, and the children I do envy Dimitra. Nothing else. Sour grapes, Mamma would say. No. Dimitra, each time she catches Louka out, attacks the woman. I with my small experience had more sense. She sobs and shrieks. She spat at one in the restaurant, pulled another one's hair. Louka takes her home and humbly swears that she's his one true love. He's lucky he married Dimitra.

At the theatre once I saw *Agamemnon*. He had led grown men to the slaughter for another man's whore and for gold. So he was returning a hero to Clytemnestra, with his slave girl in tow. I have often dreamt since of her net and axe in the stone bath and Agamemnon quietly like a great fish pumping his blood through the water. She had a right to do it. He deserved death. Never for infidelity; she was unfaithful too. Death for their daughter's death. He led her into the trap at Aulis. I would strike the blow too, in Clytemnestra's place.

But not in Medea's. One summer night at a stone theatre cut into a hill among pines, the sky clear, the sea like milk, Medea writhed and growled for us and stabbed her little boys. For this she was raised in a god's gilt chariot and sat, the moon rising behind her, and gloated. Dimitra was there. It's whispered in the family that she holds this threat over Louka's head, should he dare to leave her.

When my Sophoula died, Louka, I suspect, was relieved. He

had never seen her. 'Who says I'm its father, anyway?' I'm told that he said. I prayed for Louka's death. I screamed to God for justice, of all things. I was mad for some time. I'm sane now and no longer pray or believe. I keep the fasts. I go to church with Mamma. I eat the bread sopped in wine from the priest's chalice. God doesn't lift a finger.

Lesbos is close to Turkey. I have seen from the ferry people walking in the streets of Baba in Turkey as we passed between Baba and Molyvo in the strait. Our barracks and theirs are crowded with troops. The beaches are mined. We live in dread of another war. They do too. They love children, as we do. I believe that if there is one thing that might save the world from destruction, it is our love of children. This is stronger than hate, or nothing is. This hope, or no hope.

Louka, when I next saw him after our quarrel, was at his most easy and charming, full of anecdotes about life in the army that convulsed my aunt and cousins. I was on edge, I remember. I had come to my decision. After the preserves and the coffee I stood and announced that Louka and I had arranged to meet friends at the restaurant. He looked stunned. Outside he asked me where we were going. 'Don't ask me yet,' I said. It was a sultry afternoon, the whole town sleeping. I led him to the gullies past the olive grove where couples went. We lay on the dry grass.

'Now look. Manya, darling —'

'Take me,' I said quickly. 'Make me yours.'

'Do you mean it?'

'Yes. I want you. Take me now.'

He put his arms round me. 'Manya, not here. Not now.'

'Why not?' I cried despairingly. 'What's wrong with you?'

I didn't mean it the way he took it.

He pulled his shirt off, only his shirt. In the heat his body was rank and shone like varnished wood. The hair had stuck in curls round his dark nipples. He grasped me. Our teeth clashed and I shut my eyes. Tugging under my skirt, he lay on me and forced in hard and split my legs open. The pain, my God! I clung as he thudded on me. When he rolled away there was a sucking noise. He found a drop of blood and flicked it off.

'Louka?' I was close to tears.

'I hurt you. I'm sorry.'

'It's all right. I love you.' *S'agapao. S'agapao.*

Sighing, he lit a cigarette. Then abruptly he was on his feet. 'Cover yourself,' he hissed, and four boys, local children I think, burst on us there. They exploded into joyful whinnies and ran jostling and prodding to the beach.

'*Gamo to,*' Louka swore.

That was the first and the last time in my life, let the gossips say what they like. It was two whole days after it before I saw Louka. I spent them in bed pretending to be ill, but really ill, in a torment of shame and bewilderment. There was no one I could tell it to.

When he came at dawn and whispered at my window I — well, wasn't I his now? — I flung open the shutters. Appalled, Louka gazed up, swaying on the blue cobbles, Valerie clutched to him with one arm. She struggled free when she saw me, hissed furious words at him and clattered down the steps. I slammed the shutters. For a while Louka pleaded — those hoarse endearments of his — as if nothing had happened. Finally he stumbled away.

I didn't see Louka again for years. I left Molyvo abruptly to come here. I went for long walks alone and brooded. A broken engagement was shame enough to account for my misery, and Mamma didn't pry. By autumn I knew I had to tell her. She wanted to hide me away with relatives — 'For your sake, Manya' — but I couldn't have borne to leave here.

I saw Valerie again that winter (winter, but the morning heat was heavy, very still and dusty, more like summer) at an umbrella-shaded table on the waterfront, reading. Drops of sweat glazed her red nose, her forehead and the sunbleached hairs of her upper lip. She looked up. 'Hey! Hey, Manya!'

I swung away, but she ran up behind me.

'Manya! *Tha piies kafe, kale*?'

Why not? I would have coffee. Her Greek sounded better. I nodded my ironic approval and she grinned, leading me back. The coffee ordered, we were silent, facing a sea that heaved and glittered at us. We made laborious small talk, what little we could. When the coffees and iced water came, she flicked through the little dictionary she still had and asked when the wedding was to be. 'Wedding?' I was as red as she was. Did she think me such a fool?

'Louka *s'agapao*,' she said. Louka I love you? She saw my face and tried again, pointing at me. 'Louka *s'agapao* Manya.' She meant that Louka loved me.

'*Agapaei*,' I corrected. 'Yes? How nice.'

The coffee was strong and sweet and I drank the whole glass of water. In the thick sunlight her brown legs glistened with white hairs. Many Greek women are as brown as Valerie — I am white all over like cream cheese but our body hair is dark. Some try to be rid of it; I never have. Those white-furred legs of hers Louka had opened. Did he still? I wondered, but only dully. I was weary.

'Manya *agapaei* Louka?' she was persisting. I showed her my hand with its gold ring gone. 'Ah,' and she gazed with real regret. The Athens ferry had docked further along the quay and crowds with bags and boxes were hurrying there. She tipped small change on the table, picked up her bags — on one, I remember, swimming flippers flapped like an upturned seal — and jumped up.

'Manya, I must go, forgive me.' People say that when they go: she meant nothing more by it. '*Addio*.' Kissing me on both cheeks, wishing me luck. I felt too dazed and ill to speak. She looked back once in the surge of people to wave. I thought she gaped: perhaps she had just seen my swollen belly.

I had my baby in Athens and would not give her up. Aunt Sophia, our old Communist warhorse, was godmother and gave her own name when my mother refused. When I was well enough I brought Sophoula back here. For the evening *volta*, when families parade, I wheeled her along the quay in front of everyone. I suckled her a whole year. She walked at the age of one and swam at two. Before she had all her baby teeth she died of leukemia. I never saw a child to match Sophoula. Dying, she said 'Mamma, where are you?' I was there holding her. I have worn black since that day.

It was God's judgment on my sin, people nodded. So may their sins be judged.

In this room my child and I slept: here I laid her out and waited with her for her burial. I often sit, as I sat then, at the south window and watch the sun, the moon, then the sun again. Having lived here all my life, I need its smell of paint, its floor of striped rugs, its dark points where at night the lamp will lay a gold hand on a cracked waterjug, three red stripes, a window sill.

Here in this room I painted Sophoula naked in her coffin, among pears and apples and grapes, a bunch of blue grapes in her hand. I drew in every detail of her: the ringed nipples, each crease and nail of her fingers and toes, the lips folded between her legs, her curled ears, her eyebrows with the mole under the left one. Had I been roasting the body on a spit my mother's horror could hardly have been greater, although, afraid of her mad daughter, she let me have my way.

'The pears are rotting,' was all she said. So they were, even before Sophoula was. 'Let the poor child have flowers.'

'It's not flowers that matter,' I seem to recall saying. 'It's the fruit that matters —'

'Is this what you will do to me as well?'

'— and death is the seed inside it!'

'What will become of us, Manya?' And she refused to sit up with me. I left her to receive the few mourners who came. My mother loves her visitors. I let no one in to see the child: my mother placated them. I sat alone with the candles and kept watch as Sophoula stiffened and then was limp again and her face changed. At first I talked to her. Then I brushed and plaited her hair. In daylight I painted her as she had become. Then I dressed and covered her for the last time.

I have nearly all the paintings that I did when I was mad: all interiors with figures, as these were. Mostly they were self-portraits, mostly nude. The rooms in them are full of the whiteness that snow reflects, or moonlight; and so are the bodies. I have never shown or sold these. I can only look at them myself from time to time. I know they are here against the wall, as the dead are in the earth. I know without looking.

I still paint myself nude. I have one on the easel now. It shows the blue branchings of my veins, the shadow of bones within, the slackness of my throat and breasts and swinging thighs — all my white meat run to fat, its tufts and wrinkles and moles. It shows everything. Still, it lacks what *those* had. My best work is in landscapes these days: watercolours done in precise detail. The parapets, yellow and violet-grey of the fortress. Hills and their trees. The leaning figures in black of old women who mind goats. Children with shaved heads of brown and black velvet. Birds and insects and snakes. Old men lapped in shadow at the tables *of kafeneia*, sea light wandering on them as they drowse, these long afternoons.

Dimitra came to see me before she married Louka. I was fond of her when she was little, though I had not seen her since. I would never have tolerated such questions otherwise.

'I know you were engaged to Louka once. My mother —'

'What would your mother know?'

'I don't know.' She had trouble finding words. 'She doesn't know I'm here. She won't talk about you.'

'Good.'

'I've always thought of you as my big sister, Manya.'

'Have you? Why? We never see each other.'

'I always have. I wanted to be like you. Were you — in love with Louka?' Her jaw was trembling. 'Did he — why did you go away?'

'Pride. Ask *my* mother.'

'It's just that I — am I making a mistake? Should I really marry him?' At this point she hid her face in my shoulder. She was warm to hold. I stroked her plait of hair.

'Well, but you love him, don't you? You want to.'

'But will we be happy?'

'Sometimes. Why not?' She gazed with wet eyes. 'I hope you will,' I said. This was my pride speaking. 'Look,' I said then, and turned one of the nude self-portraits that I never show around to show her. 'What do you think?'

'It's beautiful.' She blushed and looked away. 'But you should have asked first.'

'It's not you, Dimitroula.' She looked amazed. In fact it was exactly like her but for the eyes. Hers were, and are, like brown glass; mine, like green. 'Look at the eyes,' I said.

'Yes. But, Manya, even so —' She was white now.

'I did it years ago. How strange life is! If I painted the eyes brown I could give this to you. As an engagement present.'

'No.' She shuddered. 'Oh, don't. No.'

At a friend's wedding once, when Louka and Dimitra were showing off their first baby, Louka clinked his glass on mine, leaned over and wondered in a hoarse whisper how I had stayed so beautiful. He said I was his one true love. He was, as usual, drunk. 'Darling,' he mumbled. 'Do you still love me a little?'

'To *our* child,' I said, and clinked his glass with mine, smiling even more sweetly. 'She should have been ten this year.'

He went back to his seat next to Dimitra.

Our garden is a few kilometres out along the flat coast on a lagoon full of seaweed and sandbanks. I hardly ever leave it now except to shop in Mytilene once a week. I love the crammed old shops that smell of roasting coffee, anchovies and cumin and olive oil. Skeins of late grapes glow there, withering, fermenting. At a waterfront table I sip my coffee, knee-deep in shopping bags. At twilight the harbour water is still. Darkness frills the images of boats at anchor and of sharp-winged gulls. Boys lolling on the edge fish among lights and stars.

I visit my old art teacher shivering in her frayed villa, its tiles all tufts and nests, its windows cracked by a giant magnolia that is her pride. Excrement from empty swallows' nests trails down her walls inside and out. She is sitting for me. Children jeer at her gate and scramble to safety. 'Mad old Maria,' they shrill. Her eyes water. She turns off the table lamp to hide the tears. Maria is my name, of course: Manya, Maria. Is this how I will end, I wonder? A palsied crone mocked by children — I who love children?

My mother fears arthritis and angina. She fears death. Last year the village secretary wrote that they had found Uncle Manoli, her sister's widower, dead in the snow one morning. Mamma was full of such grief, so many tears! 'Well, you have a hard heart, Manya,' she said. 'You won't even shed tears for me.' But what was old Manoli to Mamma? No. It was just — Death.

Our life is calm. My companion, apart from Mamma, is a cat patterned in black and white like a penguin. He lies breathing on a velvet sofa with his pink paws in the air. He is a shining seal; an owl when his black eyes shrink to gold plate with one black split from top to bottom and his blink is stern; a fanged snake when he yawns. He is everything in one, but his name is Fidaki, Little Snake. As a girl I once tried, from a sense of duty, to kill a snake I found writhing on my path. I threw rocks and silently the snake dodged, jerking and scraping, its gold eyes wild. All my rocks missed. Ashamed, I stood back and let it slide into a field of maize, its tongue touching ahead of it each bronze clod of clay.

Maybe snakes hunt in our own garden, but if so I've never seen one. Fidaki himself hunts, but he is belled, the birds tease him. Mamma said that Little Snake was no name for a cat. I said that the Garden could do without Adam and Eve, but it must have its snake.

'Well, so it has. You are its snake,' she smiled. 'Yes, you are, Manya! Its fallen angel,' Smiling, but I could see she meant it.

SUMMER ON ICE

The first time Caroline goes skating the cold shocks her, such motionless cold and in summer. Her breath fumes. The building, a hollow barn she remembers from her childhood, is uglier, darker, older than ever. Long drops of water fall from the ceiling to make blue lumps on the ice. She has been imagining ice like deep glass, bluish and with long needles of air frozen in it, but no: it is frosted, slashed and scarred, although no one else is there. A net hangs behind where the hockey goal was last night. She regrets having come.

A grinning boy hands her a pair of skates. She laces them tight as she has read she should, and clumps to the swing door, on to the ice. She slithers, clinging with both frozen hands to the fence to drag herself along. Her feet sting with the cold then go numb. After a dogged hour she can propel herself with one hand. No one else has turned up. Records of rock songs boom now and then over the loudspeakers. A cone of sun burns through a skylight. Dark trees flicker at its glass. When there is no music her skates scrape and thump and she remembers how her skis thumped on the hard snow of a sunlit mountain top the first time she dared go up so high; her terror then as she crouched curling down and down.

She prances out of the rink on suddenly light feet, pleased with herself. The bay is opaque olive green this morning. Yachts on it flutter their wet sails. In the haze of the western shore, the towers of Melbourne are grey slabs, tombstones. In a week it will be Christmas.

A scrawled postcard in her letter box, the first: the Statue of Liberty and a New York postmark.

My darling,
Remember how we lay and drank champagne and dreamed of being here together? I miss you terribly — a million things to tell you. Found you some

books you'll adore in the Gotham — not telling what — and mailed them yesterday. They should arrive soon after I do, some time in mid-Feb., I hope. It's freezing here ...

He gives the address of a post office in Greenwich Village where she can write to him, and signs off: '*Take care, sweet.*'

Has he remembered that they quarrelled then as they lay and drank champagne? He hasn't, it seems.

'I wish you were coming with me,' he murmured.

'Well, I would. I could afford the affair.'

'What did you say?'

'The fare. I could afford the fare.' They both laughed.

'Will you wait for me, Caro?'

'Oh, probably.'

'Eight weeks.' His eyes were fixed in anger. She sat up.

'All right, it's not eternity. I know. Eight weeks is eight weeks — of jaunts and sensual joy in the Big Apple while I sit waiting.'

'It won't be joy. I'll be thinking of you the whole time. You know that.'

'I'll think of you.'

'Promise you'll wait?'

'No! What gives you the right to ask?'

'Caro, listen. I can't not take her. She's been looking forward to it all year. All our friends know we're coming over. I can't do it to her.'

'But I don't *want* you to. Have I ever said I did?'

'But you won't wait?'

'Won't promise to. I can't. On principle I can't. It's something time will tell.'

'I see. Yet another of those somethings of yours that time will tell.'

'That's right. Like: "I told you so." '

He started to dress, talking over his shoulder.

'You claim to love me.'

'Yes. Not the point, though, is it?'

'I think it is.'

'You love me, you claim. You're going with her.'

'She *is* my wife.'

'Yes. *That's* the point.'

'I'm coming *back.*'

'I'll be here.' She shrugged.

'Will you? Alone?'

'As far as I know.'

With a gasp of anger he walked out. She cried, but noticing he'd kept his key she didn't lose hope. The next day she sent (to his work address) a card with a Pre-Raphaelite Ophelia afloat in skirts like a peacock's tail, on the back of which she had written: '*Look in my face; my name is Might-have-been. (D. G. Rossetti — SONNET 98)*'. On the third day he came. They lay in bed all afternoon and listened to a broadcast of the New World Symphony. He promised they'd live together when he got back. She promised to wait.

Against her will, as one who prides herself on being free of possessiveness — relatively free — Caroline imagines him arm-in-arm with his wife, a jolly figure though faceless, strolling along Fifth Avenue. Caroline has never been to America. She buys a book of photographs of New York and studies the sunset sky-scrapers, the squirrels and snowdrifts of Central Park, slums in the Bronx on fire. In one photograph a small tree of grey twigs on some avenue is spun all over with webs of white lights, for Christmas, she thinks. Has he seen it?

She finds a photograph in her book of a man at a block party in the Village, swaggering on a stoop, one thumb in his belt and his curled chest bare. A glass of beer in the other fist. His stance, though not his face, reminds her of her lover and she puts a marker at that page. Soon the book starts opening there of its own accord. She takes the marker out.

Am I compulsive? she writes in her diary. *Am I old-maidish? I'm thirty-two. Am I becoming a tedious woman? I was never so mild and quiet, such a mouse. Be fearless and joyful. Make him love me.*

She takes over her sister's flat near the beach. Her sister is working in Sydney. Packing and scrubbing out the old flat and moving her things keeps her too busy for a couple of days to feel lonely. She has told him her sister's number but no calls come. Is he trying and not getting through? She writes to him about the flat, Poste Restante. What, she worries, if in a new flat she seems like a stranger to him? She does to herself.

At last he rings her from a coin phone in Manhattan in a downpour. For her it's another sultry Melbourne night. They spar and hedge, off-key, and say nothing in the end.

'I do miss you, Caro. Really.'

'Oh, good. Now and then would be nice.'

'All the time. Was that a laugh?'

'A cynical snort, more like it.'

'Undeserved.'

'Is it? I miss you too.'

'Good.'

'Darling, it's four in the morning! If I'm not making sense, make allowances.'

'I wanted to catch you in. I hoped you wouldn't mind.'

'I don't. You're sure of your welcome.'

'Actually, I'm not. Far from it.'

'You always seem sure.'

'It's the best policy.'

'Better than honesty?'

'Much.' He pauses. 'You seem sure yourself.'

'I do? What do I seem sure of?'

'Me, for one.'

'Baby, you gotta be kidding.'

'Well, you can be.'

'Yeah?'

'Hey, I'm the one should talk American. Yeah.'

'Put it down to my sceptical nature.'

In no time the three minutes are up. She lies on her bed with the lamp on, wishing she had let the phone ring. He is standing bitter in the rain now, he who hates rain. She has lost ground, and lies wondering with a chill of panic if she has ever believed that he loves her, and what does a married man mean by saying he loves her? Anyway.

Anyway, darling, the flat's in a narrow street with a little yellow-grey Gothic church at one end and at the other is the bay. From the balcony you can see right across. Now and then today a shifting wind has been blurring the sea.

Then it comes still and clear again as if a glass dome had been put back on. The facade of the old baths is intact, and the one round white turret that I can see from here looks like a whitewashed chapel on some island. Mykonos, Ios. In the evening I lie getting brown on the sand. I hope you like your women brown? I eat down there and before I come home sow my handful of crumbs although only one gull is even in sight — far out at sea, circling. In a long swoop it comes crying and others follow and stalk around. They arch their grey wings like scythes, ruffle themselves and jab the sand.

The lights go on in the city and along the bridge — a sudden golden bow. Freighters at sea flick on their white lights.

I close the French window and see my room move with the glass across the darkening sea and sky: a yellow lamp, a table with books, a chair on a white rug.

The second time she goes skating the lights and the plant have been turned off. No one is there but two boys cleaning up. Water swills glittering around the blades of her skates. She wavers, anxious not to fall and be soaked, so half an hour passes before she lets go of the fence. She hovers over the hockey circles, trying to balance on one foot at a time but never daring. There is music, then the needle sticks and it is switched off. The two boys circle, sweeping off the ice. She imagines him, back from New York earlier than he said, coming here to find her: herself catching sight of his smile of admiration and pride. She will be gliding, whirling in her mist of breath, in the spotlight that the sun makes falling on the creamy ice.

'You'll fall flat at his feet,' she says aloud, amazing the boys. Her laugh echoes.

After the turkey and Christmas pudding at her mother's farm, the family goes on drinking in the garden while she and her mother wash up. This year, though, they leave the dishes to soak, and walk to the apple orchard. Her mother is worried, Caro can tell, and wants her to talk about him. What is there to say? As she talks on, her mother breathes sunlit smoke; watching it, not Caro.

'Is he going to leave his wife for you?' she interrupts.

'Only if she consents,' says Caro.

'Consents? Oh, Caro darling! You and your dream world!'

There are days when Caro does feel as if she is living a dream. She is not real; or she is fading, becoming invisible; or is left behind by time. She lies awake all night. No one knows that they are — were? — lovers. Are we? Were we? she wonders.

Another postcard, the Chrysler building this time.

> *... So you're learning to skate these holidays, my darling? There's an open-air rink here at the Rockefeller Centre. Center. Some of the skaters are serious and waltz eyeball-to-eyeball as in their young days in old Prague and Budapest. The young guys clown around pretty girls in tutus who loftily ignore them. Lovely to think of my darling in a tutu. Had any falls yet? Take care, as they all say here. I love you ...*

He mentions that he has been to see a revival of *West Side Story* on Broadway. He always writes 'I' not 'we'. She is reminded of one morning when, arriving unexpectedly, he found her still in bed and joined her there and later got up to make coffee. Naked at her little stove he swayed and sang 'I feel pretty', a cigarette dangling. His smile when she laughed was full of innocent bafflement. She wonders if he was reminded too: he doesn't mention it. She tries not to feel hurt.

She writes in her diary: *Is he thinking, poor little Caroline, writing his postcards?*

Caroline, stop it.

Caroline has started indulging in exotic foods. Am I trying to sublimate desire? she wonders. She buys a smoked fish in its cloth of gold, sullen-mouthed and swarthy. Creamy avocadoes in coarse black shells. Pumpernickel like sour plum pudding. Cheese crusted with black peppercorns or riddled with blue mould in crumbs or dimly veined with wine. A round Edam in red wax like a toffee apple. She eats her cheese with morello cherry jam by the saucerful. She buys quantities of Turkish coffee and tart Chianti in straw. At one sitting she eats a whole jar of peanut butter. She bakes a tray each of pumpkin and sweet potato in the oven of her new flat, filling it with smoke in which lurk the ghosts of other tenants' burnt dinners, and her sister's probably. In reaction she eats nothing for a week but fruit: mandarines with spongy skins, bananas and sour early apricots and plums. She buys a glossy oval crimson fruit which a poster in the shop names a tamarillo. It looks like the glowing eggs baked into plaits of bread in the Greek shops over Easter. Cut, it is orange, studded with dark seeds in a butterfly shape. It tastes of passionfruit and pawpaw together and Caroline savours every bite. The tamarillo, she reads, is a winter fruit.

She takes herself off to various good restaurants with a book and a half-bottle of fine wine. She reads *Pale Fire, A Lost Lady, Washington Square.* She orders Chicken Maryland, Manhattan Clam Chowder, Pastrami, things he must be eating. She is a slow eater and a fast reader. She keeps her head down. She hopes people are not looking at her in sly amusement.

I'm not a bold person, she writes in her diary. *Not an innovator or a rebel. Not the life of the party. But I am self-sufficient and don't much mind if strangers patronise me.*

He'll forget me. Worse, I'll seem drab and dull when he gets back. I listen to concerts recorded in San Marco's in Venice, in New College, Oxford — places I've been to — and wonder how my life can have shrunk so small. Someone vivid will catch his eye. He'll drop me.

In an Italian restaurant she eats little sea creatures stewed in wine and tomatoes: whole baby squids and mussels, scallops, shrimps and clams tangled on the plate in what looks like red seaweed. She drinks her green Italian wine. It is raining, a summer storm. From her window table she sees puddles begin to swarm with rain. Restaurants in New York have glassed-in verandahs like train carriages flush with the footpaths. She has seen them in her book. She imagines she is with him inside the golden glass of one of them, rain shivering down it and people rushing past, heads bent, smiling in at them from a black and silver Manhattan street. The waitress brings fruits, grapes and peaches and watermelon, unasked with the coffee. He said so in a letter. A candle, she thinks; a bowl of autumn fruits, a green bottle; our hands clasped on the red cloth. Afterwards, running home in this rain. No. On iced footpaths, sidewalks, slithering, hand-in-hand, our breath white: like skaters.

The third time there is a mist over the ice. Two other women are there practising leaps and figures. They smile sympathetically at Caroline's wobbles. The sunlight is a bobbin wound with gold mist and, dazzled, she can easily imagine that she is not here but in Central Park. Or the Rockefeller Centre. Center. In a letter he has mentioned smoking pretzel carts and puffs of steam from under the streets like white balloons hovering, or on a windy day flung shredded between glass walls and fluttering in the mirrors the walls make. She weaves — but in blue jeans, not a tutu — through the mist. She will amaze him at the Rockefeller Center one day, one day.

After two hours she can go round and round the rink quite fast without ever holding on and the two women smile and say how well she's doing.

He writes a lot. He writes, for example, about the hotels he (they) stay at, in rooms on the thirtieth and fortieth floors. 'Like in a helicopter, a huge ferris wheel. You sleep among stars.' She imagines him (them) high up at the summits of glass towers all gold and silver light, webbed with their long lamps and hung among stars. To make love up there, she dreams, though heights freeze her with terror. And what if they sway in the wind? She goes to Luna Park and grimly rides the ferris wheel above the glittering city.

Then he writes that he's moved to the Village now, to a friend's apartment.

> *Greenwich Village has all these red tenements caged with fire escapes. Basement rooms with lamps on all day. You've read* Washington Square, *haven't you? I was there today. The fountain was empty, just a skin of grey water and dead leaves. A pale boy was sitting on the rim gazing in, his feet bloated, red raw. I've never known such cold. You must have in Europe. There were trees, lamps, lonely wanderers. Sleet, the puddles dark red as night fell, and then red-lit coffee shops with guitarists (of a sort), bright fruit shops and souvenir and book shops: one day we'll browse in the Strand together. Again no letter from you today. Write to me, Caro, will you?*

New Year she spends in her flat waiting for him to ring but he never does. She tints her hair Granada Muscat so that it glows unexpectedly with a crimson burnish and shocks her when she meets it in plate glass windows. She has dinner with old friends, drinks too much and talks too much about him. She apologises too much, and they say not to be silly, what on earth are friends for?

'What I like about skating,' she assures her friends, 'is that I'm really getting somewhere, I'm making progress. I'm not just waiting for the time to pass. I'm getting results. I'm growing, I'm improving. Aren't I? It's visible progress.' Giggling, she waves her brandy balloon. 'It's all in the balance!' They just look, concern on their faces.

Caroline, who has been so sure that certain afternoons were really unforgettable, finds they have gone. Like a film only intermittently in focus, all the rest a mist. In dreams she relives moments and wakes burning and overjoyed. The dreams fade quickly. If he's forgetting too, she thinks in a panic, what is there left?

She looks at the five photographs, all that she has of him. Whenever she thinks of him now his face is in one or other of the five expressions. Is she forgetting what he looks like? When she sees him again, will she find herself trying to match his face to the photographs? She goes over old conversations. They are being eroded, and the expressions don't fit them at all. If only I'd written them down, she thinks.

She writes in her diary: *WRITE THINGS DOWN.* She finds scribbled lines:

> *Look in my face; my name is Might-have-been;*
> *I am also called No-more, Too-late, Farewell ...*
> *D.G. Rossetti.*

She goes out in the simmering streets and sees him on this corner or the next. He's back and he hasn't told her. It's always — well, of *course* it is! — someone else. She goes to the rink most days. Cats doze on verandahs, on a sprouting old settee left out as garbage, on brick walls. A tortoiseshell cat and a snail-coloured tabby cat, coiled and humped and with ears like horns, follow her then vanish. One day she finds a caterpillar with sparse long black fur and a hump, arching hurriedly on a wall. It looks like a tiny moulting kitten. Days later there it is again, yards further on. She is absurdly pleased. The next day it is deep under grey layers of a spider web. So what was she expecting? Immortality? Brown broken glass glows. Vomit lies on the hot footpath in clots.

She writes to him about all this and hopes he will understand. She tells him she is thinking of getting a cat: for company, she adds. So he'll know she's alone. She tells him she loves him.

She imagines that he is walking towards her. He stops to talk, seeing that she has seen him. With a smile more like a wince, out of pure courtesy he tries to chat. His shirt is open at the neck. She could lean forward and touch her lips to the hairs of his chest, except that he doesn't want her to. She remembers on a beach the hairs of his belly and groin all sunlit. Shadows of a dark tree broke over him.

'I must go, sweet,' he would say as soon as he could. 'We'll have a lunch one day, will we?'

One night, five weeks now since he left, the phone is suddenly ringing. His voice is heavy, blurred, and she is vague from sleep. The operator tells her to wait while he drops quarters in a coin phone. 'Darling, I can't stand it any longer,' his stifled voice is saying. 'I'm going to have to tell her. It can't go on like this. She can tell there's something wrong. I can't go on saying there's nothing *wrong* day in day out —'

'Oh, but listen. Wait!' Is he as drunk as he sounds?

'We'll get a flat,' he said. 'Look for a flat. She can have the house. Don't tell me you've changed your mind now?'

'*No.* Let's not be rash. Let's wait till you get back and we can talk about it. We never *have.* We need time —'

' "Time will say nothing," how does it go again?'

'Oh darling.'

'Don't want me now. I see.'

'I *do.* You know I do.'

'Your three minutes are up,' the operator says. 'Are you extending your call, sir?'

Caroline persuades him to ring her again right away, reversing the charges. 'Lady ain't tired a me yet, you hear her?' he drawls to the new operator, who sniffs. He is determined, truculent, heavily offended that she is raising objections now. They ring off, both promising a letter that will explain everything. 'My mind's made up,' he insists. 'I'm going ahead and telling her tonight.'

Caroline lies awake. His too-eager eyes urge her and on their brown surface she doesn't recognise herself. Justify this, they are saying. Justify me, seduce me, adore me. Be what I dream. Am I having to pay a great price all for nothing? Her heart thudding, she lies rigid all night.

That day she rings her mother, who is both pleased and horrified. She tells the friends she had dinner with and looks up Flats To Let in the newspaper. She waits for his letter, but none comes. She tries to write to him and can't. She skates, walks in the hot streets, swims when the bay is clean. No more phone calls wake her.

A week later there is a letter from New York: a funny recycled New Year card mailed weeks ago. He writes of having gone to Mass on Christmas Eve at St Patrick's. Long before you reach it, he says, you can see reflections of a white spire ... And she sees it jagged, a white spire curling and melting, swooning in glass. In a marble nave he gracefully genuflects as if in a dance. She, raised a Protestant, has never learnt to genuflect, or to dance for that matter. Her movements are not fluid but tight and graceless as a chilled swimmer's.

Wine is a help, she thinks. Wine does help, it warms and frees me. Remember to drink wine before he comes, she writes in her diary, and be bold and wild, sinuous! With the help of Chianti she answers his letter from the past. Her memory is starting to jam on times when things went wrong between them. This is fatal, she tells herself. At the moment of doubt the skater falls.

> *Darling,*
> *When your letter came, your New Year card, I went to the little church at the end of my street. I bought guava jelly at the stall they were holding, and went through an archway with a cool tree and lilies. From outside, the windows are embroideries of iron on glass; from inside, saints in robes of flame on their deep sky. The stone is draped like vines in Tuscany. How I wish it could bud in spring and be warmly hung with golden leaves and grapes in autumn, like the mast of Dionysos's ship — holding out its fruit in the darkness ...*
>
> *Tell me, do the skyscrapers* (but did the hotels is what she meant) *sway in a high wind? And is there skating in summer at the Rockefeller Centre? I can skate now. I haven't fallen yet. I won't, I refuse to. I'll show you!*

It's probably too late for her letter to reach him before he leaves New York, but she mails it anyway, backdating it to before his phone call. Then she sits eating guava jelly with a spoon, regretting the letter. It reads like an essay. What has its voice to do with her voice on the phone or with his? Is there any point at which their lives touch now?

Will we be happy living together (she writes in her diary)? *The only time he could stay all night wasn't a success. We were nervous and drank too much. I felt his disappointment, though he hid it courteously, without knowing what I'd done. Two days later he told me. 'You're such a selfish lover,' he added.*

'But of course I care if you're not satisfied!' I protested. 'You mean you faked?'

'Well, I had to. You were so damn happy.'

'I spent $300 on new bedcovers for one night, does that look like I didn't care?'

Again that gasp of impatience, his hand in that gesture of despair or anger: okay, let's just forget it. On the night I just lay there in an anguish of propitiation. I thought he was feeling guilty. *He left earlier in the morning than he needed to. Yet we got over this. We were overcoming our misunderstandings. Surely we'll come through?*

Don't tell me he's having religious scruples now. I don't believe this!

One hot afternoon the phone rings and she grabs it wildly, but it's her mother full of news about a neighbour's grassfire turned back just in time, a dog lost and found lame. A rooster crows on the farm, miles away, glossy and smug under gumtrees heavy with dust. Sheep are grizzling on all the dry hills. To splash on horseback, she thinks, through shadows at the amber creek.

'Caroline. Is he back yet?'

'No. Well, I don't know.'

'You haven't heard at all? The bastard. He hasn't rung you?'

'He will soon, I expect.'

'Well, come up to the farm, why don't you. Come and pick apples. What's the use of languishing alone?' She laughs. 'Sorry. Mother hen. Anyway, you know. Always welcome and all that.'

'I will come up. Yes, I will. But not yet. Who have you got lined up for me now?'

She puts the phone down before her mother can think up a denial. Checkmate. Her mother will be smiling now by the west windows, the phone still in her hand. Smiling herself, Caroline takes *Couples*, a towel and a bag of nectarines and lies on the hot sand, and swims, and dries off in the late red sun.

A postcard then — the Lincoln Center by night — but all it says is that he's coming back on schedule, two days from the day she gets it. He can't say what flight. She is elated at first and then succumbs to a frenzied panic. What does that mean: *can't say what flight?* She doesn't, of course, dare go to the airport on the day. She waits at home. He doesn't come or ring. Speechless with dread she drags through the night and the next day. At five he knocks: he hasn't a key to this flat. They embrace, but tentatively. He is certainly himself and she has not been forgetting him at all. He exclaims how brown she is and how much thinner. He has brought cuttings, book reviews for her to read. She pours what's left of the Chianti that has got her through these last two days into glasses full of ice cubes. The ice glows red around the glittering splinters of air inside it. The glasses mist over. She tries to read while he sips and smokes and listens to a new record she has bought for the occasion, the New World Symphony. Then he gets up to go. She gazes at him.

'I can't stay, darling.' He is discomforted rather than apologetic. 'It's this welcome-back party we're going to. God, I'm a zombie from jetlag. Don't look like that. I'll stay longer some other time.'

'But we haven't talked.'

'Darling, some other time.'

She nods and tries to smile, jiggling her red ice. 'What you said on the phone? Can't you tell me what's happened?'

'Nothing's *happened*.'

'It *has*. You don't love me now.'

'Sweet, that's *not* true.'

'*Please*.'

He sits down sighing. 'I don't know. I was sure I did. I even told her so, for God's sake, once when I was blind drunk. Oh, you know, I rang you. We went through hell for days after that, all over Manhattan. But we came through. You know, I think we're closer now than we've ever been. Hell, Caro, you don't want to listen to this. Sorry. Was it a good summer, sweet? Tell me about you.'

'I got by. It wasn't waited. *Wasted.* I learned to skate. Wait till you see Caro on ice!' But he is shaking his head. 'Let me guess: the deal is you give me up?'

He nods. 'A clean break.'

'Oh, right. Keep it clean. What did you tell her about me?'

'Not much. What could I? We don't talk about it any more. Though she did ask today —'

'Does she know you're here now?'

'No. She did ask today if I had any regrets about — you know. "Breaking with Caroline." I said no. No regrets.'

'Not a bad curtain line. Delivered with more conviction.'

'I meant it, Caro.'

'At the time.'

He looks at the time. 'God, *look* at the time,' he says, and stands up. 'It was fun, though, wasn't it? Caro, you were great.' A light kiss, and he is gone.

She drinks her wine, pulls thick woollens and gloves on, then wanders out on to the sunny Esplanade. Palms stoop and swish, sails shake on the foam of the bay. Leaves, torn off the trees, rise and sink about her as if in a fire. Summer is as good as over. And no bones broken either. Already Caro can see herself glide, a long blue shape on the ice among the other skaters, flaring through the sun's path with dust and mist and veils of snowy breath behind her; dazzled, transfigured, she turns and glides.

ON THE PIER

On the pier I am a familiar sight, a gaunt old woman with her shopping-buggy and her old dog on a lead. With the regulars squatting among their lines and crushed whitebait I exchange a nod and a smile. I sit against a bollard warm as a pillar of white flesh after a day's sun. The moored yachts jingle. White sails flutter, bowing and slithering towards the marina. There is sometimes a ship rimmed in gold at Station Pier, where your father used to take us for a drive, if you remember, when ships were leaving, to see them pull away from the wharf and drift out, turning, a gold bead on the sky. Salt winds and a squall of gulls, and streamers tossing. From the pier the new bridge looks like a high-prowed two-master in the west over by the refineries. At night they are towers of ice, the refineries, or frigates spun out of hot glass, glittering, and each has a flag of fire.

Mary, my dear, we are not close. Are you wondering why I am burdening you with this now? I am not in need of sympathy or help, only of a witness. Why you? You're my only child and I owe it to you to make myself understood. Why now? Well, you will know by the time you read it.

Do you remember how gloomy this house was in winter in the old days? Tossed in a storm, or sunk to the eaves in a cold mist? On that burning day you brought me home from hospital I thought: Whenever did our old house turn so chilly, so mean and dark? Even in winter it was never so bad. Red brick should look warm with the sunlight falling on it through the cherry-plum leaves. Inside the plaster was cracked, damp in every room. The frilled china fish that was the mouth of the bath tap had lost its snout and dribbled rust. When had it happened? The grate in the sitting-room was black and even after months of nothing but radiators it still smelled of ashes. All the old photographs were there; the books — mine and poor Frank's — and the crystal vases, which your Aunt Ida *will* cram with sheaves of dried flowers; even the wireless Frank made as a boy, with the valves at the back that still glow and crackle through the dust when you turn it on. A boom, and the faint voices. What did any of it matter now?

Children are yowling out in the street.

'Crazy old ladies!'

'I dare you to go in.'

'Nah.'

'Go on. Scared? He's scared of the dog. Here doggie!'

'Nah. Stone'll fix him.'

'Bullshit. Go on, then.'

'What for?'

'He's chicken.'

I remember waking from time to time and fumbling in the egg-stained sheets which I would only let you change on my good days, in a bed full of urine and musty flesh. Frank was long gone. There went my tattered cabbage head, poking out, then ducking under when you came near. You kept your temper. But when had my winsome girl become so terse and worn?

You flew home to the children and Ida came to stay. Frank's little sister, my old enemy. I've suspected myself now and then of living on just to spite Ida — we're forever sniping and bridling — but I see now it was for Toby's sake. The dachshund, Toby. You remember. He waited at my bedside day after day. Later he came tottering after me from room to room, then from street to street, gazing up with his toffee eyes. Tired, he would sink down at my feet and nuzzle at his rolls of belly with sucks and groans.

Poor old Toby's gone. Which is why I'm writing.

When I recovered I had forgotten half my life. I had forgotten what a death is like, though month after month I had to look on as Frank withered. I remember now. Afraid of the cold bedroom, he liked me to read him to sleep in here by the fire with the lamps and the fire bronze on the warm floorboards. In the last few years he'd had pupils to tea once a month, two or three at a time. I would bake scones, whip cream, spoon out my plum jam: preside, as Frank said, at the teapot. His stories of Navy life always went down well. Then he took down a book, shook off the dust and asked them to read aloud. Those owlish pink boys and their voices cracking through Tennyson, Byron, Donne! *'Death, be* not *proud!'* Afterwards as we heard them laugh and yell, scuffling once they were safely out under the street lamps, he smiled, catching my look, and shrugged. 'I can but sow the seed,' he said.

So in this room, with its stained-glass peacocks in the bow-window and the eternal chrome yellow of its lamplit gloom, I was reading to him when he died. Since he retired, only one of the old boys had been to see him, once.

The cries of gulls in the night. A peacock's screech. Or is it a cat? Even now, startled out of sleep I sometimes think: there's Mary crying. Do you remember inking in faces on the clothes pegs while I hung out the wash? You made dough-babies to bake on Sundays with the roast. Your canary, Dicky, died and broke your heart. You stood jiggling on the kitchen table while I battled with your hems. You always stirred the jam for me. There aren't any plums this summer to make jam. The trees are scraggy and old. Schoolboys keep picking what plums there are and pelting each other with them. The first time Toby snarled and barked, and one of the boys kicked him. I kept him inside after that. The footpath and the brown lawn are oozing all over with burst plums.

Yesterday afternoon I took Toby shopping and then for a walk in the quiet streets near the canal. Not much has changed. The white bridge, brown banks rimmed in the flat sun with slime and mud. A rowboat was tied to the shallow water, which is the sherry colour of creeks in the bush now. After sunset when we crossed back it was a broad black river under a rippling sky, and the boat looked the size of a ship. Street lamps shone around it and beyond to where the canal spreads into the sea.

Flashing its headlights, a car roared round the corner and hurtled close to us, braked, and blared its horn. Toby wailed. Confused in the white glare and deafened, I must have dropped his lead. He was huddled in the middle of the road. Tyres squealing, the car went round in a wide loop, heads poking out of the windows. Someone cheered. 'Toby!' I screamed. It just missed me and hit Toby. He was breathing, groaning. One of the heads was crumpled in shock. 'Please,' I said. He could have been saved. But the car lurched down a side street.

I dragged Toby to the footpath, where I laid the shopping-buggy flat and eased him in. Sobbing and panting, I talked all the way home to soothe him. Each shimmering street lamp showed the dark splashes over me. When we reached home he was cold.

I crammed him in a plastic rubbish bag and then another, and made room for him, despite Ida's outrage, in the freezer in the wash-house.

Last night I was out watering the garden. Dismembered dogs lay all over it, the grey fur frozen on them, red fleas in webs about them like spiders. The dogs had raw cavities where the bones shone yellow. They were making small, painful movements.

By the fence was a white pot of cloudy yellow liquid. 'Plum juice,' I said. 'I'll make wine.' Water spattered the gold mirror of its surface as I turned on the hose.

From the path Frank came and took my hand. I held the hose away as I kissed him, pouring darkness over a garden hung with plums like lamps. Darkness, a black veil. My hose put the day out.

'Look, Gwennie,' he warned.

'I know,' I said.

One dog had assembled itself under the battering from my whip of water, and it was our Toby, his torn limbs working as red flies and ants moved in his left hip; in his right; in his shred-hung skull.

I awoke in horror. The flash of white headlights in the window! But it was the moon through a gap in the curtains. When my heart quietened I padded out to the passage. The moon was there too, full of shadows, so I put on the light. The ritual creak of protest came from Ida's room. I went to the toilet and then to the bathroom where I bent to suck cold water from the hollow of my palms. The house shifted, sighed. I could not make myself switch off the passage light. I left my door open, pulled the curtain shut and sank with a creak which Ida's bed answered from the depths.

I lay in a sweat, eyes closed tight. In the morning this matter of the light would, I knew, be raised. I have insisted on Ida's paying half the household bills since the day she called me a Bolshevik.

When I trundled at dawn on to the pier with the shopping-buggy nobody was there. In that cool light the rim of the city was a spangled cloud. I was too tired to look for deep water. Just past the pavilion I tipped the frozen bag out, added stones from the breakwater, fastened it and rolled it over the edge. It swelled, the pale waters writhed and he sank deep.

Oh, Ida was fractious today. First came the pointed remarks about the passage light. Then an offer, which I declined, to 'help dig poor Toby a grave'. Not having slept well, I lay down. All morning I could hear her hard at work scrubbing and swilling out the toilet, bathroom, kitchen and wash-house. She refused to eat lunch. Later I found her on her knees darning a hole in the underfelt which has to serve for carpet in her room.

'Well, I'd hate you to think, Gwen,' — settling her glasses in place — 'that I was causing wear and tear to your house.'

'That's very good of you, Ida.'

'After all, you took me in without a penny.'

'Are you sure green thread is best, Ida?' I said. 'I'd have thought — maybe light grey.'

How she glared, I know, at my back! Now she has shut herself in.

We went fishing more often, your father and I, after he retired, on the pier and twice a couple we know with a caravan, another teacher and his wife, drove us to Swan Bay at night to camp by the boathouse. Weird screeches echoed over the water: not seagulls, more like cats, but it was peacocks, satin peacocks posing on a roof in the orange sunrise. We rowed out a long way and waited for whiting to bite in the reedy shallows. The dazzle and salt air burned once the sun came up. So many mailed fish alive in the sea, their gold-eyed heads agape in a stiff snarl. In the clamour of the gulls we cleaned and washed our fish together, and came home before the heat of the day.

'Death by water,' he said once, 'I used to fear most. No, fire most, then water. Gwennie, this is worse than either.'

It was so long drawn out. Not that I don't fear death by water myself. But I've checked the tide tables. I'll go out on the turn when it's dark with no one around, and at least this way I will never be just so much helpless flesh in a bed again.

I have some keepsakes with me: my wedding ring — the opal brooch and your grandmother's locket are for you — and the box of Frank's ashes and chunks of bone. *He* chose the fire for himself. Believe it or not. Also my miniature Coleridge with the blue ribbon. Did I ever tell you that he took his Dante with him into the fire? — the three little navy blue Everyman volumes that had the Italian and English facing on onion skin paper. I picked up the envelope with your first tooth and lock of hair and then it struck me as a dreadful omen, inauspicious, and I put it back. So as not to cause Ida too much bother I have left her a note of explanation which she'll find when she deigns to come out. Also a sum of money in my will, which is with the deeds in the crystal cabinet. You are my sole heir and executor. Everything is in order. All that's left now is to make my way to the post office and send this by certified airmail. Then to the pier, where I am a familiar sight. I wish you a long life free of pain or despair.

This has been a still and burning afternoon. I will lean against a bollard and watch the sunset until the lights come on.

CAFFE VENETO

Her father is there already when Anne comes. She sees him first, smoking under a streetlamp outside the misted windows with their gilt scrawl: *Caffe Veneto*. The seedballs and fingered leaves of a plane tree are touching him with shadows.

'You found it, then,' she calls out. 'Sorry if I'm late. I was held up at rehearsal.' He is holding a bottle wrapped in brown paper. 'Is this a celebration?'

'A Cabernet Sauvignon. Good to see you!'

'Yes. It's been a while. Two months?'

'Or three. Since Easter.'

'That's right. Well. What a strange phone call!' This furtive smile of his is strange as well; and how much he has aged since then. In this light his skin seems to have faded and creased, settled more slackly in the hollows of bones. His eyes are smaller. Even his teeth seem smaller, patched and stained, exposed in his uneasy smiles. This austerity of age, in his of all faces, is at the same time intimidating and pitiable. She wonders if he has seen it himself in mirrors.

'Is this place fit for the Cabernet Sauvignon?' she says. 'We could look for somewhere fancier.'

'No, why? They've only changed the name. I have been here before, I remember now.'

'Student food.'

'I live on it. The spaghetti's good, come on.'

The glass door opens and a laughing group pushes out. The bead curtains rattle. Then two barefooted girls go inside; a warm gust, a smell of coffee and smoke blow out as visibly as breath. He holds the beads aside for her, and the door open. Lamps hang inside, round and red like upturned glasses of wine. In the blurred light they shed, Anne leads him past crowded stools at the counter to the only table free, a long bench against a wall of theatre posters. Its top is carved like a school desk. Her father sits at her side tracing initials on it with his finger while their order is taken and the table set. Only when he pours the wine does he give her his usual undaunted, boyish smile.

'This whole table to ourselves? Well, cheers.'

'Cheers. A 1975! Napa Valley. Californian? Oh, it's nice.' The wine, plummy and dark, stings and makes her shudder. 'So we *are* celebrating?'

'No.'

'No?'

He shakes his head, lighting another cigarette.

'Is Mum all right?'

'Fine. She's minding the children for your Aunt Sheila. She said to give you her love and talk you into coming back for a coffee.'

'Oh. I only signed out for ten-thirty, though.'

He checks his watch. 'How's College?'

'Great.'

'What was that about a rehearsal?'

'Oh yes. The Drama Club's putting on *The Seagull*. Chekhov? You have to come.'

'Of course. Are you Nina?'

'No, only Masha. Poor dreary Masha in black.'

'Well, we must come.' His voice falters. 'When's it on?'

'In two weeks. I'll look after the tickets. Now tell me,' she smiles and holds up her wine glass, 'what we're *not* celebrating.'

'What if we eat first, talk later.'

'No, now. Come on.'

'Well — my study leave's come through.'

'Well, good! I thought you'd decided to withdraw your application.'

'I had. But I'd have missed out altogether. It was now or never.'

' "It's now or never. My love won't wait." So you'll be going to America after all?'

'That was the idea. Funny you should say that.' He gives a short laugh. 'I've fallen in love.'

'Oh Daddy, again?' Her smile is stiff from the wine. 'Not that I can talk. I have, too.'

'*Have* you? What's his name?'

'I don't know him very well.'

'Don't know his name.'

'Not telling. Not yet. He's — he's married. Separated.'

'That's what they *all* say, they say.'

'Is it now? Anyway, she's moved to Sydney and he's here.'

'Well. What can I say? So long as you're happy.'

'It has its moments. You?'

'Yes. And no.'

'Do I know this one?'

'No.' He hesitates. 'She's one of my post-grad students. She's doing her thesis on Sylvia Plath. Oh, she's mature-age,' he adds quickly. 'She's thirty-nine.'

'Married?'

'Divorced with one daughter. As a matter of fact, she's a student here: Microbiology, I think. The daughter. Jenny.'

She nods. 'You've met the daughter. What's the mother's name?'

'Sandra.' He gulps more wine and wipes his lips with a finger.

'So this is not a celebration because now you wish you weren't going to America.'

'In a way.' He fixes earnest eyes on her. 'You haven't seen your mother all this time, Annie, have you?'

'There's never a moment free. There are extra tutorials when you live in at College. And this play. And essays all —'

'I know.' He breathes out smoke. 'I just wondered. When you didn't come home at the end of first term.'

'Did she complain, did she? But she knew I was going camping!'

'No. All I'm saying really, darling, is that now your mother's going to need all your love and support. Please.'

'She doesn't *know,* does she?'

'No. She doesn't.'

'Well. Good.'

'I may have to tell her.' He bows his head and she sees that his grizzled curls, redder under this lamp, are thinning at the crown. 'This time it's the real thing. I may have to leave your mother.'

'For this — for Sandra?'

'When you meet her, you'll understand.'

'Hang on. Hang on.' Bowls of spaghetti thud into place under their noses. She watches her own hand pick up a fork and coil red hanks round and round it, too disconcerted by his lack of composure to take in what he is saying. 'Why *me*?'

'We've always been close.' He tries to smile. 'Trial run?'

'Oh, so it's all *settled*?'

'Darling, nothing's *settled* yet.'

'It sounds settled to me.'

'Not so.'

He stubs out his cigarette and lights another. Anne bends over her spaghetti. She should eat, being, unused to wine. She gulps one hot mouthful, feeling her whole head swill with tears; tears of shock.

'Annie.'

'It's the spaghetti. Hot.'

'Damn,' mutters her father. Two people are seating themselves opposite them at the table, backs to the wall, a boy in a football guernsey and a woman in black suede. As alike as the Mother and Child in an ikon — though he must be eight or nine, Anne thinks — they look at each other with pleased black eyes set widely under round brows in their amber faces. Anne moves the wine glasses to make room and the woman smiles.

'It's the only table left.' Anne shrugs, pushing her plate away. She wipes her nose. 'I won't meet Sandra. How could you suggest it? You should know better.'

'I admit I was hoping, well, at least that you'd be more —'

'Amenable?'

'Just understanding.'

'Oh yes. I *understand*.'

'Not how I feel. Do you?'

'Why not? I've understood the other times. I've kept your secrets. Commiserated when it was over. Haven't I? What I *don't* understand is why this time my mother would deserve to be left.'

'Darling, you don't leave people because they *deserve* it. Or stay with them, either.'

'If that's true, then no one's ever secure.'

'That's how it is. There's no security.'

'If people were *faithful* —'

'Yes, in an ideal world, people would all be faithful and all be secure. I agree. Or there'd be no love and so no insecurity.'

'They go together, do they?'

'I'd say so. Wouldn't you?'

'No!' At her tone the woman opposite glances up from her struggle to tuck the boy's napkin round his neck, while he digs into ravioli; full of mournful surprise, her eyes meet Anne's. She thinks we're lovers quarrelling, Anne thinks, and looks away, down at her hands. They have been tearing a hunk of bread into crumbs. She picks some up on a fingertip and eats them.

'When do you have until?' she whispers.

'Not long. America, you mean?'

'Yes. Mum must have been thrilled about that?'

'I haven't told her, Annie.'

'Why not?'

'I can't decide, don't you see?' His hand is crepe-skinned and the bones show, bent round the red glass. He sees her looking and looks too, holding his thick fingers outspread.

'I just can't take it in. When will you tell her?'

He winces. 'Oh, we'll more than likely call the whole thing off.'

'Call America off? Because of Sandra?' He stares at her. 'She — Sandra — must have known all along you were married.'

'Of course. Of course. Sorry. I thought you meant when would I tell your mother about Sandra.'

Maybe I did, Anne thinks. She gulps down the tart red wine, feeling dazed. 'How long have you known her?'

'About six months.'

'Six *months*.'

'Sssh. We've been lovers for two. Three.'

'Since Easter. You can't be sure, then. It's too soon.'

'That's what she says.'

'Well?'

'Just that it isn't true. I do love her. I'm only not a hundred-per-cent sure if she's worth the price. If anyone is, I mean. No, I am sure.'

'You mean, worth what *you* will have to pay.'

'Yes.'

'That's — don't you see that's selfish?'

'In a sense it's selfish, I suppose.'

This is what love does, she thinks. Puts us at the mercy of the other's selfishness. And of our own.

'If you believe in love,' he says, 'you pay the price.'

'Except that Mum will be paying the most. And she's always been faithful to you, in spite of your other women.'

'Doesn't that in itself say something about our marriage?'

'Maybe just about marriage.'

'When you get married —'

'I won't.'

'Let's keep our voices down. What's he like?' He smiles. 'This fellow you're in love with? Not that History tutor, is it? What's his name again?'

'I'm never getting married. Never.'

He shrugs. 'Up to you.'

Already he doesn't care, then. 'You know,' she says, 'if you leave her now she'll feel that her life has been wasted.'

'Her love, perhaps. Not her life. Most love is wasted.'

'Her whole *life*.'

'Past life. Okay. Which is it worse to waste, I wonder? The past or the future?'

'Mum, of course, would be concerned about *her* future.'

'She's still a very attractive woman, darling. She'll find someone else.'

'Will she, though? She hasn't had the practice you've had.' There is a grim silence. She stares at the peeling theatre posters: there is one for *The Seagull*. Her mouth is parched, her throat swollen and furred. 'Besides,' she whimpers, 'she loves *you*. Doesn't that count?'

'Annie,' he sighs, 'we have to be mature about this.'

'Are you being?'

'Do you think love is immature?'

'Not in itself.'

He rubs his greying head. The hair on his chest, she remembers from last summer, is greying too, above and about his nipples. He has a young man's belly. Like a tree in autumn he is withering from the top down. Not since the upheavals of puberty has she been so aware of men, the presence of the male, as now. Is it because she has a lover now? Maybe all women feel like this. And men? I still know next to nothing about love, she thinks: and I'll suffer for it.

'You always said to take love lightly,' she says.

He sighs, breathing smoke out. 'I can't be sure I can even go on hiding my feelings at home.'

'But that's not a reason to leave! That doesn't make sense!'

'Why doesn't it?'

'If you can't hide it, tell her. She probably knows.'

'No, I'd know if she did.'

'She always has before.' He stares at her. 'I never told her. Of course not. She never told me straight out that she knew. She just — hinted. "I think you're like me," she said last time. "I let lying dogs sleep," and we laughed. You didn't take it seriously, so ... And that's what she's doing now.'

'Why didn't you ever ...?' He shrugs.

'Tell you? You *know* why. I didn't tell Mum what you told me either, did I? You both trusted me. And I would never have dared, anyway. Why do you think I wanted to live in at College? Because I was out of my depth at home.'

She sees herself wading for the first time beside the huge white legs of her mother and father into cold green slabs of water that tilted high and hurled her off her feet. Screaming, she clutched a hand, a knee, clambered on a slippery thigh. They carried her back to the sandbank. Lapped in pale water, she sat there alone wailing while they waded back in without her, deeper and deeper, until they disappeared.

'Secrecy. Lies. Hints,' her father is saying. 'Why wouldn't she say, if she knew? I didn't want to hurt her, that's all.'

'Oh, *what* can I say? Can't you just wait a while? You can't spring a thing like this on her. At least, give her time.'

'Time! That's just it. I'm afraid Sandra won't wait.'

'Won't wait?'

'Won't wait, I mean, if I go off to America for months with your mother.'

'Why not?'

'It'd be asking too much of her credulity, she says.'

'But if she loves you?'

'It's faith that she lacks. Not love. Faith and hope.'

'It sounds like she's blackmailing you.' He is silent. This is what he sometimes suspects. Resentfully, in spite of himself, he pictures Sandra curled and smug on her bed reading at this moment, the lamplight around her in flounces of smoke like a mosquito net; while he fights his daughter for her sake. 'Blackmailing you,' Anne says. 'She'll wait, if you go alone.'

'You still don't understand.'

'*Tell* me.'

'I can't not take your mother, can I,' he mutters, 'if I'm living at home?'

'You can't mean that you want to take *Sandra* to *America*!'

'Annie, enough now. Please. This is dreadful.'

'You do! You do! How *could* you? You can't *mean* it.'

'Annie, for God's sake.'

'You're my father and I love you. You know that. Maybe more than Mummy. But if you leave her, I'll be on her side. I won't even see you again.' She wonders as she says this if it is true; and if he would care. 'I mean that.'

'*Well*!' He pushes his untouched plate away in turn. The boy opposite pauses to stare curiously from the cold tangles of spaghetti to their faces, and back. 'What shall we talk about now?'

'Nothing. I'll go.' But, as he half-expects, she makes no move to. He fills the glasses, drinks his down, and lights a cigarette.

'Big match tomorrow,' he tosses defiantly across the table.

'Yeah!' The boy grins back at him.

'How do you like your chances?'

'Gunna win!' The boy looks for approval at his mother, who gives him an imploring smile. She has finished her ravioli. 'Great ravioli, Mum,' the boy announces, clearly to please her; and she looks pleased.

'I *fear* for my mother!' Anne shouts. 'I fear for her! How will she bear it?'

'Darling!' Shock makes him spill his wine. With his napkin he stanches the dark puddle, wondering if she can be drunk. After all, she has eaten only the bread. He gapes at her in such evident mute dismay that again he strikes her as boyish, an elderly bad boy, and a spasm of laughter crosses her face. Yes, she is, he decides. Grinning with relief, he throws his arm around her shoulders to pull her to him for a moment and she smells suddenly the drenching sweetness in the armpits of men who smoke. But she draws back from him.

'Gunna win, no worries.'

'I don't know, though,' her father teases. 'You're up against the best team, just about.'

'We aren't, they are! And my dad's playing!'

'Your dad, is he? Go on!'

'He's the captain!'

'Is he now? What's his name?'

Again the boy refers to his mother, then leans forward and whispers it.

'He's your dad? Well, good God!' The woman nods, ruefully, it seems to Anne; the dark eyes glimmer and close. 'You going to be as good as your dad?'

'Better!'

'Going to see him play?'

'Too right!'

'Might see you there.'

'Finish, finish.' His mother nudges him: heads are turning in the red haze. He scoops up his last shreds of ravioli, while her father turns his jovial smile on the mother. 'His dad's a magnificent footballer. One of the greats. And you,' he tells the boy, 'must be very proud.' The boy nods gravely, wiping his chin.

The woman springs up. 'Yes, goodnight.' Her voice shakes and she opens her pale palms in a beseeching gesture. 'We going now.' She stoops to the boy's ear. 'Come on. We going.'

'Oh? Can't I have a gelato?'

'Yes, in a cornet. Please, the bill.' She tugs the waiter's sleeve. But the boy wants to hear more. She wavers, but bends her head, blotting her cheeks with her black lapels, and rushes alone to the counter.

Anne leans forward. 'Your mother wants you.'

A black suede arm is beckoning.

'Yeah, I better go.'

'Well, nice meeting you.' Her father puts out his hand; the boy's tawny hand is lost in it. Confused, he stands smiling at them, glancing now and then towards his mother until at last he can detach himself and run to her.

'How about that?' Her father sits back. 'Nice kid. If he turns out half the man his dad is!'

'I think she was crying.'

He looks round, but they have gone. 'Sorry?'

'She was crying. That's why she rushed off.'

'Why would she be?'

'I think because of you. All that about his father.'

'He's a great player. Why shouldn't his kid be proud of him?'

'He takes after her,' Anne says. 'Both honey-coloured.'

'So are we in this light.'

'Dark honey. Like a Byzantine Madonna and Child.'

'I thought they looked Indian.'

'Yes? Or Maori.'

'Maybe.' He considers. 'Or Indonesian.'

'The thing is, they were so happy. A dinner out at the Caffe Veneto. She should have been safe.'

'From?'

'She was hurt. Shamed.'

'Why, though?'

'Who knows? The boy's father may have *done her wrong*. Anything. It's none of our business, that's all.'

'Well, she's not his wife. I've met his wife.'

'My point.'

'Anne, all I did was pay tribute to a marvellous bloody footballer!'

'You overdid it.'

'*Did* I.'

'What right had you to make her cry?'

'How was I to know?'

'*I* knew.'

'Well, I didn't, I'm afraid. Sorry.' Stung, he makes a hurt face. 'I see nothing I do or say tonight is going to find favour. Poor me.' His lined eyes meet hers. 'Cast into outer darkness.'

'It's all of a piece, that's all.' She tips her head back to empty her glass, and her face glows under the lamp. 'You can choose not to know you're doing it, but still the damage is done. People suffer. Lives are ruined.'

'*You're* overdoing it.'

'You really don't care.' She gazes in disillusion as he sighs. The impetuosity which all her life she has loved in him is not, after all, boyish. In the light of this evening it is shown up as shallow and rash; even, perhaps, brutal. 'You ride roughshod. You'll always get away with it.'

'All right. I'm a clumsy galoot. That boy's mother's life is ruined. *Mea culpa.*'

'In a small way it does go to show,' she says, and holds out her glass for more, 'that you can make strange errors of judgement. Admit that. May I have some more American wine?'

'Just what I was about to say of you.' He fills her glass. His suddenly amused lips look as if they are bleeding, black from the wine. He watches her turn her glass so that the glow of wine moves on the table. 'Can this be our practical Annie?'

'Why can't it?'

'Burning incense to the Madonna of the Caffe Veneto.'

'She thought we were lovers quarrelling.'

'Did she? She can't have heard much.' He glances round. 'I'll bet she was on your side.'

'Being practical,' she says, 'if that's what's expected, tell me: have your loves ever lasted? Has love ever made you happy for long?'

He takes her hands. 'What has happiness got to do with love? "To love is to suffer," didn't Goethe say? "One is compelled to love, one does not want to." ' She shakes her head and pulls free. 'Annie.' But she turns away, one hand folded to hide her face.

He foresees himself at the moment when she will stand on tiptoe to kiss him goodnight holding her by the shoulders and pressing with his closed lips a kiss of finality on her stained lips; holding her away, then, to look in her eyes and compel not only resignation. Consent, absolution, belief. When he sees that she can't move first, he holds the bottle up under the lamp and shakes it. 'All gone,' he pouts. He sniffs it: the dregs have a smell of olives. She looks at him. 'Like a coffee?'

'No, thanks.'

'Sure?'

'No, I'd better get back.'

He glances at his watch. 'Let's go? It's after ten.'

While he pays she droops at his side staring at her shoes on the bare planks, in an attitude of reproach, as he notes wryly. Whatever gave me the idea, he thinks, that I could convince her of the imperatives of love? My shy and scrupulous daughter, of all people! No, her mother's daughter now. He holds her coat open for her to grope into. 'Drive you back to College?'

'I think I'll walk.'

'Walk you back?'

'All right.'

It is clammily cold. They walk on a wide path past shadowy trees holding their few brown leaves still in the mist. A full moon glimmers. His daughter's shoulders are folded in; her hair hangs in two rusty skeins along the line of her nose. At eighteen she is no longer a girl. Prettier now, yes, but shedding her young freshness. She will be late, as fearful of hurt as she is, to come to ripeness. She has a shrouded look, he thinks; her eyes, when for a moment she glances up, seem full of sorrow and foreboding.

'Give my love to Mum,' she says once. 'Tell her I'll ring.'

'I will.'

'You'll come to the play?'

'Of course. You'll see to the tickets?'

'You have to go to America. Don't you?'

'Yes.'

'With Mum or with Sandra.'

'Yes.'

'What's she like?'

'Beautiful.'

'You were my household gods,' she says as if to herself. 'Warm and luminous. One each side of the fire.'

'Oh, Annie.'

'Oh, I grew out of it.'

She has her hands in her pockets and is staring down at heaps of leaves as she shuffles through them, not close enough for an arm around her shoulders to seem unforced. She is exhausted, of course; so is he, barely able to speak. He breathes long trails of smoke out, thinking of Sandra reading; and of Margaret, at home with his sister's children, waiting.

They come round the crescent and the brick hump of her college stands black on the glow of the sky. Under the trees it is deeply dark. She catches a plane leaf as it floats loose: brown on one side, pale with brown veins on the other, like an imploring hand.

'Have a wish?'

'You know.' She looks at him. 'Daddy, you won't do it. Will you?'

'No.' He turns his stubbornly pleading face to her, but she is looking down again. 'No, I don't suppose I can.'

'You mustn't.'

'I won't. No.'

On the gravel at the entrance she turns abruptly and kisses him, her hands on his shoulders, and runs up the steps. Her mouth tastes of tears. I never asked about her love affair, he thinks. He starts back, his shoes crunching in the mist. But she is inside the blurred glass door, which is slowly closing. Her shape stoops, signing in. The light goes out, and the lock clicks.

PUMPKIN

'Just look at the men,' Barbara says, so Jill rolls over to look, brushing the sand off. Andoni and Marcus are loudly giving little Vassilaki a swimming lesson. Barbara waves as Andoni glances their way, but he fails to notice. 'When he's wet he looks like a copper statue. Or a glass one, filled with honey.' (Not like Jill's husband: Marcus is all bones and blisters.) 'Well, he does!' Because Jill has smiled. 'If you look carefully.'

Waving now as the two sisters sit up, Andoni passes his little boy to Marcus and dives under. Still with her smile, Jill watches Barbara wait until Andoni's black head springs up and shakes a spray of drops off before she will lie down again. Marcus is wading deeper with the boy on his shoulders.

'Life's good here, Jilly,' Barbara sighs.

'So I see!'

'I could live in Greece forever. Will it last, though?'

'Probably not.'

'But you keep smiling.'

'Not a crying matter yet.'

'You and Marcus? Problems?'

'Oh no.' Jill hesitates. 'Not really problems.'

'Then tell me: why probably not? Since you've gone all wise in your old age.'

'Not wise. Just old.'

'Not old. I'll be thirty myself in three years. Anyway, it will last. Andoni's mother tells fortunes.'

'God.'

'In coffee cups. I'm having long life and six kids.'

'You're joking.'

'Maybe not six. Five.'

'At least she must like you.'

'Yes. I'm one of the family.'

The shadow of a gull darts over the sand, sharp, more like a dipping swallow. Jill yawns. She rolls on to her broad brown back to brush sand off her belly. She looks like a beached seal, Barbara thinks. Jill catches her eye. They smile at each other ruefully. So much for having a *real* talk, the smiles say. But it is hot on the sand, watching the wallow and flash of the sun. Sometimes a wind ruffles their flanks and flickers away. The shadows of birds waver on them. Then the whole sky stills, as hot and bright as a ball of glass, and they are embedded in it. A searing din of cicadas numbs them. When they go in for a swim, the water pouring over them silences them; icy and deep, marbling them, making Barbara so white that beside her sister's tawny bulk she looks jade green. Their shadows reach out and touch on the sand of the sea floor: it is an illusion.

'Aren't you lucky you can tan?' Barbara has to huddle in the sand-crusted tent of her towel to save her skin from burning. 'You could pass for a Greek. I never will.'

'Not with that hair, no. Why should you?'

'Sometimes I'd like to.' Barbara shakes her head, scattering water drops. 'Vassilaki's lucky he's got Andoni's colouring. His big chocolate eyes.'

'Nothing wrong with grey. He's blond, anyhow.'

'Yes, but so was Andoni until he was six, his mother says. And his sisters too.'

'What does it matter? There must be blond and redheaded Greeks.'

'Oh, there are. Not where we live, though. They're all dark.'

'Dye your hair dark, then.'

'Mmm. Vassilaki's is going dark.'

'So long as you don't feed him on pumpkin!'

'Ha *ha*. They don't even have pumpkins here.'

It is irritating Barbara that Jill has harped on that old joke since she got here; has even been calling her 'Pumpkin', as their father used to, having convinced both little girls that pumpkin turned hair that colour. She has always hated her hair. Now that it is going dark, though, she dyes it back: as if she were not Barbara without orange-gold hair that the sun turns to brass. (Has Jill guessed that she dyes it?) Andoni is proud of his wife's hair, there being little else to be proud of. Her skin is freckled; she is too tall, too thin. That is what they think in Greece: nice, but so ugly, poor girl. She smiles, watching Andoni and Marcus tow Vassilaki to the shallows. Strangers will take Jill for Andoni's wife, her for Marcus's.

'No pumpkins? What do you live on?' Jill is saying.

'*Other* things. What do you? They don't have passion fruit here either,' she goes on, because she has spoken too sharply. 'Dad's going to airmail me some from Australia.'

'Passion fruit?'

'Well, what do you think? Pumpkins? Look at Vassilaki.'

Marcus is tottering in the shallows with Vassilaki on his back. Everyone on the beach is looking. Marcus stands out as foreign even more than Barbara, with the grey-blond wisps of his hair flying and his face still babyish in middle age. He waves to Barbara and pretends to duck Vassilaki, who squeals. His grin is bracketed by long wrinkles. Barbara feels ill at ease with him. Have I forgotten how to talk to Australian men? she wonders.

'He's calling me "Auntie" now,' Jill says. 'And Marcus is "Marco".'

'He loves you.'

'Everybody.'

'You two especially. We're expecting you to go all clucky. Especially Andoni's mother.'

'Me? I'm not having any kids.'

'Why *not*?'

'Why *yes*?'

Barbara can hardly believe it. 'You were always saying you wanted lots of kids!'

'Oh, when we were little!'

'And after. Really, not even one?'

'Freedom before progeny,' Jill declaims.

'Have both. Well, why not?' She sits up with a squeal as Vassilaki squats dripping astride her belly. 'You're wet! You're squashing me!' He laughs. The men are calling, waving. 'Oh, let's go back in,' she says. 'It's too hot to talk.'

We're more like strangers now than sisters, Barbara thinks: it's been too long. Was it a mistake to come here? Jill is asking herself. Am I sorry we came?

* *

Lunch at the *taverna* behind the sea wall is no different from lunch at home at twice the price, as Andoni's mother is always remarking. The same fritters of eggplant and marrow; salad and *feta* cheese and olives; one platter of fried *sardelles* and one of various other fish in a tomato stew. The *retsina,* because drunk in the heat of afternoon, seethes in their stomachs and dazes them. On their plates flies and wasps stumble, drenching themselves among sun-glossed bones and fish heads with white eyes. Listlessly Andoni's mother goes on spoon-feeding Vassilaki, until he baulks and runs off.

'Give the kid a go,' Marcus grumbles.

'It's a mother's duty to forcefeed. I'm falling down on the job. Not a good mother.'

'Stick up for what *you* think. They'll respect you for that.'

'Easy for you, Marco. You don't live here. Vassilaki! Stay in the shade! You'll burn, darling.' Andoni's mother looks sardonic. Vassilaki has climbed into a peeling canoe tied on the sand, and is struggling with the paddles. At last they jerk and thud. He looks up for applause.

'Mamma! Baba! Marco!'

'Bravo! Bravo!' Marcus waves, grinning, and Vassilaki laughs. 'Let's get some more of this piss, will we?' He beckons a waiter dodging by with plates lined up both arms, but the waiter ignores him.

'Let's go home to bed,' Jill says. 'My head's bursting.' It was she who insisted on making the long detour through Greece to Barbara's fishing village. It seemed such a good idea. She sighs.

'Come on. Since when did you take siestas? The house'll be like an oven.'

His gesturings have caught the eye of the *lantziera,* the old kitchen woman, and she stands up scowling anxiously, her short grey hair on end. Every afternoon she sits crouched over a bucket in the shade of the pine trees and peels potato after potato, making potatoes roll and bubble in her cold water. Now she gapes as this bald *Anglos* mouths *'Retsina'* and jabs at the empty bottles. At last, her toothless face showing a slow enlightenment, she stops the waiter for them. Sullenly he brings a bottle and opens it.

'*Kaka*, Mamma.' Vassilaki is calling.

'Is that what I think it is, Pumpkin?'

'Oh damn.'

Vassilaki is squatting in the shadow of the canoe, gazing round at the brown pile he has deposited in the sand. People at other tables, their voices blurring, turn to look. Barbara unsticks her elbows from the plastic tablecloth to hurry down and wipe his bottom. Redfaced, she wraps the soft mass in the tissues and crams it into a waste basket. '*Ochi ekei*,' she scolds. 'Not there, little one. You know that.' He smiles up. She carries him back and sits rocking him. '*Nani*,' she murmurs. 'Sleep.'

'*Oriste*,' booms a proud voice. The old woman has hobbled to their table.

'What's up?'

'She delivered the goods.'

'Did she? So she did. Good on you, *madame*. *Bravo*.' He nods to her, pouting *retsina* into all the glasses except Andoni's mother's; she has her hand over hers. The kitchen woman is tremulous with joy at the word '*madame*'; and now the *Anglos*, before anyone else notices, is pointing to a clean glass and raising his white eyebrows at her over his mirror glasses. She licks her dry lips, and he fills the glass.

'Oh no,' mutters Barbara.

'Snob.'

'I'm not. We'll never get rid of her now.'

'*S'ygeia*,' says the woman. 'Marigoula.'

Marcus cocks his head. 'Cheers,' Barbara explains. 'Her name's Marigoula.'

'Cheers, Marigoula. Bottoms up.' He and Marigoula drink. 'All, all. *Bravo*, Marigoula!'

She puts her empty glass down. '*Xenos einai?*' Giggling, she chooses Jill to ask. Jill shrugs.

'See. They all think *you're* Greek, Jilly.'

'*Nai*,' Andoni's mother suddenly says: yes.

'*Anglos? Germanos?*'

'*Afstralos*,' Barbara says.

'Aah! Xereis kai milas? Bravo!'

'Now what's she on about?' says Marcus.

'Pleased I can speak Greek.'

Families at other tables are watching, amused. Andoni glares at Marigoula, who smiles, raises a knotted arm to expose the wet grey tuft of her armpit, and fingers a curl of Barbara's hair. *'Oraia mallia,'* she croaks. *'San chrysafi. Megalonoun?'*

'My hair. Beautiful, like gold.' Barbara makes a face at Jill. 'I think she's asking if it grows.'

'If it *grows*?'

'She thinks it's fur. She's not the full quid.' To Marigoula she miaows and says, *'Ti nomizeis? Gata eimai ego?'* Do you think I'm a cat? At which Marigoula gives a delighted snort and pokes Barbara's shoulder. Vassilaki stirs and grasps a fistful of hair.

'Mallia,' he murmurs.

'Ta vafeis ta mallia sou, kale?'

'Mi.' Barbara shoves away the heavy cold hand.

'*Now* what?'

'She wants to know if I dye it?'

'God. Do you?'

'Well, sort of. I do use a blonding rinse. Sometimes.' She sees Andoni make an angry grimace at his mother.

Vassilaki wriggles, hot and heavy, his white eyelids flickering.

'Well, say so and be done with it.'

'Say you ate too much pumpkin when you were little,' Jill says.

'She wouldn't get it.'

'Try her. What's "pumpkin"?'

'Kolokithi.'

'Kolokithi — right. "Eater"?'

'Troei poli kolokithi.'

'Troei poli kolokithi,' repeats Jill with a grin. Marigoula's jaw falls and she stares from one sister to the other.

'Don't be so stupid,' Andoni snaps.

'It's just a family joke,' says Jill.

'Not this femily.' He jabs at a soggy slice of fried marrow. 'She think you want — thet.' Marigoula's eyes go round. With the grey nail of her little finger she is picking a scab on her neck; but the blood distracts her only for a moment.

'What? The zucchini?' laughs Jill, patting Barbara's hair.

'Same word.'

'*Kolokithi?*' crows Marigoula. She turns to Andoni's mother, who frowns and looks away. '*Ti leei touti?*' What's she saying?

'Jesus,' moans Marcus, pouring the last of the *retsina*.

'Well, you started it!'

'Right. I'll finish it. What the hell's "yes"?'

'*Nai.*'

'So what's "no"?'

'*Ochi.*'

'Right.' He stands up. '*Nai*,' he says loudly. Marigoula flinches. '*Nai, nai.* Now piss off.' And she totters gasping back to her bucket where she cowers, open-mouthed. 'Right. Everyone had enough? Well, let's go, then.'

They trail behind him up the sullen street with all its shutters tight against the sun. Andoni stalks beside his mother, his fretful little boy swaying on his shoulders, hands clamped in his father's hair. Jill puts an arm round Barbara's shoulders with a grimace of sympathy, but it is too hot to walk far like this. Their clothes are sweaty and prickle them. She lets her arm fall. No one speaks until halfway home Marcus lets Andoni catch him up.

'Game of chess, mate?'

'I want to zleep.'

The shutters of their room are fastened, but the window panes are spread wide open, back against the walls. In one and then the other she sees her dim reflection. A white shape, a clown's bright wig. She kicks off her sandals. Her arms and legs are rough, speckled with sand. The sounds of splashing and little squeals come up from the yard: Marcus and Jill, hosing each other down. Sand goes trickling under her dress.

Andoni is taking his time.

She hovers over a half-eaten bunch of grapes in a bowl of water on the table. The stalk is curled over the last grapes like a scorpion striking, branched legs thrust out. When she touches one black grape, a blowfly she has not seen on the stalk jolts away. She springs back. Sizzling, it blunders here and there against glass, thudding now on to the framed mirror, now on the panes. She pads over to unfasten the shutters and it is like walking on sugar.

Andoni walks in, shuts the door, and lays Vassilaki, washed and dressed and asleep again, on to his white bed. 'Mamma?' he murmurs. Andoni tucks the sheet under his chin.

'Don't open,' Andoni says. 'Is too hot.'

'There's a blowfly. *Vromomyga.*'

'Where is?' Andoni grabs her exercise book, gazes, and slams the heavy fly against the wall. 'I get her.'

'My book!'

The fly's crushed black panels have oozed a cream of eggs on the red cover.

'Sorry.' With a fingernail he flicks it off the book on to the floor. 'It come off. All right?' With a disgusted glare she grabs her book back; he stares back coldly. 'You come to bed?'

'I'm all sandy.'

'Me too. Doesn't matter.'

Their bed is made up with coarse hand-loomed sheets. On a small table beside it, with the necessary cross-stitched cloth, they have a glass of water, the black grapes, a cup full of pens and pencils, the red exercise book with its dark smear, and a folded newspaper, *TA NEA*. But Andoni is not going to read. He is already in bed with nothing on but his dry bathers. She rasps her sandy soles one against the other and slips in beside him. He lies still. Silently she picks up a pencil and her book.

'You *hev* to say you paint your hairs?'

'Why not? Since I do.'

'You hev to say to everybody.'

'Why not?'

'Because thet old woman ask you, you hev to say?'

'Marcus said.'

'You say first.'

'Oh, Andoni. She's simple-minded, poor old Marigoula. What does it matter?'

'Other people listening too. Aren't you shame?'

'No. Sorry. Should I be?'

'You should be proud?'

'Oh, that's enough! Leave me alone, I'm tired.'

'You mek fool yourself,' he says, 'and me too.'

'How come?'

'Womans never paint their hairs here. Not good womans.'

'I've seen plenty who do.'

'No.'

'Let me tell you. Your own sisters in Thessaloniki do. I've seen it in their bathrooms. It's no secret.'

'So?'

'So. Some good womans do.'

'If they do, they shut up about it.'

'Good on them. Why don't *we* do that?'

She turns her back and drags the coarse sheet up over her head, which feels bruised from the wine and heat and unshed tears. Vassilaki cries out once, and sleeps on. She watches Andoni's dark face breathing deeply, until she is sure he is asleep, her copper Andoni; then she creeps out to the balcony. The sun has just swung on to the gold west wall, the row of bedrooms with shutters clamped.

'You tired or what?'

She starts and turns. 'No.'

'You say you are before.'

'I'm not now. I want to catch up on my diary.'

'Tomorrow.' He reaches for her arm, but she moves. 'Come back.'

'No. I never have a free minute. I'm sick of it.'

'Oh. This is new. I see. I see.'

'I really don't *feel* well.'

'Don't give me that shit.'

'I *don't*. Leave me alone!' She has spoken louder than she meant to. Andoni pales. Jill's door opens suddenly and she looks out, puffy and tousled.

'Pumpkin, what's wrong?'

' "Punky"? What is?'

'My old nickname. My — *paratsoukli*.'

'What's for this name?'

'Oh, my hair of course. My bloody hair!' Barbara holds up tassels of it. Another door creaks: Andoni's mother, gazing, shocked. Andoni swings round to Jill.

'Is time you go,' he says. 'You only mek trouble for Varvara and me. First time this happen.'

'They'll stay as long as they like!' Barbara can hardly breathe. 'Jill's my *family*. My flesh and blood!'

'Not mine,' he says. 'I'm the bloody boss here.'

'So *what*!'

'Look, calm down. It's all right.' Jill's voice twangs. 'That's fine with us, Andoni. Is tomorrow morning okay?'

'Is okay.'

'*No!* You only just got here! After all these years and years!'

'It's not working. He's right, it's hopeless. Look, we'll keep writing. Won't we? There'll never be time for a real talk now.'

'Tonight?' Barbara whispers.

'You're *jo*king!'

'Please.'

'I know: come as far as Athens with us! Just for a few days. Oh, come on, you'd love it. You said you'd hardly seen Athens!'

Barbara glances: Andoni's face shows nothing. 'How can I?' she says. 'What about Vassilaki?'

'Vassilaki too, of course.'

'No,' says Andoni. 'Sorry. Not Vassilaki.'

'I think, some other time, Jilly.' Barbara forces a smile.

'You see?' Jill shrugs. 'That's progeny.' She pats Barbara's cheek and without another word goes into her room; they glimpse Marcus's sleeping head, before the door closes. Andoni's mother closes her door. Andoni stares at Barbara with twisted lips. Then he walks into their room and slams the door on himself and the child.

MATRIMONIAL HOME

He rang an hour ago, so his wife is expecting him, or he would turn back. The verandah lamp is on for him, throwing lights and shadows like a fire behind the rainy branches and the black iron fence, and the door is propped half-open. The gate squeals as he shuts it. A black cat sprinkled with rain strolls past him into the house. Not knowing if he should knock or call or go straight in, he dawdles on the verandah. Among the branches gold fruits are hanging. He remembers the persimmon tree and fondles one, cold and glassy and squat, heavier than it looks. And not gold, it was the lamp, but as dark as a ripe apricot.

'Hullo.' Margaret, in shadow by the door.

'Hullo!' He turns with a stiff smile.

'You're wet.'

'*Il pleut doucement sur la ville,*' he recites.

'I know how you hate the rain. Well, come in.'

'I was just admiring the persimmon tree.'

'Yes, it's never had so many. You must take some home with you.'

'Home.'

'Doesn't Sandra like them?'

'I told you. I'm at my sister's.'

'Your sister loves them.' She waits for him to follow her in and latches the door.

'No wonder Annie called it the Persimmon Tree House,' he says, for something to say.

'What did you say?'

'Annie. The Persimmon Tree House.'

A log fire burning gives the sittingroom its only light. In front of it the wet cat sprawls and preens its belly. It makes a smudge of black among flames that the floorboards mirror.

'Oh,' his wife says. 'When she was little. We don't call it that any more,' she adds after a moment.

'Why not?'

'It's the Matrimonial Home these days.'

'I wrote to the solicitors, Marg. I told them to call it off.'

'They wrote, yes.'

'You know I don't want the divorce.'

'It was the marriage you didn't want the last time I saw you. Now it's the divorce. No pleasing you, is there.'

'I wasn't really expecting to be welcomed with open arms.'

'I wouldn't put it past you.' She takes his sodden coat and hangs it up. 'Come and sit down.'

He sinks into the velvet chair that used to be his, spreads his legs out to the fire, lights a cigarette. Blinking scornfully, the cat jumps up and sniffs the seat of the other velvet chair, but his wife pushes it off.

'New cat.' He hates cats. She knows he does.

'He was a consolation present. He has a nasty nature but he's beautiful, or the other way round.' She is babbling. 'Coffee, or wine? You have had dinner?'

'Yes, thanks. Sorry, I meant to bring a bottle.'

'No need. These are yours. There's a chardonnay in the fridge, or there's red. French, or are you tired of French wines? There's some Napa Valley red.'

'The chardonnay, please. I'll open it.'

'No you won't. I will.'

He laughs. 'Why?'

'I can fend for myself. You're my guest. Not that you're not legally entitled to be in the Matrimonial Home, if it comes to that. I assume it won't tonight.'

'Margie, don't.'

'I'm behaving badly.'

'I deserve it.'

He stands by the fire until she comes back and pours green-yellow wine into two glasses.

'Cheers.' He raises his glass.

'Cheers. Well, welcome back. I thought the idea was to stay in America till June.'

'I wound things up earlier. I just had to get back by Easter. I wrote to you about all —'

'Yes, I got it.'

'Oh.'

'I started to answer it but I tore it up. It seemed more sensible to wait and see, considering.'

'Considering?'

'How much your letter didn't say.' A log shifts, covering itself in eddies of flame, and cuts off what she is saying next. For the first time he looks back at her. 'Annie,' she says. 'Our *daughter.* Have you seen her yet?'

'Ah, she met the plane. She didn't tell you?'

'She rang and asked me your flight number. She must have found out somehow. I thought she wanted to stay neutral.'

'Annie? Oh, come on. She's on your side all the way. Never once wavered.'

'Is she?'

'She's *dy*ing to see us back together again.'

'Oh. That's my side? Well, it *was*, of course. Before you turned up in Paris. You and Sandra.'

'I see.' He takes a deep drag of his cigarette, finishes his wine too fast and chokes. He can feel his face reddening. 'Then it's my side she's on.'

'As always. Poor Annie, she's a romantic. So are you, I suppose.'

'I suppose.' He splutters and ducks his head. 'Well, I can do with any help that's going.'

'Thump your back?'

'In a general way, I meant.' He pours more wine.

'We're to live happily ever after, is that the idea?'

'No good?'

'And what about Sandra?'

'All over. Ages ago.'

'Ages?' She is staring into the fire. 'What do you mean, ages? Have you been to her place since you got back?'

'She wasn't there, I just took my things. I think she's going to stay in the States another week or so. She said she might, at the airport. She has a friend she wants to see in Boston.'

'How's her thesis? Finished?'

'Nearly. As far as I know. She was too depressed to work on it much, she said. It has passages of real inspiration.'

'Praise from you, praise indeed. So she saw you off. Is last week *ages* ago?'

'We were under the one roof. Domiciled, is that the word? — under the one roof. Even that was bad enough, after we got back from Paris.'

'Why was that?'

'I told her I'd go home to you. If you'd have me.'

'You didn't tell *me*.'

'She said she'd go whenever I said. She didn't want to go. She wouldn't admit we'd failed. She sat tight and wouldn't be provoked into a quarrel —'

'That's weak.'

'I know. She's a totally passive woman. Dogged and deadpan no matter what you do or say. She won't argue. Won't fight.'

'Weak.'

He nods. 'What I think myself.' Then he catches her eye. 'You're leading me on, aren't you? What am I saying wrong? You're trying to trap me.'

'*You* were weak, that's all. Go on.'

'*I* was? It was a deadlock, we were barely speaking, a disastrous paralysis of the will. I was dying for a showdown and dreading the thought of it. I couldn't throw her out in cold blood, could I? And it dragged on and on.'

'Of course you were sleeping with her.'

'Oh Margie.'

'No right to ask?'

'Of course. Every right.'

He watches her stroke the cat as it winds itself round her ankles. Both, of them are dark-haired and glazed by the firelight, their eyes almost shut.

'Well? Were you?' she says.

'Now and then.'

'You *see*.'

'You don't. She was just there. That's all it was. It didn't mean a thing to me. Even to her in the end, I think. It was even shocking, how little it had come to mean.'

'You'd say that, of course.'

'No credit for owning up to it?'

'How else could she have stayed? Of course you were sleeping together.'

'I'm trying to tell you what happened. The truth, as a matter of fact.'

'Same old story, isn't it? I hope she's over it by now. More likely she's hoping you'll go back to *her*.'

'All I can say,' and he winces at his own pomposity, 'is that I've never given her the slightest reason for hoping that.'

'What will you do?'

'It seems to be out of my hands now.' This is petulance, when resignation is what he's trying for: angrily he gets up and pours more wine. The bottle has lost its jacket of frost and feels warm, but the wine chills his mouth. She sips and sits staring through the quivering wine in her glass at the flurries and pools the fire makes. He lights a cigarette. 'Not smoking?' he says.

'No.' She grins at him. 'I've given up.'

'More willpower than I've got.' He blows out smoke.

'I should hope so.'

'Isn't that the black dress you bought in Paris?'

'That you bought me in Paris.'

'That you finally let me buy you in Paris.'

'*Enfin* — yes. As it happens.'

'You said you'd never wear it again. When we quarrelled in the Brasserie Lipp. You said it had brought you bad luck.'

'I wonder if Sandra wears hers.' But he doesn't follow. 'Whatever you bought *her*, and don't tell me you didn't.'

'To tell the truth, I did —'

'Of course. To restore parity.'

'I did offer to buy her a dress. I'd let slip about yours and she hadn't said anything but I could sense it was on her mind. She turned it down, though.'

'Silly woman.'

He shrugs. 'She'd rather have books, she said. So I never bought her a thing to wear the whole time we were away.'

'Why the triumphant tone?'

'Why? I did buy her *books*. Lots of old Colettes. There we were in our hotel under our two lamps in a dark little room in the rain, reading Colette and blaming our misery on each other.'

'On each other.' That makes her smile.

'And on ourselves.'

'It never changes anything,' she says wearily. 'Let's not talk about it. I used to think about it all the time. You'd kept me in the dark and I'd never know the whole story. But it's so long since —'

'Not so long, is it? You said —'

'It's so long since I cared what your life with Sandra was like. Is it just sour grapes? I don't think so.'

He is staring from a face suddenly still and grey.

'Are you sure of that?' he says at last.

'You think I want to hurt you, get my own back, don't you? It's not that. Why meet at all now, if we won't be honest with each other? Don't look like that. What *can* you have been expecting?'

'Not a life sentence.'

'I'm not the judge. I was the victim. That's how *I* felt on the morning you packed and went to live with Sandra. You had sentenced me to despair. I was left wondering how to live through even one day of it.' She stands, rustling her black dress. 'I'll make coffee.'

Clumsily he stands and puts his arms round her, his head in the hollow of her neck. His hair tickles her. 'Coffee already?' he murmurs.

'Please.' She wipes her eyes. 'Listen to me. You haven't been listening.'

'Is there someone else? Is that it?'

'We're at cross purposes, aren't we? There's no one *else*. There's no one.'

'All our years together. Surely —'

'That was what *I* said. Did it make any impression on you?'

'Of course. It did on Sandra too.'

'You went and told Sandra what I'd said?'

'Only that. She was always bringing it up. "We've been together for twenty-one days," she'd say, "to your twenty-one years with Margaret." Things like that. Darling, is your hair still black? It looks like honey in the firelight.'

He moves strands of her hair in his freckled hands. It is still black, with here and there a glint of white. Like the cat with raindrops on it, he thinks, and strokes her hair.

'No, don't.' She sits down. 'What did *you* say?'

'Not much I could.'

'She was asking for reassurance, or so it sounds.'

'Reassurance! Exactly.' Sitting, he runs both hands through his own greying ginger hair, a new mannerism of his.

'Why not? You were sure enough before.'

'That was before.'

'She didn't come up to expectations.'

He shakes his head.

'Why did you think *I* would? What do I have to gain by a reconciliation now? Except financially, of course. Obviously we both have a vested interest in staying married.'

'That's not why. At least have the fairness to —'

'*How fair were you*?'

'Okay, sorry. You know very well that money has nothing to do with it, though. Don't you?'

'What has?'

'Love?'

'Security?'

'Love and security, fine. Not financial security.'

'Why, though, would I represent security?' She frowns. 'Unless it's because I represent the past. There's nothing so secure as the past, I suppose. We're like crabs that have had to fight their way out of their old shells. We wish we could crawl back into them. We're afraid the new shells won't harden.'

'*What* new shells?' He pours more wine. 'In a sense you are the past, of course. You're the future as well. The only future that makes sense. At present, I'm stranded.'

'Like me. When I got back from Paris —'

'Oh God. You didn't understand. I *had* to go to Paris —'

'I couldn't face coming straight home. I stopped off in London. I was only away six weeks, but you'd have thought it was six months, to look at the house. Of course it was summer here. But the past! Nothing stays safely the way it was. I'm not the same.'

He says nothing, his gaze on the glowing floor, on the cat nodding, rasping one shoulder with its sharp tongue.

There was such a chilliness, a scum of neglect over everything, she could hardly believe it. Dust sticky on all the glass. The lights blurred and strung with cobwebs. In the bath was a dead baby mouse, stuck there by its black tail, its ears curled and its eyes glinting, its body as light and dry as a moth. In a cupboard potatoes had shrivelled and put out white and purple shoots, two of them long and jointed like feelers. It was as if the house was under water and in its recesses silent creatures flickered, crabs, lobsters.

'Even the garden,' she says aloud. 'Weeds and slugs, white spiders in white webs. A crow always grating and swooping, even wasps. Am I imagining this? I thought I might go mad, I was so alone. You were never out of reach before. There were other women, but you lived with *me*, they never lasted. When an affair was over I always knew, you were so sorrowful. Anxious for comfort — reassurance — which you got. And I could comfort myself while you slept with the thought that you were at least *here*, and you couldn't go on betraying me for *ever.* Little enough to look forward to, wouldn't you think? But you're falling harder all the time. You've even left me.'

'Marg. I *wasn't* out of reach.'

'Oh! Not out of reach in America? And before that, all the nonsense about your secret hideaway? Not telling a soul her — *your* — address? Ringing me every few hours from public phones to make sure I hadn't slit my *throat*, for God's sake —'

'I know I behaved irrationally —'

'Confessing and then hurtling out with your bags in that *head*long rush —'

'It was the only way I *could* go —'

'Of course people were very kind. Most people just thought you were overseas as planned, on your study leave. The ones who did know said not to worry. He'll be back, dear. It's only the male menopause. Keep his dinner hot. Here's a lovely kitten for you. It'll be company.'

He grimaces. 'I shaved and showered and got dressed in the

middle of the second night. I was on the point of coming home. She was so devastated I couldn't do it.'

'She got you to leave *me*. It would have served her right.'

'She did and she didn't. She never had much faith in it. God knows, I soon lost mine. It was as if some other clown in my skin had taken over. While I looked on in horror.'

'That lets you out, then.'

'I know it doesn't. I'm trying to explain.'

'Why didn't she have much faith in it?'

'We hardly knew each other, she said. It was too soon.'

'True enough. Four or five months, wasn't it?'

'I knew I'd lose her if I went to America without her. She'd — she wouldn't stay faithful. And I can't share a woman, you know how I feel about that.'

'Did she say she wouldn't?'

'Virtually.'

'If she was at all honest, she must have known — oh, never mind.' She picks up her glass, but it's empty. He tips the last yellow trickle into the glasses.

'She was honest,' he says doubtfully.

'Up to a point, perhaps.'

'Aren't we all.'

'Oho! You're a special case. So's she, if her honesty can handle sneaking off with married men.'

'She never thought I'd leave you. She knew all along that I was letting infatuation carry me away. She was always saying that.'

'How annoying.'

'Oh, it was.' He gives a short laugh. 'Still, since she was right ...'

'How smoothly you say it. I was always saying it too.'

'I know it's unforgivable.'

'It would be, for you. We both know that.' It annoys her that he won't look straight at her. 'I always trusted you absolutely not to leave me. That was *my* security.' She picks up the glasses and the bottle, all empty. 'What's the use? It's getting late. Let's have coffee.'

'Late?' He looks amazed.

'I have a class in the morning.'

Lately, she thinks, I've made a ceremony of going to bed. I turn off the lights and break up the embers in the grate. I consign myself carefully to bed, now that I sleep alone. This is late for me.

She leans close to the kitchen window to make its gold reflections vanish when her shadow touches them. A wet moon lies over the shallow garden. Its light is not moving in the milky puddles: the rain has stopped. She can see scrolls of lilies and a bowed white tree, no taller than she is, its long red branches spilled like hair brushed up from a white nape. The pear tree with its fruits against the whitewashed wall. At the top of a column of spines, one many-branched stalk in midair, clustered with pale bells. She steps back. Now the yellow room settles on the glass again. She fills the copper kettle and lights the gas.

He comes out and puts his arms lightly round her from behind. She stands away stiffly, but he pretends not to notice. 'I let the cat out,' he says. 'Okay?'

'Yes.'

'It wanted to go.' She just shrugs. 'Margie?'

'Mmm?'

'*I* don't. Can't I stay?' He presses his face against her hair, patient. 'For old times' sake. Just for tonight.'

'Just for tonight.'

'I'll go quietly in the morning. Anything you say.'

'Tell me the truth: where *are* you staying?'

'At my sister's. At Sheila's. I told you.'

'I'll ask her.'

'Go ahead and ask her.'

'You didn't exactly rush here. What's the rush now?'

'I've walked past here at least ten times in the last four nights.'

'Why's that? Nostalgia?'

'I don't believe I can live without you.'

'Let's talk some other time. I'm tired.'

'What if you get into bed and I bring the coffee in?'

Shrugging, she goes without a word to undress by the slanted light of the lamp by her bed. She brushes her hair, making it swing and crackle in the mirror. She is a pillar of wax, tufted in three places and melting, dwindling, on her arms and shoulders and yellow hips. Look at my hands, she thinks as she pulls back the covers and slips underneath: like hens' claws. We grow old and none the wiser. She hears him light a match; sigh, as he breathes in smoke. He makes a deft clatter of spoons and cups. He feels at home now. A cigarette in his demurely smiling mouth, he pads in naked, with one hand holding the coffees and an ashtray and with the other cupping himself shyly.

'*Where* are your clothes?'

'By the fire.'

'*Why*?'

'I'm *freezing*. Ow. I'll *drop* something.'

'All right. Get in, then. Come on.'

He shakes the bed and the table beside it, spilling the light of the lamp on his back. He looks like a swimmer in sunny water, spotted with light and faded freckles, reaching for the cups once he is in bed. She smells his sweat, like hay, as she remembers, or like wattle flowers, sweet and yeasty, overripe.

The telephone rings in the kitchen.

'I bet that's Sandra.' She crashes her coffee down and drags her bathrobe over her shoulders. 'If it is, she'll be sorry.'

'It won't be,' he says blandly. 'She wouldn't ring here.'

'Anyone's capable of anything, I'm finding.' She hurries out. He smokes quickly, sipping his coffee; he can just hear her murmuring, then a sudden laugh and the bell as she hangs up.

'Annie,' she says, crawling in next to him. 'Being daughterly.'

'Ah.'

'She did at least try to sound surprised that you're here.'

'Ah, well.' He smiles. 'I may have mentioned —'

'So it would seem. At this time of night, too. I've hardly seen her since I got back from Paris, but she's always ringing up. I told her all about it, of course.' She makes a face.'*Joyeux Noel à Paris*, and there you were on the doorstep. With Sandra in tow.'

'My worst Christmas. Three days of hell.'

'When did you know you *had* to go to Paris? You never told me.'

'When you wrote that *you* were there. I had to see you. Sandra knew, I suppose. She insisted on coming with me.'

'I wouldn't have told you which hotel if I'd imagined you'd do that.'

'Wouldn't you really?' He has finished his coffee already.

She sighs. 'Did you have lots of snow? Back in America?'

'Snow, ice. Everything was white. It wasn't as cold as Paris, though. It never stopped raining, remember?'

'Il pleut sur la ville —'

'Comme il pleure dans mon coeur.'

'I'll never forgive you, you know. Not as long as I live.'

'No, I know. I'll make it up to you.'

'Not the *temps perdu.*'

'Everything.'

There is a book face-down under the lamp on the table. He peers at the title: Colette's *La Naissance du jour.* She is looking away, so he says nothing. At the edge of the golden light, on the dressing table under the mirror, he notices a deep wooden bowl of persimmons from the tree. The tree itself is outside this window, dripping and moving its tangle of shadows slowly on the blind. 'The Matrimonial Home,' he murmurs reproachfully. She says nothing. He puts his cup down and stubs out his cigarette. 'Peel you a persimmon?' he says.

'No!' She smiles. 'They're too messy to eat in bed. Those aren't even ripe, they're sour. They're for looking at.'

'I'd rather look at you.'

'Don't overdo it, now.'

'Me? When I've missed you so unspeakably?' He takes her empty cup and then lies on his back beside her.

'Turn over,' she says, 'and I'll hold you.' She puts her arm along the curly bulk of his thigh and doesn't speak for so long that he thinks she's asleep, her breath warm on his back. Then he hears her murmur, 'You'll only leave me again.'

'I won't.'

'Don't, please.' And her lips warm on his shoulder.

'Darling, I won't.' He hides his exultation. Turning, he lifts her hair and runs his thumb along the damp white skin of her throat, which is like a lily as the songs say, or like a camelia petal, pale and faintly crazed. Her pulse flickers in it. Two red mounds rise on it like nipples where a mosquito must have bitten her. He licks them. 'Asleep?' he whispers. But she makes a long turn and lies on her back, one arm over him, her eyes in shadow, lightly closed.

All the familiar women with their long white throats and breasts, he thinks. Their soft thighs, where they're warmest, and the rough wet hair between.

With a swish and a rattle of blinds the rain starts again.

'*Il pleut*,' she whispers. 'I can't send you out in this.'

'Good.'

'What were you thinking just now?' Her eyes are open now, dark and wet. He kisses them to close them, then kisses her mouth. 'You were remembering *her*,' she says. 'You can tell me the truth.'

It's not really the truth. 'But Marg, I *wasn't*,' he cries out; too despairingly, because he feels her start and recoil. He lights a cigarette. He breathes the smoke in heavily. They move apart in their bed and lie listening to the loud rain.

THE CAPTAIN'S HOUSE

Home, in the five years that Barbara had been married to Andoni Dimitriou, had been one rented house or flat after another. This summer, for the second time, home was the Captain's house, as everyone called it, in a fishing town in Halkidiki not far from Mount Athos.

A two-storey villa in a back street fenced with dusty oleanders, it glowed white in the summer sun and moved its shadow like a cape around it on the rough earth. Spare and shabby, the house of a plain fisherman who owned the town's sole fishing *kaïki*, it had rooms washed in sea colours of white, green, grey, blue. In the upstairs rooms all five Dimitrious slept: the baby in with Andoni and Barbara; three-year-old Vassilaki with his grandmother, whom Barbara called Mamma and thought of as Andoni's Mother. These rooms all had splintered shutters that had warped and floors of grey planks which formed the ceiling of the one long room below. From downstairs, when the lights went on upstairs, each plank glowed, rimmed with gold. It was like looking up from the shallow water under a jetty. In all the ground-floor windows — their ledges painted dark green and so deep-set that Barbara soon took to sitting there and reading in the afternoon when the household slept — branches of oleander and hazelnut made even the light green.

'Always reading, Varvara *mou*,' Andoni's mother chided her.

'I hardly ever get the chance,' said Barbara in her careful Greek. 'I never would, without you here to help me.' Which was true. 'Besides, I keep falling asleep.'

Andoni's mother smiled. 'Always Australian books. You should at least read Greek books.'

'Mamma, I do. More Greek books than Andoni.'

'Well, Andoni doesn't need to.'

Andoni's mother did more than help, she ran the house. There was no refrigerator, so Andoni's mother borrowed from the

Kapetanissa, their landlady, three wire cages to hang from the ceiling to keep food cool and safe. She found a neighbour with a Maltese cow to sell them milk for Vassilaki. She sent Andoni to buy fish alive, and at a discount, from the Kapetanios, when the boats came in at daybreak on wave after wave of faint water. All the melons, tomatoes and cucumbers and peppers, yellow peaches and grapes that the family could want were sold door to door by yelling hawkers with donkey carts and brass-panned scales: no one could haggle like Andoni's mother. She had befriended the Kapetanissa, who was in and out all day with a new-laid egg for Vassilaki, a handful of figs, a cup of gritty honey. They even went to church together.

Voula, the Kapetanissa's unmarried daughter, had taken to the Dimitrious no less eagerly.

'Anyone would think Voula had no home to go to,' Andoni's mother muttered to Barbara as they made lunch.

'Are you tired of her?' Voula's squeals and trills of laughter rang out upstairs, where she was romping with Vassilaki. 'Vassilaki adores her, though.'

'Well. She is a teacher.'

Not that that explained it. How many such sumptuous honey-skinned girls would waste their time on a small boy?

'I suppose she must love children. And she can practise her English on us.' Because Barbara spoke English to Vassilaki, to Andoni's mother's secret annoyance.

'You think that? And you're not jealous? More fool you, then.'

'Why? I want him to be happy.'

'Who, Varvara?'

'Vassilaki. Who else?'

'One way to a man's heart, for what that's worth,' said Andoni's mother drily, 'is through his children.'

'Is it? When I am not so tired,' said Barbara no less drily, 'I must try it.' She chopped an onion savagely.

Andoni's mother shrugged. Typically, Varvara had missed the point. What use were warnings? No, Varvara was so tired!

So when Andoni's brother and his wife burst into the Captain's house during lunch, insisting that they were taking everyone — everyone, yes, Voula too — for a drive to Ouranoupoli in that bright new Fiat parked outside: and Barbara said no, she was so tired ...

'You *go*!' Andoni's mother snapped. '*Ma*, what's wrong with the woman? So *tired*!'

Everyone gaped.

'*Aptokinito*,' gloated Vassilaki. 'Mamma, *aptokinito*.' He loved cars.

'*Affftokinito*,' said Barbara automatically.

Andoni's mother glared. 'With Voula, eight,' she said. 'Eight in one car. Ridiculous. And the car is too hot for the baby, remember the bus trip here? I am more tired,' she told Barbara. 'I will stay and mind the baby.'

'But, Mamma! What about his feeds?'

'I can find a bottle. He can have cow's milk. Once won't hurt him. Varvara, did I raise six of my own to manhood, or did I not?'

'Please, I'd rather stay home.' They had planned to bottle figs that afternoon, she and Andoni's mother and the Kapetanissa.

It was no use arguing. Barbara went: wedged in the back between her sister-in-law and Voula, with Vassilaki on her lap; the brothers sat arguing in the front about Greece and NATO.

They had intended to go no further than Ouranoupoli. It had a bay with boats, shops and *tavernes*, and a medieval tower, gaunt and unsteady, where an Australian woman was said to live: swallows swooped shrilling up and down its walls. But the town beach turned out to be stony and the water turbid green, so they drove on to the end of the road, the border of Mount Athos. Athos, the Holy Mountain, had a border with fences and gates, and a hut with a low wall for the guard. Signs in foreign languages forbade females and wheeled vehicles to enter. Andoni's brother parked here, under pine trees simmering with sun and cicadas. Beyond glittered the sea and a beach of fine white sand like salt, where the only shade was a twisted pinnacle of grey rock here and there, some knee deep in sand, others in water. Barbara hurried Vassilaki to the shelter of the biggest rock to change. Everyone else, tugging bathers on, flinging clothes off, hopping on scorched feet, went thundering straight in with a yell.

'At last,' sighed Barbara, lying in the shallows among the standing rocks with Vassilaki.

The water was so warm, so nearly invisible, it was as if they two were afloat in air. To every hair on their bodies bright bubbles clung, magnified.

A catamaran had anchored just offshore.

'Look at that!' Andoni's brother spat water out.

'Foreigners. All over our best beaches.'

'More foreigners?' called Barbara.

'Not you, Varvara. We brought you.'

Two white heads on brown bodies clambered up on to the catamaran, bronze buttocks glistening.

'Wonderful,' snarled Andoni's brother. 'Germans, I bet. Or Swedes.' The catamaran was souring his joy in his ruby Fiat.

'Who cares?' shouted Andoni. 'Where's the ball?'

'Here!' Voula threw it. 'Catch!'

They plunged deeper. 'Come on, Vassilaki,' called Andoni. 'Come and play ball!'

'Nao! Nao!' he yelled in frantic English.

'Ach, Andoni,' Barbara reproached him.

' "Ach, Andoni," ' whined Andoni. 'Why can't he swim?'

'He's only little.'

'Your face is all red. You're burning.'

'Already?' Barbara's white skin would only ever burn and freckle and peel; no suncream could stop it. Vassilaki burned easily too. 'How much?' But he shrugged, swimming off to the others.

She towed Vassilaki by his hands to the beach: being a boat was a good game. A promise of sandcastles and he let her carry him to the short shadow of their rock. She dragged her dress on, stiff with dry milk. 'Boo!' Down came his oiled shirt over his straw head. 'Now. Sandcastles.'

But: 'Vassila-ki! Vassilaki, *balla*!' echoed across the water. And Andoni was thrashing and wallowing, waving his copper arms at him, tossing the ball. 'Vassilaki!'

'Why I can't swim?' wailed Vassilaki. 'Why, Mamma?'

'We'll go back in soon,' she said.

'Now I want.'

'First let's make a sandcastle. One like this rock.'

'H-how?'

'Watch.'

Crouching at the water line she packed wet sand into a mound first, then squeezed soggy handfuls over it, trickling the sand down like candlewax until there it was: a twisted pinnacle. Vassilaki dug out more wet sand. Joyfully they made another one.

'Look!' He waded in kneedeep to call the others. 'Come and see what I made!'

'Bravo, bravo,' called his father.

Voula splashed out. 'What a clever darling!' She swooped to kiss him.

'Yes.' He was shyly proud.

'Is one for me?'

'They mine,' he said doubtfully. 'Mine and Mamma's.'

'Then I'm going.' Laughing, she ran back in.

'You make some too!' Vassilaki wailed after her. 'Voula *mou*! Voula *mou*.'

'When she comes back.' Barbara hugged him. 'Let's go and sleep under a tree.'

'I thirsty.'

'Come on, then.'

She carried him on her back up the hot sand to the pine trees where the car stood glowing. There was still some water in a bottle glittering on the front seat. He drank, and made a face. She drank too. Then he licked the last hot drops. 'Who that man?' he said.

On the holy side of the border wall a little man in black was fussing about, pulling up a bucket from the well, clicking to his dusty hens, chopping a blood-red watermelon open. Vassilaki trotted over, but the man had gone into the hut. Yawning, Barbara took a woven *kilimi* from the car and spread it on the pine needles.

'Madame!' The man was calling her. *'E, madame*!'

You fanatical old prude, Barbara thought. But no: he was beckoning her. And as she faltered, he grinned and hoisted two fat slices of watermelon up, one in each withered hand.

'Karpouzi!' gloated Vassilaki.

The guard brightened. Never mind their pale hair and sunburn, they were not complete foreigners.

"*Efharisto.*' Barbara bowed, accepting the slices. A bench had been built into the wall on both sides, like a stile: the guard sat there and motioned to them to sit opposite. Vassilaki huddled close, gazing. 'What do you say?' she prompted.

'*Paristo.*' The guard looked as pleased as if he had got it right. Boldly Vassilaki sank his face into the melon. 'Can we see in your house?' he mumbled.

'Sssh, no,' Barbara said. 'Mamma can't.'

'Oh. *Why?*'

'The Panagia said,' smiled the guard. 'The Mother of God. The Holy Mountain is Hers, it is Her garden. No other females can come here.'

Hens can, Barbara thought. Aloud she said, 'I've never believed all that.' The guard blinked. She ploughed on in her stilted Greek. 'Can it be true that the Panagia is jealous and hates other females? What if She wanted the Holy Mountain for females only? But the Church changed it round?'

'Ha ha!' But he was ruffled. 'You tourists. You're all Catholics and Reds and Anarchists. Why don't you stay home? Antichrists!'

'I live in Greece.'

'Since when, *madame*? If I may ask?'

'Six years.'

'*Po po.* Only? You have too much to learn, *madame*. May the Panagia grant you enlightenment.'

Every bite of the melon uncovered seeds sown like stones in snow, thawing red snow. She flicked them out with a finger and bit deep. The guard spat his seeds through a gap in his furred teeth straight at the Fiat: pfoo pfoo. Vassilaki stared; then he tried it. Barbara laughed. At once the guard relented.

'If I may ask.' He gave a dry cackle. 'You come from Italy?'

'No. Greece.' She pointed. 'See. Greek plates.'

'Before six years?'

'Ah yes. Australia.'

'*Ma! Afstraleea!*' As if that explained it. 'Why do you live so far from home?'

'Home is here now.' Home, for now, was the Captain's house.

'My husband is Greek. And our boys. Life is beautiful here.' She stood up. Her head was thumping. 'Well, time for sleep,' she announced.

'Nao! Pfoo!'

'Po po,' frowned the guard, 'Is that how good boys speak to their Mammas? Wash him down first, Mamma,' he said in much the same tone. Red juice was drying on Vassilaki's throat and arms. 'Do you want the bees to eat him? Wait.'

He took the green rinds away and brought a jug of well water. She sluiced Vassilaki down, and then herself. The water made tracks in their coating of salt and sand. With a sigh she settled down with her arms round Vassilaki on the hairy stripes of the *kilimi.*

'Melissa!' Vassilaki cried out: there was a bee, or a wasp. But it floated heavily away, vanished among the pines. 'Will the bees eat me?'

'Not now you're washed.'

'Where are the bees?'

'Asleep.'

'What do they eat?'

'Honey.'

'Mamma, I still thirsty.'

'Oh, darling.'

'I want a drink.'

'There isn't anything. Well water's bad.'

'Moolk.'

'No milk. Only this milk.' She patted her taut breasts.

'That moolk for our baby.'

'He's not here.'

Vassilaki squirmed. 'Nao!' he giggled.

'Have some.' She unbuttoned her dress. 'Just suck like our baby. Don't bite me!'

'Nao!'

'All right, nao. I'm going to sleep.'

She had closed her eyes, dozed off, before she felt him fumble, then firmly close his lips on her nipple. She sighed as her milk let down. Vassilaki recoiled; milk sprayed him. She felt him rub his eyes. But she had not moved, so he came back to the hard nipple and sucked. Languidly she stretched, as if asleep, when the first breast had gone slack, to bring the other one closer. Then they must both have fallen asleep, for when she opened her eyes with a shiver the shadows were longer over them, and cooler, and Vassilaki was in her arms with his back against her. 'Wake up,' she murmured. He moaned, his eyes flickered. No one was in sight, not even the guard, but from the beach came music and voices, laughing: Andoni's hooting laugh, a descant from Voula. 'Wake up.' She nudged him again. He yawned, stretching.

'Want to swim now?'

'Yes!'

'Want to do *tsisia*?' They never called it weewee, always *tsisia.*

'Nao.'

Holding his hand she trudged down the shadow-pitted sand, past the others (there they were, dancing to disco music on the radio), past the sandcastles. The catamaran was fluttering out to sea. '*Addio, varka,*' Vassilaki told it sorrowfully. '*Paei.* Mamma. *Pou paei?*'

'A long way away.'

'*Spiti paei?*'

'Yes. It's going home. Come on.' They surged loudly in, gasping as the cold clutched them. The others called, waved, then chased them in with shrieks and swam into deeper water. Long furrows and flurries followed them. In the low sun the shallows were as warm and golden as creek water.

'Mamma, *tsisia.*'

'Oh. You said no.'

'*Tsisia!*' And the water clouded for a moment about his plump legs. He blushed; his mouth crumpled.

'Darling. It doesn't matter.'

'*Tsisia* in the water?'

'You couldn't help it. It was the watermelon.'

'Why?'

'Just kick it away,' she said. 'No one will know.' Relieved, he kicked and pounded and splashed. It was too much: wading further away, she let her own *tsisia* flow warm between her thighs and dim the water. Airily she backstroked to where Vassilaki was.

'Ooh! Mamma!'

'What?'

'You did *tsisia*!'

'I did not.'

'I saw you.'

'You were too far. It was sand you saw.'

Forcing a smile, she kicked up a cloud of sand in the golden water. But he pouted. He knew she was lying. 'All right, I did *tsisia*,' she said. 'Don't tell anyone.'

'I will!'

'No. Don't.'

Vassilaki's uncle and aunt were calling him from the shore: they had found a crab. Vassilaki plunged away and Barbara made for the deep water at last. If he did tell, how scornful they would be, she thought. Andoni's dowdy placid Australian cow, bony and speckled; oozing milk in her sleep; pissing where she stood ... She splashed in long duck-dives into darker, cooler water and surfaced out of breath alongside Voula and Andoni.

They had not seen her coming. They sprang apart straight away. But Andoni had been holding Voula's arm with such a look on his face — of tender regret, of consolation, of sympathy — that now Barbara knew.

She knew. Voula gasped, whipped her arm free with a mutter of words to Andoni, indistinct words. And Andoni smiled. 'Race you two to the beach,' he sang out, and set off with arms thrashing, half-hidden in froth.

"Ach, Varvara *mou*,' said Voula, rubbing her arm. 'A big jellyfish sting me. You coming?'

Barbara stared in silence as Voula swam in Andoni's wake to the shore, only once stopping to float, her head dipped back to let her hair stream out on the shaken tawny water. You were right, Mamma, Barbara foresaw herself saying at home. But no; how could she? Andoni was wading ashore. He and Voula would go on pretending nothing had happened. Childishly, Barbara felt cheated. As if, just because they were caught, they had to stop playing! Varvara *mou*, Andoni's mother would smile: You think that?

Chilled, she struggled ashore, and flopped down on her towel in sand like warm corn meal. She squeezed her salty eyes shut.

Her breasts were fat white bags again. Why had she come? What if the baby was crying? Had he taken a bottle for Andoni's mother? Maybe he wouldn't. She imagined him crying, hungry: his red and crumpled little face! And Andoni's mother and the Kapetanissa in the green-gold kitchen below, much too busy boiling figs in syrup to hear him cry. If only she had stayed home! Besides, the baby never slept well in the afternoons. Then the sun burned on the upstairs walls of the Captain's house, so that its heavy light filled the rooms with golden slats and with shadows. Even with the shutters closed and the panes wide open there was no movement in the air that lay over the sweat-soaked sheets; only small flies humming in circles.

'You all right?' Andoni spoke behind her in a stifled voice; for the first time all day, in English.

'Me? Yes.' Their shadows joined, long on the sand. The sun was withering. 'It's the baby,' she said.

'My mother look after him.'

He rested his head on the curve of her shoulder: the nearest his pride would let him come to saying sorry.

'Ach, Andoni,' she sighed.

'We be home soon. Before night we be home.'

She lightly kissed his rough hair. Home for long weeks to come was the Captain's house.

OUR LADY OF THE BEEHIVES

1

Barbara, in the dark beside Andoni, felt swollen all over, raw and gritty from the day's sun and salt and sand. Like a hard-boiled egg her body held the heat in. She had dreamt again that some great whining insect, a bee or a wasp, had stung her. In this dream she was asleep on the beach in the noon sun. Waking as the sting pierced her, she was alarmed to see darkness. The harsh slow sound she heard was not waves, but Andoni's breathing.

Vassilaki cried out in his sleep. She got up and knelt with her cheek against his. 'Mamma?' he murmured.

'*Nani*,' she said. 'Go to sleep.' But he was fast asleep.

She sighed. It was too hot to lie awake. Instead she crept into the shadows of the sittingroom, switched on the hard light and tore two pages out of her diary to write a letter to her sister.

> *Dear Jill* (she would address it Poste Restante),
> *I hope you arrived safely and love Athens. We're all fine here. It was great to see you and Marcus. We've just moved into a better house, the Captain's no less, two floors furnished. The bedrooms are upstairs, with homespun sheets and lots of chairs, a table, but the rooms are large and full of heat — bare planks for floors. Downstairs we cook and eat and keep cool. We have a marble-slabbed bench with a sink and a* tap *— running water! — and a portable gas stovetop with two large burners and a little one for the coffee* briki. *(If we run out of gas a neighbour's child will run to the* kafeneion *for* us *and along will come the* kafedjis *with a new bottle on his motor scooter.) The Captain and family have moved next door. His wife has left us plates, cups, glasses, cutlery, pots, pans, baskets ... There's a large round dining table, painted shiny green, and ten rush-bottomed chairs. There are spiky bundles of herbs — mostly* rigani *— hung like birch brooms on the wall, and plaits of onions and garlic, and shrivelled hot red peppers on a string: we are to help ourselves. Her yellow tabby sits on guard day and night.*
>
> *And as if all that were not enough, this house has a lid!*
>
> *Well, it has an indoor staircase, as well as the usual cement outside one:*

an indoor ladder, really, fixed into the floor and leading to a trapdoor set in the planks above. The kapaki, *they call it: the lid. The older houses all have one. It props open on its hinges, or there's a ring in the wall to hook it into, or you can keep it shut — the sensible thing, Andoni's mother says, when there's a child to worry about. The lid looks too heavy for Vassilaki, but it's not, only awkward to lift. Besides, any one of us, being unused to houses with lids, might step into space where floor should be. (She looks on the dark side.) So we don't let Vassilaki go near it. (The Captain's wife agrees.)*

It's like Treasure Island!

For the rest: no bath, but as the Captain said, with the sea so near who needs one in summer? And in an annexe behind the kitchen there's a cubicle with a sit-down toilet, a sewered one, a bucket of water to flush it, and a plastic waste-paper basket for the used paper which we mustn't ever flush, only burn.

As for the washing, we heat water in a sooty pan of the Kapetanissa's, kindling a fire under it in the yard with twigs and brambles, wads of newspaper and (yes) used toilet paper. We wash the clothes in plastic basins and rinse them in the wheelbarrow with the hose ... In short, it's bliss!

I wish you could come and see, but of course you have to get back to London. Tell Marcus the whole town asks after him ('that brother of yours, is it, that Marko') and please write soon.

Much love,
Barbara.

It was not what she had meant to write, but it would have to do. In the yellow glare she flicked over the pages she had written when Vassilaki was a baby. A couple of pages, that was all, in two years. She was always tired.

He lies in my arms (she read).

To sleep he has to suck one fist and clamp the other in my hair, or in his own.

When he cries and I pick him up he sobs, pushing his face into my armpit, like our old cat.

I unwrap his heavy napkin. He has a small pink bag, seamed and ruched, and above it a pink stalk that extends itself and squirts, like some sea creature.

With a grunt he squeezes out mustard, soft lobster mustard.

He presses on the white bags that give him milk, and opens and shuts his vague eyes.

It might be a girl this time, she thought. We can call her Eirini and that will gratify Andoni's mother. Andoni would have to be told soon, when the time was right. It was a wonder he hadn't guessed. He had something on his mind.

When she sank back on the bed in the dark, Andoni took her in his arms and drove fiercely inside her. Neither of them spoke. He was slippery all over. He hissed like a dolphin surfacing, and then subsided. They drifted back into sleep.

Tomorrow, thought Kyria Eirini, waking as the house sighed and crackled in the dark, tomorrow I'll go to the church. To the Panagia of the Beehives. For Varvara's sake.

The Panagia *sta Melissia,* as it was known, was hardly a church at all, compared to the proper one in the town square, Agios Nikolaos, the patron saint of sailors. The Panagia's was little more than a *parekklesi,* a chapel built to honour a promise by the grandfather of the man who kept the bees now. If the Panagia would save his sons in the storm that had wrecked the fishing boats — he stood watching from the hill among the torn acacia trees — he would build Her a chapel, he vowed. He built it in the shape of a bee box, but with a small square tower, and mixed blue in the whitewash to make it the same colour as the hives. The oil lamp before the ikon of the Panagia would never go out, the old mothers of the town made sure of that.

Inside there was a rustling, never pure silence, even when no one was there; and when the lamps were lit for a *litourgeia* an amber light filled it. The candles on sale at the entrance were made of the pale beeswax, and smelled of honey as they burned. An itinerant artist, having covered the walls and ceiling with images of haloed saints, had painted the shawled Panagia Herself with a gilded Child in skirts, in a garden full of lilies and large brown bees.

Kyria Eirini, turning over on her bed in the hot house, told herself to go and light a candle to the Panagia in the morning. Two candles: one for her dead Vassili, whose sins were forgiven; and one to ask Her to do something. And this morning I won't wake Andoni to go and buy fish, I'll let him off. I'll make *imam bayildi* for lunch instead, she thought; and fell asleep again.

The Captain's daughter, Voula, lying awake in her room next

door, saw the gold lozenge of their sittingroom light fall on the balcony, and later disappear. It was Andoni, she thought. 'I love you, Voula, my darling,' she whispered in English, though she had only ever heard Andoni speak Greek. She saw herself on the balcony again, brushing out her hair in swathes, hair smelling of rain water; and Andoni looking on. How could such a man have married a thin ginger-yellow oblivious foreign broomstick of a woman like Barbara?

It was almost as if he were not married at all.

She stood up. Her mother was snoring in the next room. She crept out of the cracking house, past other moon-white houses and along a dusty path fenced with sharp thistles to a beach out of sight of the town. The lights of the *grigri* boats were as small as the stars. She dropped her clothes on the dry sand and padded across the black suede of the wet sand with its cold pools of stars, knotting her hair in a crown as she went, to keep it dry. Then she ran straight into the thick water. The shock of it made her shudder. It was so cold it was as if she had been cut in half. she could neither feel nor see herself below the waist. She bobbed down and quickly up. Her breasts glowed, dropping glints of water. Her feet stung now where thistles had scratched them. Blood pounded in her head.

If she floated, her face lying on the water would be a mirror of the moon. But then she would wet her hair. She would be found out. A moon afloat in black ice.

The heroine of a book she had read swam alone at night. She was a sea-girl too, a fisherman's daughter, the foundling child of a mermaid; and a man watched her, watched Smaragdi in the water. But that was not why, Voula insisted to herself: I love swimming at night and I always have and I always will.

But she knew that this time she was hoping that Andoni, unable to sleep, would sense where she was and follow her.

'Who's there?' she would say, splashing to make a surface of froth to cover her.

'Andoni,' he would say. 'Did I frighten you?'

What would she say? 'No. It's all right.'

'What?' he would falter. He would not be sure.

'A little. But don't go. It's all right.' She moved her cold hands over her breasts. His hands would be dry, warm.

A whimper came from the shore. She stiffened, horrified. On the grey sand a shadow was moving towards her clothes. With a gasp she sank to her nose to hide. She could see a white body, long-legged, white-scarved: no, it was a goat. 'Meh,' it said.

With a snort of alarmed laughter Voula splashed out. '*Fige*,' she hissed, and it stared at her. '*Fige*!' She slapped its burry rump and it trotted off, its frayed rope hopping behind it. Glancing anxiously at shadows, she dragged her clothes on to her wet skin and hurried along the path. Thistles slashed her. The goat, looking back, leaped and was gone. Moonlight lay heavy and white on shuttered walls. Nothing moved. Her shadow was sharp, and at every streetlamp a dim one joined it, grew and dwindled away. It reminded her of the game she played with Vassilaki's shadow when they went to the beach; Andoni's little boy. Her step was light as the shadows falling. No one seeing her out at this time of night would doubt why.

The door creaked, but her mother snored on. She laid herself cool and dry on her bed, and yawned. Bubbles of blood stung on her ankles. The moon was blue stripes on a wall.

A loud door creaked, waking Barbara, but no other sound followed. The house creaked a lot as the night cooled. She lay and thought that the air in the room was like coal in a fire, black and steadily smouldering. It would be good to walk through the grey dust of the streets now. The boats would be converging out at sea, gathering in the net. *Savridia*, she thought; *kefalopoula, marides, barbounia, fagri, sardelles*. She knew more fish in Greek than in English. It would be good to wade into cold black water flickering with fish. But there would be a scandal if anyone saw her. Besides, she was tired.

With a sigh she turned her soaked body over. A donkey sobbed, a goat gave a sudden meh-eh-eh. Soon the roosters would wake. Soon Andoni's mother would knock on the door and call Andoni to go and buy fish, unless she slept in. Soon Vassilaki would wake, waking them all.

She closed her eyes and slept.

2

Voula met Andoni coming out of the water with his speargun and flippers, pushing his mask up on to his rough hair. 'Hullo, did you catch any?' she said.

'No. None there.'

'Bad luck.'

'You're looking very beautiful today.'

'I look very beautiful every day.'

'Is that so?'

She only smiled and swung away, ruffling the surface. That he was watching her made her aware of all her colours and shapes intensified in the morning sea. In a few minutes he waded back in and floated and swam lazily some metres away. But neither of them spoke again.

This morning as usual Barbara had clothes and napkins to wash, soaking in a basin on the back *taratsa*. She wrung them out and with a grunt hurled the dirty water into the vegetable garden. Hens skittered. She poured powder and hot clean water on the clothes and pumped and kneaded them. There were ripe grapes already in the vine above her head, and flies crowded in them. The morning sun shone through grapes and leaves; she looked on the ground for green reflections, as if they were made of glass; but the shadows were black. They were sharp in the still light. Strange, thought Barbara, brushing sweat off her eyebrows, how shadows look sharper on a still day, as if a wind would blur air as it blurs water. Bubbles catching the sun in her basins of clothes were like white opals.

Kyria Eirini swept the leaves and hens' droppings off the dry earth of the yard with a straw broom with no handle, then rinsed and wrung out the clothes with Barbara and helped her hang them out. Then she went in to tidy up. When she opened the shutters and panes to air the rooms, the sun fell in thickly and whatever was inside glowed, furred with gold. No matter how often she dusted, more dust drifted in and settled. At least it's fresh dust, thought Kyria Eirini. Insects buzzed in and out.

She was glad when Barbara and Vassilaki went to the beach at last, to the same spot as always, so she knew where to find them.

She would rather stay and be alone in the Kapetanissa's kitchen. She boiled rice in milk and honey to make *rizogalo*, stirred it and poured it on to plates to cool before she tapped cinnamon over its tightening lumpy skin. Andoni and Vassilaki loved her *rizogalo*. She sliced doughy eggplants and salted them, sliced onions and garlic and tomatoes. She breathed in the smell as the olive oil smoked in her hot pans. 'God be praised,' she muttered. 'Everything we need, He gives us.' She slid slices of eggplant in so that the oil frothed over them.

Barbara came to life only in the sea. Her speckled body glowed, magnified, and made its green gestures metres above her shadow on the sea floor. Pebbles were suddenly large then small as the water moved. She dived to grasp one. A bird must feel like this, she thought as she dived and twisted, gasped, the bubbles pounding in her ears: a bird flying in rain. When she came up a white net of light enfolded her lazily.

When she came out of the water she lay on a towel with another towel over her back to keep off the sun. Dazed, she watched the sea. Whenever she blinked she saw a flare of red; then the green sea, then the red flare again, as regular as a lighthouse lamp.

Kyria Eirini bent over her eggplants arranged like small black boats in the pan, ladling the filling of onions and tomatoes more carefully than usual into each one: the pan would be on show in the baker's oven. Barbara would be annoyed with her for struggling down the hot road to the bakery with it, when they could have had something easy for lunch. The thought of Barbara's annoyance was almost as pleasant as the thought of how Andoni would carry the pan home, sucking his fingers coppery with oil when he arrived because he had picked at it on the way.

So she struggled, hot in her black clothes, down the road to the baker's, exchanging greetings as she went. She pointed out to the baker exactly where she wanted her pan, and he told her that he knew his oven as he knew his own hand. She bought a hot white loaf and went on to the Melissia to light a candle to the Panagia, which was after all the real reason she was there.

The church was stuffy and dim, with a rosemary smell of old burnt incense. The glazed faces of the saints stared. Kyria Eirini crossed herself and slipped her drachmas into the box for two candles. One she stuck in the tray of sand, for the dead; one in the iron bracket, for the living. The Panagia held her dwarfish Christ to one blue shoulder, her hollow eyes stern.

'It's not for myself,' she thought to the ikon. 'It's for my daughter-in-law. The Australian one. Fool though she is. *Aman.* Has she no pride? Enlighten her, help her, I pray. And the girl too, save her from temptation. Andoni is turning out just like his father was, whose sins are forgiven.'

As she was leaving, a bee settled on her sleeve. She shook it off. It hovered. 'Xout!' she said. They blundered together out into the sunlight.

At home she wrapped the bread in a cloth. Her dress was stuck to her. She swilled cold water from a bucket over the speckled kitchen floor to wash it. Its stones came to life, all their colours, like shingle on a sea floor. The cat that came with the house, and spent the mornings dozing under the table, sprang up on a chair and spat at her. 'Xout!' spat Kyria Eirini. The cat fled to the window sill and hunched there with a brazen scowl.

When Andoni walked in, Kyria Eirini was scrubbing spots out of the washing before Barbara got home. She started and looked guilty. 'You're home early,' she said.

'I said I'd buy the bread.'

'I bought it.'

'Why? When I told you I'd go!'

'I wanted to light a candle. It was on my way. I took a pan *of imam bayildi* as well. You can get that if you like.'

'*Aman*, Mamma! You could just as easily cook it here.'

'Yes, but you like it better baked.'

'Not when it's so much more work.'

'But since it's better?'

'Tiring yourself out for nothing. It's madness.'

Andoni's reaction was all she could have hoped.

'Kyria Eirini?' came Voula's voice at the gate. Still in her bathing suit, she was hugging a pile of striped *kilimia.* 'We thought — my mother and I thought — do you need more blankets at night?'

'Ach.' Flustered, Kyria Eirini waved her soapy hands. 'Thank you. That's very kind.'

'I'll leave them upstairs, will I?'

'Yes, there's a good girl. Thank you.'

Voula, padding into the dark kitchen, ran into Andoni before she saw him, he was so dark himself.

'Careful.' He climbed up ahead to hold the *kapaki* open.

Voula laughed. 'I grew up in this house.'

'All the same.'

'My father fell through once. He was drunk at the time.'

'Didn't you ever fall through?'

'I wasn't allowed to go near it.'

'So you never did?' He followed her and shut the trapdoor.

'No, I was a good girl.'

'Was. And now you're not.'

'Is that what you think, is it?'

'I'm hoping to find out. How old are you?'

She blushed. 'Old enough.' No, this was going too far: she looked round for something safe to remark on, and saw waxy lilies in a vase of her mother's. 'Pretty,' she said.

'Take one.' He lifted one out, its cuffed stalk dripping.

'Oh, no.' She stepped back. 'Are they from Kyria Magda?'

'Why not? Some old woman with whiskers gave them to your mother. Her goat got out and ate half your mother's beans last night, haven't you heard? You will. You're getting a bucket of milk too. Your mother hates them, she says, so here they are.' He nodded the lily at her. 'Take it, come on.'

'They make her sneeze,' she explained.

'Too big to wear.' He held it up to her hair. 'Pity.'

'How can I take it? It would look — I can't.'

With a stare he dropped the lily out the window. Shocked, Voula ran into the sittingroom with the *kilimia*. He climbed back down to wait, letting the *kapaki* slam shut. But Voula left the house, trembling, by the outside stairs.

Andoni trudged off to the bakery.

3

It was a relief when lunch was over. Barbara and Andoni assured

Kyria Eirini that the *imam bayildi* was delicious. But the baker had burnt one edge of it, and besides she thought there was just a little too much salt. They didn't think so. Vassilaki refused to eat any and filled up on all the *rizogalo.*

The washing was dry by then, hooked on the barbed wire fence among the speckled pods, green and red, of the Kapetanissa's climbing beans. Drops of water, falling from their bathers, rolled and were coated with dust. A shirt and a napkin had fallen on to the red earth. They would have to be washed all over again. Barbara sighed. Nothing seemed to dry without its earth or rust or bird stain.

The Kapetanissa had green onions and garlic growing as well as beans, and eggplants with leaves like torn felt, and cucumbers, potatoes, tomatoes, wilting melon vines. Her hens and the rooster had squeezed through the wire and were scratching and jabbing among the watered roots. Brown papery birds, murmuring to themselves, their eyes half-closed. Weary of summer.

Vassilaki had seen them too. He ran in by the gate to chase them out, but they pranced loudly into hiding. 'Xout!' he shouted.

'Vassilaki?' She had folded the clothes and was up to the napkins now. 'Where are you?' He came padding out. She pulled the wire over the gatepost. He was holding a long funnel-shaped pale flower.

'*Kitta,* Mamma,' he said. 'Look.' His mother had different words for everything.

'Mm. It's a lily. Where was it?' she said. Then: 'Put it down quick. Quick! There's a bee in it.'

So there was, when he looked. A bee with brown fur was crouched, its legs twitching, in the buttery glow at the bottom of his lily.

'Why?'

'It wants that yellow dust, see? On those little horns? It wants to make honey. *Meli.* Put it down now.'

'Why?'

'It might bite.'

'Why?' He held it out at arm's length.

'It might think you want to hurt it.'

'Nao,' he told it.

'Just put it down.'

'*Echo melissa,*' he called over the fence to the Kapetanissa and Voula, who had come out to see why the hens were squawking, and were packing the earth back round the roots with their sandalled feet.

'Careful, she bite you!' Voula called back, but softly in case she woke the neighbours.

'*Ela,* Voula!'

'Put it *down,* Vassilaki!'

He dropped his lily. The bee flew out, made a faltering circle and then was lost among the oleanders.

'*Paei,*' he sighed.

'Yes. It's gone.'

'*Paei spiti?*'

'Yes, it's gone home.'

'*Poundo spiti?*'

'In a bee box. On the hill near the church.' He looked puzzled. '*Konda stin ekklesia.*'

'Why?'

'*Paei na kanei meli,*' smiled Voula, shading her eyes. She followed her mother inside.

'Mamma?'

'Yes. It's gone to make honey.'

'*Einai kakia.*'

'Who's bad? Voula?'

'Bee.'

'No, it's not, it's good — *kali.* But you have to leave it alone. You can pick up the lily now it's gone.'

'Nao.' They left it lying there.

He went ahead of her up the outside stairs — the wall was too hot to touch — and through the empty sittingroom behind the balcony. He had gone when she came up with the washing. '*Pou eisai?*' she whispered. 'Keep away from the *kapaki.*' When there was no answer she looked in the bedroom: only Andoni, asleep. She found Vassilaki in the next room, on his back on the bed beside the black heap that was his grandmother. His eyelids fluttered as she kissed his cheek; he brushed the kiss away with a loose hand. His hair was damp. *'Nani,'* she whispered. He was already asleep. The room burned with a buttery glow like that inside the lily.

The floor creaked as she crept in, her soles rasped the planks, but Andoni stayed asleep, as if stunned, his mouth open. He had thrown the sheet off. He glistened, brown all over and shadowed with black hairs, barred as well with shadows that fell from the window over him. She lay down beside him in her dress: they would all be getting up soon. The rough cotton was stuck to her. Her breasts ached. Andoni muttered something indistinct. She sighed, hearing a mosquito whine. Our four bodies in the house, she thought, four bubbles of blood, and a fifth still forming, afloat on our white beds. A hollow light seeped through the shutters. Time and the sun stood still.

4

When they awoke, the women always brought coffee and glasses of water up to the balcony. Andoni read the newspapers there. The shadows grew longer almost as they watched, until the street was filled with them. Sometimes a sea breeze rose: the *batis.* Ach, *o batis*, people would say to each other with relief. Sometimes — especially when there was no sea breeze — the family went back to the beach for a late swim, in water warmer and brighter, tawny-shadowed and full of reflections different from its morning ones. Then the sun shrank, spilling its last light along the hoods of the waves.

This afternoon there was no sea breeze.

'Will you drink a little coffee?' And Barbara woke with a start. Kyria Eirini's grey head was at the door. 'Sorry, Varvara. Were you asleep? Vassilaki's awake.'

'Oh, not just yet, Mamma, thank you.'

'Well, whenever you like.' She closed the door. Barbara lay blinking in the hot stillness. There was a crushed hollow beside her; she had not heard Andoni go. Her wrists and ankles itched and had red lumps all over them. She found a mosquito on the dim wall, slapped it, and was trying to wipe off the red smear with spit when the door opened again.

'Varvara, sorry. Vassilaki wants to go to the beach. Ach, not a mosquito? I sprayed too.'

'One. Look at me.'

'It's your sweet blood, you see. Vassilaki is insisting. Can you see any more?' They both peered up. 'No, it was just that one, Varvara *mou*.'

Vassilaki was insisting. '*Thalassa, thalassa, thalassa*,' he chanted.

'We were there all morning,' Barbara moaned.

'*Thalassa pame*, Mamma!'

'Mamma *nani*,' reproached his grandmother, stopping him in the doorway.

'Let his father take him,' Barbara said.

'He go to buy newspaper,' came Voula's voice in English. 'I take him, if you like.'

'Voula, would you? Come in.'

Voula came to the doorway, a coffee cup in her hand, with the other hand gathering her hair at her nape then letting it flow free. Vassilaki pushed past her: 'Mamma!' Kyria Eirini made an apologetic face at Barbara and plucked at his shirt. '*Mi*, Yiayia? And he shook her hand off.

'Come with me today?' Voula squatted beside him.

'*Pou*?'

'*Sti thalassa*?'

'Mamma?'

'Mamma *nani*.'

He faltered, scowling, but finally took her hand. They went downstairs to the shadowed garden to get a towel from the wire fence and find his bucket and spade. Then they came hand in hand out into the yellow evening. When he started to drag his feet, Voula dodged to make her shadow cover his, and he laughed, remembering how she always played the shadow game; and she remembered the moonlit streetlamps. 'What! You have no shadow!' she said.

'I have so!' He made his shadow escape and caper ahead.

'You have not!' Hers pounced on it again. 'You see? Where it is?'

'There!'

Families sitting on balconies looked on smiling.

Going past Kyria Magda's Voula saw from the comer of her eye that the ivory-necked lilies had gone from the pots on the *taratsa.* The white goat, tied to a post, fixed its slit brass eyes on Voula and said, 'Meh-eh.'

'Meh-eh. Meh-eh,' said Vassilaki. '*Alogaki*?' If it was a horse, then he could ride it.

'*Katsika einai,*' explained Voula, not knowing the English word. '*Echei gala.*'

'*Pou*?'

She pointed to the pink bag bouncing between the stiff hind legs; Vassilaki stooped to look, and giggled. Kyria Magda, screeching hullo, staggered across the yard with a bucket of water. 'All right then, drink, you little whore': and the goat, in its thirst, plunged its chin and ears deep, and sneezed, rearing. 'Run away, will you?' said Kyria Magda, her hands on her hips. 'I'll teach you. Yes, I'll teach her,' she told the watchers; a sour smile crossed her face.

'*Kakia yiayia,*' said Vassilaki when they were well past.

All the way to the beach Voula let him keep ahead of her with his shadow, making little rushes forward whenever he flagged, so that they arrived sweaty and out of breath. She dipped herself in the water, no more, not wanting to take her eyes off him for a moment; though he always paddled in the shallows and if he did stray further out there was a sandbank. Waistdeep, he was filling his bucket with water and spilling it on his head. It splashed all round him and sent ripples flickering up. From his hair, darker and flatter now, bright drops went on falling.

'Ooh! *Kitta,* Voula!'

She sprang to her feet. '*Ti*?'

'*Kitta! Psarakia!*'

'*Pou*?'

'*Na*!' He pointed. There were the little fish, when she looked, first like silver needles, then like black ones. He sank his bucket in bubbles to the bottom to catch them. She lay down again, resting on her elbows. In the distance the boats were tied to the pier. A small one was pulled up on the sand nearby with an octopus spread to dry over its lamps, swarming with wasps. No one else had come down to the beach. I am beautiful, Voula decided; but he's not here to see. Over the sandbank the water was a honeycomb, a golden net. Vassilaki was intent. Now with his bucket, now with his spread hands, he bent to catch fish. '*Psarakia*?' he pleaded. '*Psarakia*?'

They stayed until the sun turned the long shoals red.

Andoni, hunched over a newspaper, saw them coming home along the street, its dark patches not only shadow now but wet dust where the shopkeepers had hosed it. At the other end of the balcony his mother and the Kapetanissa sat making lace with crochet hooks, each of them ignoring her own quick fingers to covertly watch the other's.

'When it's wet it smells like coffee,' remarked Kyria Eirini. 'The earth, I mean.'

'Here comes Vassilaki,' said Andoni.

'Ach, good!' She swung round. 'Yes, here they are!' Sounding too relieved, she knew: the Kapetanissa bridled. Did they think the child might not have been safe with her Voula, did they? She raised her heavy brows.

'Are they late, perhaps?'

'No! Not at all!' They were laughing, licking icecreams. 'Look, she bought icecreams.' Kyria Eirini made her voice soothing. 'She gets on so well with him, doesn't she?'

The Kapetanissa was not satisfied. Andoni picked a sprig of basil from the nearest pot, rubbed it and sniffed at the green mash his fingers made. His mother waved to Voula and Vassilaki, who waved back.

'I noticed yesterday what a beautiful swimmer she is,' Kyria Eirini went on, making it clear that of course he had been in good hands. 'May we not cast the Evil Eye on her,' she added, as custom demanded after praise, and pretended to spit. The Kapetanissa smiled at her, appeased.

'Yes, she's a genuine mermaid. Everyone says so.'

'Who's a mermaid?' Barbara called lazily from inside, having caught the one word *gorgona*.

'Voula. They're home,' answered Andoni's mother.

'Oh, good.' Barbara went on reading. She knew she was a better swimmer than Voula any day.

Vassilaki's chest had pink trickles on it where icecream had dripped through the soggy tip of the cone faster than he could suck it. Voula flapped the towel — it had lumps of wet sand on it — and hung it on the fence. 'Have a wash?' she said, and pulled the slack hose through from the garden. Vassilaki loved the first wash, the sun-warmed water in the hose. He pulled his shorts open and squeezed his eyes shut waiting for the silver water to come coiling over him. When it did he gave a yell. Voula stooped down to swill the sand and the icecream off him. But the water was running cold now and he squirmed away, giggling as if it tickled.

'Come here.' She was giggling too.

'Nao!'

'There is sand on you!'

'Nao!'

Neither of them had heard any buzzing or seen a wasp or a bee hanging, its wings rippling the air. But now Voula felt a searing stab in her thigh. She screamed with pain and shock.

'*Ti*?' shrieked Vassilaki.

Voula was slapping at her thigh, staring round wildly. Whatever it was fell twitching in a puddle. She bent over it: impossible to tell now if it was a wasp or a bee. She crushed it with her hard heel.

'*Melissa*!' Vassilaki shrieked again. He peered at the crushed shell. Was it his bee? Would it dart up and sting him next? A hen jabbed and took it, spraying mud on him as she skipped away. '*Paei*!' yelled Vassilaki. 'Voula *mou*!'

But this was not his Voula, cupping her stung thigh, her face red and twisted. Vassilaki stared. This was not his Voula. He stumbled into the kitchen. No one. 'Mamma *mou*! Mamma!' He bolted up the wooden steps and raised the trapdoor.

'Vassilaki!' screamed his mother's voice. He swung around in bewilderment — where was she? — and the trapdoor fell shut with a thud above him, jamming his fingers. He screamed loudly, lost his balance and tumbled down the steps on to the floor.

5

At first everyone had thought that the screams they heard were part of the game with the garden hose. Now they all came running. Barbara scrambled through the trapdoor and down the steps to pick Vassilaki up. She sat on the cold floor of the kitchen holding him against her. For long moments he held his mouth open in a silent roar, turning dark red. Then at last sobs and tears burst out. 'Oh, oh, oh,' moaned Barbara in the Greek way that always soothed him best, rocking with each 'oh'.

'*Ponaei*!' he wailed.

'Oh, oh, *poulaki mou*,' she murmured helplessly.

Andoni crouched over him and ran his hands over the wet quivering little body, the yellow mat of hair. There was a lump there and blood seeping; grey splinters showed in the plump flesh of his arms and legs; but no bones were broken. Red tangles were printed on Barbara's dress where he had laid his head.

'What happened?' said Andoni.

'The *kapaki*. He fell downstairs.'

'I know that.'

'*Ponaei*!' Vassilaki touched his head and shrieked when he saw blood on his hands.

'Oh, don't cry, no, no. It'll be better soon.' She kissed his hair.

'*Melissa*, Mamma,' he snuffled.

They looked, but there was no sign of a bee sting.

'*Ma pou, poulaki mou*?'

'*Ti* Voula.' He pointed.

Voula, her face swollen with crying and as red as his, was standing in her bathing suit at the kitchen doorway. 'A *melissa* bite me and he frighten,' she said. 'And he hurt his self. The *kapaki* fall on him.' Her thigh bulged with a lump as big as a tennis ball: she had found the barb in it.

'Luckily he's not badly hurt,' said Kyria Eirini.

'He got a fright. I'm sorry,' Voula explained gratefully, because Kyria Eirini spoke no English. With a gasp of pain she squatted on her heels to face Barbara. 'It happen so quick!' she said tearfully; and met with shock a bitter relentless glare from Andoni.

'*Kakia* Voula!' Vassilaki hid his face.

'No, no, no,' said Barbara.

'But it was an accident,' said Kyria Eirini to everyone. 'These things happen. They can happen to anyone.'

The Kapetanissa gave her a grateful look. She had warned

them about the *kapaki*, but this was not the time to say so; and besides she blamed all such accidents on the Evil Eye, but she could hardly say that either. Instead she hustled Voula home to take out the barb and dab vinegar on the sting, at the same time questioning her at length. Voula burst into more sobs: Andoni had blamed her without a word. She blamed herself, she told her mother, who stoutly told her she was being stupid. It was the Evil Eye, it was written, it was the will of God; she crossed herself.

'Yes, but they all hate me now,' said Voula.

Vassilaki, his sobs dwindling to sniffles and hiccups, was still clamped fast to Barbara on the floor. '*Ponaei*,' he whimpered now and then, when she tried to move; but it was clear that he wasn't badly hurt. When his grandmother knelt beside them with a bowl of milky antiseptic and a tuft of cotton wool, he knew what was coming: '*Ochi! Ochi! Ochi*!' he wailed, wriggling.

'Ach, *poulaki mou*.' His grandmother's eyes watered.

'I'll do it,' said Andoni.

'*Ochi*! Nao!'

'Vassilaki! Vassilaki *mou*!' His grandmother snapped on the light and ran up the steps, calling. He peered, blinking in the yellow glare, from behind his wet fists. '*Da da*!' she shouted, and punched the trapdoor. '*Da da to kapaki! Da! Da! Da*!'

Vassilaki gave a wheezy laugh. '*Da da pali*, Yiayia!' he commanded; so she beat it again, and again, until her arms ached and he decided that the *kapaki* was punished enough. And by then Andoni had swabbed the blood away.

As soon as Vassilaki was asleep Andoni inspected his head with a bright torch he had found, parting the damp tufts.

'He's all right. Really,' Barbara said.

'He could get delayed concussion,' muttered Andoni.

'I don't think so.'

'It's your job to look after him. Why did you leave it to Voula?'

'She offered. Vassilaki wanted her to take him.'

'He could have been killed.'

'It was an accident. It could have happened to anyone.'

'Did you call him to go up that way?'

'No, of course not!' Barbara jumped up.

'But you called him.'

'That was after he lifted it up.'

'I hope that's true.'

'I don't tell lies, Andoni.'

'You don't do anything much any more, do you?'

'No? Do you know why? I'm tired.'

'Tired!' He turned away.

'Tired, yes. Because I'm pregnant.'

It was some time before he turned to her; the torch in his hand threw winged shadows. He stood staring.

'You're not pleased.'

'Yes, I am. Yes. Are you sure? When will it be?'

'Mid-January, I think.'

'Does Mamma know yet?'

'Most likely.'

He smiled at that.

'He's sleeping normally,' she said. 'He really will be all right.'

'I might just go for a walk, then. Just down to the *kafeneion* for a while, I'll burst if I stay here.' He bent over Vassilaki, then handed her the torch and went down into the street. From the balcony she watched him appear under each streetlamp, and disappear again.

After searching all over the sittingroom, she found her diary under a pile of *kilimia*, striped red and green and black, which she didn't remember having seen before; and took out the two pages of her letter to her sister. She had more to tell her. A moth flapped at the torch, its shadow rocking the gold walls.

> *P.S. Jilly, I'm pregnant. I was going to tell you when you were here, but somehow it never seemed to be the right time. They will wish me* kali eleftheria *when I tell them: it means* good freedom *— by which they mean* good *(easy)* birth.
>
> *Be happy,*
> *B.*

As they did every night, Voula and the Kapetanissa watched the boats get ready to go out in a jumble of nets and crates and lamps. Half the town was wandering along the waterfront and up and down the pier by then, dressed in their best for the *volta.* The streets were very dark now, except under the lights: people tripped over stones and tree roots. The sea held its oyster colours of yellow and grey longer, even when the *kaïki* and its little boats were chugging across to the fishing grounds, lamps strung in a row over the ringed wakes.

Later they sat with the families of the crew sharing bottles of beer and ouzo and plates of *mezedes* at the *kafeneion.* Moths fell against them. Often there was no other sound but the thump of the hurtling powdery moths. At every table children insisted, to the men's satisfaction, on sipping the froth from every glass of beer; soon they fell asleep in their mother's laps. Cats yowled under the chairs. Their fur twitching, they would put a calm paw on top of a cricket, then let it limp free, then cover it again. Their eyes flashed green. Beyond the yellow edges of the lamplight more crickets started creaking under the pines. Out at sea the boats gathered under a milky dome of colder light. A gull cried out; then another.

Voula, standing to pass her aunt a plate of *kalamari,* suddenly saw Andoni on the beach. But he looked away and walked on into the dark.

'Wasn't that your tenant? What's his name?' her aunt asked, munching loudly.

'No. I don't think so,' Voula said. She longed to be alone. Her stung thigh throbbed.

There were no lights on next door, when Voula and the Kapetanissa came home. They went straight to bed. The house was too hot for sleep, and held its heat and silence the whole night.

In the next room Vassilaki said in English a word like a bell, but woke only his grandmother. She could see the slatted moon from where she lay. There will be dew, she thought, by morning, and the houses will look like blocks of *feta* straight out of the brine, until the moon sets. At dawn they will be blue. I must wake Andoni to buy fish, she decided, because once the moon is full the boats know better than to go out with their little lamps. For a week we'll be without fish.

It was too hot to sleep, and besides she was no longer sleepy, having gone to bed earlier than usual when Barbara did. They had sat in the light of an amber lamp in the kitchen and eaten cold what was left of the *imam bayildi,* just the two of them mopping their plates with bread and talking quietly, almost secretively. They felt fonder of each other than they had for a long time, and they both knew this, and so were shy with each other. She thought of asking Barbara if she might be pregnant, but it was not the right time yet. When Vassilaki woke tousled and grizzling, they soothed and dandled him. They spoonfed him an egg that she soft-boiled in the coffee *briki* and on which Barbara drew a naughty face, a little Vassilaki. His pallor was gone. He sipped the egg greedily and then ate some bread with grainy honey and a peach like a yellow rose that she had saved for him. She wanted to read Barbara a prayer from the *Theia Litourgeia,* but the lamplight, heavy with moths and beetles, was making her eyes sore. They are like fish in a yellow sea, Barbara said, waving insects away. They carried Vassilaki, fast asleep, up the outside stairs to bed. She heard Andoni come up soon after.

For all she knew, good might have come of the child's fall, since Andoni blamed the girl for it; though who knew how long the good would last or what harm might come of it? In any case, it was not how she would have gone about it. The child hurt, the girl stung, the bee dead. A bee had come blundering into the sun out of the Panagia *sta Melissia.* Was it that bee? Was a bee's life of so little account to the Panagia, that she sent it to die? Thy will be done: she crossed herself. It's not for me to say. Maybe our lives are of no more account than a bee's, if the truth be known.

She must nail up the *kapaki* in the morning.

Out in the night a click of hoofs and a faint 'meh' made her sigh. There was a goat loose again. It must have come for the rest of the Kapetanissa's climbing beans; it would finish the lot off tonight, no doubt, and the Kapetanissa would talk of nothing else tomorrow. How did the Garden of Eden ever survive with goats in it? Goats eat every green shoot that pokes up. They're a ruin, goats are, though the milk makes up for it.

Is that bee alive now in the next world, she wondered; and is there honey there? Water, and milk and eggs, bread and wine? Shall we all have other forms, or none and be made of air? We boil wheat with sugar to make the *kollyva* for the dead; but it's only we, the living, who eat it. Or so it seems. For us of this world, at least. it tastes good, salty and sweet together. Like sardines fried in sweet green oil; or watermelon with a slab of briny *feta*, or any dry cheese; honey on rough bread; grapes, rich heavy muscat grapes, dipped in the sea to wash them.

Pain is like salt, in a way, she thought; it can make the sweetness stronger, unless there's too much of it. Pain and sorrow and loss.

There was too much salt in the *imam bayildi* today. Never mind. Well.

My poor Vassili, whose sins are forgiven: that was a salty old joke he loved to tell, the one about honey. Only a man could have made that joke up. A man might even believe it, who knows?

A gypsy (he put on a wheedling voice) came to an old widow, I forget why, and said, 'What is your wish, my lady? I can give you one of two things. A fine young man to marry, or a pot of honey. Just tell me which you want.'

'Now what sort of a choice do you call that?' (And he cackled like an old widow.) 'I couldn't eat the honey, could I? There's not a tooth in my head, is there?' (At which he laughed angrily as if he knew all about old widows, and disliked what he knew.)

She breathed deeply of the shuttered air, cooler now with the dew towards daybreak, and pulled the rough sheet up over her folded throat. In the next world may we all be young again, she fell asleep wishing. All of us young and at peace by the sea for ever.

A MAN IN THE LAUNDRETTE

She never wants to disturb him but she has to sometimes, as this room in which he studies and writes and reads is the only way in and out of his apartment. Now that he has got up to make coffee in the kitchen, though, she can put on her boots and coat and rummage in the wardrobe for the glossy black garbage bag where they keep their dirty clothes, and not be disturbing him. 'I'll only be an hour or two,' she says quickly when he comes back in. She holds up the bag to show why.

'Are you sure?' His eyebrows lift. 'It must be my turn by now.' They were scrupulous about such matters when she first moved in.

'I'm sure. I must get out more. Meet the people.' She shrugs at his stare. 'I want to see what I can of life in the States, after all.'

'Not to be with me.'

She smiles. 'Of course to be with you. You know that.'

'I thought you had a story you wanted to finish.'

'I had. It's finished. You know you don't have time to go, and I like going.'

He stands there unsmiling, holding the two mugs. 'I made you a coffee,' he says.

'Thanks.' She perches on the bed and drinks little scalding sips while, turned in his chair, he stares out at the sky.

His window is above the street and on brighter afternoons than this it catches the whole heavy sun as it goes down. He always works in front of the window but facing the wall, a dark profile.

He says, 'Look how dark it's getting.'

'It's just clouds,' she says. 'It's only a little after three.'

'Still. Why today? Saturday.'

'Why not? That's your last shirt.'

'It's mostly my clothes, I suppose.' It always is. She washes hers in the bathroom basin and hangs them on the pipes. He has never said that this bothers him; but then she has never asked. He shrugs. 'You don't know your way round too well. That's all.'

'I do! Enough for the laundrette.'

'Well. Okay. You've got Fred's number?'

She nods. Fred, who lives on the floor above, has the only telephone in the building and is sick of having to fetch his neighbours to take calls. She rang Fred's number once. She gets up without finishing her coffee.

'Okay. Take care.' He settles at the table with his back turned to her and to the door and to his bed in which she sleeps at night even now, lying with the arm that shades her eyes chilled and stiff, sallowed by the lamp, while he works late. Sighing, he switches this lamp on now and holds his coffee up to it in both hands, watching the steam fray.

Quietly she shuts the door.

The apartment houses have lamps on already under their green awnings. They are old three-storey brick mansions, red ivy shawling them. Old elms all the way along his street are golden-leaved and full of quick squirrels: the air is bright with leaves falling. The few clumps that were left this morning of the first snow of the season have all dripped away now. As she comes down the stoop a cold wind throws leaves over her, drops of rain as sharp as snow prickle her face. The wind shuffles her and her clumsy bag around the corner, under the viaduct, down block after weedy block of the patched bare roadway. The laundrette seems further away than it should be. Has she lost her way? No, there it is at last on the next corner: D.K.'s Bar and Laundrette. With a shudder, slamming the glass door behind her, she seals herself in the warm steam and rumble, and looks round.

There are more people here than ever before. Saturday would be a busy day, she should have known that. Everywhere solemn grey-haired black couples are sitting in silence side by side, their hands folded. Four small black girls with pigtails and ribbons erect on their furrowed scalps give her gap-toothed smiles. A scowling fat white woman is the only other white. All the washers are going. Worse, the coins in her pocket turn out not to be quarters but Australian coins, useless. All she has in US currency is a couple of dollar notes. There is a hatch for change with a buzzer in one wall, opening, she remembers, into a back room of the bar; but no one answers it when she presses the buzzer. Too shy to ask anyone there for the change, she hurries out to ask in D.K.'s Bar instead. In the dark room into which she falters, wind-whipped, her own head meets her afloat among lamps in mirrors. Eyes in smoky booths turn and stare. She waits, fingering her dollar notes, but no one goes behind the bar. She creeps out again. The wind shoves her into the laundrette.

This time she keeps on pressing and pressing the buzzer until a voice bawls, 'Aw, *shit*,' and the hatch thuds open on the usual surly old Irishman in his grey hat.

'Hul*lo*!' Her voice sounds too bright. 'I thought you weren't *here*!' She hands him her two dollars.

'Always here.' He flicks his cigarette. 'Big fight's on cable.' A roar from the TV set and he jerks away, slapping down her eight quarters, slamming the hatch.

She is in luck. A washer has just been emptied and no one else is claiming it. Red-faced, she tips her clothes in. Once she has got the washer churning she sits on a chair nearby with her garbage bag, fumbling in it for her writing pad and pen. She always writes in the laundrette.

> *She never wants to disturb him,* she scrawls on a new page, *but she has to sometimes, as this room in which he studies and writes and reads is the only way in and out of his apartment.*

A side door opens for a moment on to the layered smoke of the bar. A young black man, hefty in a padded jacket, lurches out almost on top of her and stands swaying. His stained white jeans come closer each time to her bent head. She edges away.

> *Now that he has got up to make coffee in the kitchen, though, she can put on her boots and coat and rummage in the wardrobe for the glossy black garbage bag where they keep their dirty clothes, and not be disturbing him.*

'Pretty handwriting,' purrs a voice in her ear. When she stares up, he smiles. Under his moustache he has front teeth missing, and one eyetooth is a furred brown stump. 'What's *that* say?' A pale fingernail taps her pad.

'Uh, nothing.'

'*Show* me.' He flaps the pad over. Its cover is a photograph of the white-hooded Opera House. 'Sydney, Australia,' he spells out. 'You from Australia?'

'Yes.'

'Stayin' long?'

'Just visiting.'

'I *said* are you stayin' *long*?'

'No.'

'Don' like the U-nited States?'

She shrugs. 'It's time I went home.'

'Home to Australia. Well now. My teacher were from Australia, my music teacher. She were a nice Australian lady. She got me into the Yale School of Music.' He waits.

'That's good.' She gives him a brief smile, hunching over her writing pad.

'I'll only be an hour or two,' she says quickly when he comes back in. She holds up the bag to show why.

'Are you sure?' His eyebrows lift. 'It must be my turn by now.'

'What you writin'?'

'A story.'

'Story, huh? I write songs. I'm a musician. I was four years at the Yale School of Music. That's *good*, is it?' He thrusts his face close to hers and she smells rotting teeth and fumes of something — bourbon, perhaps, or rum. So that's what it is: he is drunk. He has a bunched brown paper bag with a bottle in it, which he unscrews with difficulty and wags at her. 'Have some.' She shakes her head. Shrugging, he throws his head back to swallow, chokes and splutters on the floor. He wipes his lips on the back of his hand, glaring round. Everyone is carefully not looking. One small black girl snorts and they all fall into giggles. He bows to them.

'I work in a piana bar. You listenin', hey *you*, I ain' talkin' to myself.' She looks up. 'That's *better.* My mother and father own it so you wanna hear me sing I get you in for free. Hey, you wanna hear me sing or don't you?' She nods. 'All *right*.' What he sings in a slow, hoarse tremolo sounds like a spiritual, though the few words she picks up make no sense. The black girls writhe. The couples sitting in front of the dryers exchange an unwilling smile and shake of the head.

'You like that, huh?' She nods. 'She *like* that. Now I sing you all another little number I wrote. I write all my own numbers and I call this little number *Calypso Blues*.' Then he sings more, as far as she can tell, of the same song.

They were scrupulous about such matters when she first moved in.
'I'm sure. I must get out more. Meet the people.' She shrugs at his stare. 'I want to see what I can of life in the States, after all.'

'Like that one? My mother and father — *hey* — they real rich peoples, ain' just the piana bar, they got three houses. Trucks. Boats too. I don' go along with that shit. Ownin' things, makin' money, that's all shit. What you say your name was? Hey, *you*. You hear me talkin' to you?'

'Uh, Anne,' she lies, her head bowed.

'Pretty.' He leans over to finger her hair. 'Long yeller hair. Real ... pretty.'

'Don't.'

' "I want to see what I can of life in the States after" — after *what*?'

'*All*.' She crams the pad into her garbage bag.

'You sha' or somethin'?'

'What?'

'You sha'? You deaf or somethin'? You *shacked*?'

'Oh! Shacked? Shacked — yes, I am. Yes.' She keeps glancing at the door. The first few times that it was her turn to do the laundry he came along anyway after a while, smiling self-consciously, whispering, 'I missed you.' But not today, she knows. She stares at somebody's clothes flapping and soaring in a dryer. She could take hers home wet, though they would be heavy: but then this man might follow her home.

'So where you live?'

'Never mind,' she mutters.

'What's that?'

'I don't *know*. Oh, down the road.'

'Well, you can tell me.'

'No, I'd — I don't *know* its name.'

'I just wanna talk to you — *Anne*. I just wanna be friends. You don' wanna be friends, that what you sayin'? You think I got somethin' nasty in my mind, well I think *you* do.' He snorts. 'My lady she a white lady like you an' let me tell *you* you ain' nothin' alongside of her. *You* ain' *nothin'*.'

She stares down. He prods her arm. 'Don't,' she says.

'Don' what?'

'Just don't.'

'Hear me, bitch?'

'Don't talk to me like that.'

'Oh, don' talk to you like that? I wanna talk to you, I talk to you how I like, don't you order *me* roun' tell me how I can talk to you.' He jabs his fist at her shoulder then holds it against her ear. 'Go on, look out the door. Expectin' somebody?'

'My friend's coming.'

'Huh. She expectin' *her friend*.' The couples look back gravely. 'My brothers they all gangsters,' he shouts, 'an' one word from me gets anybody I *want* killed. We gonna kill them *all*.' He is sweaty and shaking now. 'We gonna kill them and dig them up and kill them all *over* again. Trouble with you, Miss Australia, you don' like the black peoples, that's trouble with you. Well we gonna kill you *all*.' He drinks and gasps, licking his lips.

The door opens. She jumps up. With a whoop the wind pushes in two Puerto Rican couples with garbage bags. Leaves and papers come rattling over the floor to her feet. One of the Puerto Ricans buzzes and knocks at the hatch for change, but no one opens it; in the end they pool what quarters they find in their pockets, start their washers and sit in a quiet row on a table. Her machine has stopped now. There is a dryer free. She throws the tangled clothes in, twists two quarters in the slot and sits hunched on another chair to wait.

He has lost her. He spits into the corner, staggering, wiping his sweat with a sleeve, then begs a cigarette from the sullen white woman, who turns scornfully away without a word. 'Bitch,' he growls: a jet of spit just misses her boot. One of the Puerto Ricans offers him an open pack. Mumbling, he picks one, gets it lit, splutters it out and squats shakily to pick it up out of his splash of spit. He sucks smoke in, sighs it out. Staring round, he finds her again and stumbles over. 'Where you get to?' He coughs smoke in her face. His bottle is empty: not a drop comes out when he tips it up over his mouth. 'God*dam*,' he wails, and lets it drop on the floor, where it smashes. 'Goddam mothers, you all givin' me *shit*!'

'No one doin' that,' mutters a wrinkled black man.

He has swaggered up close, his fly almost touching her forehead. *'Don't,'* she says despairingly.

'Don't, don't. Why not? I like you, Miss Australia.' He gives a wide grin. 'Gotta go next door for a minute. Wanna come? No? Okay. Don' nobody bother her now. Don' nobody interfere. She *my* lady.'

He stumbles to the side door and opens it on a darkness slashed with red mirrors. Once the door shuts the black couples slump and sigh. One old woman hustles the little black girls out on to the street. An old man leans forward and says, 'He your friend, miss?'

'No! I've never seen him before.'

The old man and his wife roll their eyes, their faces netting with anxious wrinkles. 'You better watch out,' he says.

'What if he follows me home?'

They nod. 'He a load of trouble, that boy. Oh, his poor mother.'

'Maybe he'll stay in there and won't come back.' she says.

'Best thing is you call a cab, go on home. They got a pay phone here.'

'Oh, *where*?'

'In the bar.'

'Where!'

The side door slams open, then shut, and they all sit back guiltily. She huddles, not looking round. Her clothes float down in the dryer, so she opens it and stoops into the hot dark barrel to pick them out, tangled still and clinging to each other. Suddenly he is bending over her, his hands braced on the wall above the dryer, his belly thrust hard against her back. She twists angrily out from under him, clutching hot shirts.

'Now stop that! That's enough!'

'Not for me it ain', not yet.'

'Leave me alone!'

'I wanna talk. Wanna talk to you.'

'No! Go away!' She crams the clothes into her garbage bag.

'Hey, you not well, man,' mumbles the old black. 'Better go on home now. Go on home.'

'Who you, man, you gonna tell *me* what to do?' He throws a wide punch and falls to the floor. With a shriek of rage and terror the old woman runs to the side door and pounds on it. It slaps open, just missing her, and two white men tumble in.

'Okay,' one grunts. 'What's trouble here?'

'Where you *been*? You supposed to keep *order*!' she wails, and the old man hushes her. The young man is on his knees, shaking his frizzy head with both his hands.

With gestures of horrified embarrassment to everyone she sees watching her, she swings the glass door open on to the dim street. A man has followed her: one of the two Puerto Ricans. 'Is okay. I see you safe home,' he says, and slings her bag over his shoulder.

'Oh, thank you! But your wife's still in there.'

'My brother is there.' He takes her arm, almost dragging her away.

'He was so drunk,' she says. 'What made him act like that. I mean, why me?'

His fine black hair flaps in the wind. 'You didn't handle him right,' he says.

'What's *right*?'

'You dunno. Everybody see that. Just whatever you did, you got the guy mad, you know?'

They are far enough away to risk looking back. He is out on the road, his body arched, yelling at three white men: the old Irishman in the hat has joined the other two and they are barring his way at the door of the laundrette. There is something of forbearance, even of compunction, in their stance. 'They'll leave him alone, won't they?' she asks.

He nods. 'Looks like they know him.'

He has seen her all the way to the corner before she can persuade him, thanking him fervently, that she can look after herself from here on. He stands guard in the wind, his white face uneasily smiling whenever she turns to grin and wave him on. The wind thrashes her along their street. In the west the clouds are fraying, letting a glint of light through, but the streetlamps are coming on already with a milky fluttering, bluish-white, among the gold tossings of the elms.

A squirrel on their fence fixes one black resentful eye on her: it whirls and stands erect, its hands folded and its muzzle twitching, until abruptly it darts away, stops once to look back, and the silver spray of its tail follows it up an elm.

The lamp is on in his window — none of the windows in these streets has curtains — and he is still in front of it, a shadow. She fumbles with her key. Rushing in, she disturbs him.

'Am I late? Sorry! There was this terrible man in the laundrette.' Panting, she leans against the dim wall to tell him the story. Halfway through she sees that his face is stiff and grey.

'You're thinking I brought it on myself.'

'Didn't you?'

'By going out, you mean? By not wanting to be rude?' He stares. 'No, you wouldn't. What did I do that was wrong?'

'A man can always tell if a woman fancies him.'

'Infallibly?' He shrugs. 'I led him on, is that what you mean?'

'Didn't you?'

'Why would I?'

'You can't seem to help it.'

'Why do you think that?'

'I've seen you in action.'

'*When*?'

'Whenever you talk to a man, it's there.'

'This is sick,' she says. He shakes his head. 'Well, *what's* there?' But he turns back without a word to the lamplit papers on his table.

Shivering, she folds his shirts on the wooden settle in the passage, hangs up his trousers, pairs his socks. Her few things she drops into her suitcase, open on the floor of the wardrobe; she has never properly unpacked. Now she never will. There is no light in this passage, at one end of which is his hood of yellow lamplight and at the other the twin yellow bubbles of hers, wastefully left on while she was out. The tall windows behind her lamps are nailed shut. A crack in one glitters like a blade. Wasps dying of the cold have nested in the shaggy corners. In the panes, as in those of his window, only a greyness like still water is left of the day.

But set at eye level in the wall of the passage where she is standing with her garbage bag is a strip of window overgrown with ivy, one small casement of which she creeps up at night from his bed to prise open, and he later to close: and here a slant of sun strikes. Leaves all the colours of fire flicker and tap the glass.

'Look. You'd think it was stained glass, wouldn't you? Look,' she is suddenly saying aloud. 'I'll never forget this window.'

He could be a statue or the shadow of one, a hard edge to the lamplight. He gives no sign of having heard.

Wasps are slithering, whining over her window panes. One comes bumbling in hesitant orbits round her head. It has yellow legs and rasps across her papers jerking its long ringed belly. She slaps it with a newspaper and sweeps it on to the floor, afraid to touch it in case a dead wasp can still sting, if you touch the sting. Then she sits down at the table under the lamps with her writing pad and pen and scrawls on, though her hand, she sees, is shaking.

'Not to be with me.'

She smiles. 'Of course to be with you. You know that.'

'I thought you had a story you wanted to finish.'

'I had. It's finished.'

A WOMAN WITH BLACK HAIR

Her front door locks, but not her back door. Like the doors on many houses in her suburb, they are panelled and stained old pine ones, doors solid enough for a fortress: but the back one opens with a push straight into her wooden kitchen. Moonlight coats in icy shapes and shadows the floor and walls which I know to be golden pine, knotted and scuffed, having seen them in sunlight and cloudlight as often as I have needed to; having seen them lamplit too, cut into small gold pictures by the wooden frames of the window, thirty small panes, while I stood unseen on the back verandah. (The lampshades are lacy baskets and sway in draughts, rocking the room as if it were a ship's cabin and the light off waves at sunset or sunrise washed lacily inside it. Trails like smoke wavering their shadows over the ceiling are not smoke, but cobwebs blowing loose.) These autumn nights she has a log fire burning, and another in her front room just beyond. With the lights all off, the embers shine like glass. They fill the house all night with a warm breath of fire.

An old clock over the kitchen fire chimes the hours. One. Two.

Off the passage from her front room is a wooden staircase. Her two small daughters sleep upstairs, soundly all night. Beyond the staircase a thick door is left half-open: this is her room. In its white walls the three thin windows are slits of green light by day, their curtains of red velvet drawn apart like lips. There is a fireplace, never used; hardly any furniture. A worn rug, one cane armchair, a desk with a lamp stooped over books and papers (children's essays and poems drawn over in coloured pencil, marked in red ink); old books on dark shelves; a bed with a puffed red quilt where she sleeps. Alone, her hair lying in black ripples on the pillow.

For me a woman has to have black hair.

This one's hair is long and she is richly fleshed, the colour of warm milk with honey. Her eyes are thick-lidded: I have never been sure what colour they are. (She is mostly reading when I can watch her.) They seem now pale, now dark, as if they changed like water. On fine mornings she lies and reads the paper on the cane sofa under her shaggy green grapevine. She is out a lot during the day. She and the children eat dinner by the kitchen fire — her glass of wine glitters and throws red reflections — and then watch television for an hour or two in the front room. After the children go up to bed, she sits on and reads until long past midnight, the lamplight shifting over her. Some evenings visitors come — couples, the children's father but no one stays the night. And she has a dog: an aged blond labrador, half-blind, that grins and dribbles when it hears me coming and nuzzles for the steak I bring. It has lolloped after me in and around the house, its tail sweeping and its nails clicking on the boards. It spends the night on the back verandah, snoring and farting in its sleep.

The little girls — I think the smaller is five or six, the other not more than two years older — have blond hair tied high in a sheaf, like pampas grass. (The father is also blond.)

Tonight, though the moon is nearly full, it is misted over. I may not even really need the black silk balaclava, stitched in red, that I bought for these visits, though I am wearing it anyway, since it has become part of the ritual. I am stripped to a slit black tracksuit — slit because it had no fly — from which I unpicked all the labels. I have the knife safe in its sheath, and my regular tracksuit folded in my haversack ready for my morning jog when I leave the house.

Tonight when the clock chimed one she turned all the lights out. When it chimed two I came in, sat by the breathing fire, and waited. There is no hurry. I nibble one by one the small brown grapes I picked, throwing the skins and the wet pips into its flames of glass, making them hiss. Nothing moves in the house.

When the clock chimes three I creep into her room — one curtain is half-open, as it always has been — to stand watching the puddle of dimness that is her pillow; the dark hair over it.

I saw her once out in the sun untangling her wet hair with her fingers. It flowed over her face and over her naked shoulders like heavy dark water over sandstone. The grass around her was all shafts of green light, each leaf of clover held light. There were clambering bees.

There is a creek a couple of streets down the hill from here. I wish I could take her there. It reminds me of a creek I used to fish in when I was a boy. There were round speckled rocks swathed with green-yellow silky weed, like so many wet blond heads combed by the fingers of the water. (My hair was — is still — blond.) I used to wish I could live a water life and leave my human one: I would live in the creek and be speckled, weedy-haired, never coming out except in rain. I lay on the bank in spools and flutters of water light. A maternal ant dragged a seed over my foot; a dragon-fly hung in the blurred air; a small dusty lizard propped, tilted its head to take me in, and hid in the grass under my shadow.

Over the weeks since I found this woman I have given her hints, clues, signs that she has been chosen. First I took her white nightgown — old ivory satin, not white, but paler than her skin — and pulled it on and lay in her bed one day. It smelled of hair and roses. I left it torn at the seams on the sofa under the grapevine that shades her back verandah. I suppose she found it that night and was puzzled, perhaps alarmed, but thought the dog had done it; anyone might think so. Another day I left an ivory rose, edged with red, in a bowl on her kitchen table. She picked it up, surprised, and put it in a glass of water. She accused her daughters of picking it, I could tell from where I was standing by the kitchen window (though of course what she was saying was inaudible), and they shook their heads. Their denials made her angry; the older girl burst into loud sobs. Another frilled rose was waiting on the pillow in the room with the three red-lipped windows. I wonder what she made of that. They looked as if they were crumpled up then dipped in blood.

I drop a hint now: I sit down in the cane armchair, which creaks, and utter a soft sigh. Her breathing stops. She is transfixed. When it starts again, it is almost as slow as it was when she was asleep, but deeper: in spite of her efforts, harsher. Her heart shudders. For long minutes I take care not to let my breathing overlap hers; I keep to her rhythm. She does not dare to stop breathing for a moment to listen, warning whoever is there, if anyone is, that she is awake. And at last — the kitchen clock chimes four — she starts to fall asleep again, having made herself believe what she must believe. There is no one there, the noise was outside, it was a dream, she is only being silly.

I make the chair creak again.

She breathes sharply, softly now, and with a moan as if in her sleep — this is how she hopes to deceive whoever is there, because someone is, someone *is* — she turns slowly over to lie and face the chair. Her eyes are all shadow. Certainly she opens them now, staring until they water, those eyes the colours of water. But I am too deep in the dark for her to see me: too far from the grey glow at the only tall window with its curtains left apart.

This time it takes longer for her to convince herself that there is nothing here to be afraid of. I wait until I hear her breathing slow down. Then, as lightly as the drizzle that is just starting to hiss in the tree by her window, I let her hear me breathing faster.

'Who is it?' she whispers. They all whisper.

'Quiet.' I kneel by her head with the grey knife out.

'Please.'

'Quiet.'

The clock chimes. We both jump like rabbits. One. Two. Three. Four. Five. I hold the knife to her throat and watch her eyes sink and her mouth gape open. Terror makes her face a skull. 'Going to keep quiet?' I whisper, and she makes a clicking in her throat and nods a little, as much as she dares to move. 'Yes or no?'

She clicks.

'It's sharp. Watch this.' I slice off a lock of her black hair and stuff it in my pocket. 'Well?'

Click.

'*Well*?'

'Yesss.'

When I hold her head clear of the quilt by her hair and stroke the knife down the side of her throat, black drops swell along the line it makes, like buds on a twig.

'Good. We wouldn't want to wake the girls up, would we?' I say. I let that sink in, let her imagine those two little girls running in moonlit gowns to snap on the light in the doorway. Then I say their names. That really makes the pulse thump in her throat. 'They *won't* wake up, will they?'

'No,' she whispers.

'Good.'

I press my lips on hers. My mouth tastes of the grapes I ate by her still fire, both our mouths slither and taste of the brown sweet grapes. I keep my tight grip of my knife and her hair. She has to stay humble. I am still the master.

'I love you,' I say. Her tongue touches mine. 'I want you.' Terror stiffens and swells in her at that. 'Say it,' I say.

'I — love you,' she whispers. I wait. 'I — want you.'

Now there is not another minute to wait. I throw the quilt off and lift her nightgown. She moves her heavy thighs and the slit nest above them of curled black hair. There is a hot smell of roses and summer grasses. I lie on top of her. 'Put it in,' I say, and she slips me in as a child's mouth takes the nipple. 'Move,' I say. She makes a jerky thrust. 'No, no. Make it nice.' Her eyes twitch; panting, she rocks and sways under me.

I have to close her labouring mouth with my hand now; in case the knife at her throat slips, I put it by her head on the pillow (its steel not cold, as hot as we are), and it makes a smear where the frilled rose was. Her nightgown tears over her breasts, black strands of her hair scrawl in red over the smooth mounds of them, warm wet breasts that I drink. Is this the nightgown? Yes. Yes. Then we are throbbing and convulsing and our blood beats like waves crashing on waves.

None of these women ever says to me, How is your little grub enjoying itself? Is it in yet? Are you sure? Can it feel anything? Oh, well, that's all right. Mind if I go back to sleep now? No, move, I say, and they move. Move nicely. Now keep still. And they do.

'Now keep still,' I say, picking up the knife again. She lies rigid. The clatter of the first train tells me it is time. Day is breaking. Already the grey light in the window is too strong to be still moonlight, and the dark tree has started to shrink, though not yet to be green and brown. 'I have to go. I'll come again,' I say as I get up. She nods. 'You want me to. Don't you.' She nods, her eyes on the hand with the knife.

I never will. I never do. Once is all I want. At night she will lie awake thinking I will come to her again. Just as she thinks I might cut her throat and not just slit the skin; and so I might. But their death is not part of the ritual. The knife is like a lion-tamer's whip: the threat is enough. Of course if the threat fails, I will have to kill her. She, for that matter, would turn the knife on me if she could. Chance would then make her a killer. Chance, which has made me the man I am, might yet make me a killer: I squat stroking the knife.

'Well, say it,' I say.

'Yes.'

'You won't call the police.' She shakes her head. 'Or will you? Of course you will.' My smile cracks a glaze of blood and spittle around my mouth. In the grey mass on the pillow I watch her eyes roll, bloodshot, bruised, still colourless. 'I want you to wait, though. I know: wait till the bird hits the window.' A bird flies at her window every morning. I see her realise that I even know that; I see her thinking, Oh God, what doesn't he know? 'That's if you love your little girls.' Her eyes writhe. 'You do, don't you. Anyone would.' Girls with hair like pampas grass. 'So you will wait, won't you.' She nods. 'Well?'

'Yes.'

Her coils of dark hair are ropy with her sweat and her red slobber, and so is her torn gown, the torn ivory gown that I put on once, that she never even bothered to mend. A puddle of yellow haloes her on the sheet. She is nothing but a cringing sack of stained skin, this black-haired woman who for weeks has been an idol that I worshipped, my life's centre. The knowledge that I have got of her just sickens me now. Let them get a good look at what their mother really is — what women all are — today when they come running down to breakfast, her little girls in their sunlit gowns. 'You slut,' I say, and rip her rags off her. 'You foul slut.' Just having to gag her, turn her and tie her wrists behind her and then tie her ankles together makes me want to retch aloud. Having to touch her. But I stop myself. Turning her over to face the wall, I pull the quilt up over the nakedness and the stink of her. I wipe my face and hands, drop the knife and the balaclava into my haversack, and get dressed quickly.

The dark rooms smell of ash. Light glows in their panes, red glass in their fireplaces. The heavy door closes with a jolt. I break off a bunch of brown grapes with the gloss of the rain still on them. The dog snuffles. Blinking one eye, it bats its sleepy tail once or twice on the verandah.

I have made a study of how to lose myself in these hushed suburban mornings. (The drizzle stopped long ago. Now a loose mist is rising in tufts, and the rolled clouds are bright-rimmed.) I am as much at home in her suburb as I am in her house, or in my own for that matter, though I will never go near the house or the suburb, or the woman, again. (I will find other women in other houses and suburbs when the time comes. Move, I will say, and they will move. Move nicely. They will. Keep still. Then they will keep still.) And when the sirens whoop out, as of course they will soon, I will be out of the way. I will wash myself clean.

I am a solitary jogger over yellow leaves on the echoing footpaths. No one sees me. I cram the grapes in my haversack for later.

I know that soon after sunrise every morning a small brown bird dashes itself like brown bunched grapes, like clodded earth, at the bare window of her room, the one with its red curtains agape. Again and again it launches itself from a twig that is still shaking when the bird has fallen into the long dry grass and is panting there unseen, gathering its strength for another dash. (The garden slopes away under her room: no one can stand and look in at her window.) It thuds in a brown flurry on to its own image shaken in the glass. It startled me, in the garden the first morning. I think of her half-waking, those other mornings, thinking, It's the bird, as the brown mass thudded and fell and fluttered up to clutch at the twig again: thinking, Only the bird, and turning over slowly into her safe sleep.

But she is awake this morning. She is awake thinking, Oh God, the bird, when will the bird? Twisting to free her hands and turn over: Please, the bird. Her shoulders and her breasts and throat are all ravelled with red lace. Her hair falling over them is like dark water.

SAINT KAY'S DAY

How warm even a cold white room became when you turned on the light! Any light would do the trick. Candlelight was best of all, though, with its little shadowy fires. And a room that faced the sunset was like a cave behind a waterfall, when you lit candles in it and made shadows arch their wings like bats on its walls and ceiling. With the shutters closed you could be anywhere in the world. With them open, you were in Greece: over the balcony rail was Mount Olympus, printed indigo on the hot sky, and all the still gulf in between had little boats pulling threads in the silk of it. What did it matter if the room that faced the sunset was the only room you had, except of course for a narrow kitchen, and a dark bathroom no bigger than a telephone box? (And if little pale celluloid cockroaches scurried into the air vent whenever you switched the light on in that bathroom.) Even if the power did keep failing. And her flat was small and dark and so icy — and this was only November, late November — that she ached and shuddered all day.

Sunset was when the lizard crept out and spread his sleek bronze skin on the warm glow of one wall. He was company, the rippling lizard.

'Aren't you lonely there, Kay?' Letters from home kept asking that. 'When are you coming home? What's Thessaloniki got that Sydney hasn't?'

Thessaloniki has Aleko, her letters never said in reply: Aleko was still too new. Besides, was it only Aleko?

'We miss you, you know,' pleaded the letters.

'Well, I miss you,' she wrote back. 'But Thessaloniki is very beautiful and strange. More than Athens even. I've hardly begun to see the real Thessaloniki.'

'We're not getting any younger as you know.' Her father wrote as he spoke, flatly. 'Your Mum and I were hoping you'd be back this Christmas. First it was "my studies". Now it's "my working holiday". That's all very well, but you have to settle down sometime, don't you.'

'I've taken on students for English lessons. I can't let them down and just leave, can I?'

'But *aren't* you lonely, dear?' That was her mother.

'Well, you see, there's this lizard,' she wrote, 'and a sweet little Burmese cat …' The letters ignored that.

It *was* sweet, a spoilt coquette of a little cat, in this city of starved strays too. It came faithfully to her door every day after the siesta for its plate of warm milk. When she stroked it, it closed its eyes in its bat-eared black face and stretched itself in poses of pure lust. Its deep-furred bony little body vibrated warmly; it was just beautiful. It gave her hope that her own bony body would, when — if — the time came, be beautiful for Aleko. She told Aleko, in Greek, that she loved the cat because it spoke English: just as she hoped, he laughed aloud. He was at his most handsome then. His mouth, widening, lost its petulant droop. Because there was something petulant and spoilt about Aleko at times. He *was* selfish, he was vain. But he would grow out of it. He had a kind heart. Once he asked, looking down, looking at her hands as thin as dry leaves on the table: 'Why you are alone in your life, Kay?' So she told him about the man in Australia that she had loved and never really got over …

'It spik Greek too, this clever cat,' spluttered Aleko, in English. 'Ask it if it spik Burmese!' And, why she didn't know, but they collapsed at this and laughed together till they cried.

Aleko came for a lesson twice a week at around sunset. He always stayed on, though, drinking coffee in her chilly kitchen long after the hour was up. She was always free: in her two months in Thessaloniki Aleko was the only student she had found. The sixty drachmas that he paid her twice a week covered the rent; that was only five hundred a month. For everthing else but the rent she had to withdraw savings. Any day now she hoped to find more students: it was hard without a telephone or a work permit. Her notices in English in the two libraries were still up: ENGLISHWOMAN (because no one wanted an Australian accent): M.A.GRADUATE: SEEKS ADULT STUDENTS FOR ENGLISH

LESSONS IN YOUR OWN HOME: 60 DRACHMAS PER HOUR (and her name and her address).

Aleko came to her place, his had no privacy. Aleko had written out notices in Greek for her. He might know someone who wanted lessons, or so he had hinted. He enjoyed hinting.

'Is your name's day next Thursday, you know thet,' he said after the last lesson, when they were waiting for the lift. 'We hev little party, okay, Kay? I bring a cake.'

'*My* name's day? Saint *Kay*?'

'Agia Aikaterini. Is the same. Aikaterini, Katerina, Katy, Kay.' With a quick smile as the lift bumped and opened: 'We be hev good time. Okay? Kay?' It amused him to say that.

'Okay, okay!' And the lift closed. When he comes, she decided, we mustn't fail, we must come to the point. Why have I been so prim all this time? (Who am I keeping it for?) I'll ask him to stay and we'll have dinner ... No, not here, how can I?

How could she, when all she had to cook on was a portable Camping Gaz with one burner? On this she fried her eggs and vegetables and sardines, she boiled spaghetti and then sauce, she brewed Greek coffee in a copper *briki*, she cooked her morning porridge, having found oats here at last, imported from Holland and very dear, in a grocer's near the flower market. What a luxury, after so long, to stir the thickening mass of oats until it plopped and then add honey in a trickle like a brass wire and eat it out of the saucepan! She always ate at home. Even in Sydney she was too shy ever to eat out alone; here women just didn't. In the covered market she bought her quarter-kilo of leeks here; her quarter-kilo of spilt sardines rusty with blood there; here an eighth of a kilo of olives, there a half-litre of dry red — '*brousko*', she insisted — Cretan wine. Shopkeepers exchanged resigned smiles when they saw her coming. On the way home, she stared in the steamy windows of the restaurants along Odos Egnatias at the crusted golden beans in earthenware, at roast meats wrapped in their film of fat.

I'll ask him out to a restaurant, she decided. I'll pay. Aleko can choose where. And then — what?

Her life had never seemed so empty to her as it did now that Aleko was the centre of it. She went on the bus to a cinema sometimes. She shopped and window-shopped. The streets were windy and stank of diesel fumes. She read in the warmth of the two libraries, the British Council one on the sea front and the United States Information Service one on Aristotelous Square, which was where Aleko had seen her notice offering lessons. (But he never happened to come in again while she was in there.) She borrowed books to take home, and returned them mostly unread: she was too cold, too restless, to be bothered.

On grey days her room could have been a cube of air cut inside an iceberg.

Once or twice a week she did her washing in the sink and pegged it out on a rope along the balcony, or up on the *taratsa*, the flat roof, with everyone else's, strung among dusty chimney pots and aerials; or even in the kitchen when it rained, and then her weak yellow bulb was screened by layers of washing that shed drips and shadows. She spread old newspapers — the *Times*, the airmail *Guardian*, bought for reading aloud with Aleko — over the powdery cement mosaic of her kitchen floor. She had a dream the morning of one washing day. She was hanging out a wet sheet in the wind when it became a sail, and a woman — who? — on a shore somewhere was leaning forward to tell her reproachfully, 'Life is so *ephemeral.*' The word itself was like a puff of air: *ephemeral.* It stayed with her. She even looked it up in Greek: *efimero*, the same. Life was *efimero.* For days she was filled with a sense of urgency, of waste time. She was as housebound as an old widow, and she was all of twenty-eight.

She made herself go out for long walks. She sat on benches in the parks and ate the roast chestnuts or the corncobs that she bought on street corners, or a *souvlaki* in a paper bag. Men pestered her, gypsy women begged, gypsy boys smeared shoe polish on her suede boots and sneered in her protesting face. '*Raus*!' they called after her: all blond people were Germans.

One gypsy woman in particular, nursing a limp little baby, worried Kay so much that she told Aleko about it: a gaunt woman who whined at her out of a greasy scarf that hid all but the long brown nose and teeth. Kay gave her ten drachmas. Aleko whistled at that. 'She'll remember *your* face,' he said. And was the baby really hers? — since everyone knew the gypsy women took turns, all with the same baby. 'My child! Lady, my child is sick!' But it really was sick, it was yellow, with a crusted rash. Then there was the beggar woman at the Post Office counters, roaring with her hand stretched out at you, a tongueless and toothless giantess like a dead tree. She never failed to corner Kay. And sure enough, that gypsy with the sick baby ran into Kay all over the place as she photographed ruins — 'One earthquack do that,' Aleko explained — and huts and churches, and sculpted faces in the crowd. 'Tou*rist*?' furtive young men whispered behind her. 'Spik English, miss? Tou*rist*?'

No, she thought, never answering them though: I *live* in Thessaloniki. I live in Greece now.

The neighbours greeted her curtly when they met in the building. They shrieked at her when she swilled water on her balcony to wash the dust off and it piddled down the spout in a murky arc on to the footpath: though they all washed their balconies. They exchanged dark looks when they caught her seeing Aleko off at the lift. He was five years younger than she was, and looked younger still: their eyes said that this beautiful young man had undersold himself, because doubtless she was supporting him. How ludicrous she was, this lovesick broomstick, this *Anglida* of his! Kay took to not wearing her glasses, to make herself more worthy of Aleko. She knew her way in the blurred streets by now, and at home she could see everything except glasses and bottles, whose contents seemed to hang in mid-air in some disturbance of the light. During lessons — at the card table under her dim kitchen bulb — she sometimes had to bend in front of Aleko until her nose was on the page. She blushed. Could he see through her? If so, she thought, all he saw would be a burning scarlet flood of light.

On the morning of Saint Katerina's day Kay washed her hair, something she did less often now, it took so long to dry. She had what they called here a telephone shower, hand-held (but no bath or shower recess, so that it flooded the floor) and shivered in its lukewarm trickle every day. In September when she first came, she could squat on the *taratsa* and her hair ran like hot toffee over her bare knees, drying in minutes. Even on fine days now the sun had no warmth. That morning she dried her hair kneeling in front of the red bars of the radiator and pulling her fingers through the knots. With hours to fill in, on impulse she caught a throbbing blue bus to the city, to a tourist shop she knew, where she bought coloured candles and four hand-woven woollen *tagaria,* to use not as shoulder bags but as cushions. They made beautiful cushions with her summer clothes crammed in them, scattered on her bed — which was not ostentatiously her *bed,* since it was a rubber mat on the waxed planks of the bedroom floor with a *flokati* rug of tufted greasy wool over it instead of blankets. It wouldn't look too obvious, if they had their party there. *We hev little party:* that was sweet of him. She had coffee, sugar, brandy. The brandy was getting low, but a new bottle now would cut into the restaurant money. She stared in the mirror and spread over her velvet shoulders the polished stripes of her long hair. Would the sun never set? She lit the candles, switched on the radiator. Again and again, her heart jumping, she held her watch to her ear.

When at last the bell rang, she counted to ten first, before she opened the door. There stood Aleko, holding a large white box, red ribbons curled all over it. And beside him, a plump Greek girl. Gypsy-eyed, richly dark.

'Kay, hullo!' he shouted. '*Chronia polla*! Many heppy years!' He passed her the box, which automatically she took, her eyes fixed on his in her consternation. The girl, stepping forward, grabbed Kay's free hand in her warm brown one and shook it. '*Chronia polla,*' she said, 'Nitsa.'

'Nitsa?'

'... Yes. This is Nitsa,' Aleko said, his voice choked with self-consciousness and pride. 'Nitsa, this is my English teacher. This is Kay.'

They smiled, and Nitsa fluffed her tails of black hair loose with her hand. The corridor light clicked. They were in darkness. 'Well, come *in.*' Kay held the door open. 'Please, Nitsa, Aleko. Come in and sit down.' Who was it? Was she supposed to know? One of his sisters? She shut the door and with an embarrassed laugh led them to the *flokati* in her flickering room. They sat side by side on it, their backs to the wall, stretching their legs out to the red bars. Kay hovered in the doorway. 'May I open it?' She peeped, and did: in the box were six cream sponge cakes of the kind called *pastes*, thickly piped with cream and sanded with roast nuts. 'Oh look, *pastes*!' she managed — she who loathed cream.

'You like it?'

'*Love* it, thank you. Both. They look delicious.'

'Is *okay*, Kay.'

'You hev a goot view,' offered the girl, Nitsa. The lamps had come on in the street, dripping and swaying at the water's edge. The *volta* was beginning, shadows were shuffling past. The whole sea was a dying fire. Beyond it the dark mountain stood; white lights glittered on it like sparks astray in winds.

'Mount Olympus,' Kay said reverently.

'Yes, you know Olimbos? He hev a lot of snow nown.'

'Now,' smiled Kay.

'Yes, nown snow. Is winter nown.'

Aleko rewarded Nitsa with a dazed smile and took her hand.

'These beautiful *pastes*. Let's have them now.' Kay held up the box and nodded to Nitsa. 'Nown?'

'No, no, Kay! Is all for you this one!'

'Aleko, I'd *die*. You have to help me. Well, excuse me, won't you?' They would. They smiled ecstatically.

In the kitchen she was frantic to remember. Aleko had mentioned sisters, hadn't he? Two sisters? Well, then! But no, one's name was Maria and the other one's? Toula. Nitsa must be a cousin. Young men were expected to escort their cousins too. Her hands quivering, Kay lit the Camping Gaz and stirred coffee and water and sugar in the *briki*. She found plates and forks for the *pastes*. Pouring two glasses of her dark brandy, she drank one down, rinsed and refilled the glass. The coffee frothed. She tipped it into the cups — at least she had three *cups*. Please, Agia Aikaterini, Katerina, Katy, let Nitsa be a cousin, she thought. They were very quiet in there on the *flokati*.

Nitsa's hair was a shawl over Aleko, until they saw her and sat bolt upright. And Nitsa was not a cousin.

'*Stin ygeia sou*, Kay,' they chanted, tossing down their brandies. She served them a *pasta* each and, putting the tray of coffees on the floorboards near them, sat on a *tagari* cushion to munch her way through hers. They jabbed and licked and gulped. Once

Aleko bent and stole a chunk off Nitsa's fork. 'Ach!' she squealed, delighted, and slapped his thigh. His teeth when he grinned were lathered with the cream. Kay smiled maternally.

'Aren't they delicious!' She rinsed her mouth with coffee. 'Where did you get them?'

'From very goot shop. Terkenli, you know, Kay,' he boasted. 'Is near to the American library.'

'They must have cost a fortune. You shouldn't have.'

'You hev to eat!' He sucked his coffee. 'Look at you, all bones, is no goot for your healthy. Not *you*, you too fet.' He poked Nitsa's waist. '*Patata eisai esi.* One big fet patato.'

'*Niata threfo*,' Nitsa said loftily. Kay raised her brows.

'She hev to feed her youngness, she say. Young pipple need to eat *too much*.'

'*Kala lei*,' agreed Kay. Her tone was dry; not that they noticed.

'*Ya!*' Nitsa grinned at her and gave Aleko a triumphant shove that sent him sprawling. They giggled. How old was Nitsa? Kay could just make out their faces on the coppery wall, half lit among shadows and reflected in the glass door now that the sky was dark. Perhaps sixteen; eighteen at the most. She licked her white fork.

'Well, I'm still hungry.' She made her voice light. 'I'm going to bring the other *pastes* now.'

'No, no,' said Aleko feebly. She took their plates anyway and dished out the other three *pastes* in the kitchen. This time she remembered water, pouring them two glasses that turned the gold of beer when she brought them in.

'And now more coffee,' she said.

'No, no. No, really, Kay.'

'You always have two or three coffees!'

'Yes, but no, Kay, sorry. We carn stay nown.'

They couldn't stay. So that was that.

'I hev auntie in Melvourni,' mumbled Nitsa with her mouth full. 'You come from Melvourni?'

'No, Sydney.'

'Ach, Sydnayee.'

'Is nice place, Sydnayee, Kay?'

'Yes. It's like here in some ways. A city on the sea — '

'Like here? Is so cold?'

'Well, no — it's summer there now, of course.'

'*Po po!* Summer there nown!' Nitsa giggled with a great shudder. Aleko tugged the *flokati* up around her shoulders.

'You look like Eskimo,' he said happily, combing her back with dark fingers. 'One big fet Eskimo bear.'

Kay shut her eyes to remember Sydney and in what ways it was like here. But Sydney was a set of faded transparencies. What her parents wanted was their old Kay back. As for those of her old friends who were still there, what did she have to say to them? As much as she had to say to these two. *I zoï,* she thought she might say, as one who leans earnestly forward across widening water: *I zoï einai toso efimeri* —

'We hev to visit another Katerinas, many Katerinas tonight,' Nitsa was explaining. Kay nodded.

'You lookink too sed, Kay.' He bent to help Nitsa up, brushing her crumbs off. 'I think so you hev nostalgear nown.'

'Oh, a little bit. No, not really. I'm happy.' She scrambled up. 'It's been a lovely party, thank you both.'

'Well, I see you next lesson. Hey, silly me!' He glowed, all eagerness. 'I forgot to say you. Din I say I find you one new student? Well: Nitsa want to learn with me English!'

'... Oh. Yes, Nitsa? Oh, good.'

'We learnink together, okay? Is more funny.'

'Fun. Yes, I see.' Kay laughed indignantly, and he mistook her.

'We come together and both of us payink you sixty *drachmes*,' he said quickly. 'One hundred twenty. Okay — Kay?'

'Okay. That will be fun.' She smiled back at them. When they come next time, she thought, I can always say that my mother's sick and I have to go home. I don't have to stay in Thessaloniki or in Greece if I don't want to. Can I stay here now? How the neighbours would laugh if they knew! They laughed anyway.

She got rid of Aleko and Nitsa (who were more than anxious to be gone) and rinsed the dishes, leaving them to dry on the marble, the real marble, of the draining board. In her room she locked the balcony shutters and straightened the still-warm *flokati*, which smelled of Arpege. To think I hoped he could love *me*, she thought: it never even crossed his mind. (Though it must have crossed Nitsa's, clever little Nitsa's.) It seemed to Kay now that nothing more would ever happen to her; her life would never be any fuller than it was at this moment, in this lonely city or another.

Mewings, scratchings at the front door: wearily she let the cat in. It was greedy and luxurious, not lovable at all. It sniffed, peering round. She gave it its milk cold. It wet its nose, gazed up with a mew, backed away. When it was sure the milk wouldn't warm itself, it stalked to her cushion and curled up with its back to her. The lizard hadn't come out. Nitsa must have alarmed it: it knew Aleko. Maybe it was going torpid and would freeze stiff in this cold, not coming alive till spring. So might she, here. A moth, quivering loudly at her ear, stumbled away among the candle flames. Fire would eat the moth, or the cat would, or the lizard. *Efimero, efimero!* As for her, she had nothing to eat in the flat, not even a drop of *brousko* wine. She had to keep her strength up. How had Nitsa put it? *Niata threfo. Niata,* youth: well, hardly.

Kay took out her tin of oats and ran her fingers through the flakes. She could always have porridge for dinner, porridge with bright honey. But wasn't there something stringy in the oats? She stared. Webs of them clung to her fingers. Yes, the oats were strung on webs, like corks on a fishing net. She could have wailed aloud. Weevils had got into the oats!

No, it was too much. Biting her lips, she lit the Camping Gaz and put the tin of oats on the flame. Let them bake in it like silkworms in their cocoons: why should she throw her Dutch oats out? As she watched, though, a little horrified, a white grub broke the surface of the flakes and reared, waved itself at full length, hopped and hurled itself first on to the red-hot rim, then on to the floor. She knelt and peered. Where was it on the cement mosaic? What a heroic escape! She had read, in an American magazine at the library, about a man tied with ropes and thrown on to an anthill in a pit rearing like that: covered in red skeins of ants he reared to his feet, to his full height, in the agony of death. The grub had done that. But it was still alive, wasn't it? It had to be!

She turned the Camping Gaz off — there might be others still alive — and jammed on her glasses. In the thick yellow light she crouched down, slanting to throw her shadow aside, and felt with her fingertips every chip and speckle of the floor where the grub had fallen. But she found only dust.

Against her shoulder the Burmese cat came pushing its warm head, purring. Then it hunched, stared, danced around the table legs and, before Kay could move, patted something and licked it up. '*Pussy*!' she groaned. It closed blissful eyes, in its mincing delicacy like a furred brown spider. Pinching its scruff in her powdery fingers, she dropped it outside in the dark of the corridor and slammed the door. The flat reeked of singed oats.

'You blight on the earth,' she told her reflection in the pane. 'The futility of you!' Her face flashed, goggling back. She pulled off her glasses to wipe her eyes. And then: 'Crying over a dead grub! What would the neighbours think of the mad *Anglida* if they saw you now? Wouldn't they be right, too?' Because she could see the ludicrous side of it all, but only as if at a great distance ... Saint Kay's day! Life is so *efimeri*! Oh dear, oh dear. I *will* go out, she thought suddenly, I'll go out for dinner anyway. At one of those restaurants with steamy panes in Odos Egnatias (but I'll take a book with me). I'll have Cretan *brousko* wine, blood-red in the copper measuring beaker, and crusty beans or meat out of an earthenware baking dish ... She would go somewhere warm with fuzzy gold lights and an uproarious crowd, where you stayed as long as you wanted: out there in the real Thessaloniki. And then? Then — come back here?

Besides, she wasn't hungry any more, not after the *pastes*, not after the oats.

In the cave of her bedroom she lay back with her hair spread out on the hot tufts of the *flokati*. The radiator hummed its one note. Veils of the candlelight began their frilling and soft unravelling on the whitewash. After a while the lizard came out and sunned himself. After a while, she could have been anywhere in the world. Saint Kay's day was as good as over. One month to Christmas Day, she thought: and knew that, wherever in the world she was at Christmas, she would be there among strangers. The shadows of small flames quivered over her. She was sleepy now. She lay, a log in a sinking fire.

MARKET DAY

The market town stayed green even now, when the fields of ripe wheat and barley all around for mile after mile were scorched and the simmering air wavered in ripples over them. The stork, its long legs trailing back like a mosquito's, dipped over its frayed shadow, landing to prod the stubble. Over fields and cracked creek beds the crows flapped: ka ka ka ka-o.

But the market town stayed green. Everywhere leaves dripped over mossy stone and the carved wood of balconies, and the sound that underlay all other sounds there even in midsummer was the sound of water moving. Mikri Elpida had noticed that about the market town even as a child who could see. Now that she was blind, it was what she loved most. On every market day that the family went she insisted on going, jolting and stifled in the bus from the village. Even then there were all the sounds of water, even on market days, when the *pazari* drew in the buses roaring from every village, honking and farting; and tractors and motor *trikykla,* trucks and cars and horses and carts all crowded in; and felted donkeys minced along the damp streets between tiers of tomatoes, peppers, peaches packed in boxes. It was always the same. Then, as now, ragged women offered their crumbles of white butter folded in leaves. In the laneway, where whiffs of coffee and cumin and charring *souvlakia* caught at you as you passed, rows of plucked chickens hung their red necks out of windows. Soldiers and priests, gentlemen in suits, gypsies and grim little pigtailed widows pattered past, as they always had. Jostling strangers pounced, called your name and turned out to be relatives, all with some thrilling piece of news to tell.

When you were tired, you found a table outside one of the three *kafeneia* under the plane trees of the Square, as near to the spilling, rippling fountain as you could, and revived over a coffee, an ouzo with salty *mezedes* to eat, a cold *limonada.* It was the same year in year out, season by season. When it snowed you sat inside round the stove. The mountain thawed and all the street gutters swelled with ringing tunnels of glass, and soon the Square was overhung with wisteria in bunches. In midsummer all the great plane trees dropped darkness over the tables and the fountain, over your lifted face.

Mikri Elpida always took her knitting, for company, she said: and she was glad of it today. Her brother's daughter, Nitsa, sipping her *limonada* opposite, was sunk in silence. Nitsa's silences were new these summer holidays, no one knew why. Her mother, Megali Elpida, had dumped her with Mikri Elpida and dragged the rest of the family off to carry shopping. Click click, chattered Mikri Elpida's needles. In the family, jokes — worn thin — now were still made sometimes about their names. Big Hope and Little Hope: just because Mikri Elpida's brother had happened to marry another, taller and slightly older Elpida, and since they all lived in the one house ... But Big Hope, Little Hope! People had to smile. Little hope indeed, for a blind girl with no dowry! Still, you never knew. Elpida smiled. Click click, click click. The wool tickled her cool hands.

'You're like a knitting machine,' Nitsa whined.

Elpida's hands clenched. 'I always knit. I'm sorry.'

'No — you're so good at it, that's what I mean.' Nitsa's voice warmed, by way of apology. Poor Aunt Elpida. But life was so cruel! Always alone, yet never alone for a moment! And must men keep staring like that? Those soldiers by the fountain ... She had an impulse to tell Elpida her secret. What would Elpida know about love, though? She was like a quail in a cage. A dry little nun.

'You can knit just as well!' trilled Elpida. Hadn't she herself taught Nitsa? 'Don't you flatter me, now!' Nitsa, with a peevish shrug, decided: no. And now two of the soldiers were strolling over. Elpida went on laughing. Even her laugh was birdlike, in shrill staccato chirps. We must look like two schoolgirls, she was thinking, to anyone who doesn't know us. Maybe not *school*girls, no. Besides, wasn't Nitsa a full-bodied woman now? She had been for two summers: since she was — yes, fourteen ...

Just then the two soldiers, as if they had every right, scraped back chairs at their table, and one said hotly, boldly, in Mikri Elpida's ear, 'You don't mind if we sit with you, do you, Yiayia?'

'Yiayia?' Did they take her for Nitsa's grandmother? 'Yiayia? Me? Imagine!' tinkled Elpida. Nobody heard. The soldiers and Nitsa were all suddenly talking at once: Nitsa was furious. The soldiers shambled off, Nitsa's shout of 'Who do you think you are?' lashing their backs.

'Imagine! He called me Yiayia,' Elpida persisted.

Nitsa snorted. 'They've got a nerve! Soldier boys! No, thank you!' She sucked on her straw. And burning behind her dark glasses, Elpida knitted.

A grandmother? Nitsa smiled. She looked nothing like one; just like a little brown aunt. She was thin, she was agile and sprightly. With her plaits and her always eagerly tilted face, she looked young: until you saw that the face had set as heavy as clay behind the black glasses, and the hair under the crown of plaits was grey. When she dried it in the sun, the bronze cape of it swept close to the ground. But down to her armpits it made a grey veil. 'Your plaits look as if you knitted them on,' Nitsa remarked.

'Really, do they?'

'Yes, a thick grey and brown knitted cap. If I bought the wool, what if you knitted me a pullover? Would you? Those exact colours, I think.'

Mikri Elpida was open-mouthed.

'Oh, not for me.' Nitsa hesitated. 'Listen — can you keep a secret?'

Grey! A thick grey and brown knitted cap! Worse, worse than being called Yiayia! Elpida's lips shook. Of course, there had to be some grey in it by now, but —

'*How* grey?' she burst out.

'... What? Oh, well, not at the ends, only on top. It's like the rings of a tree, isn't it? You can read your whole life in it. If I buy the wool, will you knit me a thick pullover? Will you? Say yes.'

'We'll see.' Elpida's lips were stiff now. No one had ever told her. She was a grey *yiayia*, she who had hardly lived. She was a knitting machine.

Megali Elpida pounced on them then and bore them off to the hospital on the leafy hill, where an old aunt from another village had recently had a gangrenous leg amputated. The corridors and the wards breathed ether and phenol, sweat and hot linoleum. Eyes everywhere tracked them past. Megali and Mikri Elpida sat on Aunt Lena's bed, holding a papery hand each. Nitsa, discomforted, took the peaches they had brought over to the washbasin and rinsed them until their velvet skins darkened. The ward filled with the rosy smell of peaches. Now and then Aunt Lena muttered, clutching the hands to her cheeks, 'Ach, Elpida! Elpida!' That there was no hope all of them knew. Tears seeped down their faces.

Out in the sun, rowdy as children let out of school, they marched down arm-in-arm to sit by the fountain again and drink cold ouzo and savour the strong *mezedes* fiercely: the black bitterness of olives, sour peppered cheese with a green gloss of oil, hair-boned anchovies crusted with salt. Before they could finish, the family swooped and rushed them staggering off to catch the last bus. Bags of shopping punched their knees. Hoisted up by the elbows, stifling her gasps, Elpida stumbled along. *Bouzoukia* jangled. In the smoky oven of their bus — nobody would hear of opening a window — she fell asleep on Nitsa's shoulder, her stitches dropping, and woke only when the bus braked in its own dust at the village stop.

Oozing dusty sweat, Elpida said she was tired and went straight upstairs to lie down. In the kitchen, meatballs began to sputter in hot oil. The hens in the yard squabbled. Then the sun slid away and water was pounding into the bucket: the tired cow came clattering home. Elpida unplaited her hot hair. You can read your whole life in it! Your wasted life. I won't go to the *pazari* again, she decided. Never. Never. Coolness flowed in at the window. A cat wailed.

At nightfall the cats, sprawled moth-eaten furs all day, came alive and squatted outside to stab their green gaze at beetles and moths and mice. All the family sat in a circle in the yard, with only the kitchen light on, and the radio, though nobody listened. Neighbours and relatives strolling along the road were called over. Megali Elpida and Nitsa brought out plate after plate of meatballs, fried potatoes, bread. Our kitchen is a lantern in the dark, Nitsa thought, dropping crumbs for the cats: everyone gathers like moths outside it. Everyone, she saw, except Mikri Elpida — who more than anyone loved to sit outside in the dark.

'Where's my aunt?' she asked Megali Elpida.

'Lying down. Let her rest.'

Knocking, Nitsa swept in without waiting to be told. Mikri Elpida was huddled by the window, her loose hair pooling in her lap. 'Who? No!' Her voice quavered. 'Leave the light off!'

'Why are you up here by yourself?'

'I have a headache.'

'Oh, me too!' Nitsa flopped on the bed. 'It's the *pazari*. The heat.' Against the light thrown up from the yard, Elpida was a draped bronze statuette. Nitsa told her so. The answer was like a sob. 'Don't *cry*!' she protested, going nearer. But you never knew when Elpida was crying, even when you could see her eyes. They always looked tightly squeezed; no white edge showed. 'You *are* crying, aren't you? What's wrong?'

'Nothing!'

'Then come down. Come on.'

'Later.'

'What's *wrong*?'

'*Aman*, Nitsa. Don't be such a baby.'

Nitsa dipped her hand under the hair to press it to her aunt's forehead. 'Is the pain there?'

'No, in my heart,' Elpida muttered unexpectedly; straight away her face burned Nitso's palm.

'Ach, me too,' Nitsa crooned. 'Where's your brush?' She pulled the brush through rustling handfuls of Elpida's spilt hair. 'Isn't it sad how cruel life is?'

'How would you know?'

'Everyone knows.'

Which might be so, for all Elpida knew.

'Is it Aunt Lena?'

'Oh, everything.'

'Because of your eyes too?' murmured Nitsa.

'It's my own business.'

'You can tell me, I won't tell.'

'Well, my eyes, I suppose. In a way. Yes.'

'Do you remember when you could see?'

'Of course. I'm not so old ... I see dreams every night.'

'Tell me how it happened.'

'But I have.' Everyone knew the story.

'Again.'

'All right. We children had climbed that red hill above the road into town, where everyone's grapevines were. Some of those old vines are still bearing, they're hidden behind the fig trees.' Her hair crackled round her as Nitsa brushed. 'Our mothers had given us baskets to pick the figs and grapes. I remember figs that the birds had torn open, hanging down like thick purple flowers, the seeds spilling. Heavy rains had washed tree roots out and made gullies full of red mud. Saki found a smooth shape buried in one. It looked like glass. "Treasure!" he shouted. Yordani found a mattock and we all crowded round. Then the mud erupted, we were thrown down. That's all I remember. When I dream about it, that's how it ends: a blaze of noise and when I wake up — I can't see.'

Nitsa hugged her. 'It was a German shell,' she prompted.

'... A live German shell. There are still some left, people say. Six of us were injured. Saki and Yordani died, torn open like the ripe figs ... I remember when I could see, but times change. So I can't be sure of knowing what anything looks like now, I suppose.' She swung her hair. 'Today, by the fountain —'

Nitsa stopped brushing. 'What do you think *I* look like?'

'Like a — silly, how would I know?'

'Am I pretty?'

'Well, are you?'

'I know someone who thinks so!'

'What's this?'

'You won't tell, if I tell you a secret?' she whispered. 'Well — I'm in love.'

'Don't *tell* me!' Elpida jumped up. 'And I *thought* maybe — by the fountain today — a thick pullover! *Oh yes*, I thought. *It's for a man*,' and instantly she was sure she had thought that by the fountain.

'So can we buy the wool at the next *pazari*?'

'Slow, slow. Who is he? Do we know him?'

'You won't tell?'

'Never.'

'Well, his name's Aleko. He lives in Thessaloniki and he's a student.'

'And is he in love with you?'

Nitsa giggled. '*Madly*!'

'So life's *cruel*, is it?' scoffed Elpida.

'But I can't see him, can I? Not for weeks! I'll be stuck here in the village all summer till school starts and he's in Thessaloniki!'

'You'll work something out. What if — could he come to our *pazari*, do you think?'

'*Yes*!' Nitsa hugged her. 'Will you help us?'

'How?'

'To be alone together for a while?'

'You be sensible! You hear?'

'I will, I will. Now come down and eat. Please?'

'My hair!' protested Elpida.

'Nitsa, are you upstairs? Nitsa!' shouted Megali Elpida from the yard.

'Now what?' Nitsa leaned out. 'Coming!' She sighed. ' "Nitsa, Nitsa," ' Elpida's fingers were twitching in and out of her dim skeins of hair. 'Tomorrow,' Nitsa said, 'I want you to plait my hair like that.'

'You can do it. It's easy.'

'It isn't. I can't.'

'We'll make a thick black cap of it, will we?'

'Not as thick as yours.'

'Flattering me again! Go on down, I won't be long.'

'Let me get you something to eat. Meatballs? Salad? All right?'

Elpida bit back her usual proud rejection of help. 'All right,' she said.

'Remember — it's our secret!' Nitsa flung the door open, clattered downstairs. Elpida sighed. Market day certainly tired you out. But how exciting! What a thrilling piece of news! Tubby, wilful little Nitsa — a fine sweet woman she was turning out, and in what seemed no time at all! Yet wasn't it a little shocking? In love, already! Aleko. Was he handsome, young, brilliant? He must be. He loved Nitsa — *madly*. Remember, our secret. How mystified everyone would be when they saw her knitting, the same as always, a thick pullover — for no one knew who! For Aleko. She would sit in the dark of the plane trees, the water beside her bubbling, brimming over — she remembered how the water looked — with splashed shadows of leaves and clouds. People might even think *she* was the one ... Mikri Elpida's laugh trilled out. Voices answered. Dancing with impatience in the doorway, she pinned up her bronze crown.

HOME TIME

By late afternoon the sky is a deep funnel of wind, damp and white. She remarks as she passes through the lamplight around his desk on her way to the bathroom: 'Doesn't it look like snow!'

'Do you think?' He squints out the window.

'That hollowness of the light.'

'It's early for snow.'

'*Casablanca*'s going to be on TV tonight at eight,' she says before he can look down again. 'Why don't we go to that bar and see it and then have dinner somewhere after?'

'Mmm.'

The room is grey; only the light around him is warm and moving with shadows. The steam pipes are silent. Whenever will they start clanking and hissing and defrost the apartment? '*Isn't* it cold, though!' she says brightly.

'Mmm.'

'Maybe I should go for a walk downtown, take some photos of the lights coming on,' she says.

'It's a lot colder outside.'

'Walking would warm me up.'

'Okay.'

'Oh, maybe not,' she says. 'I might write letters home instead.' Home is Australia. It's summer there. 'Until it's time for *Casablanca*.'

He sighs and waits for silence.

She has an electric radiator on in her room — the sitting-room really, but she works in here. She has twin lamps of frilly glass at twin tall windows inside which wasps sizzle and cling and trap themselves in shreds of cobweb. The table she writes at faces the windows. Three times a day she pushes books to one side and turns papers face down, since this is also the table they eat at. The kitchen is next to it, bare and icy, smelling of gas. She pulls her radiator over by the couch and lies curled up in the red glow with her head on a velvet cushion.

Later she half-wakes: he has walked past into the kitchen. When he switches her lamps on and hands her a mug of coffee she is stiffly sitting up to make room. 'Did you get much written?' She yawns, stretching an arm warm with sleep along his shoulders.

'Fair bit.' He grins. 'Did you?'

She is glad she stayed in. 'No. What's the time?'

'Hell, yes.' He looks. 'Ten past eight.'

'Oh, we've missed it!'

'No, we haven't. Only the start.'

They gulp their coffee and help each other drag coats and boots on. 'You must have seen it, haven't you?' he says.

'Oh, yes. Hasn't everyone?'

'Then what's the — ?'

She shuts his mouth with a kiss. 'I want to see it with *you*. In America.'

He smiles at that. They fling open the door and stop short. Snow is falling, must have been falling for hours, heavy and slow, whirling round the white streetlamps. 'Oh, *snow*!' She dashes back inside for her camera and takes photo after photo from the stoop, of fir branches shouldering slabs of snow, drooping in gardens, and elms still with gold leaves and a fine white skin all over, and lawns and cars and rooftops thickly fleeced. Passing cars have drawn zips on the white road.

'Now we're really late,' he says. Hand in hand they tramp and slither the few blocks to the bar they like, bright as a fire with the lamps on. Outside it two young men are throwing snowballs. She gasps as one leaps on the other and they flounder giggling at her feet.

'Pussy cat!' one jeers. 'That's *all* you is!'

Her man is holding the blurred glass door open. Heads along the bar turn away from *Casablanca* to stare at them. He leads her to a stool, orders a red wine and an Irish coffee and stands at her back. Ingrid Bergman's face fills the screen.

The door opens on a white flurry and the young men stamping in, shaking the snow off. The heads turn and stare. 'Celebrate the first *snow*!' one young man announces. 'Have a *drink*, every-buddy!' A cheer goes up. The barman brings her another red wine and him another Irish coffee. The young men have flopped crosslegged on the carpet and are gazing at the screen.

'Oh, they're so young,' a voice murmurs in her ear; the grey-haired woman beside her is smiling. She smiles in answer and gives herself over to *Casablanca*. He is at her back with his arms round her. When it ends he goes to the men's room.

The old woman is dabbing her eyes. 'Oh dear!' She makes a face. 'Do you come here a lot? I do. We live just down the road.'

Do you come here a lot? I do. We live just down the road. You can see this bar from our stoop and I tell you it's a real temptation, glowing away down here. With that lantern at the door with snowflakes spinning round it and the way the elm leaves flap against it like yellow butterflies — it's like some place in a fairy tale. And here inside it's as bright and warm as inside a Halloween pumpkin. Those lamps everywhere, and the bottles burning in the mirror. And whenever the door opens, a breath of snow blows in and the lights all shift under and over the shadows. Even if *Casablanca* wasn't on the TV I'd have come tonight.

What'll you have, honey, another one of those? What is that, red wine? Jimmy, another one of those red wines and I'll have a Jack Daniels. Yes, rocks. And wipe that silly grin off your face, have you no soul, what kind of a man laughs at *Casablanca*? Thanks, Jimmy. Keep it.

Look through that archway, the couples at their little tables, all so solemn and proper with their vintage wine and their candles — look, their heads are hollow, like the candles burnt their eyes out. They might all have stories just as sad as *Casablanca*, but who cares? It's *Casablanca* breaks our hearts, over and over. You cried at the end, I saw you. So did that nice man of yours. Oh, a bar's the place to watch it, a bar's the perfect place. I cry every single time, I can't help myself, it's so noble and sad and innocent and — hell, you know. I couldn't watch it home, anyway. Bill, he's my husband, gets mad when I cry. He walks out. 'Why, am I supposed to stay and watch you slobber over this shit?' he said last time it was on. 'Most people got all they need to slobber about in real life.'

'You're what I got,' I said right back.

That's him there, over at the pool table. That your man he's talking to? I thought so. They're lighting up cigarettes and getting acquainted. Isn't that a coincidence? He looks a nice easy-going kind of a guy. But then so does Bill. I love Bill, I love him a lot. I've known that man thirteen years, I could tell you things ... I'm not blind to anything about Bill, I love him anyway. He loves *me*, though it doesn't feel like being loved much of the time. He needs me. He has to punish me for that. There he is, an older man than he acts. His hair has a grey sheen and his skin hangs loose all over, see the crazed skin on his neck. He's affable and a bit loud with the drink, everybody's pal. Well, when we get home there won't be a word out of him. Under the skin and the smile he's a bitter, fearful man and nobody gets close to him.

He's a second comer, for one thing. He can't forget that. He's my second husband. Yours is a second comer too, is he, honey? Don't mind me sticking my nose in. It's just I can tell. You two are a mite too considerate, too careful with one another, know what I mean? It shows, that's all, if you can read the signs. So what if you are Australians. Oh no. Look, I don't mean you haven't got a nice relationship. But it's only the first time you give your whole self. After that, like it or not, you hold back. You've gotten wise — and you can't pretend *other*wise!

We've been married ten years this Thursday — Thanksgiving Day. You got to laugh. Cheers. Isn't that something, though. My first marriage never got to double figures. I had twenty years alone in between.

Do you remember the first time you saw *Casablanca*? Mine was in 1943, when it first came out, on my honeymoon with Andy. That's reason enough to cry. Bill knows. It's something he can't stand to be reminded of. He pretends it's only Rick and Ilsa making me *slobber.* Men — you tell a man the truth about your life, you end up paying for *ever.* Remember that.

1943! Andy was nineteen, I was seventeen, his ship was sailing for Europe in a week. Our parents said no, you're too young, but we said we'd only run away, so they gave in. We had one weekend for a honeymoon in New York City. The hotel was an awful old ruin — it still is — full of cockroaches and noisy plumbing. We were so embarrassed, you could hear every drop, every trickle. Our room was on the top floor. Through the fire escape we could see the river, and the moon in the mist like a brass knob behind a curtain, and the lights of Manhattan. So it's not a bed of roses, Andy said: it's a bed of lights instead. We saw *Casablanca* and we cried. We were such babies. He was going to be a hero and I was going to wait ... We danced round the room like Rick and Ilsa did. We sure didn't sleep much. We didn't even know how to *do* it, you know. We were scared. Oh, we soon got the hang of it. And then his ship sailed.

He came back, oh, he came back. He'd won medals in Italy, he was a hero. But he wouldn't ever talk about it. Whatever happened over there, it finished Andy. He started drinking, then he lost his job, and soon he couldn't hold down any job, he just drank and gambled and played the black market. He'd come home once, twice a week, then sleep for days ...

One night he started hitting me. Everything was my fault, he said. Then he cried. He promised he never would again. I was fool enough to believe it. If they've hit you once and gotten away with it, honey, you're in trouble. It can only get worse.

So, one night I woke up on the kitchen floor. The table lamp was still on, the beer that he spilt looked like butter melting under it. I remember I saw the pattern of brown triangles on the linoleum every time my eyes came open, they looked wet and red, but I couldn't see sharp enough to be sure. The window was black — so it was still night time — and had silver edges like knives where he smashed it. The curtain was half torn down, sopping up the beer on the table and moving in the wind, a white curtain like a wedding veil. *Help me!* I called out. My head felt crushed. The wind must have blown my hair on my face, hair was stuck to it. A long way away something was — snuffling. My nose was flat on my cheek, red bubbles blew out. Andy *wasn't there.* I held my head still and pulled myself up by the table leg: broken glasses, slabs of the window pane, the wet curtain, but no note. No nothing. The room was going all watery and dim as if the floor was hot as fire and yet it was so icy when I lay down, I pulled the curtain down over me to keep warm.

It wasn't till morning that I saw he'd taken all his stuff. God knows there wasn't much, poor Andy. Then I got started all over again: *Don't leave me! Don't leave me alone now! I love you!* Even now I dream — I wake up and for a moment I'm on that floor again knowing I've lost Andy, he's gone for *ever.* Oh, I've never gotten over it.

I'm sorry. Don't be embarrassed. I'll be all right in a moment. Thank you, yes, another Jack Daniels would be nice. Yes, thank you.

Funny thing was, when I got up off the floor next day and my nose was smashed and my eyes looked like two squashed plums and I was shaking so hard I thought my teeth would crack — I ran out into the street in case I could see him and maybe catch him up and all the time I was whimpering, *After all you've done to me, you just get up and go?* I looked in the kitchen window. It was empty, all shadowy gold behind the edges of glass.

Another funny thing — I had a vision in the night, a ballerina came in. (I wanted to be a dancer, I was good, but first the War started, then I got married ...) Anyway, this ballerina in white was waving her arms and bowing. It must have been the curtain that I saw. She bent down to lift me then she lay beside me, sobbing, I remember that.

Look at us there in the mirror, like two ghosts among the whisky bottles. Okay, Jimmy, laugh. He thinks I'm admiring myself. I'm not that far gone, though I'm getting there. Cheers. Is that really me, that scrawny thing with the spiky grey hair? You'd never think I was a ballet dancer. Bill hates ballet. He says that because the pain and exertion and ugliness aren't allowed to show, it's one big lie. Tinsel and sweat, he says. Dancers smell like horses, someone famous says, so Bill has to read it to me out of the newspaper. Horses aren't any less beautiful for the way they smell, I say. Horses are dancers too and dancers love them. Anyway, I say, I like the way they smell. You would, he says, you're not what you'd call fussy, are you. Now wasn't that asking for it? *No, well, I married you!* I let it pass, though, and he gives me points for not saying it: just a flicker of the eyelids, but enough.

Most of our quarrels end like that. They're harmless. Nothing Bill says or does can get to the quick of me like it did with Andy whether he meant it or not. Bill can make me ache with misery when he wants, but somewhere deep down inside me now there's this little tough muscle braces itself so the barbs can't go too far in. Bill knows. He's the same. Maybe by now it would have been like that with Andy, who knows? I don't even know if he's alive or dead. My parents came and made me get a divorce. They told him I said he couldn't see me or the kids ever again.

Let me tell you the *worst* thing — let's have another drink? — the worst thing — oh, God, I've never told a living soul this. Jimmy, more of these and have one on me, okay? The worst thing is, when he had me on the floor that night — just pushed me down — and started smashing things and yelling that he wanted *out*, I rolled over and hung on to his trouser leg for dear life and begged him not to leave me. I just wouldn't let go. I slobbered and howled and — and I kissed his muddy shoe. So he slammed his other shoe in my face. That's when my nose got broken. I mean, that's why.

I thank God the kids weren't home, they didn't see that. They saw him hit me other times, but not that. They were only little. Rick was about five, Ilsa was just a baby. Something like that, though — if they saw it happen, it'd leave a scar on them. 'I won't let Daddy hurt you,' Ricky used to say to me. They were at my parents' place in New Jersey because I had to get a job so I couldn't look after them. We called them Rick and Ilsa — well, *you* know why! Ilsa's married, she's in Alaska now, she's a nurse. Rick's dead. He got killed in Vietnam. Got a medal doing it, too. If his Daddy ever heard about it, I suppose he must have felt proud. Or maybe not.

Don't get me wrong. I believe in sacrifice, and love and honour and loyalty, even if it turns out they were wasted — else why would I love *Casablanca*? Rick and Ilsa, they had something or someone they'd give up everything for. I only wish I still did. Real people have their moments of glory. Time goes on for them though, they can't live up to it. But the glory lives on in memory. Bill won't see that. Face facts, he says. You and your glory and your wallowing in the past. It's shit, that's all it is, shit preserved in syrup. That's better than shit preserved in vinegar, the way yours is, I say. Oh, that's good, he says. Make with the witty repartee, babe, you know I dig that. (Bill can never let go of anything. All his past is still there inside of him, pickled.) Why better, honey? Shit's still shit, he says then. Who knows the truth? I say. You refuse to, *he* says, and round and round we go.

What you never really get over, I suppose, is finding out love's not enough. Loving someone's no *use.* And you only find out the hard way. No one can tell you. You believe in love when you're young, you believe it's forever, it's the only thing that matters, it'll save you both, if you just hang in there and give more and more. I wonder if Ilsa would have gone with Rick — given up everything and gone with him — would it have ended up with her on the floor with her nose smashed? You never know.

Here they come. Look, they're wondering what we're saying. Look at those suspicious eyes and butter wouldn't melt smiles of theirs! Your man's been watching you all this time. Here's looking at you, kid! Easy to see you're new. It's great while it lasts, make the most. The couples have had their wine and candlelight and now they're leaving. Don't you just love a black and white night like this after snow, when it echoes? And you slide and fall down on top of each other all the way and rub each other's feet dry and warm once you're inside. Okay, fellers, home time? I've lost my coat. Thanks, honey. I feel so lit up it's a wonder you can't see me shining through it! I'm sure I don't know why I've been telling you the story of my life. You cried at the end of *Casablanca.* I suppose that's why.

'Can I read that?'

'Read what?'

Her hands have instinctively spread across the pages of blue scrawl. He raises his eyebrows: 'What you've been writing half the night.'

She passes them over her shoulder. The couch creaks and the pages rustle until at last he tosses them back on the table and goes to make coffee. She stares at them, sweat prickling her. The heating is on full.

'Thank you,' she says when he brings her mug.

'Is this finished?'

'Oh, for now, anyway. I was just coming to bed — I'm sorry. Haven't you been asleep?'

'I used to respect writers rather a lot,' he murmurs. 'Now I'm not sure.'

'You're writing your thesis on one.'

'Mmm. There's writing and writing. To my mind this' — he points — 'is more like scavenging.' He waits while she swallows hot coffee. 'Perhaps if you wore a badge, a brand on your forehead that meant: *Beware of the scavenger*? Then people would know they were fair game.'

'You think *that's* being *fair*?'

'She trusted you, it seems, with the story of her life.'

'I hope I can do it justice.'

'Justice.' He sighs.

She has nothing to say. He finishes his coffee sip by sip, takes his mug and rinses it, then comes back to stand behind her chair. Her mug is clenched in both hands; the light of the two lamps blurs in her coffee.

'I am not to figure in anything you write,' comes the smooth voice again. 'Never. I hope you understand that.'

Hardly breathing, she cranes her neck forward to have a sip of coffee, but he grabs the mug from her and slams it down on the table, where it breaks. Coffee spurts up and splashes brown and blue drops over her pages. This time she knows better than to move until his footsteps creak away across the boards. His chair scrapes. She hears a match strike in the room beyond, and a sigh as he breathes smoke in.

WHITE FRIDAY

In a room somewhere Barbara wakes in anguish and lies with her eyes shut, having dreamt someone has died. Who? All that is left is the muddy trampled grass at a graveside, one mourner with her hair dark with rain over her face. Bells in towers clang. She opens blank eyes on a strange white room where she makes a void, a vortex. Still, the bells: more than most other mornings. This is Friday. And this is Greece, yes, Hydra: this is the hotel. She creeps over baked floor-tiles to push the shutters open on nothing but sunlight. '*Seismos einai?*' someone outside shouts. '*Pyrkaia!*' comes the answer. Not an earthquake. A house is on fire.

Tall smoke from a white house high on the hilltop lays itself flat over the town and the harbour. The sea clouds over. Bells in the square clock tower toll, bells in the filigree one, bells further away; then the clock strikes the half-hour. Seven-thirty. '*Kai nero den echei!*' And there is no water! Even if there were, there is no road up to there, only cobbled stairways, and only donkeys to carry it. Shouts echo in the streets. Figures are massing under the stout white walls. Sprouting at the eaves, flames hang like corn-cobs stored for winter. They are no brighter than corn in the smoky sunlight. Then with a turbulence in the smoke and a great shout the roof caves in.

Late autumn, on a dry island. Yesterday she walked along the cliff road, past the headland with the cannons and the windmill, hoping it led to the monastery that hung among the rocks in a white silence. Here and there an olive, a cypress. But it led to smoke rising, and an avalanche of rotting rubbish poured down to a gulf like a slit in the sky with a rowing boat anchored. The wind ripped tufts of fire out. Furry bodies moved: cats, spitting, cringing, hundreds of them among the charring papers and tooth-edged cans and the bones of roasted animals.

The grave in the dream was not my mother's, she thinks,

though it was in Australia. My mother was cremated. Whose, then? Whose hair trickled rain?

Her arms are clinging to the marble window sill as if to ice. She comes inside. With the immersion heater she boils water in her teapot that she takes everywhere — pure white but for two black flecks on the curve under the handle, like moles in an armpit — then adds the tealeaves. She makes her bed the island way, smoothing the starched sheet, folding the blanket at the foot; pours the tea into her mug; sits on the blanket to drink it. The room has warmed, breathing the smoke in. A beautiful room, its ceiling has dark brown ribs that match the shutters and the slatted bench on which she leaves her bag and *Memoirs of Hadrian* open face-down. She reads a few pages aloud every night, her hands warm round the mug, while tea steams in her face and the room hums round her.

The day she came she wrote in her diary:

This is a place of serenity. Wherever I live I want white walls and the sun coming in. Folded all day in warm light, after dark I would turn on all the lamps. When I went out, a lamp left burning would wait.

Now she opens her diary with her free hand and writes:

A solid house on the hill, like this hotel, burned to ashes as I watched — no water to save it.

A drop of tea splashes her white thigh. Wiping the stain away, she remembers the poem she scrawled on an envelope before she slept — yes, there it is — and copies it into the diary.

Winter-white, my thighs
are rippled, high-water-marked:
fine like rice paper.

She canters down stairways bright with fallen leaves between solid houses with pipe-tiled roofs and heavy doors, blue, red, green, that close over courtyards and have as knockers iron heads of lions or goddesses or ringed hands. Iron bars on the windows curve plumply out like grooves in pumpkins. Cats sunning themselves on doorsteps cringe as her shadow falls. Flies burn bronze in the donkey dung. At souvenir shops she asks where the OTE is: faces open to her once she speaks in Greek. She has to ring the man she loves in Australia. After these weeks apart, he might prefer her not to. She recoils from the thought that, taken by surprise, he might betray — annoyance? But the dream has alarmed her; and the fire. She has to.

The OTE office is a stale, dingy hall, with an impatient queue for every telephone. When her turn comes she dials again and again: whistles, clicks, silence. At last there are five double rings and then he speaks.

And he is pleased to hear her voice!

He has left the taps running to fill the bath, with his children and their toys in it already, so he can't talk long. Of course, Friday — his children have come down. She tells him she had this dream. Well, he is all right, he says, and so are the children. Everything he talks about makes her heart sink, he is so far away. She says she will be back next Friday. Good, he says. In fact she is in two minds. She has not confirmed her booking; she might stay here. Goodbye, they both say.

The cashier hides a smile. The call has cost her 2850 drachmas, about $30. The bath must have overflowed.

They are all splashing, laughing, in his bathroom in its downy light (it is evening there). A spiderweb strung high on the window frame catches on each movement of the air. Spider threads rig a toy yacht with no sails on the shelf. Weeks since she was there. And she might stay here.

Or stay in Athens, where the olives hung ripe two weeks ago, oozing oil, among the ruins and the statues. Or in Thessaloniki, where three weeks ago the yellow leaves froze stiff, and pomegranates blazed, where her sons and their father live now. Darker, heavier boys than she remembers, they sat in waterfront squares at sunset. eating *loukoumades* with her, hotly exchanging glances and giggles with each other. Syrupy kisses they pressed on her lips; goodbye, Mum. She came to Greece to see them.

Only this minute, sun-blinded at the door of the OTE, does she think her dream might have meant *them.*

Surely the grave was in Australia? Still, she turns and queues again: rings Thessaloniki. Their father is curt. Everyone is all right. The boys are out. At school, yes. No, never mind. Yes. Goodbye.

* *

Past saddled donkeys and boats she walks along the road round the point into a warm wind, hoping to find the sea cave. Soon she comes to platforms, cannons, broken concrete steps. Dribbling rust, the iron ladders in the rocks have their feet in the ruffled sea. She climbs down one to dip her hands and face for the first time in years in the Aegean — warm, salty, fine to swim in, though the sun has clouded over. Further round she finds the cave, a dome of dark blue light with a hole in the top, a hollow whale of a cave. She would love to swim into it, if people, donkeys, even gravel trucks, would stop going past. Suddenly a dozen Japanese tourists with cameras are clambering on the rocks. Wishing she could turn transparent in the water — surely there are fish that do? — she goes and sits out of sight beside a small blowhole breathing like a dolphin. Across the water are cloud-pale hills in folds; threads of smoke blow off them. Close to shore a fishing boat throbs past, its seabirds squealing in loops. The sun is more like a full moon, shifting among screens of the mist.

Another parade of tourists is coming near.

Panting, she scrambles uphill. A scatter of sweet rain furs the sea behind her, pricks her skin. Birds cry out in astonishment. The darkening earth breathes out warm smells. Above the white windmill on the far side of the harbour a rainbow comes into being. Out of the rusty grey rocks where she is, pine trees and gums are growing, Australian gums, and thorns and thistles. Her feet slither on red pine needles. She sits on a stone wall to get her breath. Hens stalk away. A rooster raises its throat, dripping scarlet, to drink rain. A ladybird like a small tortoise will not move from her sleeve.

Stones rattling from above her make her jump. Startled, a white goat skips off smiling, her rope like a tufted tail behind her. 'Bebekaaa!' screeches a hag in a low doorway. The goat nibbles, bridles, falters towards Barbara; then lets her pick up the tuft and lead her home.

The hag fondles the long white ears. 'Thank you, my girl.'

The town clock strikes twelve and suddenly all the bells are ringing again. Barbara stares. 'God protect us': the hag crosses herself.

New smoke has risen over the hill, from the burnt house. They can see it from here, roofless, crammed to its white lintels with ashes. Rubble has spilt out wherever doors and windows were. A smell of wet ashes comes on the wind. But soon the smoke frills away.

'Whose house was it?' asks Barbara in Greek.

'A rich man's. They live in Athens. Don't tell me you're Greek?'

'I was.'

'How come?'

'My sons are. And their father. I'm Australian, though.'

'Australians sometimes live here. You I've never seen before.'

'We mostly lived in Thessaloniki. I've just been there to see the boys.' And angrily: 'They were born in Australia, though.' This is a lie. She is surprised at herself.

'How many? Who looks after them?'

'Two. His new wife. She's pregnant. His mother helps her. The older boy started high school in September.'

The goat tugs, the tuft of the rope jerks free; flicking her tail, she stops high on the slope to gaze down benignly. With a sigh the woman turns her back. 'Your Greek is good,' she says. 'Why not live here?' She screws up cunning eyes.

'I can't decide.' Barbara smiles. 'We still write letters. Ring, on special occasions. But we're not —'

'Over there (Bebeka!) you have someone?'

'Not since my mother died.'

In her head she adds to a letter she has been writing to him, not to be posted because won't she get back first?

I'm using up my mother's shampoos; frugality was dinned into me as a little girl. Guiltily I threw away her butts of lipsticks — the show of bravery they made.

Who, I wonder, will use up what I leave behind?

Letters never sent, or sent but not answered; if answered, not answered to the point but at an angle to it: this is how it has been with him all along, in spite of what they wanted. She suspects that it will be in silence that they lose each other, by which time he won't care.

After the silence of respect for death: 'Condolences, my girl. You have a man, I meant.'

'Oh. Well, I don't have — not *have*. There is a man I —'

'But not in wedlock.' Her face closes.

'Ah. No.'

And the woman is shrugging disparagingly: 'Your own children are here?' And turning: 'Ach! Now look where she's got to. Bebeka!' Like a baby's her grin shows gums and two stumps of bottom teeth. In a terraced tomato patch the goat props, stutters. The woman is clambering up. 'Beh-beh-ka! Come back!'

'Goodbye.' Barbara calls.

'Yes. God go with you.'

Bebeka means baby girl. Barbara is sorry not to have had a girl. (*He* has one.) In a sense it's not too late; and yet it is. She has been alone too long. The membranes that bind her to other lives have worn too thin to sustain her in motherhood. *Over there, you have someone.* Her only living relatives are the boys. Their names and the Thessaloniki address are in her passport: *in case of death or accident.* One day they will stand holding a letter from the Embassy.

Bebeka, dislodging a rock too many, smashing through the crust of tiles on some ruined house, is sure to break her neck.

Barbara sees the old woman turn to stare back over her shoulder, her hands knotted on a root in the hill.

The drizzle has stopped. I weigh lightly on the earth, Barbara thinks, picking her way round and down: what does it matter if I live here, or there? If I sold my mother's house I could afford to live here. Her abrupt and resentful spirit stalks me through its narrow rooms and shares her old bed with me. Under the dust her mirrors in the morning startle me with a face not yet hers. I will sell it. If I want to I can even go from island to island.

A cobweb quivers on his evening window.

Under dark arches and along stairways flashing with puddles she makes her way down to the harbour.

A cruise ship has docked and all the shops are open waiting. At the comer *taverna* near the monastery most of the outside tables are taken already. On the steps down to it she almost treads on white fur lying there — a sprawled cat. She recoils, crouching in horror. It has shat itself, its twitching haunch is pasted with shit and blowflies. Froth drips from its jaw. Aware of her presence, it rasps itself round on the whitewash, its paws stretched out to her. Its eye is fixed and its dry tongue points. Passers-by stare, but at her. She walks away.

The thought of eating makes her sick, but she finds a table against the sunny wall and asks for a bottle of *retsina*, since they only have bottles. Everywhere the cats are lying in wait, under the tables or on rush-bottomed chairs in the sun; some snuffle and retch, some vibrate with greed, some doze, paws folded. After two glasses of the woody wine she wanders inside and orders stuffed tomatoes. Thick bread comes with it: she eats it all, mopping up the red oil with the last crust. On the whitewashed wall at her back is a yellow light in the shape of a bottle of *retsina*.

A black cat stretches out a paw, then it lands in a blonde woman's lap, its tail a flagpole. 'Oh, what a lovely boy': she strokes its cheeks. A laughing group of Japanese tourists passing by takes everyone's photo. A team of donkeys clatters past. 'The Japanese! The new rich,' blares an Englishwoman. Cooing, the blonde flicks haricot beans one by one under the table — no, not beans: the fried eyes of fish. A scuffle of cats erupts.

A boy who looks like Barbara's sons charges the cats with a straw broom. 'Oh, don't!' Barbara calls in Greek. His impudent eyes meet hers. With a yell he scoops a tabby up, thumps it against the wall. The blonde screams. Resentfully the cook grabs the boy's shoulders and marches him inside. More donkeys plod nodding past.

Half a bottle of *retsina* throws its shape on the hot wall. When it is gone, Barbara stumbles away. The white cat is motionless now in the shade. She finds the stairway to the hotel, her head swarming, and collapses on the starched sheet.

The bells for vespers half-wake her, and the rush of rain. When she wakes properly, shivering and dry-mouthed, the sun has just set and a cruise ship on its way out is making the dim red harbour water roll. Yellow lights come flickering on. *Souroupo*, she says aloud, thinking what a lovely word for twilight: and *plio* for a boat, that sound of parted water. *To plio fevgei souroupo.* Where is [illegible]ing? Even so high up she can hear and smell the sea.

As she is picking up her teapot, it slips out of her hands to smash into the basin. Shocked, she turns on the basin light and stoops in her shadow picking up the glossy fragments and the wet tealeaves. You stupid, she tells the mirror: look at you mourning for it. As if it were alive. She washes her hands that smell like wet ashes.

Now that a light is on she closes the shutters; rainy air still flows in. Before the real rain starts again, she pulls on her yellow slicker and splashes down stairways to the bright shops, open again, to buy her evening yoghurt in the grocery she likes, a tunnel of stiff salt cod, opened tubs and barrels, chandeliers of sausage. Already rain is prickling the puddles. The red light at the headland is spilt wide. The cobbles of the harbour front, always so glossy at night that they look wet, are streaming, glimmering now. Rain falls from boats into yellow water.

At a turn in the stairway a man mutters urgently to a woman whose long hair hides her; hearing footsteps, she winces, lifts a face aflash with light, rain — tears? A *taverna* further along has its music bottled up in golden glass, and its sedate families in rows. Three girls passing her arm-in-arm chant in chords, *'Ka-li ny-chta.'* Inside the Frondistirion Anglikis Glossis an Englishwoman articulates: 'He has five pounds in his wallet. She has five pounds ...' A dog howls.

She gets back just before the heavy rain breaks. In the still light of her room she parts the shutters to look out at all the lighted windows (one blank and black where the burnt walls stand); all the yellow cascading under streetlamps. The usual shouts and laughs from the evening streets are muffled, voices underwater. A church bell chimes.

A rich man's. They live in Athens.

The shutters closed, she sits cross-legged on the sheet to eat the yoghurt, blandly sour with a crinkled skin, and spoonfuls of honey she curls out of her honey-jar. She licks her syrupy lips. Still loud, the rain; a voice in a bubble reads shadowy pages of *Memoirs of Hadrian.* Is it raining in Athens, on the statues and the olives? Raining in Thessaloniki? The boys live there. Raining where he is?

Naked in her white bed she imagines herself in his. She strokes his arms and shoulders, strokes him all over and kisses his shaggy head as it bends to her nipple. He has long eyelashes like shadows. The dark hairs of his body press soft against her. When he falls asleep he lies breathing in her arms, as confiding as a child (as his children). But he is lent, not given. He has said — to her, to others — that he can never imagine living with her. He asked once, 'If you had a man, would you want to have another child?' The words spread silently inside her like blood pooling. How should she have answered? What does it mean anyway — *have, had*?

Why did he ask?

Lying flat, she remembers the death that the old man flicking worry beads told her about on her first day here, in the grocery she likes. A girl, having grown up on this island, went home and married in Australia. One day she dressed herself again in all her white wedding clothes and put her head in her gas oven. Why? No one knew why. It was a mystery.

This has been a white day of bad dreams and omens.

Nevertheless, regardless, she leans over and on the Monday page of her diary she writes in large capitals:

OTE: RING AND CONFIRM RETURN FLIGHT THURS. 3.45 A.M.

She slips it under the pillow. She is going back, it seems. Why? Is this how decisions should be made or make themselves? Never mind. This is as good a way as any.

In Australia Saturday morning has begun. He and his children are waking up in his white front room where trees make the sunlight flutter on them. A world away, in a few hours chimes and church bells will wake her: bells flung on ropes from edge to edge, great voices bursting through the shutters, slashes of the sun.

POMEGRANATES

'Your hair's got darker,' Kyria Sophia says, 'since you came here first. Otherwise you're the same. Your Greek is still all right. I can't take it in, how it's all those years since you left our son.'

Strolling around the village on a road that has been asphalted past balconied mansions where doughy cottages used to be, she is slow: she who strode laughing and skipped over its ruts and heaps of dung. She is almost deaf. The skin of her face is baked on, her hair dead white. A grey spider like a crab is groping over threads of it; she stands still to let the younger woman flick the spider off, and absently with ridged hands strokes her woven hair smooth again.

Passing a garden, she begs a bunch of marigolds from a young householder whose moustache just covers a tolerant smile. She grabs at running children to ask each one: whose little boy, whose little girl? Outside the bakery they meet a nephew of hers, a man bald as a brass knob who always makes much of her Australian grandson whenever his father brings him here. Merrily she screws two fistfuls off the loaf he has bought. Munching hot sour bread, talking about their boy, they all walk home in the sun.

In barn after barn left open to air, garlands of tobacco are hanging like fur coats. She and the old man no longer grow any. Their barn still has sacks of grain, bales of hay and lucerne; he keeps the old horse in there, and the cow with her calf. Kyria Sophia has her vegetable garden, fenced with beans and morning glories. Her tomatoes hang in skeins among yellowing leaves. She has round peppers and long ones, deep red, and black eggplants curved like horns. Hens scratch and flounce, and two scraggy turkey cockerels. The flowers on her basil are like lilac, white and mauve.

The trees are the same, in the same warm mist as when Bell first saw them, their leaves yellowed, even the cobwebs afloat among them yellowed. Mist-glossy and black, there are the thorny acacias: dented gold pods, green fronds of leaves. Over the doorway the grapes are ripe to wrinkling and hum all day with insects, grapes so sweet that they parch the throat. Along the fence there are trees with round red fruits too bright to be apples and besides they have tails: pomegranates, full of red glass seeds.

It is seven years since Bell was here last; fourteen, since she first came in pomegranate time.

Kyria Sophia picks one now and breaks it open. She and this Australian who was her daughter-in-law sit on stools under the grapevine, nibbling the seeds.

'The boy kept saying when they came this summer that you had made up your mind to come. I didn't believe it. After all these years. And here you are.'

'I wanted to come before this.'

'I'll pick the pomegranates before you go. You can take some back to Australia for him.'

This is the time of year when the earth reddens, and the sun; and the moon, like an egg in a nest of clouds.

'Every summer they come I tell the boy, this or that is his mother's,' Kyria Sophia says coyly. 'Whenever we use your things.' Forgotten things are everywhere. They have just drunk Nescafe from the silver-rimmed Australian cups, with milk from the old blue-and-white striped jug. Today's yoghurt, in the red French casserole, is warm in an Onkaparinga blanket by the wood stove. Kyria Sophia has the earthenware baking-dish — a wedding present — on her lap: under a white crust is tomato paste, dried like blood after days in the sun. She is spooning off the crust of mould.

'All your things have been waiting here for you.' She sighs when silence answers her.

'What if I go and see if there are any eggs?' Bell jumps up.

'Go and see.'

She escapes to the barn, where the hens lay their eggs in the old mangers. Just inside, the black-lashed eyes of the calf bulge; it stumbles upright, its knees and belly wet with dung. The cow swings her head up from the manger with a snort that stirs the hay warmly. There are four smeared eggs stuck with straw beside the dummy egg.

She remembers the eggs she wrote 'B' on.

'She wrote "B" on the eggs!' Her sister-in-law Chloe's voice. 'Why should she hog them? What about my children?'

'Ssst.' That was the old woman. 'Here she is!'

'So what?'

'Here I am.' She saw Chloe grimace. 'What's wrong?'

'Nothing.'

'Something about eggs?'

'No, no, she didn't say anything.'

'I did.' Chloe pointed. 'That's not fair.'

'Because they're hard-boiled?'

'I'm sure it's just a misunderstanding, girls.'

'How come you need your initials on them?'

'Oh. The "B"? I always — it's for "Boiled". *Brasto.*'

'Oh.'

'So we can tell.'

'There! A simple misunderstanding!'

'I still don't see why you had to hard-boil four, when there aren't any fresh eggs.'

'I thought there would be. I boiled these for the salad.'

'We don't put eggs in the *salad.*'

'No? *Sorry.*'

'They'll do for a *meze* with olives. And Magdalini will have fresh eggs,' smiled Kyria Sophia. 'Let's all go and see her now.'

'Let's go and see Aunt Magdalini?' she is about to call out now, coming back with the eggs. But there is the *papas* fluttering along the road, his coppery hair and beard as if on fire under his black stovepipe hat. 'Look! It's the same *papas*! The seaman, the red one who married us.'

Kyria Sophia's mouth sets hard. 'That's him.'

'He's coming over.'

'He would.'

Both women kiss the red curls of his extended wrist. They all recite the required greetings; then he sinks into the cane armchair with a creak to wait for the cakes and coffee.

Luckily Bell has brought a ribboned box of cakes from the city. She washes her hands and the eggs, pours glasses of water and puts a cake each on three silver-rimmed plates. This *papas,* she remembers, was a wild seaman until his wife made him study theology and give her six boys, burly farmers all. 'I ploughed the waves,' he boomed. 'My boys plough the dry land.' Barbarossa.

'He looks like a pirate!'

But the old woman sniffs, stirring the coffee.

'I ploughed the waves. My boys plough the dry land.' That time, too, he was having coffee with them both. 'Are you still liking Greece, *madame*? Yes? A very different life.'

Bell quoted a proverb: 'Where there's land, there's home.'

'Good, good. Here's the place to raise children.'

'I hope to, father. One day.'

'Soon, if God wills.'

'We'll see.'

'Mmm. How many years is it?' Scratching his bright beard, he leaned forward. 'You do have contact with your husband?'

'Contact? He lives here!'

'No: contact. She doesn't understand!' He rolled his eyes at her mother-in-law, who shot them both a shifty look.

'Contact? Mamma, he can't mean —'

'Of course he does!' hissed the old woman.

'Oh.' She felt her red face gape stiffly in a grin. 'Yes. I do.'

'It's the will of God then, eh?' he said gratefully. Both women glared as he took his leave.

'And what's more, your mother put him up to it!' She was still angry when her husband came home. 'What she really wanted him to ask was if I'm on the Pill!'

'Don't start this again,' muttered her husband.

'It's *her.* She never stops.'

'Ssst. Perhaps it was a misunderstanding.'

'Sure.'

'Okay, so she wants grandchildren. What's so terrible about that?'

'Like when she took our dirty clothes —'

'She wanted to help you wash —'

'— to see if some disease was stopping me conceiving!'

'You hurt her that night. Shouting, crying, shutting yourself in.'

'Asking if I'd like to see a doctor! "This stain here on your pants — are you sure nothing's wrong?" '

'Oh God.'

'Oh yes, God, oh yes. "The will of God." '

His curly beard is sprinkled with icing-sugar; he rubs his hands and a veil of it falls. 'Is it the will of God,' he intones now, 'that the churches in your country should have women priests?'

'No!' says the old woman. 'Jesus was born a man. He wasn't born a woman!'

'Mamma, He had to be born one or the other.'

'Exactly! And He chose to be born a man. He said woman was born to be man's hostage!'

'What? Hostage!'

'He said so in the Bible. And now the Protestants have women priests! Blasphemers! God will send His fire to Earth!'

'Because of that?'

'The world will end soon in storms of fire. That's the nuclear holocaust. No wonder, when mankind has forsaken His way and let communism and divorce and women's liberation run wild. They worship the Antichrist! May God send the fire to burn them!'

'Well now, Kyria Sophia, time I was on my way.' The *papas* sighs. 'Duty calls. Have you got the names?'

'I'll bring them, father.'

Tomorrow is Psychosavvato, Souls' Saturday, when he will hold a morning service for the souls of everyone's dead. Their names will be read out and each family's *kollyva* shared among the mourners. Kyria Sophia will be the first one there.

After the afternoon sleep they go to see Aunt Magdalini, who insists on picking all her best roses and presenting them with a hug of welcome. She scuttles in the blue cave of her kitchen dishing out cherry *glyko* on glass saucers, mixing coffee, pouring iced water.

'*Aman*, Magdalini.' Kyria Sophia slaps her saucer down. 'This cherry *glyko* of yours. Nobody can eat it. Throw it away.'

'I boiled it too long,' cackles Magdalini.

'Is it *glyko* or glue?'

'Don't eat it, dear, if you don't like it,' Magdalini tells the visitor.

'Oh, but it's lovely!' she answers. It's more like toffee than jam. She scoops up the last threads and bites them off her spoon, grinning at Magdalini, who is more than ever a gnome of a little old woman. Kyria Sophia hunches her shoulders and her black brows. Magdalini, as ever, is impervious.

'I haven't boiled my *kollyva*,' she says. 'Have you?'

'Oh yes,' says Kyria Sophia.

'I haven't even cleaned the wheat.'

'Bring it here, then.'

Magdalini brings in a pan of rustling wheat. The three women sweep it with their hands, picking out stones and husks and seeds. The mist hovering in the doorway turns cool blue.

Kyria Sophia has a bowl of *kollyva* with a lighted candle stuck in it, as if for a birthday; and a little brass incense holder which she stuffs with hot coals from the *somba* before setting in it a bead of red incense like a pomegranate seed. She takes them from room to room. The smoke trails after her muttering shadow.

Back in the kitchen, sighing, she strains the evening milk and puts it on to boil.

The old man comes in cold from the *kafeneion*, hungry for chestnuts before dinner. He smokes with his eyes closed, waiting. Kyria Sophia has to remind Bell where to find the chestnuts. She remembers without being told how to slit them with a knife and shuffle them round on the iron top of the *somba* until they scorch. Singeing her fingers, she peels them then, enough for everyone; waxen, wrinkled and sweet, they sting in the mouth.

Kyria Sophia cuts bread and cheese and heats up the vegetable stew left over from lunch. The old pots flutter their lids and whistle, now and then uttering a faint crow as of roosters in the distance. The milk, as always, boils over, surrounding the pot with a frill that crackles and burns brown. They eat eggplants and peppers and beans and mop up all the red oil with their bread. The cheese is a salty white honeycomb, the grapes ripening into raisins. To celebrate her coming, they pour what's left of last year's ouzo from the demijohn, and drink it watered.

While Bell washes up, Kyria Sophia decides to inspect the eggbound hen. 'I hope she's managed to lay it. If not —' She holds up the knife. 'I'm not letting her die on me.' Soon squawks and one screech come from the henhouse. A bundle thumps on the kitchen windowsill by the pot of basil: red cords poke from speckled shoulder feathers. Kyria Sophia throws open the window — oil-yellow smoke drifts out among needles of rain — and with a pot of boiling water at her elbow she plucks and cleans the hen.

'Rain at last. Well, we'll eat her tomorrow.' She crams the carcase into the refrigerator. They have one now, and a television set too. 'In red sauce? Or egg-and-lemon, maybe.' Her bloody fingers hold up a bright pomegranate: no — the egg that she pulled out. 'Pity,' she says.

She sits by the *somba*, reading the prayer book aloud in her cracked treble, glancing over her glasses now and then. The visitor goes and leans over the sill to breathe in the cold air made lemony by the wet basil. In the mud below, the cat's eyes flash green; it sends up a yowl for more of the tattered hen. Both the old people are snoring.

So many village evenings spent yawning beside the *somba,* to the sounds of cats and snores and night birds. She has put off going to bed, because this is the same old bedroom, and the bed. Those are the two cane armchairs that made up a cot for the baby the first time he was here. These are even the honeymoon sheets that they rumpled and soaked with sweat all the first summer, night and afternoon. Now she opens the window and the hinged shutters: she leans on the sill. The rain has stopped. Drops fall from the grapes into dark puddles.

On the chest by the bed are old photographs of them all together, here and in the city and on beaches. She is holding one of her boy tossing wheat to hens long since killed and eaten, when his grandmother creeps in.

'Some hot milk?'

'No thanks, Mamma.'

'All the good times.' She points at the photograph. 'Don't they matter any more?'

'Everything matters.'

'Can a woman just walk out on her man these days, and her little boy? Don't you remember how it was?'

'I remember, or why would I be here?'

'I can't take it in.' She turns away. "Hang anything you want in this wardrobe. See, we have a wardrobe now. I'll just take my coat for church, then I won't have to wake you tomorrow.' Her voice is still reproachful. Once she would have added: Or will you come with me? She holds up a slim camelhair coat, silk-lined. 'Isn't it beautiful?'

'Yes. Let me see it on.'

She slips it on and lets her white plait loose.

'Yes, Mamma, you look very elegant.'

'I'm old.' Peering in the dull wardrobe mirror: 'Look at me. Is my hair much whiter now? Whiter than when you first saw me? It must be.' There are tears on her cheeks.

'No.' Bell puts her arms round her. 'It's the same.'

FIRE AND FLOOD

At the best of times I was — am — far from being a man of action. Joan was sometimes irritated by what she called my immovability. I've come to a standstill now.

For the past few months I've been living in an upstairs flat in Melbourne, in a street that runs alongside a railway cutting. My bedroom has two windows: the one high over the bed looks south, the other east on to the street. I leave both blinds up all night. From time to time a car grunts and slides away and its lights fling the sudden shape of the east window in at me. There is a silver birch and a streetlamp beyond it which inks in all over the room the shapes of its spotted branches and its leaves fewer each day. On rainy nights the branches themselves are black. Edged and beaded with lamplight they quiver under their weight of water. At full moon a whiter backwash floods the branches on the wall.

Tree of light and death, heaventree. For the time being I need to live alone inside a web of black branches. My mind shies away. It must take them in.

Standing there at the window I can see the top half of the trains that pass in the cutting. All evening yellow trainloads of people come and go, sitting up straight, some with their hands at the edges of newspapers. I hardly ever read a newspaper now. A pulse trembles in my walls whenever a train passes; if I lean against them I can feel it.

Last night a woman woke me, shouting: 'You've given me nothing in four years!' A silence. 'Four years! *Nothing*.'

Wasn't it six? I caught myself thinking: surely it was six? I gave you all I could, Joan. You must know that. Salvation, absolution — they weren't in my power.

But this was a woman outside, and a man's voice bellowed out once in furious reproach, '*Sarah*?' Only once. And the only answer was the sound of heels tapping away down the street.

I have lost Joan. Lost Sam. The dreams I have of them bare me to the bone.

As one window faces east, if I happen to open my eyes as day breaks (most mornings I do) I see the sky red, and trees still or windflung outspread black against it. I close my eyes and walk on bleeding earth. Lava, the earth's blood, gushes and along its banks, as with a wound, a black scab forms. The hill is smoke and ashes. Flames burst up in a gully of bracken. At their core a boy in bathers is asleep on his back. I scream: 'Sam!' The smile leaves his lips. As I bend forward he breaks up into fire coals like a log on the hearth. The window breathes in on me.

I get up for a glass of water or vodka and sit up in bed sipping it. My hand round the glass absorbs my attention as the sun comes up. The light caught in both flesh and glass fuses them into one red-gold mass. When the sun touches the wall, bird shadows are on the shadows of the branches.

This morning when I went to the other room for a drink, a sparrow had found its way in, I suppose between the blades of the exhaust fan. I heard its chirrup and ruffle of wings. Then the brown egg-shape leaped at the panes. I wound open what windows I could (this room also has two): it battered the fixed ones. Each time it flew through a ray of sunlight it flashed as if on fire. At last it hurtled out into the silver birch and I could wind the windows shut.

On the day of the fires, birds flying high above were overcome by the heat, fell and were burnt. The wings of others caught alight in midair. Falling, they set more bush on fire.

Early that morning Sam and I went to the Cascades to collect samples of water life for him to take to school.

A favourite place of ours, the Cascades were — are — reached by a bush track lit in stripes of green and gold-brown wherever the sun touches the river. Past a quarry the sky opens out over flat rocks and the river is forced down narrow slimy channels, the Cascades. When Sam was small we came to draw with chalks on the grey rocks, and paddle and fish with nets. Soon he graduated to sliding down the channels on plastic garbage bags with the big kids, smack into the deep pool at the bottom. Not this summer, though: the drought had dried up the channels. The river was a chain of dark pools covered with curds of scum like dried vomit.

We found ourselves a hollow out of the hot north wind. Above us the gums tossed and creaked; here ants and skinks tilted their long shadows, and dragonflies sped, then stayed and their wings drilled holes in the air. There were hoppings and writhings at the black lips of the pools. Sam as he dipped his jamjars sent bronze lights swaying. There was a stink of rottenness, too foul to be from the pool: someone had turned a black snake inside out and hung it over a branch, with opal flies for a skin.

The dog chained at the quarry barked. Sam laughed, barking back.

'She's a scorcher today,' people were saying in the streets. 'If a fire gets going today, we've had it.'

'Reckon there'll be a fire, Peter?' Sam said.

Sam called me Peter, not Dad: he was Joan's boy. (I have no children.) He was a few days short of his eighth birthday and after six years together we were father and son all the same.

'There's a cool change on the way,' I said. 'But if a fire does start, you make for the beach with your mother and stay there.'

'They ought to have back-burnt the bush ages ago,' he said. 'That's what Jake reckons.'

Jake was — still is, I suppose — a journalist; his boy Colin was Sam's best mate at school.

'They couldn't have this year because of the drought,' I said. 'Everything's been dry as paper for months now. They couldn't take the risk.'

'He reckons we're in for the big one all right.'

'Big or little, make for the beach and you'll be okay.'

From the school where I taught, in the industrial zone of Moorong, home was a good hour's drive round the coast. It was after four by the time I got halfway — halfway is where you first see the lighthouse on the point — and saw clouds rising over the far cliffs. Storm clouds on the coast come over with the rear and lunge of surf; they have a dark vault and fray out in slow explosions of white. But there was no water in these: they were smoke. Soon after that I nearly went hurtling into a roadblock.

They were turning all the traffic back and getting ready to evacuate the coastal towns. It's the big one all right, they said. No casualties, as far as they knew.

It was a slow crawl back to Moorong, with a couple of stops at petrol stations to try and ring Joan. From a friend's place in Moorong I kept on dialling our number, then the Beach Hotel where Joan worked some evenings, until at last I got on to her. The fire had burnt out the fringe of the town, she said: a lot of our friends' houses. It had gone east and wiped out the next two towns. The hills were burning. Our place was safe so far but there'd been spot fires. The cool change was due any minute.

'Sam all right?'

'Yes. He's up at Marie's with Colin. He's gone wild with excitement. Keeps badgering everyone with ideas for fighting the fire. Jake's out on the firetruck.'

'Shouldn't you all stay down near the beach? Look, I'll drive the long way round, I'll be home in two hours,' I said. 'The inland roads are open, aren't they?'

'No, no, don't,' she said. 'Nobody knows where it's going next. We're all safe where we are so let's stay put. You can come tomorrow.'

So all I know of the day and night of the fires is what Joan and others told me, what I heard at the inquest and read in the papers.

All that morning of intolerable heat Joan worked in her painting shed. After lunch she listlessly did the washing. Before she could peg it all out it dried in one roar of the northerly. Sam came tearing home from school with the news that a bushfire had broken out behind our hills and was heading for the town. As he said it, swollen clouds rolled over the sky. She hurried to unpeg the washing. But it was smoke.

Red and gasping, she and Sam ran to collect books, papers, photographs, her canvases, his toys, the television set, odd pieces of clothing, and cram them into the car. Breathing was painful; between trips they lay on the clammy kitchen linoleum to cool off. Dread and the heat were making her vague. At last she locked up and drove to the foreshore. Standing with Sam at her side in the shallows — a flat sea, milky jade green — she watched the dark rim of the bay burn round to the river mouth. Trees were suddenly crests of flame, then black bones, and fire brimmed in the grass. Horses set free went wandering along the water's edge, mirrored among the clouds.

Schoolmates of Sam's were down at the beach, among them his best mate Colin and his older brother. They swam around together and watched the fires for a while. When they had to go home, Sam begged to be allowed to go with them. They were having good fun. Colin's place was up the hill, but nowhere near the fires: Sam went there most afternoons, didn't he? Colin's mother didn't mind.

Worn down, Joan said he could go.

Some time after sunset — no telling when sunset was, in all the smoke — she walked back and hosed the house down, though it seemed pointless. There was no one in sight. She went in and lay down sweltering in the smoky light of a lamp. Both the radio and the television set were in the boot of the car, down on the foreshore. She rang the hotel: she wasn't feeling up to going to work. But they were short-staffed already, they said, with nearly everyone out at the fires. As they were speaking her lamp went off, and that settled it. The power was off in the house, in the street: in half the town.

So she rang Marie, Colin's mother. The power was on there and the boys were having a great time. She'd keep Sam there until Joan could pick him up after work.

Cars crammed to the roof were still crawling into the main street and the foreshore. Burnt-out families were settling with borrowed bedding in shopfronts and in the school buildings. By now mountains of red-lit smoke hung so low over the river that it seemed that the nearest rooftops were on fire.

As she served the meals in the terrace bar, the flames made their way along the hills, clear in the darkness where in daylight the smoke had hidden them. Yellow gushes of light glowed and sank back. The cool change came: the wind whipped round to the south-west, spitting rain, and took the fire with it.

She had no suspicion until the call came from the hospital, a call she couldn't make sense of. Sick with terror, she ran all the way. Marie was there, and Colin and his brother, moaning in each other's arms. Joan screamed when she saw their hands and their feet, Marie told me later: and again when she saw that Sam wasn't with them.

It seems, piecing stories together, that within minutes of the change their trees and then their eaves, their whole roof, caught fire. As Marie rushed the boys out, still in bathers and thongs but holding around themselves the blankets she had kept soaking in the bath, a burning tree torn up in the squall crashed among them. A thick branch pinned Sam down by the legs; branches all around were blazing. They had to leave him. Marie shoved her boys into the back seat and drove blindly down the hill with the fire all around her. When the engine cut out she steered somehow on to level ground, and firefighters were there to take them on to safety. She told them where Sam was. We'll get him out, they said.

Marie and her boys and Joan were kept at the hospital under sedation. I knew nothing about it. No one knew where to ring me; Joan couldn't remember.

In Moorong we tried station after station on the radio and then the television news: helicopters had got news teams in. According to them, everyone in our town was huddled on the beach or the pier watching the last houses go up. Fires, firestorms, were raging out of control in the hills near Melbourne. There were unconfirmed reports of people being burnt alive, even in cars. That can't be right, we said. Isn't that what they tell you, stay in your car? But it was right.

I got on to Joan at the hotel. She was flat out, but calm. She wrote down my friend's number and promised to try to ring after work. I probably won't get through, she said. I knew that.

I rang Marie too. 'We've got off lightly,' she said. Sam was playing cricket in the backyard, so I didn't ask to speak to him.

By then there were a few people at my friend's place, some of them with houses in the fire's path. We went through a fair amount of beer, and after a while we gave up on the radio and the television altogether and even the phone and put on records instead. Someone passed a joint or two around. At some time in the middle of all the confusion and hysteria I stretched out on the hot seagrass matting and went to sleep.

I woke over and over in smoky light — there was ash in the smoke clouds over Moorong — and then alone in darkness, sure that it must be daybreak and time to get going; until at last it was.

I drove home against a cold wind spattering rain, past the black hills and the bare black sticks of trees and the two burnt towns before ours with their flat spaces and wreckage where houses had been. Leaning telegraph poles smouldered, and road posts, each with a red and a white eye melted like wax. Against the smoke over our town a yellow helicopter shuttled with its bucket of sea water on a rope.

'The house was locked. Joan and Sam weren't there. I knew something was wrong then. It took me a while to find out where they were. Up at the hospital I saw Joan (she was still asleep) and identified Sam's body. It was Sam under the blanket. I said not to let Joan ever see that. She insisted, though; Marie told me.

Jake was there, Marie's man, black and weary after fighting the fire all night. He came up with me to their place. Half the houses on the hill were gone: nothing left but chimneys and strips and twists of corrugated iron buckled like cardboard and dumped over the rubble and ashes. At their place, glass that had melted lay in the yard in gobs like grey toffee. Rolls of black chicken-wire had been bedsteads. The garden was black stumps and tufts of smoke, a small flare in the gully, pale red-gold. The burnt tree lay where it fell. They had dug under it to get Sam out.

The opposite hill that had been thick bush was white with ash like a fall of snow. Walking over there we stumbled on mounds of flesh, torn already and loud with flies, as black as if they were mummified. A wombat, a few possums, somebody's cocker spaniel were still alive, burnt to the bone but still alive, and so we bashed their brains out. There must have been crows around, but I remember it as total silence. Silence and absence and bitter cold, as if the ash had been real snow.

We had a short service at the church, to which Sam's teachers and all the third grade came. We buried him in the cemetery on the hill. Bit by bit we gave his belongings away. We talked about living somewhere else, in or near Moorong, and perhaps we should have, but it seemed important at the time to try to go on living as normally as we could. I drove to school in Moorong and back every day. Joan worked her usual evenings at the hotel and I ate with her there after work and drove her home. She took an art class up at the school a couple of mornings a week: she wanted to drop that, but Marie talked her out of it. Marie was — is — a teacher at the school.

'The kids only want to do fire paintings,' Joan said. 'It's all they think about.'

'Maybe you should too,' I said.

'I don't feel like it.'

'Once you started —'

'I couldn't care less if I never paint again.'

She did keep on with the classes all the same. It was impossible to know what she felt. She always was like that, self-contained and solitary, careful to restrain her feelings. Except that she wore black every day now, and had lost interest in her painting, most of the time she might not have been bereaved. That was more than I could stand.

I hurt her, I suppose: I had to break through her silence.

'Talk to me, Joan, for God's sake,' I said in bed one night. 'Stop shutting me out. I've lost him too.'

'He was my child though. It's different.'

I was angry. Even in the dark she knew that.

'You'd like to blame me,' she went on. 'Say it then, why don't you: I should have made him stay with me.'

'You couldn't have known, nobody could.'

'*You* could have driven the long way round, if it comes to that.'

'I said I would. *You* said not to.'

'You didn't really want to, that's why!'

'I did want to.'

'But you didn't bother, did you?' And she ran sobbing out of the house. It was no use searching in the dark. I went back to bed and lay awake. She could have gone anywhere. There was a moon that we'd watched sway up out of the sea, heavy, full, a deep orange. High and white now above the tree at the window, it drew on the wall the precise shadow of branches, every twig and leaf sharp.

I never asked and never heard where she went. It was the first of several nights. I imagine her at the cemetery or the Cascades, or tapping on a window somewhere; tapping on some man's window.

I went out into the garden: dew and silence underfoot, like a night in snow. The houses all had dark windows. The sea was flat, no sound of surf. Beyond its rim the lights of two squid boats, thrown up to a bar of cloud, stared landward like white-browed eyes. I went back to bed.

She came back a long time later and bedded down in Sam's room — the first of many times that she slept there. I never knew when she would, or why either. Other times she clung to me all night. Sometimes we made love. Both of us woke a lot, whimpering and clenched, having had a bad dream. She wouldn't talk about her dreams.

'He was driving me mad, he wouldn't stop talking,' she woke and said aloud one night. 'I let him go to Marie's. I couldn't wait to get rid of him.' I held her. 'He lay there watching them leave him.'

'Don't. I love you,' I said, too sleepy to think what to say, and she pushed me off wearily.

'Oh, *love* — what good's *that*? Oh, leave me alone. Go back to sleep.'

I couldn't. I touched her and she turned away.

I remember one time, I woke to find her shaking me gently and murmuring, 'Wake up. It's a dream. Wake up.'

'You were in it,' I said, and at once she turned on to her back. 'I'd come in and the house was stripped. Even the plaster walls were gone, and the bath, the sink, the basin, the linoleum. There was one tap dripping on to the dust. You were bringing Sam. We were all going out somewhere. I hugged you and him, but as soon as we walked out into the sun he faded into dots and stripes like a badly tuned television. I said, "I can't see him. I can see right through him." You said he was there all right. "He's *not*," I —'

'Stop it. I don't want to hear it.'

I lay still for a while. ' "I don't want to hear it," that's you all right.'

'I have dreams too,' she said.

'Well, let's hear them! That's all I'm asking.'

She lay still. 'It makes me sick,' she said at last, 'the way you trot out your dreams as if you'd produced something *clever*.'

'That's what you think, is it?'

'I can't stand it. That's all. I can only take so much. You just have to leave me alone.'

'I thought we were together,' I said.

'We are. So far, anyway. Okay?' She turned her back.

I might have been strong enough for her, but for my own sorrow. As it was, we both started drinking heavily, apart and together: red wine for preference, in those days. Drunk, we could communicate or at least fight openly. Friends began to avoid us. In between times her silences went deeper. Silence, absence, a slow dissolution of the self: she was, I thought bitterly, as lost to me as Sam.

Then the rains came and we went to the Cascades.

The tail-end of an easterly was blowing the one time that I've made it back to our town since the flood. The other times I've tried, I've turned back at Moorong. I planned it well ahead and rented a car nothing like my own so no one would notice I was back in town. I was going to drive past our old place, and Marie's new one; and then keep well away from the centre.

Most of all since I moved to Melbourne I miss the easterlies, cold white easterlies of the coast sweeping up out of a white sky, a white ocean, and hurling froth over the beach. They blow for a week or more, summer and winter. Your hair goes stiff, your skin prickles from the salt. The seaward windows all over town film over. Perspectives flatten, as in fog or at sunset, warp as you look, so that the surrounding hills close in and hang over your head.

On the night of the fires the hills hung close like that, I've heard, as close as the rooftops.

I was ready for the first sight of the lighthouse on its bare headland. Then I saw the white surf and the long dunes, and all the tea tree dead and leafless on them like black coral. In the first town and the second, new houses had been built and the raw wooden frames of others were up. Soft in the spray, the folded hills were a sweeter green than ever, sheep were ambling sunk in grass. There was a wide concrete bridge where the old wooden one had burnt down. Most of the charred gums still had life in them: they had covered themselves with a shaggy cape of lush green that looked more like ivy than gum leaves and left the crowns bare. Their wiry black tufts poked into the sky.

I drove into town along the back streets, keeping my head down. There were lights on already in the new pinewood house they had built on Marie's land. Heads in her front window rushed past me as I drove downhill. I should go to the Cascades, I thought. Now that I was here I couldn't remember what I had wanted myself to do. I went to the cemetery.

From up there in the wind you can see most of the town and the white ocean all the way back to the lighthouse: the houses, some new, and the flat spaces, and the black trees huddled in thick new leaves, all in a roar of wind and water.

A few of the old graves have sunk and the mud has coffin shapes embedded in it. The crosses on the mounds are askew and mostly illegible. The marble and cement of gravestones a century old has cracked under the shells and the plastic flowers: Joan's family name is on some of them.

I walked the long way round to Sam's grave, a mound with no name on it, only opal ear-shells and pebbles like white eggs. Someone (Marie, I think it was) had planted flowers in the middle, freesias, grape-hyacinths, bluebells.

It was true what I had thought I remembered: trains in the distance can sound like surf.

It was too public to stay long. I picked two freesias to take home. I put them in water when I got back to the flat, and the next morning a brown spider was hanging on a thread between them, a spider from our town. Then I drove to the edge of the rainforest.

Here out of the wind was a dank stillness. New tree ferns like baby carrots were sprouting up under scorched old ones; others had fronds unscrolling, like green hands holding yoyos. New bracken hid the wet black fallen trunks of trees. I was the man sitting on a stump waiting for night to fall to make his escape. He knew there was nowhere he wanted to live but in this town, if he wanted to live. As far as he was concerned, though, it might as well still have been ringed with fire.

Long after the day of the fires the bush smouldered on. In the valley behind the coast the open-cut coal mine poured towers of smoke up. People walking miles away would find themselves on a hot crust of earth, how thick no one knew: fires were burning underground, along veins of the coal. When the rains came five weeks later, people driving at night into the town through the burnt hills saw through their streaming windscreens a glow of red here and there where trees were still burning.

Fleshy belladonna lilies were the first plants to grow out of the ash. Then grass sprouted at the roadsides, so bright that it looked like a corruption — mould on rotting matter, algae on ponds. Inland the hills stayed bare, but along the coast the green haze thickened by the day.

Close to shore the sea went dark with burnt leaves; the sand was scribbled along every tide mark with a charcoal line of leaves, and littered with black trunks lashed around with kelp.

On the day of the flood, however, the sea was grey, thick with the earth and ashes that the rivers were gouging out. I had to miss school. Burnt trees loosened by the rain had fallen and blocked the back road out of town and on the coast road the gravel ford where the bridge had burnt down was feet under water; on the third road, the long back way around, landslides were expected.

We stayed in bed most of the morning and for once we were close and gentle with each other, though nothing much was said. After lunch I was restless. I wanted to go and see the river. Joan didn't, she said, but I was feeling reprieved, overjoyed: I couldn't part from her. It would do her good. Didn't she love walks in the bush? She gave in. We walked hand in hand along the beach in the thick rain, then up the swilling river-path, our boots bogging in the silt, and past the quarry to the Cascades.

I remember that the quarry dog was howling.

Two forks of the river meet at the Cascades. On the far bank the trees were black, their leaves scorched rusty brown, but the fire had not touched the trees on the other bank. Between them, the living trees and the dead, two grey spouts of water joined with a smash like surf breaking. As we watched, a whole black tree hurtled downstream and, rolling and frothing, rammed itself against a high rock.

'I'm wet *through,*' she shouted. 'Let's go *home*!'

The loose rocks we had crossed were already under water: we would have to clamber up the bank to where the path led uphill. I went ahead, clutching at roots, slipping flat in the mud more than once and swearing. She didn't make a sound. Even in the roar of the water I think I would have heard. I *can't remember.* All I know is that when I turned round at the top I saw her — it was Sam's yellow raincoat that she had on — I saw her flying down the long, deep slopes of water that the Cascades had become.

I slithered down, ran and waded to the yellow bubble of the raincoat. She had been trapped where the dead tree was still wallowing in froth and tearing its black bark off in strips, thudding against the rocks. I screamed, 'Joan!' Our eyes met. A torn branch snapped and the tree rolled. Abruptly she sat up with the jackknife twitch of a corpse undergoing cremation. Then she was under the grey water.

I plunged in, sank, swam until I found footholds, and lost them again until at last I wrenched her free and into still water and on to the bank. Too exhausted to lift her, I had to pull her like some black log up on to the firmer mud. I loosened the clothes at her throat and, clutching her by the hair, pressed my mouth over hers and sucked, blew, sucked, blew, sucked. She didn't breathe. It was a long time, I think — I was half-drowned myself — before an old woman from the caravan park found us and went for help. Perhaps Joan was unconscious, perhaps dead, even as she reared up. In any case she was dead when help came.

Her blood was rusty in my mouth. The raincoat was still spreadeagled on the tree: I can see the yellow dance of it.

Though I stayed on at the school in Moorong till the end of first term, I hardly remember anything about it. I sold our house — an old weatherboard looking east over the ocean — easily and for more than I expected. I was thought to have left town long before I did: few of the locals ever saw me. Some of them might have taken that as an admission of guilt. Very soon, I suspect, I was a town legend. There are several. There's the old bloke in the fish story, for one. He gets home from the pier with a bucket of live salmon trout only to find his wife in bed with a neighbour. The neighbour takes off out the window and the old bloke, bellowing his rage and anguish, grabs a trout and shoves it headfirst up her cunt. Well, I'm the young bloke who not only lets his kid get trapped by a tree in the fires, he has to let another one drown his wife. It has that touch of the grotesque that makes a legend.

Some of the locals were good to me. Marie was. Since the fires she and the boys, and Jake sometimes, had been spending a lot of time at our place, now and then staying the night. They were living in a borrowed caravan. She came now as well, and stayed: What the locals couldn't take was the thought of Marie and me. That put them right against me.

In flashes of memory from time to time I confuse Marie with Joan. Not that Marie was a stand-in during those last few weeks. She knew that.

It was good to lie along her back with my arm round her shoulder, her breath a warmth that came and went on my open hand. Often I stayed awake. Hours would pass while I looked at the branches on the wall and held this warm woman in her sleep or she held me. Once when I got up and went walking round in the garden she came out — I saw her moving towards me in the white light — she came and put her arms round me, and we went back inside and lay down again. The surf was loud in the room.

I lay in her arms and told her what I had been dreaming about: the lava, the gully of burning bracken. She listened patiently. I came to the boy asleep at the core of the fire.

'*Don't*,' she said, twisting away, and I remembered.

'I'm sorry.' Her face under her hands was hot and wet. 'I didn't mean it.' I turned her round to me. It was pure thoughtlessness. I had forgotten for the moment who she was. When we were calmer she told me that Joan had seen Sam's body. That was the first I knew. They went in together, Joan and Marie, and had a look under the blanket.

At daybreak, I remember — shrill birds in the leaves at the

window — we were awake, naked, and Marie took a firm hold of my cock suddenly.

'You're a tower of ssh,' she murmured into my mouth.

'Strength?'

'Flesh. Your tower of flesh. All right, strength.'

A tower of strength. To think that she was looking to me for strength.

It was because of Sam that she was with me; but he was always between us too. Not that we talked about him much, or Joan either: it was mostly about our pasts and our futures. All the same, he was there. When her boys started staying overnight (they'd been having skin grafts at the hospital in Moorong), I couldn't bring myself to say they could have Sam's room. It was full of boxes of books, I said, and put them on camp beds in the sleepout. She must have known why and been hurt. Besides, there was Jake as well. She and Jake were in the same morass that Joan and I had been in since the fires, and he was seeing other women even before that. Still, I knew that Marie didn't take seriously the thought of any future without Jake. She was marking time.

We didn't break off abruptly. Before the final settlement at ninety days Marie moved into my place and looked after it while I shuttled between there and the flat. The new owners let her rent it from them while her house was being built. She was the only person in town who knew the address of this flat.

She wrote at Christmas. The boys were well again. Jake was back 'for now': she sounded off-hand about it, so as not to hurt me, I suppose. I answered that letter, but not the next couple. No more came.

I only rent this flat, and the house money is all in the bank — I can live on the interest. It's just as well, since I'm in poor shape, getting by on fruit, cheese, vodka. I can't see myself ever teaching again.

While I was packing I went into Joan's shed for the first time since the fires, not expecting to find anything there: bundled in newspaper were photographs, enlargements and sketches, dozens of sketches, of burnt wallabies and possums. It must have taken her days out on the hills to find so many.

She had done a painting too and scrawled in red along the bottom of it: *Firebirds*. Birds flapped on a dark ground, their wings alight, some without legs, some with charred stumps and white bones protruding.

I remembered someone at the hotel one night saying that he'd had to shoot his dog after he'd found it with its legs burnt off, and Joan asking if anyone knew a legend about a race of legless birds that have to live the whole of their lives in the air, or had she dreamt it. I was shocked, for Sam's sake — though I still didn't know she'd seen him — and for the man's. I thought she was being morbid in a repellently sentimental way. Seeing my anger, she clammed up.

I had *Firebirds* hanging on the wall for a day or two. Marie saw it. Perhaps I should have left it for her. I had to take it down and put it away. I understand better now.

I stayed up the last night at the house, checking that I had packed everything I needed and then sitting by the window looking through Joan's photographs and sketches in the lamplight. A blue morning came up, sunlight like gingery water lapping at the pane. I touched my face to the cold glass and the skin froze on the bone. The lamp, alive all night, had turned yellow and dry like a leaf.

In a dream I have, Joan is being stalked by a tiger. I write down my dreams in the hope of finding the one detail, the variation, that will change the pattern of events or give me a new key to it. A barred white and gold tiger: that could be the fire, or the charred tree trunk, its bark flayed off in stripes. I am usually a boy, Joan is my mother. Am I Sam? Sam-I-am: that was in a book Sam used to love. I have tried to warn her, but her look as the tiger leaps always accuses me, as if she thinks I'm its master. I could call it off, but I stand and gloat. In this dream the only sound is of fire or water (they sound the same).

Joan was six years older than me.

I wait for an illumination. Months go by as I wait here unable to take up the burden of my life. Doubts torture me. What look was that in her eyes? Could she have believed I was willing to let her die — stand by and let her die? Was she thinking that a death like that was what she deserved? What she wanted? Or that I thought so?

Some of the locals were sure of it. Joan's family was, especially after Marie moved in. It was a coroner's case, after all, since it was not from natural causes. An autopsy was done at the Moorong hospital and a report sent to the inquest. There was no talk of laying charges. The local sergeant was someone who had known us both for years. He took a statement from me the day after, and he and a constable went carefully over the ground taking photos and measurements. There were no suspicious circumstances, no prima facie evidence, as they put it: the inquest was a formality. That was just as well for me, I suppose, juries being what they are. They're holding an inquest, aren't they? some people said. That speaks for itself. Well, doesn't it? I got through all this somehow. My mind recoils from the effort of remembering it in any detail, let alone the thought of what a court case would have been like. The finding, anyway, was accidental death: she drowned after falling into the Skye river while it was in flood. Her head injuries and lacerations were not severe, according to the pathologist's report. The brain was not damaged.

He also reported that she was pregnant — about three months, evidently. Which document I saw this written on I can't remember. (If I can't trust my own mind, what foothold have I?) I do remember I asked a doctor friend if the pathologist could be mistaken; he only looked at me in consternation and (I think) pity. Later I asked Marie if she'd known. 'No,' she said, 'she hadn't said a word. You mean she hadn't told *you*?' she cried out. 'Oh. Peter.'

Anonymous letters arrived in the mail, made up of words cut out of newspapers and pasted on black paper:

YOU MURDERED HER YOU DROWNED HER IN COLD BLOOD

YOU WANTED THE BOTH OF THEM OUT OF THE WAY DIDN'T YOU YOU MURDERER

YOU DRANK HER BLOOD IT WAS ALL OVER YOUR MOUTH

YOU THINK YOU GOT WHAT YOU WANTED WELL HER ASHES WILL BURY YOU IN THE END

Her will — we made our wills when we bought the house — said that she was to be cremated. Her ashes are in Sam's grave. Ludicrous letters, insane of course, but they harped on my doubts. Had I hesitated for a second at the Cascades? Couldn't I be bothered, honestly, to come home on the night of the fires? I know the mind can keep its secrets from itself. But if I know anything, I know I wanted her to live and Sam to live. If I can know anything. Did I know Joan?

I showed Marie one of the letters. 'I've got one of those,' she said. But she'd burnt it.

'What did it say?'

'Oh. About Sam. Us. You can imagine the sort of spiteful bullshit.'

'Any idea who it is?'

She only shrugged.

Beyond the doubt of myself I have a worse doubt, because the coincidence is so obvious, and not only to me. If I could be sure that their two deaths grotesquely mirror each other by blind chance, well and good. I could take up my life again, abandon myself to the flux, to chaos. But what if it is as it seems, a maniacal joke? And our story seems to make clear that I was instrumental in their deaths. If so, the hand that wielded me as the instrument wished us ill. (The floods were God's tears, one old woman said.) We are set in motion by a malevolent hand, unable to know in what our actions are rooted or what fruit they will bear. Why are we?

Rather than bring harm to anyone else, let me remain suspended out of life, of time, beyond all possibility of action.

Sometimes I go to the local library to read for a while in the warmth. I walk round the streets, drive to a beach now and then for a spot of fishing off the pier. I like sitting in churches and in public bars, quiet ones with an open fire. No one disturbs me. I have nothing to say to anyone there.

The days are long, though drawing short again for the second winter. More and more are dark with rain, soft rain. Here it leaves no salt on the lips. I spend more mornings than I can count sitting up in bed in the sun with a glass of vodka and a pen and white sheets of paper. Trains trundle past. The sun catching my fingers through the paper fills them with a milky red light. I make disjointed notes:

> *The pines shelter a green shade on the foreshore. The wind shifts: a quick shine on the needles of the marram grass and the spider threads between them.*
>
> *Red wine has the rusty taste of blood. Vodka tastes of nothing, not even itself.*
>
> *If I write our story, then will it give up its secret?*

A GIRL ON THE SAND

I think I could live in almost any country now so long as I was not beyond the range of seagulls and the smell of water, salt water, lifted in on the wind.

'We Greeks, we can make a life in any country, Dimitri,' I remember my mother insisting. We chose Australia because there was work, and we have made a life. We have more or less mastered the language. We are here to stay.

This part of the coast of Australia, facing Bass Strait and the Southern Ocean, is where I want to build a house when I can afford one. Not because it reminds me of Greece. Except in its wildness it hasn't the least resemblance to any part of Greece that I knew. Maybe the wildness is why. The village of my childhood was on the plains under a ledge of mountains. Thunderstorms along this coast have all the savagery of the ones I remember, when lightning bolts struck farmers down in the fields and fireballs burst in at windows and burned children in their beds.

We talk a lot at home about the storms, the floods and droughts and iron winters, what was done in the War and then the Civil War. We feel it proves what we are made of. I have heard Australians talk with the same pride in having endured. Our countries have barrenness in common: the centre of ours is jagged rock, the centre of Australia dry sand and rock, and we take pride in this even if we never set foot there. May your soil be barren, one of our great modern poets has written — I forget his exact words. May your soil be barren so you don't have room to spread roots and so you keep groping deep.

It must be every day of fifteen years since I came to Australia with my mother and my married sisters. After the first months at General Motors I've mostly worked in restaurants and hotel kitchens, studying part time in the last few years to get a science degree. All I need now is a Diploma of Education and my mother will have a teacher for a son. This will impel her to try even harder to find me a bride. I'm forty this year and one failed marriage is more than enough, I tell her. I left all thought of marriage behind in Greece.

I spend a lot of time, in this town on the coast, in the water when I'm free during the day and fishing on the pier at night. A lot of us sit in a row on the planks with a crayfish boat on props towering over us on each side. Two cranes on the pier lower the boats into the water and hoist them out again. There are the lights of the town slithering over the water, and far across it the slow red flicker of the lighthouse. There is the creak and lap of water on wood, as if we were in a boat on calm water. It was like that, fishing from a *varka* with a lamp on the gulf at night, out of Thessaloniki. But the sea wasn't icy and wild like this sea, or not often.

If my family has found life full of harshness here, it hasn't been any more so than we were bred for.

This afternoon, the lunch rush over, the rest of the staff have gone across the road for a swim. I'm going as well as soon as I clean up. Too tired to hurry, I trudge round collecting the last cups with their saucers full of slops and sodden butts. The door handle jiggles. Someone is making wild signs against the blue glitter of the sea: Jake, a local, a friend I go fishing with, so I have to unlock the door.

'Jesus, Jim. *Jesus.*' He shakes his head. His face is yellow, his eyes wide.

'Cup of coffee?' I'm being offhand to make it clear that whatever has happened I'm not turning round to make him lunch at this time of the afternoon.

He nods. Sitting at a smeared table, he covers his face with tight hands while I make a strong short black for the both of us.

'Well?'

'I've been up at the police station.'

I wait. Jake's a journalist. He makes the most of the stories he has to tell.

'Well, I went round to Western River.' I know that; he asked me if I wanted to come. 'Went for a swim, fished off the rocks for a while, you know, time goes by.' He catches my look. 'Listen, you bastard. There'd been a quick shower, heavy for a moment but only enough to make pits in the sand and raise a hot smell. A rainbow was forming out at sea.' I know those rainbows stretched from cape to cape. 'I was looking at it and paddling back through the warm water along the edge of the river and so' — he takes a deep breath — 'I nearly trod on her before I saw she was there.'

'A woman?' A lot of Jake's stories involve a woman.

'She had her legs in the water, half in, half out. Wide apart. And not a stitch on. She was — white all over. Long black hair full of seaweed and things hopping, sandflies. Oh, Jesus.' He stirs his coffee and takes a gulp. 'She was white and sort of grainy like — I don't know — white sugar. Or sand, a sand sculpture, seaweed for hair. She had dark stains on her.'

'Was she dead?'

'Of course she bloody was.'

'There's a bit of a rip along there.'

'She was dead before she got into the water, it looks like. Or so the cops say.'

'Murdered.'

'That's what Bill reckons.' Bill, the local sergeant, is a friend of Jake's. 'Smothered or strangled. They'll have to have an autopsy. Can you manage another coffee, Jim?'

I take the cups to the machine. I know the spot he means, where the river curves past a cliff of jagged brown rocks as bright as snakeskins. The cliffs that face the ocean at Western Beach are black, damp from noon on, and their shadows darken the sea at their base. I was fishing there just the other day. The high yellow slopes of scrub and autumn grass were heat-shaken. An undertone of insects would suddenly lurch close, sun-jewelled, then away out of sound. In the dark under the ocean cliffs the beach was as cold as a cave.

'She wasn't on the ocean beach?' I put down the coffees.

'Thanks. No, up the river a bit. The tide was going out.'

'You could tell she was dead.'

'Oh, Jesus, yes, right away. There was this sweetish — funny, though, I couldn't leave her there while I went and reported it. I don't know why. I couldn't bring myself to touch her — try to drag her up on to the sand or whatever. What if I gave her arm a tug and it came off in my hand? That's been known to happen. Anyway, in the end I dropped my shirt over her and got up on to the road and stopped the first local that came past — the new bloke from the fruit shop, it was — and told him to send the police. Then I went back and waited with her. Jesus. The silence.'

'How old was she? Roughly, I mean.'

'Fucked if I know, mate. I couldn't — Jesus, how are you supposed to tell?' He knits his fingers together and stares at them. 'Bill reckons about sixteen and they're pretty sure she was pregnant. She was bloody huge. I just thought she was bloated.'

'Blotted?' A word new to me.

'Swollen up, blown up?' His hands shape a dome over his belly. 'Corpses do at a certain stage. I couldn't tell you how long it takes. Ever seen one?'

'Yes, often. In 1941 when the Germans occupied Greece. I was only a boy. I can't remember how long it took them to — blot.'

'Bloat.'

'People died in their sleep then, side by side on the footpaths. When I woke up there would be a head bent back further along the row. A mouth open on broken teeth, eyes rolled back. Rats ate the noses off live babies.'

'Jesus. I never saw her face, come to think of it. Her hair was all over it. Can I have one more coffee and then I'll go?' But as I get up to make it he grabs my wrist. 'Wait on. I haven't told you the worst thing yet, have I? Jesus. The fucking worst thing.'

'Wait till I get the coffee.'

I make one cup. When I bring it he is leaning into the corner with his head flung back so that nothing of his face shows but his trowel of ginger beard.

'Coffee.'

'Yeah. Thanks, mate.' The beard waggles.

'This worst thing.'

He heaves himself round with a sigh to face me: 'She only had one hand.'

'One —'

'Hand. Bitten off in the water, I thought. But then I got a better look after the cops arrived. Her arm ended smoothly at the wrist.

It must have come off a long time ago. Maybe she was born like that.'

'Little buds of fingers on the end of her wrist,' I say.

'That's right.' He narrows his eyes. 'How did you know?'

I shrug. 'I've seen it before.' (Where have I?) 'Why is that the worst thing?'

'Fucked if I know. It just is.' He sips the coffee. 'Ah! Good one, Jim.' I've put whisky in it.

He has nothing more to say. Neither of us has. Once he has finished his coffee and driven off, I lock the door and walk down to the beach. No one knows yet that a girl has been found, nudged by yellow ripples of water and sand. Her legs were open in the shape of a gulf. *Kolpos* means gulf in Greek; it also means vagina, which shocks my Australian friends — a word like that all over the map. The sea froths over my feet and tugs and furrows the sand under them. I no longer feel like a swim. I walk round as far as the rocks on the point (something is rising like a bubble in water to the surface of my mind) and lie down on the sand.

Kitchens have been my life. Ploughed fields were meant to be, as they were for my father; but when he was away fighting in the War and the Civil War we had to move to the city for safety. We found two downstairs rooms in a tenement in the red-light district of Thessaloniki, not far from the railway station. We slept on the floor on *kilimia*, all five of us, I and my two sisters, our mother and our grandmother. What hope did the girls have of growing up chaste, I overheard our mother ask our grandmother one night: ours would be like all the other families where brothers dishonoured sisters and ended up pimping for them.

'What rubbish, Melpo,' my grandmother said. 'Dimitri's not like that. You know he has a sense of honour.'

A sense of honour: *philotimo*. Or rather, a pride in one's honour. Of all things to saddle me with. A very selective honour, since I stole, or we would have starved. Perhaps there's no honour free of paradox; no pride either.

In 1946 when I was twelve I started work as a kitchen and water boy in a *taverna* owned by a friend of my father's. All the *tavernes* had one or two boys who worked from the early morning until midnight with an hour off in the afternoon, their shaven heads cuffed for the smallest mistake. They could scrounge a living from tips and food scraps. My tips came from the girls in a couple of nearby hotels and in the brothel, when I took meals to their rooms. They were fond of me and tried to keep me talking. They passed the time making coffee and telling fortunes in the grounds, gossiping about pimps and raids and abortions, and who had fought over whose girlfriend in what hashish den, and who had syphilis or consumption.

My mother knew this was part of my job. She wept over me and made me swear not to dishonour the family.

I wonder why I'm remembering this, after all these years. Is it because a girl with only one hand has been thrown up on the beach? She had long black hair. Maybe she was Greek. This is the moment when the bubble rises to the surface and bursts. I remember who she was.

At about half past two one dusty yellow afternoon she sidled into the *taverna* and ordered a *pilafi* and a lemonade at the counter. Our customers were working men, on the railways mostly: women didn't eat there alone. I saw her glancing nervously around, though no one, after the first stare, was taking any notice. She was a stranger, a country girl judging by her clothes (my mother would have known exactly where from) and by her bundle too, her *bogos* of worn home-woven wool which she balanced on the chair beside her. She wore a white scarf over her hair, and white gloves, in all that heat. I brought her bread and a glass of water. When her meal was served she drank the lemonade in one gulp and with the fork in her gloved hand she scooped up all the yellow rice and then she scrubbed the oil off her plate with the bread. Then she called me to ask for more water.

After I'd brought it she called me again. '*Mikre*,' she said: little one. It was how everyone called us boys. I went over, wiping my hands on my apron and wondering what she wanted this time. She had paid the waiter already. The last customers were getting up to go. 'Tell me your name?' she said, and slipped a coin into my hand.

'Why?'

She smiled. 'It's awful, calling you "*mikre*." '

'His name's Dimitri,' grinned a waiter on his way past.

'Mine's Dimitroula,' she said to me. 'Strange, isn't it? The same name.'

I shrugged. What was she getting at?

'Have you worked here long?'

'Two years,' I muttered.

'Will you help me then?' I had to bend down to hear her. 'I don't know a soul in Thessaloniki. I only just got off the bus. Do you know if there's a very cheap hotel round here that's — you know — suitable for families?'

I knew one. She sat back in relief, her hands clasped, and I saw her face, broad and brown with heavy-lidded dark eyes and a full mouth with a mole at one corner: an *elia*, an olive, as it's called in Greek.

I explained that she would have to wait outside for me. We could all see her standing there in the sun, shading her eyes to glance in from time to time. My friends and enemies all thought it was a great joke. 'What does she see in you, Dimitri?' one said. 'Can't she wait till your voice has finished breaking?'

'Shut up,' I said. 'You've got it wrong. She's my cousin on my mother's side.' They gave a yell of joy. 'She is. It's years since we saw each other. She lives in — Katerini.'

'And what's her name, Dimitri?' The waiter opened his eyes wide.

'None of your business.' She had opened her eyes like that as she said her name: I didn't believe it was Dimitroula. I had said Dimitri and she had said the first name that came into her head.

'He can't remember!'

'He forgot to ask!'

'Dimitroula!' I squeaked, to a burst of applause.

'Get on with the job, come on,' the cook growled. But he crooned 'Dimitroula *mou*' under his foul breath the whole time I was scrubbing his pots and pans. 'You've got one hour,' he called as I rushed out, and raised another laugh.

Red-faced, I hoisted the girl's bundle over my shoulder and set off with her trotting beside me down the gravelled laneways to the Hotel Epiros.

'Epiros!' She made a face.

'Well, it's respectable. It's for families.'

'Yes, all right. It was just the name. My parents live there, in a village near Albania.'

I put down her bundle on the doorstep. 'I told them at work that you're from Katerini. I had to say something.'

'A lot further than that.'

'I *know*.' Did she think I didn't know Epiros was near Albania?

'No. Where I live is much further than Katerini. Skala — I live in Skala with my aunt. I haven't seen my parents since the Germans came.'

'Seven years!'

'That's right. I don't care. Neither do they. Now the *andartes* have taken over.'

'You'd have been conscripted! They're conscripting girls.' She shrugged. 'Skala where?' There are villages called Skala this or Skala that all over the coast of Greece. She bit her lip and looked down. 'All right, don't tell me then. Suit yourself.'

The manager came: he knew me. If she hadn't been with me she would never have got in, since she had no papers on her. He handed her key to me.

The passages of the Epiros were dingy and rank and had cockroaches. Piss glistened on the bathroom floor; on the enamel footplates and in the holes of the lavatories shit of various shades was clumped. A country girl would be used to worse, I knew. The air in her room was hot, striped with dusty yellow light. But the sheets on the bed were washed and starched and the blankets were old army ones, thin but solid. Families from the villages stayed there regularly: no one would molest her.

I dropped her bundle on the stiff blanket and she sank down beside it, her scarf slipping so that her hair fell along the pillow in a flow of black.

I opened the window and went to unfasten the shutters.

'No,' she said. 'Let's leave them shut.'

'I have to go,' I said.

'No, stay a minute. Don't go, Dimitri.'

I felt uncomfortable. She saw that I did, and sat up. 'I don't know a soul. What will I do?'

'I have to get back to work.'

'I have to find a doctor.'

'What's wrong with you?'

She gave a snort and her gloved hand shaped a dome over her belly.

'Ah,' I said as if I knew.

'Three months. I have to get rid of it.' *Na to petaxo* was what she said: to throw it away.

'Ah.' Now I knew. 'Can't you get married?'

Her nose reddened and her eyes spilled out tears which she wiped on her glove.

'I've got the money. My aunt gave me plenty. It has to be straight away. She said, "You come back in that condition and I'll stick a knife through it and you." '

I hid my shock. 'I think I can find out where there's a doctor.' The whores were certain to know a good one.

'Oh, can you? Can you really? When?'

'Tonight. I'll come and tell you on my way home.'

'Will you? You promise?'

'Of course I will.'

'Dimitri, my life's in your hands.'

'I *know*. I said, I promise.'

I worked hard that night at the *taverna*, spurred on by jeers about how tired I looked. I knew who I could ask: Lina, the one I liked best, the one who made the most fuss of me. She had a lame leg, and that may have been another reason. When I went to pick up her dinner dishes — there'd been no time earlier — I asked if she'd do me a favour.

'Anything, anything, my darling,' she said.

So I stammered it out: where did she think my mother's cousin from Katerini could get a safe abortion? Lina lit a cigarette. 'You bad boy!' She goggled her black-rimmed eyes at me.

'Come on, Linaki. This is serious.'

'I'll say it is. You're telling me.' She passed me the cigarette for a quick puff. 'You could always marry the poor thing.'

I choked the smoke out. 'It isn't *mine*!'

'You all say that,' she sighed. 'Don't I know it?' She shrugged at herself in the wavy mirror, grabbing the cigarette and blowing a fan of smoke at her dark face staring back. She was enjoying herself. She went on like this for some time. Time was short, so was my temper, and the more thwarted and sullen I became, the more she teased. But she wrote a name and address at last. I grabbed her dishes and turned to go, but she took them back, put them on the dressing table and demanded a kiss. Angrily I jammed my mouth on her blotched lips.

'I won't tell,' she said. 'You be sure to take good care of your little cousin.' She stroked my cheek. 'She's in for a bad time. I should know.'

I kissed her again, and I meant it.

I ran to the hotel after work and told Dimitroula. She looked distraught and I felt bad about leaving her alone, but I was dropping with tiredness by then and my mother, as I explained, always waited up. Early next morning before work I took her to the address, a shuttered upstairs surgery. She was lucky, the nurse said: the doctor would do it that very morning. I knew I had no hope of getting off work early, so I told Dimitroula she would have to find her own way back to the hotel, but I would come straight after work and see if she needed anything.

It was well after three when I knocked on her door and called softly. 'Come in,' I heard. The door was unlocked, though she had the shutters and the window closed. In the thick heat I made out her face, a paleness as it moved on the pillow and made a ripple in her long strands of hair.

'Something to eat,' I muttered, having at great risk — a boy sacked for thieving wouldn't get another job — smuggled out a lump of stewed meat and potato wrapped in a teatowel. I presented it: the red sauce had soaked through. She gasped and turned abruptly away, flinging her brown arm up over her eyes and I saw that for the first time she wasn't wearing her gloves and — I peered closer in the dimness — *her hand had been cut off*.

I screamed.

'Take that thing away,' she groaned. 'Oh, it's all over blood. It looks like a — take it away, I'll be sick.'

I put the teatowel of food down on the floor outside her room and shut the door quietly. Her voice was thick, she had been crying. She was again, but she patted the blanket for me to sit down.

'*Why did he cut your hand off*?'

She sobbed, or laughed, and rubbed her wrist against my thigh. 'Don't be silly,' she said. 'Oh, why did you have to see it? I didn't want you to.'

'No, let me see.' I stared as she turned her arm, plump and brown on the top and white underneath like a loaf of bread. Her veined wrist ended in five small buds.

'How did it happen?'

'I was born with it like this. That's why my mother wouldn't have anything to do with me. My father's sister said she'd have me and they send her money every summer for my keep.'

'The same aunt? The one in — Skala?'

'Yes. She's fond of me in her way.' She caught my look. 'Well, she brought me up. A deformed child that no one wanted.'

'She made you come here by yourself and find a doctor.'

'She's letting me go back. Not everyone would.'

'Do you want to? After what she said about the knife?'

'Where else can I go? My own mother didn't want me to live.' Her eyes closed and tears ran into her ears and her loose hair. She whimpered something I didn't hear.

'Don't cry.'

'I'm worse than she is now. I've killed my baby.'

'They made you, though.'

'But I wanted to have it. You should have heard my aunt. "You're hard enough to marry off already," she said. I know that.' She held her arm up. 'Who wants a wife like this?'

'Can I feel it?'

She nodded. I touched the nodules with my long fingers: they felt like a baby's knuckles.

'It's not so terrible. It's only when you first —'

'There's more to it than that. Don't you understand?' She leaned forward and whispered: 'Why am I like this? How would you like to be my husband and have to wait nine months to see if the child was the same as me?' She watched me understand.

' "No wonder he ran away," my aunt said. The father. She called me a whore.'

I'll bet! Just what my mother would say if it was one of my sisters. A silence fell. 'Did you love him?' I said at last.

'He didn't even know about the baby. And a lot of men are after me, you'll be surprised to know. Crippled or not.'

'You're not *crippled*.'

'He was different. He was a boy I've always known. We were at school together. He had big ideas about saving the world and feeding the poor and all that. He never said he was a Communist. I wouldn't have cared anyway. He left home a few weeks ago. He's in Epiros with the *andartes* now. He never told me anything. That's what his best friend said.'

'You haven't heard from him?'

'No one has. He's dead or as good as dead. The *andartes* are going to get wiped out. Don't you read the newspapers?'

I didn't. 'He might come back when it's over,' I said.

'And be shot? His father's waiting. And his brothers.'

'But you still love him.'

'No.'

'Because he's an *andartis*?'

'No, because he left like that without a word. Because he didn't trust me.'

'Why did you love him?' I was, I realise now, jealous of the boy.

'Why! Why does anyone?'

'I don't know.'

'You will.' She smiled, but her face crumpled and she was whimpering again. I stroked her hair. My hands must have stunk of the meat stew but she stayed still, her eyes closed. 'I'm tired,' she said, 'and my belly hurts.' The hair close to her head was soaked with sweat, the ends dry and feathery. I smoothed it back off her forehead until her breathing went heavy. Then I crept out.

A squeal, the snake dash of a grey body, brought me up short. A rat was crouched in the corner. It had mauled the teatowel with the meat. Sick with loathing, I kicked the ragged mess down the passage a long way from her door.

On my rounds that night I took a dinner to the Epiros for her

(Epiros, where her lover had gone): they could dock the money out of my pay, I didn't care. I chose *yemista*, one pepper and two tomatoes stuffed with rice, since she liked rice; and a serving of bread and a bunch of yellow grapes. I stumbled on the gravel in the dark, and trudged along the dank passages half-afraid of what I might find. But a light was on inside and she opened the door herself. The one dirty bulb in the ceiling made yellow waves on the walls, leaving the furniture in the darkness.

'Did you sleep?' I asked sternly as she laid herself down on the bed.

'Yes, I feel better.' When she smiled her face was sleek and brown again. 'Oh, look how much you've brought! You'll have to help me eat it.'

I ate some rice to please her. She was slow but she finished it all and sopped the bread in the red oil and made me have a bite before eating that too. She lay carefully back with a sigh.

'Was it good?' I was eager for praise.

'You saved my life.' That was something the whores often said, but not the way she said it.

'It's nothing.'

'Here.' She took more drachmas than the dinner cost out of her purse and pressed them into my hand.

'No, it's all right! I'll pay.'

'Don't be silly, take it. My aunt gave me enough for my expenses. You have a family to support, haven't you? Put it in your pocket, go on.' I put it in my pocket. 'Have you got a girlfriend, Dimitri?'

'No,' I muttered. 'I'm only fourteen.'

'Is that all? You look older. I'm sixteen.'

'What a shame. You're too old for me.'

'What a shame. And you're good-looking too.' Her tone, her teasing smile: it was just what I needed. On such familiar ground I could relax. 'Don't go thinking I can't do things,' she went on. 'I can. I have a sort of leather strap that I wear on my wrist. I can cook, sew, knit, mend nets. I can embroider and use the loom. Anything.'

'You mean you've got your *proika* ready?' Even in those hard times some girls had managed to make sheets and woven blankets and clothes for their *proika.* My sisters hadn't.

'Everything. Why not?'

'Well, I can't marry for a long time,' I assured her. 'I have two unmarried sisters.'

'Bad luck.'

Traditionally the brothers have to wait until their sisters marry. A few years later, as it happened, I did marry before them. It caused a lot of bitterness in my family and gossip outside it. After ten years of murderous turmoil — war, disease, hunger — the grip of tradition had loosened. Magda, the girl I was in so much of a hurry to have, was like Dimitroula to look at, broad-faced and full-lipped. She had no physical flaw. Not even a mole.

'Aren't you going to eat the grapes?' I had to go back to work. 'They're good. Very sweet.'

'I'm too full. I'll have them for breakfast.'

I put them on the dressing table. 'You're sure you'll be all right?'

'Yes. You have to be getting back.'

'I'd stay with you if I could.' I wanted to stay.

'I know. I'll be all right, don't worry. I'll be leaving in the morning.'

'Will you come past the *taverna* and say goodbye?'

'If you want.'

'Is it the Skala near Platamona?'

She smiled. 'No. It's another one. Bend down,' she said, 'and give me a kiss.' Balancing the dishes, I knelt and kissed the mole beside her mouth. She turned her head to kiss me on the lips. 'Good night,' we both said. Her damp hair smelled of salt.

That night for all my tiredness I lay awake a long time listening to the four women who depended on me, two old and two young, breathing in the dark.

Next morning she looked in through the door of the *taverna* — I was keeping an eye out — and waited till I had a chance to come outside. She was scarved, gloved and her face was sombre. 'I should have died,' she said. 'I wish I had. Then I wouldn't have to go back.'

'You can always come and live here,' I said, sure even as I

spoke that she would never want to come back here. 'I could find you a room.' I was about to lose her.

'How would I live? Or don't you know?' I did know. She kissed my cheek, smiled, and walked off with her bundle.

With the passing of time I suppose I fell in love with her, or with the thought of her. I relived every word, every look. If I saw a white scarf in the distance, it had to be hers (and it never was). In my daydreams she came to the *taverna*, only this time I stayed the two nights at the hotel to keep her company and on the second morning she told me she was never going back to Skala. I worried when I changed my job: where would she find me now? I made up scenes, chance meetings. I would be taking meals up to the whores one night, for example, and find her among them. Or she would pass me in the street one day with a man and a child, children, and know me, or not know me.

We were fated to meet again. I was certain of it.

In the village your family is your life, or it was in those days. I was too young then to understand how she felt. When my wife Magda was caught in the arms of a neighbour who was our mortal enemy, she ran away; and the dishonour to our family drove my mother to emigrate to Australia. Maybe Dimitroula escaped by coming here, if the authorities would let her in with only one hand. She might have run away to the city; she would be easy to trace, but her aunt would hardly bother. My feeling is that she stayed in Skala and endured the darting eyes of visitors and the chatter in the street that stopped as she came near and waited for her to move on. They all knew too much about her, but she was never one of them. They smiled and kept their distance. There's no Greek word for privacy, as it's understood in English — nor for intimacy, if it comes to that. There is for loneliness: *monaxia*.

To be Dimitroula and be confined to Skala, wherever it was! I can see her as the scarved woman posed to give depth to postcard photographs: walking by a white bell tower or against fishing boats mirrored in the shallows. I saw a lot of sea ports during my national service. She might have been any one of the women — if I ever happened on the right Skala — that I saw watering geraniums in kerosene tins, hanging up herbs to dry, mending a net in a doorway, seagulls at her feet. (Did she ever think of me?)

If I did see her again, neither of us knew it. Her story has long since lost any power to move me. It must be twenty-five years since it occurred to me to wonder if she was alive, if she was happy or not. Now our lives have crossed a second time — no, drawn close without touching, a second time. Lives with their roots not spread but sunk deep.

No tide of any ocean could have washed her round the world from Skala to Western River, I know that. Even if she was living on this coast, she's forty-two now, not sixteen, and the sergeant thought the girl was sixteen. That's not the point. Whoever she turns out to have been, and whoever killed her and why, the girl that Jake found has nothing to do with me. The link is too fine and fragile.

Even if it is Dimitroula.

The police will call on the public to come forward with any information that might help them identify the body. Nothing I have to tell could do more than confuse them and raise false suspicions. (Even if it is Dimitroula.) For me to claim more part in her life than I have had would be to falsify it. My part has been to stand by once — now twice — and witness, and stay silent. Why this should be, who knows?

What do I know about her? She was a beautiful, lonely, passionate woman who took risks. They think she was also pregnant. She has died by violence and her death seems to be something I was meant to learn of. Maybe I was meant to find her body; I spend a lot of time round at Western River. She looked like white sugar, he said. Or sand. I spread hanks of hairy seaweed in a fan. With my palms I raise and smooth the shape of a breast out of the sand, a second breast and the high dome of a belly. I make her two arms and one hand. I spread her legs wide apart. Between them a gulf of sand was formed as the yellow river water sank away from her.

Surfers are riding past me in the green waves.

The rocks here on the point are blistered with sandy pools where the water is blood-hot. There are limpets and blue-black mussels and grape weed. A beaded net in a pool below a rock is the reflection of the sun's glitter on lichen on the rock. I measure the slowness of bubbles as they rise. A small flathead sways and noses under shadows. Puckering the pool, an insect trails over the sand its own magnified shadow ringed with bubbles of light in the precise form of a tea tree flower. A limpet lifts its lid as water nudges it: the tide is coming in.

What part, I wonder, does free will play? I talk of honour and endurance and love.

PLACE OF BIRTH

On the last day Bell will remember before the snow, on a blue-grey morning of high cloud, the old woman brings out a *tapsi* rolling with walnuts that she has cracked for the Christmas *baklava*. 'We'll be shut in soon enough,' she sighs, perching on a plaited stool under the grapevine with the *tapsi* on her lap. Bell, her son Grigori's wife, pulls up stools for herself and Chloe, the other daughter-in-law, the Greek one who has come to the village for Christmas; her husband's ship is at sea. The women huddle over the *tapsi* picking out and dropping curled walnuts here, shells there. Chloe's little girl, Sophoula, leans on her mother.

'Me too?' she murmurs.

'Go ahead.'

Sophoula, biting her lips, scowls over her slow fingers. With a trill of laughter Chloe pops a walnut into the child's mouth. 'My darling! Eat,' she says.

'Don't tell me she has nuts at her age?' the old woman says. 'You'll choke the child.'

'Mamma, she's three.' Chloe's face and neck turn red.

'Just the same —'

'Oh, I don't like it!' Sophoula spits and dribbles specks of walnut. The shelling goes on; under their bent heads Chloe and the old woman put on a fierce burst of speed. Suddenly all of them flare bright with sunlight and are printed over with black branches and coils of the grapevine as a gap opens in the cloud. Bell leaps to her feet and lumbers inside.

'What's wrong with you?' Chloe frowns.

'Nothing. I'm getting my camera.'

'*Aman*. Always photographs,' her mother-in-law sighs.

'It's too cold to sit out here,' Chloe says.

'Oh, please,' Bell wails from the window. 'All stay where you are!'

But the gap in the cloud has closed over by the time she gets back, so that what she will always have is a photograph all cold blues, whites, greys and browns: brittle twigs and branches against walls and clouds, the washing hung along the wire, a white hen pricking holes in mud that mirrors her, and the three heads, black, brown and bone-white, suspended over the *tapsi* of walnuts.

Because she takes all the photographs, she won't find herself in any of them.

Six weeks ago, as soon as she knew for certain, Bell wrote to her parents that they would be grandparents some time in May. 'You're the first to know,' she added, though by the time the letter got to Australia the whole village probably knew. There's no hope now of an answer until after Christmas. But at noon the postman's motorcycle roars past, a fountain of mud in his wake, and stops at the village office, so she wanders down just in case and is handed an Australian aerogram. It has taken a month to get here and is one she will mark with a cross and keep as long as she lives.

Grandma and Grand Pop, eh, scrawls her father. *And about time too. Tell Greg to take that grin off his face.*

'Are they pleased, Bella?' The old woman is kneading the pastry for the *baklava.* Her arms are floured to the shoulders.

'Of course. Dad says, "And about time too." '

'No wonder! Considering that you're thirty-one —'

'Thirty —'

'— or will be when it's born.'

'Hasten slowly.' Bell reads her mother's exclamatory, incoherent half-page, laboriously copied, then goes back to her father's.

It's been three years. You could leave it too late, you know, Bell. With a bub and all that you could find yourselves tied down before you know it. It's hard to think we mightn't live to see our only grandchild. Mum's been having dizzy turns again lately. She's had one stroke, as you know. If money's the problem, I can help you there. Also book you into the Queen Vic or wherever you like.

'What else, Bella?'

'Oh, questions. Money, hospitals. All that.'

'Surely you're booked into the Kliniki?' Chloe stares.

'No, not yet.'

'Well, you'd better do it soon! You don't want to have it in the Public Hospital! *They* have women in labour two to a bed in the corridors, it's so crowded.'

'I think I want to have it at home,' Bell hears herself say.

'At home!' Kyria Sophia is delighted. 'Why not? I had all mine here. Grigori was born in the room you sleep in!'

'It wouldn't be safe.' Chloe raises her eyebrows. 'Not with a first child. Anything can go wrong.'

'Thank you, Chloe.'

'It's the truth. Look what happened to the *papas*'s daughter!'

'The *papas*'s daughter? You know why that happened? She got a craving for fried bananas in the middle of the night and her husband wouldn't go and try to find her any. And sure enough —'

'Mamma, the cord got round her baby's neck and strangled it.'

'Mamma, not because of the bananas!'

'You're both fools! Of course it was because of the bananas!' The old woman rams a grey branch into the firebox of the *somba*. '*Aman!* How come I'm the only one who ever stokes the fire?' She brushes a wisp of hair out of her eyes and flours her face. White like her hair and arms, it sags into its net of wrinkles.

Lunch, Bell's chore today, isn't ready when the old man comes in from the *kafeneion* and finds her alone in the kitchen. Kyria Sophia has taken Sophoula with her to the bakery to leave the *baklava*. Chloe is at a neighbour's place with the baby. He sits by the *somba*, small and grey and muddy, rolling and smoking one fat cigarette after another. The *makaronia* have to be boiled to a mush, Bell knows, before she can toss them in oil and butter and crumble *feta* cheese over them. Kyria Sophia comes back exhausted hand-in-hand with Sophoula and as if the day's work wasn't enough, now she has her to spoonfeed.

They eat the *makaronia* in silence. At every mouthful a twinge, a jab of pain drills through Bell's jaw. Not a toothache, please, she prays. Not now, not here.

Sophoula pushes the spoon and her grandmother's hand away. 'Yiayia! You have to tell a story!'

'What story?' sighs the old woman.

'A story about princesses.'

'Eat up and then I will.'

'Now!' Sophoula bats the spoon on to the floor. The old woman gets another one and shovels cold lumps into the child's mouth, chanting a story by heart. Whenever she falters, the child clamps her mouth shut. Bell, stacking the dishes, isn't really listening, but when the bowl is almost empty she exclaims aloud in English, 'Snow White! No, Snow White and Rose Red!'

The old woman giggles. 'Zno Quaeet,' she mocks. 'No Zno Quaeet End —'

'Yiayia, *pes*!'

'*Aman*, Sophoula!'

'*Pes*.' She spits into the bowl.

After lunch these days Bell sleeps until it's dark. Now that she is into her fifth month she is sleepy most of the time. From under the white *flokati* she can hear Grigori's voice (so he is back from Thessaloniki with the shopping) and then Kyria Sophia's shrill one. When she wakes properly, ready for another long yellow evening by the *somba*, he is still there in the kitchen finishing a coffee. So is Chloe, red from her sleep, with the baby at her breast. 'Hullo,' Bell says, kissing Grigori's woolly crown. She fumbles with the *briki*.

'Coffee again?' Chloe mutters.

'Just one to wake me up.'

'It's so bad for the baby.'

'One won't hurt.'

'Oh well, you'd know.'

Bell turns her back to light the gas. 'Where are the old people?' She touches Grigori's shoulder.

'Milking.' His father's grey head grins in at the window; he leaves the milk saucepans on the sill. 'You got a letter, Mamma said. Are Mum and Dad all right?'

'Yes, they send their love and congratulations.' Bell rubs her jaw. There's a hollow ache in her back teeth. She empties the sizzling *briki* into a little cup and takes a furry sip of her hot coffee. The *baklava* is on the table, baked and brought home already, its pastry glossy with the syrup it's soaking in. Grigori's shopping is all around it: oranges in net bags, chestnuts, a blue can of olive oil, lemons and mandarines and — she can hardly believe it — six yellow-green crescent bananas blue-stamped *Chiquita.* 'Oh, bananas! Oh, darling, thank you!' she cries out. 'We were just talking about bananas!'

'I'm so extravagant,' Chloe simpers, 'but Sophoula simply loves them. So I gave Grigori the money to buy her some.' Her eyes dare Bell to ask for one. A pregnant woman can ask even strangers in the street for food. Bell grins at Chloe, remembering her frying mussels one day in Thessaloniki when a pregnant neighbour squealed from a balcony, 'Ach, Kyria Chloe! Mussels! I can smell them!' and Chloe had to let her have a couple. 'She never smells anything cheap,' Chloe grumbled to Bell.

'Is that so, Kyria Chloe?' Bell contents herself with saying. 'Ah, so much lovely food. We'll never eat it.'

'*You* won't.' The old woman comes in and lifts the milk saucepans inside. '*Aman*, the cold!' She slams the window. '*You* won't eat. You're fading, look at you. White as snow.'

'I *will.* That was when I had morning sickness.'

'We don't want a kitten, you know, we want a big strong baby.'

'Believe you me,' Chloe mutters, 'the bigger it is, the harder it comes out.'

'Ah, *bravo*, Chloe, *bravo*!' The old woman clatters the saucepans, straining the warm milk. 'Don't you crave anything, Bella? You must crave something.'

'Why must she?'

'Well, to tell the truth, I'd love a banana,' says Bell. 'It seems like years! Can I buy one from you, Chloe?'

'I'm sorry. There aren't enough.'

'We share in this house, Chloe! If you want a banana, Bella, you have one! Don't even ask!'

'No, no, it's all right.'

Grigori stands up. 'See you later,' he says. He grabs a mandarine and saunters outside.

'Not to the *kafeneion* already?' his mother pleads. 'You just got here.' She stares bleakly after him. 'And what would you expect?'

She rounds on her daughters-in-law. 'Doesn't a man have a right to peace and quiet?'

'Auntie?' Chloe has taught Sophoula this English word. 'Auntie Bella? Do they have Christmas where you come from?'

'Yes, of course.'

'Did you go to church?'

'No.'

'You stayed home at Christmas!'

'We went to the beach,' Bell says.

'At Christmas! You're funny, Auntie!'

'Funny, am I?' Bell crosses her eyes. With a giggle, Sophoula sits in her lap.

'Where's your baby?'

'You're sitting on it. Oh, poor baby.'

'What's its name going to be?'

'I don't know. What's your baby's name going to be?'

'We won't know till he's been christened.'

'Oh, no, I forgot.'

'If it's a girl, they'll call it after Yiayia,' Chloe interposes. 'The same as we did with you.'

'Good idea. I'll call my baby Yiayia.'

'Auntie, you can't!'

'Why can't I? Not if it's a boy, you mean?' Bell winks. 'Then I'll call it Pappou,' and she is rewarded with a peal of laughter so loud that it wakes the old woman.

'Let's eat, Mamma,' Chloe says.

'Is it late?' She blinks, squinting in the light. 'The men'll be home any minute.'

'No, they won't.' Bell lifts Sophoula down. 'Can we cut the *baklava* now? I crave *baklava*.'

'Oh. All right.' Smiling in spite of herself, Kyria Sophia cuts her a dripping slice. As Bell bites into it, the ache that has been lying in wait all day drills through her tooth and she shrieks aloud, letting syrup and specks of walnut dribble down her chin. She swills water round her mouth. The women cluck and fluster. Sophoula clings to her mother in tears of fright. The old woman mixes Bell an aspirin and she gulps it. She is helped to bed, where she curls up moaning in the darkness under the *flokati.* The light flashes on once, twice. She lies still until the door quietly closes.

Grigori is undressing with the light on. Bell rubs her watery eyes. The ache is duller now.

'Were you asleep? How's the tooth?'

'Bad.' She probes with her tongue.

He turns off the light and lies on his back with one cold arm against her. 'What's all this about having the baby here at home?'

'No! I'd be terrified.'

'Mamma said you said you wanted to.'

'No. She misunderstood. I meant — I just feel — I want to go home and have it.' She holds her breath. 'Home to Australia.'

'How come?'

'Oh. Mum and Dad. You know. Mostly, I suppose. Yes.'

'We can't afford the fares.'

'One way, we can. Dad said they'd help.'

'Ah. One way? I see.'

The moon must have risen. In the hollow glow through the shutters the *flokati* looks like a fall of snow on rough ground. 'I wonder if it'll snow for Christmas?' she says. 'It didn't the other times.'

He snorts. 'You spring a thing like this on me. What I might feel — you couldn't care less, could you! I wanted to stay in Australia three years ago, but no, you uprooted us, you — *felt* — you had to go and live in Greece. And now what? Come along, doggy, I want to go home. To Australia!'

She takes a shaky breath. 'I feel guilty, I suppose. They're old, they're not well. "You could leave it too late," Dad said.'

'You know what a pessimist he is. You used to joke about it.'

'Can we bank on it, though?' She ploughs on. 'It's not as if it would be for ever.'

'It might.'

'We can always come back.'

'Always, can we? Backwards and forwards.' He turns his back to her. 'I'll need to think it over. I'm tired.'

'There's not much time. We've got till the end of February.

That's when my smallpox vacination expires. I can't have another one while I'm pregnant and I can't enter Australia without it.'

Lying along his back, she feels him tightening against her. The nape of his neck is damp and has his hot smell. Once he pelted past her down a sand dune and was out of sight in the white waves when the hot smell from him buffeted her face. That was at Christmas.

We went to the beach at Christmas when I was little, she remembers. On Phillip Island we had dinner at the guesthouse and then Dad and I followed a track, called Lovers' Walk — there was a board nailed up, Lovers' Walk — to look for koalas as they awoke in the trees. First we walked down the wooden pier where men and their sons were fishing. Red water winding and hollowing. Crickets fell silent when I walked in the tea tree. After sunset the waves were grey and clear rolling and unrolling shadows on the sand. The trees, black now, still had their hot smell.

Some time in the early hours the toothache jerks her out of sleep. Grigori breathes on deeply. Tossing, feverish, close to tears, she stumbles to the kitchen for an aspirin and Chloe, passing through to the lavatory annexe, sees and scolds her. 'You shouldn't take any medicines now,' she says.

'One little aspirin!' Bell's smile is a snarl.

'Any medicine at all.'

'I have toothache!'

'Still, for the baby's sake.'

Bell turns and gulps it down. Back in bed the pain is relentless, it drills into her brain. After an hour, two of whimpering in her sweat she creeps back to the kitchen and in a flash of bilious light swallows down three more aspirins. No one catches her. In the passage she trips over Sophoula's potty, which they leave outside their door until morning. Splashing away over cold urine, she lets it lie where it fell. Grigori is snoring. 'Turn over,' she hisses in Greek, and he turns.

A rooster calls, the same one as every morning, then hens, then a crow, so loud that it must be in the yard. How long since she last heard a gull? It must be only a couple of weeks. When was the last time she was in Thessaloniki? Gulls are as common as pigeons in the city. It seems like years.

What does tea tree smell like in summer?

Their bedroom is white and takes up one corner of the house and of the street, 21st of April Street these days, in honour of the Colonels' coup. The two-roomed school that Grigori went to is opposite. They are on one of the busiest crossroads in the village. All through Christmas Day, Boxing Day and the next day Bell sleeps and wakes to the uproar of tractors, donkeys, carol-singers, carts, trucks with loud-speakers bellowing in her windows. Snow falls. She sits sipping milk at the family table in her pyjamas, staggers to the lavatory annexe and back to her cooling hollow under the *flokati.* She coughs. Her head pulsates. She loses count of how many aspirins. The toothache goes through her in waves. Sweat soaks her pyjamas and sheets and Kyria Sophia dries them again by the *somba.* Grigori takes refuge for two nights at his cousin Angelo's place behind the bakery. Children throwing snowballs yell and swear. The baby wails. From time to time Sophoula opens Bell's door, but slams it in panic when Bell stirs to see who it is. Chloe keeps away in case she and the children catch something. Kyria Sophia comes and sits at the end of the bed crocheting with a pan of hot coals at her feet.

Penicillin, somebody suggests, a shot of penicillin, there's a woman down the street who's qualified. Bell says yes, oh yes, please. Chloe is appalled. But no one ever comes to give the injection. Time has broken down. Sand slides shifting under the scorched soles of her feet. The scream of a gull makes her slip and clutch at the stringy trunk of a tea tree, but it must be the grapevine. No, she is flat on her back, she is clutching the *flokati* when her eyes open. It looks like snow on rough ground. That scream comes again and it's the baby screaming, Chloe's baby though, not her own, that she can hear, then all the sounds of hushing and commotion as he sobs, then whimpering and quiet.

One morning she wakes and is well, clear-headed, free of toothache and of fever. She opens the windows but the shutters won't move. She is weak, look, trembling. But it's not that: snow is heaped on the sill. She patters to the door and stares down the white street. The sun is rising behind white roofs and trees, turning the snow sand-yellow, shading in the printed feet of birds and a stray dog. The stringy grapevine has grown spindles of ice.

Stooped panting over buckets and *tapsia* of water, she spends the day washing her stiff, sour clothes and her hair, stuck in yellow strings to her head by now; and sitting with hair and clothes spread out to dry by the *somba*. She would love a bath, but not in the dank ice-chamber that the lavatory annexe has become. For one thing, other people are always wanting to get in. And in any case, it's not as if they'll notice whether she does or not, not even Grigori: for fear of a miscarriage, now that she has finally conceived they don't make love. She's well again, she won't risk catching cold. She wraps a scarf over her mouth whenever she goes outside. Now and then a twinge through her tooth alarms her, but the rivetting ache is gone.

Every day there is washing and cooking of which she does her share. When the sun is out she walks around the village photographing crystals and shadows, tufty snow and smooth. The narrowed river is crinkled, slow, with white domes on its rocks. Ovens in the deserted yards have a cap of snow over two sooty airvents and stare back at the camera like ancient helmets. White hens are invisible except for their jerking legs and combs. The storks' nest is piled high; it could be a linen basket up on top of the church tower. In the schoolyard a snowman has appeared — no, a snow woman two metres tall in a widow's scarf and a cloak of sacking under which her great round breasts and belly glisten naked.

She takes photographs of the snow woman and of children hiding to throw snowballs and of the *papas* as he flaps by, his hair and beard like a stuffing of straw that has burst out of his black robes. The family and the neighbours line up for portraits under the grey grapevine. The old man leads the cows out of the barn and poses for her standing between them on the soiled snow while they shift and blink in the light, mother and daughter.

'You can show them to your parents,' he says. So all the family knows that she is going home. No one talks about it.

She takes time exposures in the blue of evening as the windows in the houses light up and throw their long shapes on the snow outside. As often as not, Kyria Sophia, Chloe, Grigori, even the old man, can be found in one or other of the rooms, the little golden theatres, that Bell used to love being in. Now she knows the sets, the characters, the parts too well. She would rather stay home alone; she is quite happy babysitting. Having read her own few books too often, she reads Sophoula's story books about princesses. If Sophoula wakes, Bell reads aloud with the warm child in her lap. When the old man comes in they roast chestnuts on top of the *somba* until the others come. They listen in to the clandestine broadcasts on Deutsche Welle, which he calls Dolce Vita: these are banned by the Junta and the penalty for listening could be imprisonment, could be torture. He has enemies who would report him if they knew. 'The walls have ears,' he growls, the radio pressed to his grey head; he is hard of hearing himself. His wrinkles are so deep that they pull his hooded eyes into a slant and his lips into a perpetual smile around his cigarette.

On New Year's Eve Kyria Sophia announces that she is too tired even to dream of making the family *vassilopita*. 'Thank goodness my nephew's the baker,' she says. 'Angelo says he'll bring us one.'

Chloe fluffs up her hair. 'My mother always makes ours.'

'It's a lot of bother for nothing, if you ask me!' snaps the old woman. 'Who appreciates it? Look at all my *baklava* that none of you will eat!'

'Mamma, it's a wonderful *baklava*!' Bell hugs her.

'You say that. Eat some then.'

'And what about my tooth?'

'*Aman*, that woman!' Bell hears her whisper to Grigori. 'I could wring her neck,' meaning Chloe, or so Bell hopes.

Then to her further exasperation the old woman looks everywhere and can't find the *flouri*, the lucky coin that she hides in each year's *vassilopita*. Bell gives her the lucky sixpence that she brought from home, the one her mother used to put in the plum pudding.

After dinner, while Grigori and his father are still at the *kafeneion*, Angelo and his mother, Aunt Magdalini, arrive with the *vassilopita*. An elderly doll in long skirts, she falls asleep by the *somba*, steam rising from her woollen socks. Bell wakes her to eat a floury *kourabie*, and again to drink coffee. Angelo has ouzo. It blurs his sharp brown features, so like Grigori's, and makes him jocular.

'What can you see out there, Bella?' She turns from the window. 'Your man coming home?'

'The moon rising.'

'*Fengaraki mou lambro*,' recites Sophoula proudly.

'Good! What comes next?'

'*Fexe mou na perpato*!'

'I'll give you twenty drachmas,' Angelo drawls, 'if you can tell me what the moon's made of.'

'Rock?'

'You lost. It's a snowball, silly. It was thrown so high it can't ever come back to earth.'

Sophoula's jaw drops. 'Who threw it?'

'Guess.' He scratches the black wool on his head.

'A giant?'

'*I* think a bear. There's one up the mountain. There were tracks up there the other day. The hunters are out after her.'

'The poor bear!'

He peers out the window. 'That's not her in the schoolyard, is it? A huge white bear?'

'Silly.' She giggles. 'That's only the snow woman.'

'The snow woman, is it?' hisses Angelo. 'So that's who threw the moon up there!' and Sophoula screams in terror.

Kyria Sophia glares up over her glasses. 'God put the moon there.'

'Supposing she comes alive at night time? Supposing she comes and stares in all the windows while we're asleep?'

'No, no!' Sophoula clamps herself to Bell. 'Auntie, make him stop it!'

'Angelo, please?'

'Of course she doesn't!' cries Kyria Sophia. 'Aren't you ashamed to put an idea like that in the child's head?'

The door bursts open on Chloe red-faced and turbulent. 'You'll wake the baby! Can't I leave you alone here for one minute?' She drags the child by the arm into their room. There they both stay until Angelo and Aunt Magdalini have gone and Grigori and his father are home for the midnight ceremony of cutting the *vassilopita.* Then Chloe sidles sullenly in with her black hair stuck to cheeks still red with sleep or crying. 'Sophoula will have to miss it. She's asleep,' she mutters.

The old man, as head of the household, carefully divides the loaf. He sets aside a piece for the church and then for every member of the family, present and absent. The lucky sixpence turns up in Chloe's baby's piece, as it was bound to, and they all pretend surprise. Bell stuffs the sweet bread into the safe side of her mouth. Next New Year, she knows, wherever they all are by then, the *flouri* or the sixpence will turn up in her child's piece.

The New Year card games at the *kafeneion* will go on all night. Grigori walking back there is a shadow among other shadows that the moon makes in the snow.

On New Year's Day no bus comes to the village. The road in has been declared dangerous because the two narrow wooden bridges that it crosses are thick with frozen snow. No buses until further notice, bellows the village loudspeaker. People grumble. This happens every winter and every winter the government promises a new road. The mountain villages are worse off, of course; they'll be snowed in for weeks, not just a few days. Still, since no one has a car, everyone is trapped here while it lasts, except Angelo with his bread van.

Angelo goes on delivering his bread around the villages using chains, risking unmade tracks on hills and across fields to bypass the bridges. Grigori has been joining him lately for the sake of the ride and the company; now he goes on every trip in case Angelo strikes trouble and needs a hand. But Angelo won't take anyone else. 'It's not legal,' he tells everyone, 'and it's not safe.' He broke his rule twice last year, he says, and look what happened. The old man that he took to the district hospital in the back of the van survived; but the woman in labour? She lost her baby when the van hit a buried rock miles from anywhere and broke an axle. 'Never again, not for a million drachmas,' he says. 'Don't ask me.'

So that evening Bell and Chloe, sitting by the small *somba* in

Chloe's room with the work done and the children asleep, are thunderstruck when Kyria Sophia — who has made herself scarce all day — puts her head round the door to announce that by the way she and Grigori are off first thing in the morning to Thessaloniki to see her other grandchildren. Angelo is giving them a lift.

'She can't do that!' Chloe cries out, and follows her into the kitchen. 'You can't do that!' Bell hears.

'What? What can't I do?'

'What about *me*?'

'What about you?'

'I brought the children all this way to visit you and it wasn't easy on the bus and now you take it into your head to go off to Thessaloniki just like that and —'

'Look, when I need you to tell *me* what —'

'— And leave us stranded here!'

'What would you do there, anyway?' Kyria Sophia shouts. 'Your husband's away at sea for two more weeks!'

'I happen to live there. *Your* husband's here, remember? How will he feel if you go? This is your house, it's not mine. I could have gone to my own village for Christmas and New Year when they begged me to. *My* mother —'

'You're a married woman. It's your duty to come to us.'

'Duty? Oh, duty? What about your duty, then? Aren't *you* a married woman?'

'You dare to talk to me like —'

'Mamma, you have *no right* —'

'Get out of my kitchen, Chloe. You say one more word and I swear I'll hit you. I'll hit you!'

Chloe strides into the room where Bell and now Sophoula too are listening in horror; she slams the door behind her. Thuds and crashes of glass hit the wall between them.

'*Oriste mas! Oriste mas*!' come the shrieks. 'Now *she'll* tell *me* if I can go or not, will she? Twenty-five years old! *She'll* tell *me* what I can and can't do?'

'Mamma, what's Yiayia saying?' Sophoula whimpers.

'Never you mind. She's wicked. She doesn't love you or any of us.' Chloe bites her lips. 'Let the old bitch howl,' she mutters.

'She would have slapped my face in there! She knows she's in the wrong.'

The outside door slams and they jump. Footsteps splash past the shuttered window. The three of them creep to their beds. Bell is still wide awake when at last Grigori comes in and starts undressing in the dark.

'Grigori?'

'You're awake, are you? What happened here? Mamma's in a frenzy. She's beside herself.'

'She had a fight with Chloe.'

'And you?'

'Me? No! I stayed out of it.'

'You didn't try to stop her.'

'As soon try stopping a train! If Chloe wants a fight, I suppose that's her business, isn't it?'

'If she fights with her own mother it's her business. If she fights with mine it's my business and yours and all the family's.'

'So I should have stopped her.'

'You were there.' He has slid into bed without touching her. 'And your place in the family gives you the right.'

'Because I'm older than Chloe?'

'No. Because I'm the older brother and you're my wife.'

'Oh. I think Chloe was right to be upset. Is it fair of Mamma to go off and leave us like this?'

'One more day of Chloe, she says, and she'll go mad.'

'Chloe's hard to take. It's the children. They tire her out, you see.'

'Mamma does everything.'

'No, she doesn't. Chloe pulls her weight. I'm here all day and I know.'

'*You* know! You live in a world of your own! Chloe pulls her weight, does she? And what about you?'

'Tell me, what do the men do here while the women are pulling their weight? Play cards in the *kafeneion*? Stroll around Thessaloniki? If it comes to that, I'm the one who really needs to go. If I don't get to a dentist, I might lose this tooth.'

'Nice timing.'

'For every child a tooth, they say. It's to do with lack of calcium.'

She feels him shrug. 'Drink more milk.'

'I'm awash with milk already. Milk won't fill a rotten tooth, though, will it?'

'Well, bad luck,' he says wearily. 'It's stopped aching, hasn't it? There'll be a bus soon anyway, go on that. The fact is Angelo only has room for two and he needs me.'

'Well, let *me* come, then! Explain to Mamma!'

'*You* explain to Mamma.' He waits for her to think that over. 'Why all this fuss, I wonder?'

'You're going and leaving me here.'

'It's not as if it's for ever, is it?'

'Oh, that's it. I see. You want revenge.'

'You're happy to go off to Australia and leave me here.'

'Happy? I'm hoping you'll come.'

'It's more than hoping, I think. It's closer to force.'

They are lying rigidly side by side on their backs and neither moves. 'You'd be taking my child with you.'

She snorts. 'Not much choice at this stage!'

'No. There's not. So I want you to wait.'

'I can't, I told you. My smallpox vaccination.'

'I know that! I mean wait till after it's born.'

She opens her eyes wide in the darkness, so suddenly alarmed that she thinks he will hear the blood thumping through her. 'No. I'd be trapped here then,' she dares to say.

'Trapped!'

'Besides, the whole point is to be home with Mum and Dad before the birth. And then come back. If you want.'

'*Why?* Why does it matter *where* you are for the birth?'

'It just does,' she mutters. 'I'll feel safer there.'

'You're a stubborn, selfish, cold-blooded woman, Bell. You always have been and you always will be.'

'Always?'

'You want your own way in everything. Well, you're not getting it.'

Calming herself, she strokes the long arch of her belly, fingering the navel which has turned inside out and then the new feathery line of dark hair down to her groin. Once or twice a flutter inside her has made her think the baby has quickened, but it might have been only wind. Soon there'll be no mistaking it, her whole belly will hop, quake and ripple. She runs a finger along the lips that the head will burst through. 'What the fuck are you doing?' he mutters.

'Nothing.'

'You're breathing hard.'

'No, I'm not.' She forces herself to count as she breathes slowly in one two three, out one two three.

'I can hear you.'

'No.' She moves to the cold edge and listens motionless, breathing very slowly. He is silent. He has had his say.

She wakes at cockcrow when he gets dressed. She hears the van come, then go. She has stayed in bed through all the flurry of their departure, and so has Chloe. They open the kitchen door to find the *somba* burning with a bright flame, the milk boiled, the baby's napkins dried and folded, the day's eggs brought in from the barn and the table laid with bread and cheese and honey under a cloth.

'Oh, lovely!' cries Bell.

'You see?' Chloe snorts. 'She's sorry.'

'She must have been up all night!' Bell could hug the old woman.

'She was. I heard her.'

'She didn't have to do all this for us!'

Chloe stares and shrugs. 'Why shouldn't she?'

Chloe spends the morning washing and rinsing clothes, Bell taking Sophoula for a walk with the camera. The piles of soft snow were frozen overnight; so were the puddles and the clothes hung out on wires and bare brambles. There are no clouds this morning to block the sun or the faded half-moon, and everywhere they go water trickles and drips and glitters. As they come near the schoolyard Sophoula cringes, pulling at Bell.

'Carry me, Auntie Bella.'

'Why, for heaven's sake?'

'The snow woman's there.'

'It's only snow! It's only a big doll made of snow.'

'It's the wicked witch.' She huddles against Bell. 'She comes alive at night and stares in the window.'

'She does not! Look, she's melted. The poor old thing, she's vanished away. 'A heap of pitted snow sits under the pines.

'The moon's melting too, Auntie Bella!'

Sophoula keeps Bell company while she boils the potatoes and fries eggs for the four of them for lunch; Chloe is with the baby in the bedroom. But the child is grizzly and cross now and says she isn't hungry: she doesn't want potato or egg or bread or anything. 'Have a bit of banana?' Bell pleads. One banana is left. Chloe has made them last, feeding them to Sophoula inch by inch and folding the black soft skin over the stump. But no, Sophoula won't. 'I know!' On impulse Bell peels the last banana, flours it and fries it in the pan with the eggs for Sophoula. 'My darling, eat,' she says. The old man trudges in. Lunch is late again. 'Try it? For Auntie? Have some milk with it?'

'Tell a story.'

'Once upon a time,' she slips a spoonful of banana in, 'in a little cottage in the woods —'

Sophoula gags and splutters. The old man stares. 'Eat,' he growls. 'It's good for you.'

'No! Auntie, I don't like it!'

'All right, you don't have to eat it.' Blushing with shame, Bell gobbles the banana herself before Chloe comes.

'There was a banana,' Chloe says when they are peeling fruit into their empty plates later, and Bell tries to explain. Sophoula announces smugly that Auntie ate it all up. So as not to let it go to waste, Bell says, red-faced. 'You know she has them raw,' Chloe accuses. 'No more bananas!' Chloe kisses the child's hair. 'Wicked Auntie! Where will I get my darling some more?'

The old man, groping in his pockets, finds a bag of peanuts in their shells and presses it into Sophoula's hand.

'Is it *safe* to give her nuts?' Bell wonders aloud. 'They'll choke the child.'

In silence she rinses the dishes while Chloe shells peanuts by the *somba.* Abruptly Sophoula hoots and stiffens. Her back arches. Chloe bangs her, shakes her, shoves her head forward, and at last a great gush of sour curds and speckles pours out of her mouth all over her mother.

'Thank God!' Chloe hauls her jumper over her head. '*Aman*, my poor darling!' she moans, dabbing Sophoula's white face. 'They're bad, don't ever eat them! Wicked Pappou! She pushes the whole bag into the firebox and slams the iron door. The old man plods to his room. 'There,' she says, 'let them burn. He won't tell Her,' she mutters at Bell, who has brought a glass of water. 'Thanks. Don't you tell either, or we'll never hear the end of it.'

It is dark these days before the old man wakes to do the afternoon milking. The torch he takes into the barn lights up the ridge of snow at the door. His approach to the house is a clank and slop of saucepans past the window and a red point and trail of smoke, his cigarette. This time he dumps the saucepans caked with dung and hay inside on the kitchen floor and covers them. 'Who'll strain the milk?' he says loudly to no one. 'Will you boil it or use it for cheese?'

Sullen with sleep in their doorways, the women exchange looks. He is waiting. Chloe tweaks a curl off her baby's damp cheek and kisses it.

'Two daughters-in-law!' barks the old man and they all jump. The baby whines.

'Sssh.' Chloe frowns.

'Two daughters-in-law and I do it, do I? I strain the milk! I make the cheese! It's not enough to look after the cows and milk them. I can do the lot!'

The kitchen door slams. Chloe pulls Bell into her room, where they stand listening behind the door as he unlatches the window and clatters the saucepans. Then the front door clangs shut and his boots crunch away.

'He's thrown it out!' Bell mutters.

'*Two daughters-in-law and I do it, do I?*'

'Sssh. He'll hear!'

'Him, hear?'

'Sssh.'

They creep to the kitchen and turn the light on. In the square of yellow it throws outside, Bell can just make out the saucepans on end against the barn wall. The sun never comes there and the snow is still thick, with a pale puddle in it, a cat crouched at the edge, and all around a wide shawl of creamier snow. 'Oh! What a waste,' Bell sighs.

'Who cares?' Chloe looks in a jug. 'Look, there's all this left from this morning.'

'He's right, though.'

'It's Mamma's job!'

'But since she's not here.'

'I have two small children I have to do everything for.'

'Yes, I should have done it.'

'You're pregnant!'

'Only five months.' She sits down. 'I need a coffee.'

'No, come on, let's get out of this place before we go mad! We'll take the children to Aunt Magdalini's. Come on.'

At Aunt Magdalini's, the village secretary's wife tells them that the bridges have been declared safe for the time being and that a bus to Thessaloniki will run in the morning. Rowdy in her elation and relief and scorn of Kyria Sophia, who might just as well have waited, Chloe hauls Bell and Aunt Magdalini's three daughters-in-law along the crusted, muddy street to celebrate her release at the *kafeneion.*

Inside its misted windows men are smoking at small tables, watching the soccer on the grey television screen, the only one in the village, or looking on while Grigori's father plays the champion at *tavli.* The men all sit with their elbows on the chair-back and their hands flat on their chests, glancing sidelong from time to time at the table of women drinking orangeade. When Grigori's father wins the game he sends the *kafedji* over with another round, and the women raise the bottles smiling in a salute to him.

Chloe tells joke after joke uproariously and the other three are soon helpless with laughter. 'What are the men staring at?' she asks, gazing round. 'Oh, Bella, it's you!' She swoops and whispers, 'Bella, look how you're sitting.' Startled, Bell looks. 'Bella, your hands!' She has them open over each breast exactly as the men's are, but women never sit like that. She moves them to the slopes of her belly and Chloe giggles and nudges but Bell is too torpid in the smoky heat to be bothered. When the others are ready to go they wake her. The sky is all white stars, frost crackles as they tread. They link arms with Bell in the middle to keep her from a fall. Scarves of mist trail behind them. They drop her at home on the way to Aunt Magdalini's.

Alone in the cold bed, Bell is awake for the first unmistakable tremor of the quickening.

Before daybreak Bell is up to strain the milk — twice carefully through the gauze — and boil it in time for breakfast. Chloe's noisy desperation surges all around her. At last the kisses crushing or missing cheeks and she is away with the children, the old man carrying their bags to the bus, and Bell has the house to herself.

She scrubs the saucepans and puts clean water on to boil. The table is littered with crusts, plates and cups under the yellow bulb that only now she remembers to switch off; she tidies up. She has packing to do as well, letters and lists to write, but that had better wait until Grigori decides whether or not to go with her.

When her saucepans boil she carries them and another of cold water into the lavatory annexe that the old man spent all autumn building and is proud of. In case he tries to come in and wash, she pushes the heavy can of olive oil against the door. There is no light bulb in here yet, only an air vent and a candle stuck on a plate. She leans over to put a match to it and its flame lights her breasts: they are as she has never seen them, white and full, clasped with dark veins like tree roots. Shuddering in the cold, she stands in the *tapsi*, wets and soaps herself urgently, rinses the soap off. Flames go down her in runnels. She is rough all over with goosepimples except for her belly, domed in her hands, warm and smooth like some great egg.

All the water is swilling round her legs in the *tapsi* before she has got all the soap off but she rubs herself dry anyway, pulls on her clean clothes and with a grunt hoists up the *tapsi* and pours all the water into the lavatory bowl. It brims, then sinks gurgling down in froth and a gust of sweet cold rottenness from the sewer belches up in her face.

Still shuddering, she hugs herself close to the *somba,* propping the iron door open while she crams pine cones in. She sits with her clothes open. Perhaps the baby can see and hear the fire, she thinks. Did he see my hands in there, by the light of the candle? They must have made shadows on his red wall.

Here we are in a cold white house with icicles under the eaves and winter has hardly begun, but inside its walls are warm to the touch, full of firelight.

She has a couple of hours before she needs to start cooking lunch, and one full roll of fast film left: she will use them to take her last photographs. Bare interiors of sun and shade and firelight, in which as always she appears absent.

A DROP OF WATER

Tenzin who used to be Hans lives in a shack on the steep bank of a lake. His eyes open at dawn beside a long pane of glass facing the lake in which currents of mist slowly slide and lift over green-leaved grey trees along steep banks, the white skeletons of trees drowned when the river was dammed to form the lake, and the reflected images of all the trees. He is confronted every day with the suffering world at its most beautiful, the spectacle of it spread like a tanka painting at his feet to illustrate Delusion, Impermanence, the Wheel of Life.

Once, after meditating with half-open eyes which had seen nothing but his vision of the Buddha seated in front of him radiating a light which entered him in the form of white nectar, he saw the last sunlit web of mist curl away and a great white tree in the lake slant and subside like a ship into its white wake and vanish under the grey glass. Equanimity: the lake closing its silent lips, every leaf motionless.

He meditates mostly on death. He has a mala for counting mantras: at first sight, a necklace of beans or of carious teeth, white turning yellow and brown-edged, but the beads are of yak bone carved into the shapes of tiny skulls. He sees himself found lying dead here one day with the mala around the bones of his neck, one great skull and one hundred and eight bead ones and he smiles: for all the world like a gift-packed Easter egg.

After nightfall noisy possums and bush rats come round his shack. He spreads jam on bread and leaves it on the verandah, watching eager hands stretch out and snatch. Now and then he comes across a small animal lying dead in the leaves on a track, still plump and richly furred, resonant with blowflies, its mouth and eye-sockets and nostrils a red fretwork where ants are propping and tugging. Bush rats nest inside the walls. His room itself is ratproof. He will not risk the destruction of the Buddha. The rats fight and squeal at night. He wonders if a snake ever finds them and traps them in there. There are snakes around, tiger snakes mostly. He sees them less often than he hears them — a slither in the bracken, a wind fluctuating in the grass on a still day — and is always careful not to risk taking one by surprise. None, as far as he knows, has ever come into the shack, but it has dark corners during the day, and at night his candles and kerosene lamp, while they cast a golden warmth of light around, would not show up a snake.

The shack is in a hidden valley, part of an old overgrown farm being run at a loss — though there is hope for it — as a Dharma centre. Life all over the valley is ascetic, the buildings mostly ramshackle, the food eggs and goats' milk, rice and lentils and whatever else they can grow. There are power stations in the mountains, but the cost of a line to the valley puts it out of reach. Having no resident lama at the centre, they are glad of a monk, even a novice like Tenzin. The offer came at a time when he was looking for a solitary place to live. In payment for the shack all he needs to do is chop wood a few hours a week, and look after the gompa.

The gompa stands apart at the end of the paddock. The heart of the farm, formally consecrated by an abbot, it has six walls, one for each syllable of the mantra of Tibet, *Om Mani Padme Hum,* Hail the Jewel in the Lotus; one for each of the realms into which beings are reborn on the Wheel. Blond shingles cap it. Being under that roof is like being inside a pine cone. Twelve rafters, spokes of a wheel, radiate from one great black trunk in the centre; six have a silky gold curtain on a track. The floor is polished pine and when the altar candles are lit their long flickering shapes burn along it. One wall has a vast brick fireplace, beehive-shaped like ovens in old Europe. In another wall is the gompa's only source of daylight, a small, square stained-glass window with a white lotus set in a sea-blue diamond, the rest of the panes clear (as is Ether, Mind) except for a small lozenge of light at each point of the diamond: green for Water, yellow for Earth, red for Fire, blue for Air, for Sky. Hung on a red thread, a faceted pale blue bead glows and magnifies in the white corolla of the lotus. The window catches the rising sun. The jewel in the lotus flashes, and the colours and black lines of the panes spread along the floor like a lance pointing at the fire. Incense and candlesmoke waver past the altars in the waxy sunlight.

At that end of the paddock soft-leaved ginkgo trees have been planted inside wooden cages on which grey-green whiskers of lichen are growing long. A small white monument nearby, a stupa, enshrines the remains of a girl drowned years ago. At the hour when he wakes to go to the gompa, this dim shape among the cages is a child's white beanie and dress. It has a window in the front in which a brass Buddha sits in meditation, and under it are engraved on a tablet the name and dates and the Perfection of Wisdom mantra. *Om Gate Gate Paragate Parasamgate Bodhi Soha.* The window is lightly misted, as if the Buddha is breathing inside.

When Tenzin arrived at the beginning of the summer he mistrusted his intense consciousness of the place, accusing himself of letting his senses attach him to its beauty and harmony, when his whole endeavour was to go beyond the senses. Now he in his material body has become one with the place, eating the food grown there and returning his wastes to it, and it seems to him that his mind has made of it a living mandala to be used, like the mandalas and coloured Buddhas and Bodhisattvas in the tankas, as images reflected on the surface of the bubble of his emptiness.

The summer is over in the valley before he notices: the brambles in the bracken are hung with blackberries, the tall ragwort stems all over the farm have small flowers. With the first frosts the overloaded quince trees in the old orchard droop and let their woody fruits fall in the wet grass. Like almonds when they first formed, over the summer they have ripened and bulged out smooth and golden all over but for the traces of pale green vernix clinging to their hollows. Blackbirds stand pecking into them, their beaks the same butter yellow.

In autumn, he has been warned, his peace will be invaded. Before or soon after Easter the farm always holds a ten-day retreat. This year a young Tibetan lama is coming from California, one that Tenzin met in India — years ago when he was still Hans — soon after the monasteries in Tibet were destroyed and the boy fled across the Himalayas. They say his English is good now. Because families with babies are coming, Tenzin gives up his shack — wrenched, to his shame, by the loss of it — and takes his books and a few necessities to the small back room of the gompa.

The day before the retreat begins the young lama arrives and the farm people welcome him with tea in the guest quarters and take him to see the gompa. Tenzin pulls the heavy log door open. 'Tenzin?' the lama says while they are slipping their boots off. 'I know you. Have we met before?'

'Yes, in Dharamsala.' Tenzin feels his face turn hot with pleasure. 'Back in the sixties. You wouldn't remember.'

'Oh! Long time. Your name I don't remember.'

'Hans.'

'Hans, yes! Did you perhaps have very long hair?'

'That's right.' He runs a rueful hand over the grey-brown stubble on his skull.

'Like straw. You see? I remember.'

The others are standing waiting inside. The lama hurries in and does his prostrations.

All day cars come groaning up the hill. The paddock fills up with couples, children, dogs. Coloured tents balloon. Lay people, though dedicated to the Dharma, to his mind they are dabblers as he himself was for years, with barely one hesitant foot on the Path. They carry a long fallen trunk in from the bush — 'Heigh ho, heigh ho!' — and erect it on a rise with a rainbow windsock at the top. On the night before the retreat begins they pile dry logs and branches on a mound in the centre of the paddock and light a bonfire. They are burning their past errors. He remembers the bodies on the Burning Ghats at Varanasi; his eyes pick out skulls and exploding ribcages in these flames. Dogs and children run yelling with excitement as if around a fountain that might splash them, and into which they might just jump; sparks spurting out at them sizzle in the damp grass. A new moon rises, a pale line low in the blackness splashed with a milky flow of white sparks. The farm rooster crows; its call echoes, or one across the hill answers. The corpses of trees. Charred logs are still on fire when he wakes in the gompa room, and their shrunken shapes glow red into the next night and morning.

From now on Tenzin hardly ever has the gompa to himself. Hour-long meditations and discourses alternate from before sunrise to nine at night. The lama's throne has cushions of gold silk, and a red and orange canopy. On the tabletop at which he sits is a kerosene lamp, a frilled glass vase around the flame, balanced above a full glass belly like a goldfish bowl. His face in this light is brown as if finely carved of wood, his black hair sleek. Glasses hide his eyes. He leans holding up to the lamp his long white sheaves printed in Tibetan. His English is good now. Before each discourse he intones a mantra which everyone chants time and time again, some counting on malas. The discourses are on Wisdom and Compassion and Emptiness and Tenzin has heard it all ten thousand times. The lama takes frequent sips of water. The gompa is crowded with yawning, shifting strangers on cushions and matted sheepskins, rugs round their shoulders; coughs and farts echo. Children sleep, cry out and suck loudly at the breast. Emptiness, Tenzin thinks. Our bodies, our actions, our thoughts — scum on the water of the lake. Rust on the mirror. 'The mind is restless like a bird,' the young lama says. Dogs whinge among the shoes left at the doorstep.

Before dawn each day Tenzin fills the twenty-one offering bowls with water and empties them at night back into a white porcelain jug as large as a goose. He renews and lights the fire and the lamp, the incense and all the candles, red and blue. Then the brass Buddha burns like fire and interlocking waves of light move dimly over the skin of the marble one. On each side of the door is a brass bracket for a candle, lit before he beats the gong for the day's first meditation. Only a few retreaters come to this session. The lama never comes. Sometimes the fire burns down and a log falls in the grate; sparks spit, and the nearest sitter hastily pokes and settles it down.

By the second day, the occasional showers have turned into steady rain, the first good rain of the year. Each day the rain is colder, heavier, until on the fifth day there is ice in it and the tops and the long southern slopes of the mountains are white-sprinkled. Snow scattering over the lake, Tenzin thinks, but even if he had time to walk to his shack to see, he would keep away rather than risk an awkward meeting with the family living in it. Their tents flooded out, more and more campers grab their sleeping-bags and creep up into the farmhouse loft, where twenty mattresses are spread on the floor. No one has clean clothes. A sour steam rises from people warming themselves at the fire in the gompa or at the farmhouse. Rain soaks the gompa woodpile. At mealtimes children squabble and cry, their parents shout, everyone stumbles over everyone else in the gloom. Two kerosene lamps burn all day, and a third in the kitchen, but their rich light barely reaches through their glass. Angry mothers kneel by the fire to change napkins, spilling brown curds, and get soaked rushing round to the bath-house to wash their hands. 'Oh, yuk,' children yell, waving their soup spoons. Every morning someone treads in human turds half-splashed into the grass round the farmhouse.

The young lama keeps to his quarters, striding, sodden robes flapping at his ankles, over the paddock to the gompa for each session, returning straight after. He will stop for a chat if someone is hovering; he will give a child a push on the swing or a riddling answer for a riddle; anyone is free to make an appointment to ask him in private about a problem, and many do. Not Tenzin, who has no problem he could frame in words, and who senses in the lama a need for solitude as strong as his own. He wonders if the lama is feeling the cold; he himself loves winter weather.

On the sixth day at last the sky clears. From then on the days, cold at first, full of mist lifting in layers from the folds of the hills, are flooded by midmorning with hot, still sunlight. The thin gum trees are strung together high overhead with fine white webs that vanish when the sun reaches in. The tents are pitched again, lines of coloured washing slung between trees. Through the bush the lake glitters, its surface motionless. The gompa, a hive full of light and warmth while it rained, turns into a hood of darkness now. Fewer people turn up, always the same ones. Discourses and meditations, one follows the other: these days are a time out of time. Wheeling blowflies sing *Om*.

One early morning, as he pushes open the door from his room into the gompa — ashes and cloying incense, a red glint among sprawled logs in the grate — he sees the candles already burning and in their light a bald maroon figure sitting in meditation, a shadowy tree-tall monk. 'An emanation!' he exclaims aloud. Has his piety achieved such power already? The figure stands and its teeth gleam. A flesh and blood monk! He must have travelled up overnight. Tenzin is seized with sudden harsh convulsions, his face gapes, he chokes, he roars. His eyes ache and weep.

'What's the matter?'

'Laughing,' explains Tenzin. He wipes his eyes.

'I gathered that!' The strange face peering down at Tenzin is very young, smooth and blank.

And Tenzin, who has had to remind himself that this is laughing: 'I took you for an emanation!'

'So I am,' says the monk with a grin.

'So we all are. So is everything.' Tenzin has recovered himself.

'I'm Ben.'

'Tenzin.' He sees the other hide his surprise. 'Most people keep their old names, I know,' he says. 'I prefer not to.' They smile and the other sits and crosses his legs. Tenzin does his three prostrations and sits beside him. The candles burn straight and high. Their breathing disturbs the candles as little as a fish disturbs the lake.

To the huddled families this visitor must seem even more remote and cold than Tenzin does; they leave him alone with his thoughts. Tenzin is awed by such asceticism in one so young. Married life, jobs, children — he himself had all that, before he turned his back on it. He last saw his wife ten years ago, when his daughter was about fifteen, his boy seven or eight. They matter as little now as if they really were from a previous life (he won the battle against his disbelief in reincarnation, in karma, long ago); if they remember him, they have no idea where or who he is now. He is glad of the young monk's presence and of his remoteness. Enough, he thinks, that we, the two of us, serve as each other's witness and refuge.

Still, now that his shack is occupied, he has to have his one meal a day in the farmhouse, with everyone else except the lama, who eats in private. Tenzin takes his plate to a seat by the fire as night falls — the young monk nowhere to be seen — and observes the chattering retreaters, the children, the valley people there to cook and their friends there out of curiosity. Some of these come to the gompa from time to time to hear what the lama has to say. One, a thickset rowdy girl, has the same name as his daughter,

Julie. He wonders from time to time if it could be his daughter. A white-faced boy or man — he is thirty, Tenzin has overheard him say — always lies close to the fire with his bristled red head in his arms and almost in the ashes, looking up now and then to ask an abrupt question. He disconcerts most people, laughing in bursts, closing his shiny black eyes, resting his face gently against their legs like their own small children. But the valley girl has taken to giving him cigarettes and going for walks with him.

'What's your name? I mean your real name?' she asks Tenzin by the fire one night.

'What's "real"?' he says.

'Oh, you know what she means!' The boy rolls over on the hearth. 'Your given name. Originally.'

'Hans.'

'Hans? What nationality's that?'

'It could be several. I was born in Austria, though, and have been an Australian for over thirty years.'

'Must be older than you look, then.'

'I was a child when I came. Not that I'm saying I'm young! I have two grown-up children. The girl would be about your age.' He stifles the impulse to say her name. What if my daughter is this slovenly, bold, ignorant child-woman, he thinks, dismayed. Better not to know.

'So you're *married?*'

'Divorced. A long time ago.'

'My father divorced my mother,' the boy said, 'so he could marry someone else. Younger.'

'And then?'

'She went out of her mind.' He writhes and hisses. 'Isn't that a silly saying? Maybe I went out of my mind too so I could be where she was! Didn't work, though. Nothing does, does it?'

'*Are* you out of your mind?' Tenzin wishes he could be eating his rice and quinces in peace on the verandah of his shack, the lake flowing white through its drowned trees.

'Well, I want to kill my father.'

'That's quite common,' mumbles Tenzin with his mouth full.

'Oh, don't I know it! I could set up as a shrink myself by now. Oedipus Rex! Oedipus Adrian! Doctor Oedipus Adrian!' His milky face is convulsed. 'I came here,' he whispers when he gets his breath back, 'to find help. Will I ever get well?'

Tenzin is wrung with sorrow and shame. 'When the time comes,' is all he can say.

'What time?'

Tenzin opens helpless hands over the fire.

The last meditation on the last day of the retreat ends at noon. By sundown half of the people have packed and left. The tall young monk might have been an emanation, for all Tenzin has seen of him. The family in his shack is still there; Adrian as well, and the valley girl, Julie; and the young lama, who can relax for a couple of days now before his lecture tour. He asks if he can go riding so Julie catches the farm's one horse, a fat blond mare, and saddles her for him. Laughing with pleasure, he changes out of his long robes into jeans and a shirt to ride her round the paddock.

'Watch out for Ivory,' Julie yells. 'She'll throw you if she gets the chance.'

'Not me! No way I'm being a flying lama!' he shouts back. With a wave and a whoop he nudges her into a canter.

'His family are nomads,' Tenzin says beside Julie, and she swings round. 'They herd yaks and sheep in the Himalayas and the ponies they ride there are half-wild.'

'Oh, I know all that. He showed me the photos from his trip home.' Julie grins. 'Hey, you want to have a go too?'

'Me? No! I can't ride.'

'Flying monk!' the boy says.

'Ivory's fat.' Julie blows smoke in the air. 'She needs riding oftener.'

'That's the way to lose weight, eh, Julie? Want to try it?'

'Oh, ha ha.'

With the darkness a mist is slowly filling the valley. Children are being fed inside. Outside, everyone is watching the circling rider and the faint new moon coming up behind him over the hill. Someone has a flute and plays a shrill, rhythmic tune on it that falters away when the lamps and the fire are lit.

At the shack Tenzin has a tape of Tibetan priests chanting *Om.* He would like to be there again now, alone and free to play it out loud in the middle of the night, while the mist lay on the lake. When he does that, the great echo growls back from the mountains over the water to where he stands, also chanting back: *Aaa-uuu-mmmm.* Soon, he thinks.

That night no one comes to meditate. Long after the candles have been doused and the screen put in place in front of the red ashes in the grate and Tenzin has gone to bed, he hears the heavy outside door creak open. Someone has come to sit after all, he thinks, someone troubled enough to want to pass the night in meditation. But no, he hears giggles, then a thud, and footsteps come padding across the wooden floorboards. 'Where are you?' he hears the boy Adrian say, and he knows in a flash that it had to be Adrian. He goes to his door, which is not quite shut — he can just see the hollow hive of the firelit gompa — and is about to say softly, 'Here,' when he sees the girl. Wrapped in a sheepskin, she is crouched spreading a sleeping-bag in front of the fire.

'Over here,' she says.

'Where?'

'Here by the fire. Come *on*.'

Tenzin stops short, frozen with outrage, while she rummages among his logs stacked ready for the morning, stirring up the embers and making a wigwam out of sticks. 'Ah,' says the boy, holding his hands out bright red in the flames.

'Enjoy.'

'I don't think we should, Julie.'

'No one's going to know, are they? What they don't know won't hurt them.'

'What about the monk?'

'We'll get up real early,' she murmurs, 'before he gets here. How about I pull these curtains across?'

'No. All that gold silk.'

'They'd hold the warmth in.'

'No. It's enough as if I'm on stage without that.'

'On stage? Why? All the Buddhas watching, you mean? They've seen it all.' She is cross-legged as if in the lotus position, rubbing something in her lap with her fingers. Her face flares as she strikes a match. Smoke drifts from a cigarette.

'On stage as someone else. Oh, you got some more. Oh, thank

God.' He slumps over and lays his head in her lap for her to put the cigarette between his lips. Silence. Then: 'Oh, God, Why are you so nice to me?'

'I like you.'

'Nobody likes me. They put up with me. I hate people.'

'Not me.'

'Not you.'

Tenzin sniffs: he knows dope when he smells it. I should storm into the gompa and throw them out, he thinks. No, tell them more in sorrow than in anger that this is a consecrated place and they have to go. The thought of how the boy would reel away in anguish at such a rejection holds him back. Is this *compassion*, then? Does compassion compel him to let them be? Where does wisdom lie? Compassion is all very well, he thinks, but if I let this go on, what's to stop others? What's to stop an orgy in here? Where's the line to be drawn?

Not here, he decides. Much as I hate myself for letting the gompa be used as a bedroom, I'll hate myself more if I cast this boy out. So he stands transfixed while they undress murmuring to each other with dreamy slowness, and the smoke drifts over the firelight.

As he watches the girl languidly seats herself across the boy's spread thighs and puts her arms around him, her head so far back as he kisses her long throat that her hair covers the arm that is holding her to him. Tenzin feels the familiar delicious stiffening under his robes. What does this remind him of? Of making love himself, yes, but it's something more. Of course: they are the Buddha and his consort, they are the yabyum, like in the tanka: Wisdom and Compassion in eternal ecstatic embrace. They too are an emanation, he thinks, remembering the tall young monk. So are we all. Slow candlelight and firelight shift, red and gold, over them rocking and then lying down apart, both shiny with wet light, panting.

A muffled squeal makes him jump. 'What's that? A scorpion!' the girl says, crouching. One must have run out of the fireplace and been crawling shadowy on the glow of the polished floor towards them.

'Don't kill it!' The boy sits up.

'No, okay.' She takes some newspaper from the fireplace and pushes the heavy door open to flap it outside, her buttocks in the air, huge, quince-golden and downy. '0oh! Brrr!' she says, shutting it again, hugging her breasts and hurrying back to the fire and the boy. He is lying still, face-down. Humming, she runs her hands over his shoulders and back.

A fierce pang of envy takes the watcher by surprise. He has a vision of himself creeping forward into the firelight to put himself in her hands; of her with her silent head bent, hair falling dark around her face as she opens his maroon wrappings and touches his skin. Shocked, he steps back noiselessly. His room is blackness. He gropes to his bed and lies in it. A shameful lapse, he thinks. Of course, I'm only a novice. No, stop: no self-abnegation. That would be a further lapse, to make too much of it. No looking back. Equanimity. Restless as a bird. Take long slow breaths, observe the breath. Their rambling murmurs from the gompa lull him.

It is still dark when he wakes and with a smothered groan remembers the visitors. The girl said they would have gone before he could find them: he hopes so. But the gold curtains have been pulled across. Against the glow of the embers he can just make out a long quilted mound. Someone in it starts snuffling heavily. He takes a handful of shoulder, the girl's, and shakes it. 'Wake up,' he says.

'Mmmm?' She sits up abruptly. 'Oh! Oh shit! Hey!' She shakes the bag. 'Wake up, will you. Hey! He's here.'

'Please, get dressed straight away. I'll be in my room. That's my room there. I'd like to talk to you before you go.'

He turns on his heel. They seem to have no idea that he was awake and knew they were there during the night. Good. He can choose whether he tells them or not. Not, he decides. What would be the point? To tell would just be a further invasion of privacies, mine, theirs.

They are doing up buttons and folding the sleeping-bag when he comes back in.

'Sorry.' The girl looks up. 'With all these people everywhere, this was the only possible place.' She shrugs.

'Are you shocked? I bet you think we're a bit off.' The boy rocks and grins. 'Disgusting!'

'Most people prefer, don't they, to go somewhere no one can see or hear them.'

The girl looks at him with narrowed eyes. 'Well, it'd be bloody cold sleeping in the open, I'll tell you that,' the girl says.

'There's the main house.'

'With a dozen people in it, some of them kids.'

'I'm sorry,' he says, 'but the gompa is *not* a possible place, you should know that.'

'The retreat's over, isn't it? And look! We took our boots off.'

Ignoring an agonised bray of laughter from the boy, he pulls the gold curtains back. 'The gompa's a consecrated place,' he says.

'Okay. Sorry. I'm not into religion myself. Neither is Adrian, are you? But we didn't mean to *offend* anyone.'

'You haven't offended me.'

'Lucky you didn't catch us last night! Jesus, you gave me a fright. My heart's still banging.'

That reminds him. 'I won't be ringing the wake-up gong today,' he says, 'but I'm doing a guru puja. A few people have said they're coming.'

'Okay. Sure.' She shoulders the sleeping-bag. 'Well, let's dispose of the evidence. Come on, love.' She flings an arm round the boy's shoulders. 'Cup of tea time, hey.'

Three men come, prostrate three times and sit. They join in when Tenzin chants. The sun rises into the window and still they sit on. After a breakfast of porridge on the lawns, tents are packed, cars rattle down the sunlit hill to the highway. Tenzin stays in the gompa. He has cleaned out the ashes, stacked the cushions and is sweeping over the reflection of the window on the glossy wood when the door creaks. He swings round, expecting the lama, but the valley girl and Adrian are on the doorstep, and she is holding a shaggy bunch of yellow flowers and bronze-green fronds which she hands to him. He stares.

'Oh, you're still here,' she says. 'We picked these for the gompa. Got a vase?'

He gets an empty jar from his back room and puts it into the boy's hands. 'Wait,' he says, 'I'll get some water.' He fills the jar from the heavy white jug by the altar, and she crams the stems in.

'Ragwort and bracken. Aren't they noxious weeds?' giggles the boy.

'Yep. It's what there is here in the valley.' She leans sideways to brush wisps of grass and leaf out of her brown hair. 'Where'll I put them?'

'On the floor in front of the throne would be best,' he says.

'There. They look good, eh? Match the gold silk.'

'They look very good.'

'I love flowers. *Live* ones.' She fingers the dried chrysanthemums round the candlesticks. 'Do you *live* in that little room?'

'No, in a shack, usually. Down by the lake.'

'Oh, I know! The one those people with the twins had. They're going after lunch.'

So he will have his shack back today. In a few hours he will pack his kitbag and go home, put his books and pictures back in their places and himself with them, and it had slipped his mind until now.

'Good,' he says aloud. 'I can pack my things. Move out of here.'

'Oh, that's all right.'

'Yes,' he says, mystified.

'No, thanks all the same, there's no need. We're going today too.'

Tenzin gapes. The boy jerks his body in his blind, gulping laugh: 'Last night was our first and last night, father. How sad.'

'Call me Tenzin.'

'I like Hans better,' the girl says.

'It's no longer my name.'

'I don't get you. You're not Tibetan. All this dressing up and mumbo jumbo — it's all very well for the lama, he was born to it. But for you it's just an act.'

'Julie!'

'Oh, he doesn't mind. Do you?'

'I don't mind. But it's not an act.'

'That's what it looks like to me.'

'That's the problem, of course. How to tell the form from the substance. If it's worth trying to do.'

'All these golden Buddhas. Radiating nectar, isn't that it? I don't know. I reckon I'll stick to nature. This is beautiful, I suppose. The window, look — it's lovely.'

'Yes, I love the window.'

Her finger traces the lead lines of the lotus petals. 'There aren't any waterlilies in the lake.' He shakes his head. 'Where did they get the idea for this one?'

'They put it there *because* there aren't any in the lake. Idiot,' giggles the boy.

'Oh, you!' She grabs at him and roughly rumples his hair. He dodges, squealing.

'Are we awful? Don't you think we're awful? Look, he's smiling. We're his chance to practise forbearance. Bless you my children,' the boy prates with a papal gesture.

'If you call *be what you are* a blessing.'

'*Be what you are?* I don't call that a blessing, it's a curse. Oedipus! Be what you are!'

'I think the best —'

'Heard of the mummy's curse? That's nothing, folks. Meet the daddy of all curses!'

'I think the best way to see it,' Tenzin says, 'is as being neither a curse nor a blessing.'

'Oh well, if the *father* says it's neither, of course. But what if it's both? What then?'

'Not *being* a father —' Tenzin says.

'Hear that? He's *not* my father.'

'Come on, love. I want a swim in the lake.'

'In a minute. *Not being your father ...?*'

'Not being *a* father, I was going to say, please don't call me that.'

'You said you had two kids?' Julie says quickly.

'I mean "father" is for priests. Monks aren't called "father".'

The boy is gulping in front of them, struggling to speak. His face wrenches. At last he hurls one warding arm over the bristles of his head and stumbles out into the paddock.

'He's got this problem, you know?' the girl says.

'About his father?'

'Yes.'

'He's always on like that about Oedipus? He's on tranquillisers. I got him to go and talk to the lama and all *he* did was show us photos of *his* father. I reckon I've helped him a bit. Believe it or not.'

'I do. Why not?'

'I know you think I'm a slut.'

'The longer I live the closer I come to the knowledge,' he says, 'that everyone's everything.'

'What's the good of that, though, when everything's nothing?'

'Not *nothing*. Empty.'

'Same difference, I reckon. What's this for?' She fingers the faceted bead, making it flash in the sun. 'Look,' she says. 'Pretty though, isn't it? Like a big drop of water. Well. See you round, hey. Tenzin Hans.'

The boy is face-up in the long grass beyond the stupa, a tiny skull edged with brown. She goes and lies down with an arm across him. Tenzin, replacing the candle-stumps above the door, watches her pull the boy up and lead him through the far gate on to the lake path.

They thought I was offering my room for tonight, he thinks, and feels the rumbles and quivers inside him that had overcome him at his mistake with the young monk. In his heart he is suddenly roaring, rolling on the floor in the grip of pummelling laughter. He is still smiling irresistibly when he starts his walking meditation, pacing with careful slowness clockwise round and round the inside walls of the gompa, treading his wheel. The vision comes into his mind of the young lama cantering joyfully round the paddock in the twilight as the new moon rose and a flute sang. He walks on until his attention has alighted on everything — the flickering Buddhas, the empty paddock through the lotus window, the hollow grate — and so can draw itself in, oblivious. He knows that the task of the mind is to come to the realisation that everything is empty of inherent existence: not that it is nothing, but that it is empty. Nor can the mind come there picking its way through negation, through denial. No, it must take in emptiness whole. And he knows the mind has as much chance of taking in emptiness whole as a drop of water has, say, of taking in the lake …

'First,' he says aloud, 'let the mind be like a drop of water.'

Already with the thought of the lake his mind — the mind is restless — is flying off to the empty shack waiting for him above the mirrored silent trees. Firmly he brings it back inside, walking on.

AMONG PIGEONS

Our house was near the river, deep in the city, one of a row of narrow brick houses half-hidden under shaggy creepers. Green and red leaves and yellowish ones like singed wax-paper hung and fell, shone through its barred windows, flickered in spider webs. A long glass room tacked on at the back opened into a courtyard. We slept upstairs and woke to pigeons, clusters of them on the bricks and branches, wheezy bubbles bursting in their throats. When I fed them they came fanning up to my shoulder and pecked in my palm, one eye watching, ready to edge their plump warmth away. Some would let me stroke a crown, a mother-of-pearl neck. I remember their eyes: luminously red.

It was in the autumn of my seventh year that my father left this house to live by himself in a house in the Dandenongs, and the first I knew of it was when my mother took me to the park on the way home from school. Over my shoulder while she was pushing me on the swing she said that my father had gone away to another house to live and that I was to be a good boy for her from now on. In the watery green air the words hung shuttling, loud, soft, loud. Then we walked home over the sodden grass hand in hand. His things were all gone when we got home. They were at his new house, she said, but he was coming to see us this and every Saturday afternoon.

Auntie Jan (who was our friend, not a real aunt) was in by the fire with my sisters, and in the courtyard a man not my father sat slumped over a beer and some pizza. This was Uncle David, my mother said, and he had brought Auntie Jan's things over for her, now that she was going to live in our spare room and mind us when my mother went out.

'Who's Uncle David?'

'He's a friend of Jan's. He's an actor.'

'On TV!'

'Not yet,' she said. 'Hey, the pigeons know you're here, Luke.'

They were crowding round. As I went out with the bag of bread I saw one suddenly whir up and snatch out of the man's hand the red crust he was holding to his mouth. At the same moment a splodge squirted from its fantail on to the pizza tray. The man jumped, clenching his ginger brows until they joined with a ridge like his moustache, and this astonishment wrung a wild laugh out of me. But he had grabbed the bird, pushed it down flat to the table: staring at me, he lifted one arm and clawed his hand above the trapped grey head. At my shriek my mother ran out. 'Luke!' she said. 'What's going on?'

'Rub its nose in it,' he growled. 'Its beak. Teach it a lesson.'

'No! Mum!'

'Fair go.' She touched his shoulder. 'No teasing my boy. Come in by the fire?' Grinning, he lifted his hand; the pigeon fluttered off. I scattered the bread by the sandpit, my back to the warm glass room, my shoulders and shoes heavy with pigeons.

'Who was that man?' She was putting me to bed. The girls were asleep already.

'I told you, love. Auntie Jan's friend. He'll probably help her mind you sometimes.'

I hung round her neck. 'But I don't like him.'

'You will once you get to know him. He's just not used to relating to kids, that's all. He's had a hard life.'

'It thought he was *feeding* it. The pigeon.'

'I know.'

'But he *hurt* it!'

'Let go, now you're hurting me. He was teasing you.'

'Dad doesn't tease.'

'Everyone's different. Just give him a go, love. Please?'

'I want Dad to mind us,' I whined. No answer. 'Why can't Dad?'

My father came down on Saturdays to take us to the pictures or the park and on to McDonalds, though he would always refuse to come inside or round the back. I waited on the front porch every Saturday afternoon for his car to stop and the door to creak open. The sun was on the front of the house by then; leaves of ivy like flames crawled up knotted branches all over the walls and across windows as dark and clear as ponds. My mother kept an eye out from inside, rcady to send my sisters running out when he arrived. They were only three. Auntie Jan remarked to my mother that they didn't really miss him. I was six, though, nearly seven. I missed him.

He had a long drive from the hills to Melbourne and back. A Saturday came when he had to ring up to say he was stranded and couldn't make it. My mother shouted into the phone, slamming it down before I could speak to him. I sobbed on my bed, unable to believe it, while she and Auntie Jan had one of their fights about who had to stay home and mind us. Auntie Jan moved out soon after that and I was relieved, I think. I fought fiercely against being left with the babysitter who sometimes came and minded the twins: my mother only tried it that once. Another frosty Saturday afternoon she dressed us all and I stood on the porch for an hour watching the pigeons among leaves as red and shiny as apples, until she came running out and hugged me, lifted me up in her arms (and I was heavy): 'He mustn't be coming, love,' she said. 'Come in now and we'll watch TV.'

'Did he ring up?' She shook her head. 'No! I want Dad!' I struggled. I howled. The sky turned yellow before I would give in. My head was exploding. My bad headaches had started about that time and a hot bath helped to take the pain away; that night when she walked in to soap my back she found me doubled over with my face in the water and in her fear she made me sleep in her bed that night, the first of many. I was put on sedatives. The headaches lasted whole days. I cried and vomited. I fell asleep a lot in class and at playtimes I hid in the grounds of the tall church of which my school was part, a grey stone monument with ruffles of cold leaves alive with pigeons.

The Saturday outings lapsed after that and instead my father started picking me up once a fortnight and taking me for the night (my sisters were too small, he said) through silvery gum trees to his windy house on the hill. Bellbirds and crows woke us there. We walked through bracken to a creek spilling over a staircase of brown stones and paddled with numb feet, drank out of numb hands. He wanted to live there now, not with us. Why did he? Well, they fought too much, he and my mother: I'd understand one day. Yes, I said, but there was still us children. None of it made sense.

Now that it was harder for my mother to go out, she filled the house with visitors all weekend. Not many old friends came. These were new ones, strangers in coloured leather clothes, who if they had children came without them. They ignored us, crowding into the courtyard or on cushions around the fireplace, their flagons of black wine flickering, jazz on the stereo; we children played games and watched television upstairs. The babysitter was all right, I had conceded, as long as my mother was still in the house.

'I want Dad.' That was my refrain, and I did, but back home where we both belonged. Every weekend in the hills was lonelier and sadder than the last. Nevertheless, the first time he cancelled one I plunged into a panic. I was packed and waiting when the phone rang. 'At this short notice?' my mother shouted. 'I'm going out, that's why. He won't stay with the babysitter, he goes berserk. Jan *can't*. I told you she's *left*.' She stood and sobbed. So I knew: I was ready for her with sobs of my own. She held my fists and tried reasoning with me. She made phone calls. In the end, sighing, she cancelled the babysitter and read aloud on my bed until the girls fell asleep and my eyes were glazing. She kissed us all goodnight. I jammed my face in the pillow.

Some time later I woke up hot, wet, my head aching, and having struggled out of my pyjamas, lay there covered with nothing but the dusty still light of the lamp that stayed on all night by the bed. The girls inside their white plaits shone like china dolls. If my mother was asleep it would be naughty to wake her. But I heard her laugh and a splash, so I wandered along the passage. The bathroom door half-hid the steamy light. She was standing with her back to me with a glass of red wine in one hand and the soap in the other, and thunderstruck, I saw beyond her my father's head and knees above a dazzling swirl of water.

'On your knees and I'll do your back,' she said, the way she always used to, and he rose up and sent a surge of water out over the tiles, but instead of scolding she laughed. Only he wasn't Dad. This was some other man whose large soft thighs and genitals were striped with shadows, spotted with long plaques of light inside a loincloth of bubbles. He sipped her wine while her hands spread froth in spirals around his shoulders. Froth clung to her dress, her best, most beautiful dress, a grey silk that moved with the opal shimmer of a pigeon's neck. Suddenly she shoved his head under, so suddenly that the wave he made surfacing, snorting, splashed over her.

'Oh!' She tugged the darkening silk open.

'See. I told you to take it off,' he said, twisting her round so that she squealed, off balance, and taking a wet nipple in under his moustache — but the eyes under his wet ginger hair had caught my shadow's movement in the doorway.

'*Jesus.*' His lips spoke round her nipple as if round a cigarette and the hand holding the glass threw wine over her.

'Luke!'

'Thought you said they were in bed asleep,' he muttered.

'Mu-um?'

'What's wrong now?'

'Mum, my head's hurting.' But the wet hand that she laid on my brow I angrily shook off.

'Will I get you some medicine?'

'Yes.'

'Come on, then. Sorry.' Her hand dipped into the bath in passing. Downstairs in the bright kitchen she crushed a tablet and mixed it in a spoon with apricot jam. I leaned my head against the slimy wine-scarred belly of her dress, mumbling bitter chalk, thick sugary fruit. 'Who's that, Mum?' And gulped some water.

'Don't you know? He's been here before.'

'Mmm?' So had lots of people. 'Has he got a headache?'

'A headache?'

'When's he going home?'

'When he's out and dry. Where are your pyjamas?'

'I was too hot.'

After the stairs she gave me a piggyback to bed, bounced me on the lamplit sheets, covered me and kissed my head. 'Sleep tight,' she whispered.

I put my arms round her neck. All that autumn her eyes were

red and puffy, but that night they were more than usual. 'Stay here, Mum.'

'No, it's time you went to sleep.'

'Can I come into your bed?'

'Not tonight.'

'Why?'

'The pain'll be gone in a minute.'

'Why can't I, Mum?'

'Just do as you're told.'

'I want Dad!'

'Ssh. You'll wake the girls.'

'I want Dad.'

I should have been there with him in his windy house.

'I'm going to get angry with you in a minute.'

I wailed for a long time and she rocked me, whispering 'Ssh,' her hand on my forehead, until with a quick kiss she left. The twins, who had slept through it, sighed, slowly breathing. When I heard that the house was still I crept out again to the door of the spare room. Closed. My mother's. Closed. In there I thought I heard her rustling, but I was too dazed with tiredness and bafflement to be sure. I thought of opening the door, stumbling in and putting my head on the pillow beside my mother's, sobbing, waiting for her arm to go round me. 'Mum, my head's still sore,' I mouthed. But she might get angry with me. Why should she? She never had before. In the end tiredness and the cold sent me back to bed.

I woke to find the courtyard already full to the brim with sunlight like warm water in a pool edged with red weed, though above the walls a high wild wind was spinning the leaves off trees. The girls were dressed and in the sandpit. My mother had set the table outside. A few of the Sunday crowd were there already. A woman with orange hair popped open some champagne, half of which frothed over the bricks. There was a cheer. Scowling across the table waving his arms was the man who had been in the bath. 'Well, hullo.' He raised his ginger brows at me: 'Luke Sleepwalker, eh? Bugger you pigeons,' he muttered, and now I knew who he was.

Someone snickered. My mother was there with a basket of

toast and hot jam croissants wrapped in cloths. 'Watch out,' she said, 'the pigeons'll fight you for these.'

I tugged at her sleeve. 'Where's Auntie Jan?' It was a while since Auntie Jan had been to our place.

'Later, Luke, I'm busy now, love.'

I only wanted one croissant but I had to have toast first and not be greedy. Everyone had toast except the man, whose every move I was watching: he only had croissants. They were all talking at once. My mother washed the twins' hands under the tap, sat them up and fed them and let them down to play again. I shook out the cloths. The pigeons gathered round with soft sounds like sobs. When she poured the tea she put some in my milk, so that black leaves spun down to the bottom of my glass and settled. Someone played a jazz tape and a couple danced. The man, Uncle David, sang along. A flagon of claret passed round. A soft ache had taken root in my head. I dug and filled buckets with the twins, drifted in and watched television and out again.

A pair of hard hands suddenly grabbed me round the ribs. With a yell I fought free. He roared laughing in my face: Uncle David. I said, 'Don't.'

'Hop on my knee,' he said, and my mother nodded to me, giggling, red in the face. People were looking on. I hung my head and did as I was told.

'What a lump of lard. Hey. Give us a tickle, Luke,' he said, and I scrabbled my hands in his armpits while he sat there stiffly frowning. 'My turn,' he said and tickled hard. I yelled and gasped and rolled, clamped relentlessly. His beer glass fell with a splash on the cloth. 'Hell. Stronger than he looks. Now hit me. Go on, I know you want to. I want you to. I'm telling you to. Biff, come on. Biff! Ready set? Go!'

I writhed, throwing myself back against him as if he were still fiercely tickling me, laughing in deep, rhythmic, helpless barks. 'No,' I gargled. 'No! Mum!' I flung her a glance: she was standing his glass upright, her face set in its smile, her head on one side.

'Go easy, Dave.'

'Luke can take it.' His moustache rasped hot on my ear: 'I mean it. Hit me hard! Are you a sook or what? No? Go on, then!'

I reared up and twisted to face him, my eyes watering, my fists clenched at my throat until I dared to shoot the left one out hard against his cheek. 'Biff!' I yelled, and my eyebrows rose into my sweaty hair with the effort of holding my breath. With a roar his head whipped back. My mother spluttered, widening her smile. At that I burst into a high quaver of a laugh, so my mouth was wide open when his open palm, swung wide from the shoulder, smashed into it and sent me thumping on to the bricks at his feet like a sack of flour.

'Luke!' All I could see was dew-slopped ivy leaves on moss and bricks. The breath from her mouth was a chilly flow along my cheek and down my collar. Parts of my face stung hot and numb. She touched them and her fingers came away dipped in red. 'Why did you do that?' she shrieked up into the silence.

'Got a blood nose, has he? Give us a look.'

A boot stepped forward. I flung an arm over my head and screamed as the sleeve grazed my split lip.

'Why did you do that?'

'That's what life's like. You know it. I know it. I reckon the sooner he knows it, the better off he'll be.'

'Get out.' She turned. 'Get him out, for God's sake, someone. Don't you *ever* come near us again.' Tears were dripping down her chin. She sat and hoisted me into her arms. 'Open your mouth, love, come on,' she kept saying into my hair until with a whimper I did as I was told. Her finger running over my teeth wobbled some of them. My mouth tasted inky. A burning lump was sprouting in the wetness of the temple where I had landed. She wiped the tail of blood dangling out of my nose. 'Is it broken? Thank God.'

'That's what life's like,' I heard him protesting as they took him away. 'You all know that, don't you? I know that —'

'You're going to have a black eye by the look of it,' she said. 'Come on, love. A nice hot bath's what you want.'

'No!'

'Yes, it'll help to take the pain away. You know that.'

'No! I want Dad!'

'Come on, I'll carry you.'

'No,' I howled. 'No!' I pushed and kicked at her but she was holding me too tight and in her rough hair, ropy and wet against my throat, I could feel sobs bubbling and bursting, hers, my own.

VASE WITH RED FISHES

At the beginning of summer she invites him down to stay at the Point in the house in the tea trees in the lee of the dunes which she is minding for a friend. 'No strings,' she says. 'Come and paint,' and he accepts. He arrives late one night bringing wine and a framed print as a present.

'Oh, thank you!' She props it up. 'Oh, I love this.'

'I thought you would.'

' "Henri Matisse. *Vase with Red Fishes* (1914). Centre G. Pompidou" — I wonder where he painted it.'

They lie in bed together sipping the wine. 'They're moving,' she says. 'Look. The fish.'

'Fish-es.'

'They're negative of us. White inside, red out.'

'Mmm.' He wants to sleep now, not talk.

'If we immersed it in water they could swim off.'

'You dare!'

'Fresh water, of course. Salt water'd be fatal. They'd float away with their bellies up. Over the balcony and off into the flooded square where gulls would swoop and snatch them away.'

On a stand with long grey wooden legs is a jar of thick glass more than half-full of water in which are circling two goldfish, *poissons rouges,* red-gold fishes nosing at the fragmenting shrunken and swollen shadows they inhabit. They are in the window of a dark blue room, seen by someone inside leaning back to take in the wooden chair-back, the divan with square cushions, the pot or jug of pale green water in the foreground. A pillar stands behind the vase. Black iron is curled round the blue of the balcony. The sun strikes one side of the tall building across the square, its tower hooded with black tiles, slate tiles like the scales of a giant fish; its other side, four storeys of wall with narrow windows, is in shade. Next to it is a sunny facade with black loops for windows. The sky is thick blue. Carts crawl over the square. A terracotta flowerpot by the vase holds two long black stems out over the balcony, which has a top rail of darker red. There is an archway below. Serrations, a staircase. The perspective is fractured, refracted.

It is hot, a hot summer evening in the south of France. Out of sight beyond the frame two people are sitting in the dark interior, which, like the painting, is touched here and there with red and gold — the bright edge of a cushion, the strip of rosy light at the floor of the balcony. A man, a woman. They are translucent. They have just woken up from the siesta. Colours flow from and over them listening to watery piano pieces: Debussy, *Reflets dans l'eau, Paissons d'or, La cathédrale engloutie.* Or the record has stopped and sound — a bird, a shouted exchange of words, a cat's yowl — floats in on a silence.

He has been painting what he sees out the window. She sits watching the fishes. They are two ripples of blood that dissolve and twine, red whips in the light of the water. In the glass with them are fragments of the hot blue and wheat-brown square with its turret and loophole windows sunk in a slab of shade. Their eyes, hollow black, look out at her. As if in a concave mirror they see hollow towering walls and encased in them a red bubble, which is the woman. She has put on a long red robe today and the folds and shadows of its silk lap her whiteness, trailing loose from her arms and on the floor at her feet. The silk feels like cool water.

They have been lent this room by a friend. They will feed the goldfish and water the overgrown potplant; walk about on the green floor of the square under the stone walls in the cool of the evening. She knows a beach that disappears and reappears with the tides. The tide will be low, she says, at sunset, if he wants a swim. There is a long metal staircase down from the clifftop. When you walk on it in wooden-soled shoes each step chimes; when you run, the small sounds shimmer together like gamelan music. The whole staircase thrums. At its foot lie two flat round rocks with a fan of flutings on their backs like giant scallops. Black straps of kelp twist on the sand and in pools. The waves in the shallows turn cloudy gold as they rise, full of sand they have scooped up. He can watch the moon rise, she says, the lighthouses flicker under their green helmets, ships edge by into the open sea. And the other bay at low tide is all sweeps of pale water and sand, she says, tangles of kelp and red weed, and birds gathering, rowing boats tilted to one side half a mile out, lying on broken mirrors.

'Low tide. I love low tide,' he says.

'Yes, it's best at low tide,' she says, 'here at least.'

'How come?'

'When the tide's in, the water comes right up to the foot of the cliff and the sea wall. But there's sand at low tide.'

' "As I Ebbed with the Ocean of Life." '

'Yes. Fancy you remembering that. Well, I ebb and flow. I still love Walt Whitman. Remember you said we all do at one stage and then we grow out of him? "Your summer wind was warm enough, yet the air I breathed froze me ..." I'm less depressive than I once was.'

'Good.' And he squeezes her arm. 'That's good.'

'Why do you love low tide?'

'Seeing what's hidden at other times. I think that must be why. Revelations. It's like love, don't you think? Like revisiting a past love. Each time the sheets are pulled down and then up again. The water sheets.'

He goes out on the dunes to paint. Sandstone is honeycomb in the late summer sun, pitted with swallows' nests. All this beach is the same colour — sand, rock and rock pool. The small mouse-shrieks of swallows skim and soar. The wave-shaped, whale-shaped headland is dark in the spray of the western sky and into the eastern sky a ship surges from behind the lighthouse. Its surfaces flash. A point like a star pierces the masthead. Its smoke is a rope pulling it away. His footprints flatten the crisp arrow-heads left by gulls. At the high tide mark, along the hairline of the marram grass, he sees a soaked spaniel head, but it's a drowned penguin, its dense wings folded under and hanging out like earlobes. Here and there are splashes of jellyfish. Long pink and white eggs are cuttlefish bones, in nests of seaweed.

He sees her down on the beach lying in a dark gold rock pool and paints the small sandy prongs of her stretched out, weedy head back, hands open on the edge out of the water. He shows her that night. 'Want to have a look at this, Narcissus?' he says.

'Me, Narcissus? Oh, this is lovely! Monochrome, is it? Yes, it's tawny all over. Were you up on the cliff this afternoon? Why didn't you come in for a swim?'

Later, looking at the painting again, she says: 'You were looking in the pool, I was what you saw. That makes *you* Narcissus.'

'And you, now that *you're* looking in the pool.'

She smiles. 'Okay. But Narcissus can only be a man. Only a man can be Narcissus.'

'He was human, ultimately. Both male and female.'

'No, women don't see themselves in him. He doesn't reflect — echo! — anything in women.'

'Echo! He's the Self, it seems to me, in search of the Other, brought up against the impossibility of finding an Other. The boundary of the Self as a mirror. It's not a matter of male or female.'

'Men made Narcissus. In their own image, or so it seems to me. He's a male myth.'

'All right. But one that transcends gender.'

'I think it's an illusion,' she says, 'that human beings can transcend gender.'

He sighs.

A wooden table stands against one wall, with a second chair. In the next room is an iron bed under a window with shutters; the window faces the back and fills up with hot strips of light every day. So they lie back against the blue wall in the front room, sipping wine or tea and watching the coolly spiralling fiery fishes.

'The heart of the painting,' she says one day, 'is the red fishes.'

'*And* the vase. You could take out the fishes and still the vase would be the heart.'

'Not if the fishes weren't there it wouldn't.'

'You're wrong. The vase is enough. By itself.'

'I don't think so. I think that sunlit building would dominate. I wonder what it is? A town hall? A convent? Of course, we're used to it as it is. If we'd seen it first without the fishes or the vase ...'

One afternoon she comes in from the water, drives over to the fish-shop boat moored at the pier and buys two red fish for dinner. While he is still out sketching she uses his paints, on the glass not on the print, to hide the fishes; she fills the vase with the colours of the water. He sees as soon as he walks back in that they are missing and his face smiles, dark with annoyance at the mutilation of his gift.

'A glass of wine?'

'Thanks. And thanks for proving my point. I suppose next thing you'll go off and paint the vasc out.'

'Your point or mine? Look at that bright building. Anyway I have other things to do just now. Such as dinner. What if I bake the fishes?'

'Oh, right? Bake the fishes, eh?'

'They'd taste quite good baked. With herbs in their bellies, stuffed inside the slit, and a little garlic. Lemon juice. Or I could slash and oil them and grill them whole, if you like.'

'Oh, yes. Grill them whole. Great idea.'

'You don't believe me.'

'Have you got loaves as well?'

'See.' And she opens out the wet newspaper.

'Red fishes!'

They are not red-skinned; they have silvery white skin tightly covered in a mesh, a red net with a sheen, densest at the peak of the back. They have a rack of spines and their long-lipped jaws sag. Blood has leaked in and tarnished their ringed eyes; through the pupils you can see into the dim caves in their skulls. At the base of the great wound behind the head and in the skin along the edges of the slit belly is a bluish pearly gleam. Their fins are braided bright vermilion.

Grilled, they are toast-brown with black bubbles and their eyes are as white as the flakes of flesh and the skeleton.

Early next morning she has wiped her paint off the glass and the fishes are back. 'Look,' he says, ignoring that, pointing at his mug of tea. '*Poissons bleus.*' The white mugs have a blue fish painted on the outside.

'That room, that window, must be in France. The Côte d'Azur.'

'*Poissons d'azur.*' He turns the print over. 'We could probably find out. Let's see: 1914.'

'Fancy you remembering my birthday.'

'1914?'

'No! The Matisse. Wasn't it for my birthday?'

'Was it your birthday?' He raises his glass. 'I didn't remember. I just thought I'd give it to you. Happy birthday, eh? What does that make you?'

'Older.'

'Indeed. I meant your star sign.'

'You don't know?'

'Don't go in for star signs myself.'

'Pisces!'

'No!'

'You knew.'

'It was pure coincidence.'

'It was fate. Or maybe you were remembering my ring.'

Her ring has a stone, a clear bright bubble of amber with dark flecks, some close to the surface, some resting on the silver bottom. In the silver on each side of the stone a fish is embossed. The two full-lipped identical fishes face opposite ways, so that their movement is a clockwise circling of the stone. She slips her finger in.

'*Poissons d'argent*. Remember it now?'

'Never set eyes on it. Never seen you in a ring.'

'In a ring! No, well, I don't wear it all that often, it's too heavy.'

'Honey turned to stone.'

'I love amber as clear as this. Sometimes it's opaque like butterscotch. Like bottle glass from the sea. They harvest amber on seashores, don't they? On the Baltic, I think I've read. Imagine fossicking for shells and starfish and bottle glass, and suddenly — this! What's your star sign, anyway?'

'Gemini.'

'No!'

'Don't say they're compatible?'

'No idea. They ought to be, though, don't you think? They're both mirror images, twin fish and twin boys. Swan-begotten, water-born. They match.'

They ought to be. Are they? They have moments of felt intimacy, but different ones, that quickly seem to have been illusions. Their conversations leave them stranded in silence. Each is a past love of the other's. Each moves through the house, night and day. They sleep in the one bed. Alone and together they go to the beach, to the dunes. He is a painter. Of interiors? Exteriors? Where to draw the line? She serves as his model. The images of her in his mind are flat, all shape, so much like a sole or a flounder, those moon fish, that it would hardly surprise him if she had a dark underside to match the pearly belly he is labouring on. The shadow where the flesh sags down from the hipbone ... He peers, brush high. His astonishment on first entering her is repeated, though more mildly, every time. Suddenly she is three-dimensional, four, yes; suddenly he finds himself engulfed, embedded in a warm and clinging soft mass moving over and under. His eyes had given him no foreknowledge of this. He is as astonished as if he had fallen into the canvas into this embrace. He could go on pushing more and more of himself in with every thrust, all of himself until he is wholly contained in her. But as if in his thrusting he had touched some giant sting in the deepest part of her, he convulses. And burns, and is paralysed. Later, chilled, he opens his eyes to detach himself carefully. She is glistening and limp in her sleep, glazed, translucent, yes, a stranded jellyfish. The hair under her arms and between her legs has a damp, mossy savour which stays on his fingers long after she goes back to her pose and he to his easel. Soon he has forgotten what it is that his fingers smell of. The sea comes into his mind. Seaweed on the sand.

The dunes are growing fine long green hairs all over. Their skin shows through.

The waves are the loudest sound in the room at night. Twice she slides out from under the sheet in the dark, pulls a tracksuit on over the damp mass of her body and walks to the lighthouse. Both times the tide is out and so is the moon. Restless, she walks on the sand, peering in pools in the light of the tide-lanterns (green one time, red the other) and of the turning lantern in the great helmet, Orion at its ear. The first time the water is rough, a turbulence of green froth; the next time she slips off the tracksuit and lies in one of her pools, in red-glinting water in which she can only just see herself. Silently she comes back to the room, to the bed with the man in its centre, who sighs in his sleep and turns to lie along her back with a hand on her cold thigh.

One day while she is posing for him she says with a laugh, out of the blue, that when she is ready to go she will end her life here by wading out to sea with the tide. 'Better to end up as sweet strong meat for fishes,' she says. 'Not liquify in a grave or be dry ashes.'

'Or food for seagulls. Dogs loose on the beach. Feral cats. Rats.'

'Not if you study the tides.'

'What's the difference, if it comes to that?'

'Fish are clean. Clean beasts.'

'Hmm,' he says. And later, staring into space: 'Well, I can't help you with this one, love. Whatever it is. Sorry.'

She sits and watches the fishes. They are two ripples of blood that dissolve and twine, two red whips. In the glass with them are fragments of the hot blue and wheat-brown square with its turret and loophole windows sunk in a slab of shade. The fish gasp; their films of fin flutter in hot midair. Their bubbles mirror that other bubble, the vase. They see hollow walls towering and encased in them a red bubble, the woman. She has a long red silk robe on; cool folds and shadows lap her whiteness, trailing loose from her arms down over her feet. She is a shape, a pearl, a vase with handles. Shutting her eyes she sees red silk.

She reaches for a white mug of water on the table inside the room, outside the frame, but the water has gone, the darkness inside is only shadow, hot shadow. She has no recollection of drinking the water. Perhaps it evaporated in the intense heat over the space of the afternoon, or is such a thing not possible? She is not at the moment able to coerce her brain into remembering whether or not it is possible. If it is, though, wouldn't the water in the vase also have to be no more than shadow? With the fish lying in draggled lumps on the thick glass of the bottom like the hanks of red seaweed the high tide leaves on the sand?

A blue fish latticed with scales is curled high and dry on the outside of the mug. It has a barbed back and a twin-barbed fan-tail. A shadow of it shows on the inside, inscribed in the white porcelain.

So as not to have to get up for a drink of water, she tells herself she is lying in sea water, in a deep pool of blue rock. Tails of red weed drift rocking around her wrists and ankles. The under-surface of the water is a mirror in which the pool is held and in it she sees that the two red fishes are fluttering at the weedy edges, each following the other and each a mirror of the other. So without turning her head she knows that the vase on the sill is empty for the time being. Empty, that is, of fishes: almost full of empty water.

'Thirsty?' He stretches, finished for now. 'I'll make the tea.'

Sometimes he comes to the beach with her and they swim around each other among the honey-coloured rocks in shallow water flecked with weed on the surface or on the bottom. Wherever he has gone to paint he swims as well, diving in, pounding through the waves until he has cooled off. She lies in pools and dries off in the sun, moving up and down the beach with the tide. 'There was a Matisse book in the local library,' he says one evening at a restaurant with a mirror wall facing east over the sea. 'I had a look. It's got your picture in it, but called *Interior with Goldfish.*'

'Not "Vase"? Oh well, yes. Different translators. And the vase being *their* interior as well makes it a double interior. That's nice.'

'He did a whole series of goldfish paintings. There was a Moroccan one with *three* fishes, and a *Woman and Goldfish* with four, yellow ones. He *was* in Nice in 1914 but he came back for the winter to 19 quai St-Michel and there he painted —'

'He painted it in winter! Then he had summer in mind. *Quai* St-Michel, did you say? On the Seine? The arch is a bridge, then! No, it can't be, it's not wide enough. But then —'

'That would be the span that crosses to the Ile de la Cité?'

'Oh, then the arch is the Pont Neuf? No. It can't be.'

'Pont St-Michel?'

'If you could see your smirk! Okay, then, what's the building?'

'With the morning sun on it?'

'Afternoon —'

'Whatever. I don't know for sure. I wish I could remember. The

Palais de Justice is over there, and Notre Dame, but facing the other way. So it has to be the Louvre. Over on the Right Bank.'

'I see. You wish you could remember!'

'I can't, sad to say. I consulted the *Blue Guide*.'

'The *Blue Guide*!' She stares. 'You went to all that trouble!'

'No, no trouble, it was a pleasure. It brought Paris back.'

'I see. So, now we know. This was a certain room, in Paris, in the winter of 1914.'

'It was that roof, that steep slate roof that —'

'Oh, stop it, will you.'

'Sorry?'

'You and your *Blue Guide*?'

'*Guide bleu. Guide d'azur.* What's got into you?'

'Nothing. Nothing. Now if I ever go to Paris again I can make my little pilgrimage to the quai St-Michel, can't I? Armed with my *Guide bleu.* And go and see the original at the Pompidou Centre — right? Though the original, don't forget, is much larger and for all we know its colours are different. So often with prints ... *My* print is still a window in summer on the Côte d'Azur. It's an interior of the *mind* —'

'Complete with goldfish —'

'Where it's as hot as here. And close to the sea. That blue in the air: clearly it comes from water —'

'The Seine —'

'And its light is the same as in the vase. It's a submerged room.'

The window and the mirror brim over with water. There is a haze of pink over the town on the hill, its black roofs and trees and lighthouse, and over the water. From behind it rises a faint pink balloon turning small, cold and sharp in midair.

The tide is going out when they walk round under the cliff to the lighthouse on the point. Its red glass panels and the dark clear ones that face out to sea enclose a lantern like a gold beehive, a Chinese paper lantern staining the ceiling with a light no brighter than the lamps in houses. Dark shapes wander on the walls inside. The sky is red-gold. Beyond the last rim of the rock pools a ship low in the water carries its girdle of lights away, its red smokestack like a candle burning.

In the morning she wakes knowing before she sees that all his things are gone. She thinks there is no message left for her this time, no small painting to keep. But there is one of each. On the table he has scribbled on the back of an envelope:

A thick gloom fell through the sunshine and darken'd me,
Must I change my triumphant songs? said I to myself,
Must I indeed learn to chant the cold dirges of the baffled?
And sullen hymns of defeat?

Walt Whitman

And on the Matisse, one of the red fishes has been perfectly painted out. She peers: yes, perfectly. Not on the glass, on the print. The other fish hangs ringed in its glass and reflected there it glimpses fragments of red-gold, an apparition, a sufficient self.

BLACK GENOA

In Memoriam: Marjorie Barnard

She had moved to the south coast in autumn to live in the house she had bought, an old weatherboard with long windows and old trees growing against them into the sun. One room in particular, the one behind the apple tree next door, glowed all day as if there were a lamp on inside as the sunlight moved over one wooden wall after another. The walls smelled of incense and quivered in the light wind; on every sunny day a banner with large characters on thin gold silk went wavering in the wind on one wall or another with every flicker in the branches at the window. The characters changed in size and shape and so, no doubt, in meaning. She put her bed in here, and hung a dark blue paper blind with white gulls stencilled on it over the window, though as often as not, and without fail when there was a moon, she would roll it up again once her bedlamp was out. Day by day more apple leaves fell until, with all but the last few stained leaves gone, the whole beach showed at this window when she woke, opaque and still on some mornings, glittering on others, or turbulent, white and dark blue.

She wrote a poem about the window and on impulse sent it in a note to an old friend, Joanna, who lived in the city but had grown up on this coast. *There's a spare bed if you'd like to come down and stay,* she added. *All these clear cool beaches — that's if you can get away, of course.* (Joanna had three children still at school.)

WINDOW

Branches at this pane
turn it into gold lead light
in the winter sun,
they spread a large butterfly
on each wooden wall in turn,

who comes in early,
settling where she's supposed to,
poising each black-veined
wing at the right slant, only
twitching in a wind, or when

birds happen to perch
on a vein — all are black birds,
turned wingpatches. Black,
all the new buds. She'll be blocked
in, blocked out, when the leaves grow.

On full moon nights, two slabs of white marble stretched under her two bare front windows; and the bedroom window was white marble, watered with shadows. So quiet was the wash of the sea that she heard the engines of boats in the Rip. Sometimes in the middle of the night a loud rattling made her sit up and switch the bedlamp on. It was one of the mirrors quivering on the wooden wall, and as she watched the other mirror began and the double sound shuddered in the hollow space between that wall and the wall of the next room, then in the spaces of the rooms themselves until the whole house was throbbing aloud for as long as it took for the ship to edge through the passage.

She slept lightly in the house and had more dreams than usual. In one, her friend Joanna wrote back that she had cancer. Soon afterwards they met by chance and stood talking, so weighed down with intense sorrow that Joanna had to lie down in the grass. She was impossible to lift; trying only made the bones come away out of her like a baked fish's, leaving the flesh, a soft mess of pink and pearly white. Seeds, she thought, but they had a black speck and began to move. *Maggots,* she spoke aloud. Joanna said nothing more. Dumbfounded, she woke and was herself lying stretched out, but in the gold box that was her room on a bright morning.

In one of the half-read borrowed books that she was always leaving lying round she read an extract of a letter from Marina Tsvetaeva to Boris Pasternak, written in November 1922, an autumn letter, and copied it into her notebook:

My favourite form of communication is in the beyond: in dreams. To dream of someone. The second choice is correspondence. Letters are a form of communicating in the beyond, less perfect than dreams, but subject to the same laws.

Joanna rang in answer to her letter to say she would love to come down to the coast, but her father's cancer, which he had fought for months, had invaded his whole body. They had stopped the treatment and sent him home but now he was back in; now even he had to admit it was the end. She had promised to be with him while he died.

Every day she sat on the beach sketching ink edges around the pallor of it — a still scoop of water as thin as cold air, as if the bay were an empty shell, an earshell, pearl-pale and dotted inside with a line of rocks. When she was cold she walked on the sand. A wet spaniel's head she found one day at high tide in the hairline of the marram grass turned out to be a drowned penguin, its dense wings folded under and hanging out like earlobes. Between them were hunched feathers and there, poking out of them on a fine chain of bones, waggled a small skull black-beaked, formed of fretty translucent folds like bloodstained paper. Carefully she snapped the chain and carried the skull home wrapped in a sheet from her sketchbook to dry in the sun. Every day there was sun, though a wad of fog materialised over the dunes and the sea in the afternoons and often was still there until late next morning. Her house was not far from the lighthouse on the point; the horn's relentless hooting haunted her sleep. Waking, she read in the lamplight or wrote on scraps of paper.

He slips on a muddy embankment. Beside him something emits a foul sweetish stink: a corpse swelling against its buttoned jacket. It has the head of a pig, blue-tinged, dark red on the cheeks and snout. Dark red means that it is decomposing, he reasons, proud that he is still capable of reason. Everyone is starving. This is a terrain of war, covered with the dead and the dying. What did he last eat? The jacket of his uniform has a blue and dark red hand stuck in it. He climbs the embankment to a railway platform. He is busking, juggling balls, reciting a patter. He is waiting, as is his audience, to jump in front of a train when one finally comes. Meanwhile he juggles. A train hoots, hoots on a double note. It is out of sight, very far away still. The audience exclaims. A ball falls on to the gravel. Squatting to grope for it he sees in horror a thick brown pipe of flesh come out of him and prod the gravel. It disgorges a shiny brown mass. He sticks his finger in it to confirm what it is. He groans. His death has begun. He will miss the train.

After school on a dark afternoon. I am walking home from the railway station along the middle of the street between gutters full of puddles shining grey, rain-spattered, with silvery fish flickering to their surfaces. No cars come and none of the neighbours in front gardens has anything to say to me. The streetlamps blink on. I go to my room, collecting on the way clothes that my father has taken off and left on the floor. I hold his warm shirt and singlet to my face to breathe in the smell of him. My bed looks too small with him in it. There is sunlight in the flowers of the broom bush at the window; the rain has made them large and glossy as buttercups. His pyjamas are in a tangle on the floor. Scolding him, I pick them up. He turns his sleepy grey head towards my voice, his eyes still closed, waiting for a kiss. He has a grey fuzz all over his body except his knees and elbows, wherever the nap has worn off.

Joanna rang early one morning to say that her father had died quietly a few hours ago, as day broke. 'When I woke he must have just gone,' she said. 'That could have been what woke me, I suppose.' She had sat nine days and nights holding his hand. She thought she might come to the coast for a day or two, now it was over. The funeral was in four days.

Misty rain would cover the cemetery. Joanna would wear black. Old soldiers would hang around chatting, and old railwaymen, waiting for the priest to turn up; eventually a flustered substitute would arrive to mutter the words of the service while rain trickled from grey trees and a crowd of umbrellas. The box of darkness into which the coffin under its flowers would slip with a clunk was lined with creased, satiny clay.

Joanna came at nightfall and sat unable to eat, drinking wine, crying, smoking with a tremulous hand that made her strands of smoke ripple; folding, unfolding her hands between cigarettes. When the lighthouse uttered a blast she yelled. Startled awake, a dog howled in the distance. Again it blasted; again the dog howled. They opened the window a crack and fog came wisping in. No question of sleep now. They pulled on boots to walk to the lighthouse, which was invisible but for the twisting lantern until they were on the last steps; then like a rocket on the launching-pad it showed thick white. The shed that held the foghorn pumped out flurries of mist as bellow on bellow slammed through the cement platform, through their bodies. Just under the lantern, red tide-lamps burned. The tide was out of sight. From over the bay an echo came in thunderclaps.

They walked under blurred white lamps along the leggy pier, its piles gnawed black at the ankles, above black rocks and the sandy sea floor, a thong here and there of black kelp winding in a net of ripples. The lighthouse flared, boomed, flared, boomed. Under the last lamp they were met by a huge groan. The lighthouse spoke, and the echo. The whole wide shell of the bay, seafloor and lip of cliff, reverberated. They leaned on a wet rail as with a groan, a roar, a groan, a cluster of lights came into sight, slid past the end of the pier and disappeared. Chord on slow chord sounded over the water. Their two shadows stretched along the seabed as far as the whirlpool of light where the ship had been.

The metal staircase up the cliff face from the beach spilled rain with a jingling at each step. The moon was a high bright smudge. A secretive soft dripping of water from the black trees seemed to fall silent whenever they halted; frogs were creaking. They came back in after midnight with their lips salty and their hair dank and strung with bright drops, having taken the rhythmic booms so far into themselves that they were no longer hearing them, they were no more bother now than breath, than heartbeat and eyeblink. They were soaked with fog, booming. Once or more than once in the night they woke to the deep music of a ship passing the lighthouse. Loud crows in the pines woke them when it was well into the white midmorning, and still the horn was sounding.

They flung up their sleepy white arms and stretched and yawned and drank strong tea in the kitchen. 'Waking up in this house is like waking up on board ship,' Joanna said.

> *The lighthouse horn hooted all night on two notes* (she wrote in her notebook), *while I dreamed of a wrecked ship sunk into a pit so deep no light could wake it. Now in the sun the fog is lifting. The pines creak, heavy with crows.*
>
> *I opened the book by my bed and found this in a letter from Boris Pasternak to Marina Tsvetaeva in July 1926; a summer letter. 'The groan is the loudest*

> *note in the universe. I am inclined to believe that outer space is filled with* this *sound rather than with the music of the spheres ...'*

At lunchtime Joanna leaned forward into a hood of sunlight, offering a damp paper bag in her hands, which though large and strong always looked helpless; and they still had their slight tremor. The bag was full of large bruise-purple figs, with a red crack in each one, a glow of seeds.

'The last of them and look, I've squashed them. I put them in the fridge and forgot all about them,' Joanna said.

'They're only a bit squashed.' She kissed Joanna's cheek in thanks and washed them in a bowl under the tap, watching seeds move on the surface. 'I associate you with figs, you know, ripe figs, for some reason,' it occurred to her to say.

'Fat and seedy. That's me.'

'Opulent. Purple. Abundant, syrupy and gritty, bursting —'

'They called me the Purple Lady in at the hospital, did I tell you? I was a fixture. Everyone knew me. Here she is, they'd say. Hullo, Purple Lady.'

'You wore all purple clothes?'

'I wore this *one dress.* I've had it on day and night for the last two weeks. Do I stink? No? I didn't have the time to change. No, it wasn't even that — in my tiredness I just couldn't think what else to put on. Last night I could hardly walk. How did I get through it?'

'You'd put your mind to it.'

'The family are all against me. Anyone'd think all of us weren't Ray's kids too, only you were — that's what they're saying.'

'It's the strain.'

'You might as well go home, they said. It's not as if he can see or hear you, he doesn't even know you're there. But I promised Ray I'd be with him.'

'Yes. And you were.'

'He never came out of the coma.'

'Whether he knew or not, you had to stay. But I think he knew.'

'I'd lie in the armchair holding one hand then the other. I'd fail asleep and wake up holding a hand, listening to him breathe. Sometimes I dressed his wound. It was black and it stank. They stopped giving him water, did I tell you? For ten days we were wrenching his jaws apart and dabbing inside with swabs. He had a leather strap for a tongue.'

'He wouldn't have been in pain.' She tore a fig open and licked and bit flesh from its dark lining, pushing the bowl forward. Joanna grinned and shook her head, her eyes blurring again. 'Like a ripe fig, am I? I feel as dead as Ray inside.'

They went down the stairs and sat on the strip of sand in the sun while the tide washed in and the shadow of the cliff flowed down to meet it. Rocks raised their brown backs, scaled or furry, and dived under; weeds strayed in and out of channels. Joanna puffed at a cigarette. 'I keep thinking I have to get back,' she said. 'To the hospital.'

'I know.'

'I was worried every minute I wasn't in the ward. I *would* have to be asleep when he finally went, wouldn't I?'

'Don't you always have a feeling who's with you when you're asleep, though? In a coma, mightn't it be the same?'

'I keep feeling that the death happened to someone else, Ray's still in there waiting? There was always someone dying. I got to know them all, the visitors too, everyone talked in there. All of us smoking our heads off nonstop. Funny, isn't it?' She sighed smoke. 'I'm stopping when this is over.'

'Is the funeral still on Wednesday?'

'Wednesday. Yes, Wednesday at ten. Oh God. You do still want to come, then?'

'Of course.'

'Thanks. You never even got to meet him. I used to wish — oh.'

'No.' She poured more tea. 'I had a weird dream the other night. I keep having these dreams — horror dreams, some of them, and wish dreams. I try to note them down, if I wake up in time. There was this old man in a railway uniform —'

'That'd be Ray. I have frightful dreams all the time. I'm scared to go to sleep.'

When she had seen Joanna off she put the skull of the penguin, which smelled like salted cod now, on a sheet of paper beside a shell she had found and taken at first for another small emptysocketed skull, so many birds there were now washed up on the sand. A hole in the dome of it opened the shadowy ribbed chambers and the white column inside. Carefully with a fine pen she drew the skull and the shell and washed over them, blurring lines to make a watery shadow. I am an empty shell, she thought, not bothering with a signature; while my friend is brimful of feelings which spill out of her, words and tears, hour after hour.

Later, in the flickering room, beside a glass of daisies that had curled up like dead yellow spiders, she scrawled on the back of the sketch.

Dear Joanna,

I wish I could take on some of your pain. You would have taken your father's on, if pain could be shared. There you are overflowing with suffering, while I sit on the beach, empty, an empty shell.

My own father died fourteen years ago. We hadn't been close since I was small. We were shy and uncomfortable alone together.

I remember as a very small child waiting in the bathroom one winter afternoon so dark that we had the lights on waiting for him to come home from work and punish me for some misdeed that had angered my mother. I heard the front door and their cheerful voices suddenly lowered. When he stepped wearily into the bathroom I was cowering under the basin out of the greasy lamplight. He unhooked the razor strop from behind the door. I have no memory of the thrashing (of which we were never to speak), nor of the pain. I cried, I suppose. What I remember is disbelief: each of us staring at the other afterwards in a consternation of disbelief. He was never to thrash me again and that might have been in his face as well.

My father had a heart attack one winter afternoon twenty-five years later. He died suddenly, alone in the house.

The page was full. She wrote her initial, and sent it to her friend, whose white hands, folded, quivering, filled her mind. The day of the funeral she drove into the rain and back. Yellow day lilies opened and closed in the garden, a curled blue iris here and there, and daisies. In a low fork of the bare prunus tree she found a twig cup with nothing inside but dead leaves and broken shells, snail shells. Brown leaves lay all over the grass. Wandering into a garden shop one day — by then it was July, midwinter — she saw among plum and apple and apricot saplings a grafted stick with loose roots and no branches, as slender and dry as cane or dark bamboo. The label fluttered, a printed butterfly: a picture of figs, and a name a woman might have, she thought, in a book about the deep South: *Black Genoa.* She bought it and planted it where it would screen the sun at the kitchen window, digging a hole with four glistening brown walls, packing the roots in hard. As night fell the fog fell also; the lighthouse hooted. In the fuzz round the porch light, wet and cold, the skin of Black Genoa shone. Green hands would reach out of it one day, loose on spread arms; and a thousand pouches, purpling, oozing, burst apart.

LAND OF SNOWS

In the centre of the Land of Snows surrounded by great spires of rock stands a mountain with a crystal dome and two brilliant lakes at its base, Sun Lake to the east and Moon Lake to the west. Sun Lake is round, Moon Lake a crescent, its luminous surface slippery, evanescent. Sun Lake belongs to the deities of light, Moon Lake to the demons, any of whom might come striding towards you along the moon path cloaked in darkness, two stars for its eyes. While the lakes and the fish that live in them are sacred, you may drink the water and eat any fish that you happen to find cast by the storms or the tides on to their jewelled shores. This mountain is the centre of the world and also the point of intersection of this world with other worlds. Seven rings of oceans and seven rings of mountains of gold surround it. Beyond them are continents.

The seven offering-bowls of water on an altar are the size of a cupped hand. When the monk fills them in the morning with fresh water, the first bowl is frozen before the monk comes with his jug to fill the last one. A cup of tea there, buttered and salty, freezes solid before you can drink half of it. A glass of water becomes all glass as you watch; its surface, burning, clamps the skin of your fingers. There are ice stairs and walls and towers in the Land of Snows and ice tables that stand twenty and thirty feet high. There are gorges that you can pass only when the river is frozen over, and then only on foot, carrying all your belongings on your back because no pack-animal can be brought down the cliff-face or walk the river. Mirror-smooth, the surface is nonetheless flawed, choppy, woven with runnels, and through its glass, which is as fine as a shell in some places, you see that hollows of air are glowing in those split and shattered cloudy depths. The great surge of the river under the ice continues invisible, unheard. The journey might take you several days of walking and of pitching your tent on the bank at sunset by a river of frozen stars.

By way of preparing myself for a winter in the Land of Snows, yesterday I took out a glass left in a cupboard by the previous owner of this house. Small, with a rounded base, it once had a lid and a label: Vegemite, or Velveeta, or Lemon Butter. All the old houses in this land have a stock of these relics. I filled it to the brim with water and set it in the freezer, careful not to spill a drop. Not being crystal, if it should break in the ice, no matter.

High above a monastery, locked like a hermit in a sanctuary on top of a plateau with sheer walls, is a statue with the body of a man and several heads, the main one that of a bellowing horned bull black as Death. Glaring demon-heads surround the bull's head; the whole is crowned with a calm Buddha. Around its black neck hangs a rosary of human skulls and its penis is up ready to shoot seed. Yamantaka, the God of Death: death-in-generation, generation-in-death. The sanctuary is accessible only through a maze of passages cut in the rock walls.

Temples here have roofs of gold. Statues are seated in them, made of gold or copper, jewel-studded, or carved of rock, or yak butter. Some contain the embalmed remains of great lamas. As in the deserts at the centre of our own land, on certain days ceremonial sand images are made on temple floors: the monks funnel brightly dyed sands into their place in the pattern, which serves as a cage to hold whichever deity is to be invoked. Demons of terror and evil have been known to come uninvoked. These possess the Oracle, and speak through him. They can be appeased by offerings. The hermits live in frosty solitudes, having no dealings with temple or monastery. Each hermit is walled in a cell with one small opening in the rock through which his bowls are passed in and out. He also has offering cups for water and grain; sacred pictures and scrolls; sticks of incense; a little cabinet in which he keeps a demon prisoner.

Because the Hermit of Tsang, a revered ascetic lama, is known to remain all day and all night in the lotus position, the villagers, some of whom clamber up the rock wall and in strict silence leave tea and barley-meal at his cave mouth, believe that he never sleeps. He sleeps, as still as stone in the lotus position; having reached that point where sleeping and waking become one and the same.

Only the hollow earth speaks to him. A rumble, a sough, a screech: the sky speaks. Through the gap, curtained with ice, in his rock wall he looks out over plaits of mountains. The domed days and nights of the Land of Snows go by, made by his immense meditation into no more than beads of a rosary, black, turquoise, white, red, black, to be passed through indifferent hands.

One night of hard frost he knows himself to be come to a Pure Land, even the Happy Western Land of Amitabha, the Buddha of Boundless Light. There the grass in the meadow is as tall as he is, shafts of deep golden-green, spires of shadow. Globes of fire grow high above, held out in clusters among frets of fading leaf; some lie fallen and out of their skins seeps sour scarlet blood and golden seed. A few great fruits like yak-butter statues of the Buddhas hang higher still among black leaves each the size of a vulture and over them as the Hermit cranes his neck go great white and silver birds drifting like snow clouds, their wings spread flat; their sword-beaks and the talons clenched to their bellies and even their circled eyes are a brilliant coral-red. Crouched staring up into the sky long after the birds have vanished, he conceives out of nowhere the idea that these were birds from an ocean. Like all his devout fellow-lamas, the Hermit of Tsang believes in the existence of oceans, ring upon ring of oceans and gold mountains: indeed the sacred texts are adamant.

How can a rainbow span a sky that has not one drop of water in it?

Here the lamas train their disciples to run in a trance hour after hour over long distances and rough terrains without fatigue or injury. They are advised to fix their eyes on one point, such as a star. They are trained also by means of the breath to generate heat, so that sitting naked in the snow they will feel no pain and will be able to melt it under them. Wrapped in a wet robe, they will dry it on their bodies. A lama of high attainments is able to reduce his stature cubit by cubit; to incorporate himself in another; to send out into the world aspects of himself so real that all who encounter them are deceived; to create visions of the Bodhisattvas lasting many hours and visible to multitudes; to dematerialise himself. Such a lama is able to choose his successive incarnations, creating what is called here a rosary of births. After every death he enters the chosen mother at the instant of conception. His followers will seek and find the child he has become. If they fail, he will find his way to them. He will know them. He will claim his old drinking-cup, his rosary and bell. His old dog, mad with joy, will come capering around him.

Parts of the Land of Snows are so dry that, no matter how cold the weather, snow is rare; the nomads greet a snowfall there as a sign of milder weather. Coppery faces around the campfires split into white smiles; pilgrims sleep wrapped up in skins and snow; firelight gilds the white-crusted boughs of the last surviving trees.

I take out the glass of ice and look at it. Is that a crack in it? No. Upside down it is a rounded cone, a stupa. But I have made a mistake, taken the glass out too soon. A ball at its heart is loose water still, and out of it a storm of tiny bubbles springs and spirals, descending like flakes in a paperweight; faster, in a surge as I turn the glass this way and that. Then ice slips loose at the invisible edge of the glass, which has misted over; and wobbles, free. I put the glass back.

The Hermit of Tsang is standing under a tall tree with green fronds, hung with flowers like bells, like curls of butter folded t make bells. Nearby is another tall trunk with four leaves on two shrivelled and two splayed open and golden, which recognises as fig leaves. One is a hand held upright with the facing out, and the other is flat, dipping to the earth. This s tree is in the *mudra* of a Bodhisattva. Is this a sign? Can it he has entered a sacred image? *Om*. He opens his mov the mantra appropriate to this Bodhisattva. *Om. Om?* Panic grips him. He has no memory of the mantra! Is he losing, or has he lost — his mind? — his way? *Om.* He stands frozen in mute supplication.

For a stranger, one unable to speak the language, above all one of another race, it is far from easy to enter the Land of Snows and, leaving the roads and the yak-trails behind, penetrate alone to these crags. But once there you might find a cave or an abandoned hermitage with water flowing through it and a village nearby whose inhabitants, seeing that a hermit had come to live there as in the old times, would clamber up the rock face to leave warm tea and barley-meal at the mouth of the cave each day. How could the hermit have known of the old cave? people would say, their buttery faces alight in a smoke-filled yakskin tent or a stone room, the children half-asleep but listening, wrapped up naked in skins with the fur on the inside. It must be the same Hermit, the one who lived there before, in another incarnation.

Lamas who are weather-masters can hasten or hold off the rain.

There are lands where the people, the old original people, leave an offering of corn-meal by the mouth of a deer they have killed for food, to sustain it in its next world. Here in the Land of Snows if need obliges the people to slaughter an animal, thus breaking their Vows of Compassion, the herdsman asks its forgiveness, performing in exchange a ritual that will procure for it a rebirth in a higher form.

Manifold are the paths to Enlightenment. Most take the Graduated Path in the hope that in the course of maybe innumerable lifetimes they will arrive at it. The Short Path that leads to Enlightenment in one lifetime is fraught with perils. Those who choose this path and have a Guru who will guide them on it must confront the Lord of Death and all his cohorts. A monk on the hort Path to Enlightenment will, for example, be instructed to pend night after night alone where a corpse, cut in pieces, has en strewn among the rocks. There he must perform the ritual of self-sacrifice called *chöd*. The monk must dance, hitting a drum and blowing a leg-bone trumpet, and call up a female spirit to behead him. She feeds his body to the waiting demons, who munch his limbs, slit his belly and, jeering, lap his blood and his viscera as they flow out steaming. This is the Red Meal. Later the same night humbly he will call the spirits to the Black Meal, offering his ashes this time, mud-sodden, and his burnt bones. Some of the monks who persist in this practice lose their minds. Some die. For them the Short Path of *chöd* is a step over a precipice.

Here among these summits live sorcerers who have in their possession a dried human tongue whose magic power is theirs to wield. To obtain one the sorcerer must lie mouth to mouth on a corpse, embracing it while mentally reciting the magic words until it stirs, rises, struggles, makes wild leaps in the air. At the last, its icy tongue will jab into the sorcerer's mouth. Now he must bite it off, after which the corpse will fail inanimate again; or, failing, die in its arms.

This time when I take my glass out of the freezer there is no mistake. It is solid. Set upside down on the table it is a cone of ice whose resemblance to the Crystal Mountain of the Land of Snows is clear. The ice itself is far from clear; at its core is an opaque double shape, like a small egg in the act of breaking away from a larger egg below it; and this is afloat in flounces of ice like half-beaten eggwhite. Clouds, these eggs, in a sky of ice, clouds composed of a spray of millions of dense bubbles that glitter wherever the light reaches. And all around them waves, and jagged ridges, precipices, a cave mouth, a hermitage.

Immediately a crust of ice forms on the outside of the glass. I turn it right way up. Within minutes, bubbles are bursting on the surface. Soon the ice cone slips easily out of the glass and, set on the sill in the low sun, starts to dwindle. Gauzy like the wings of insects, the stilled waves catch alight; the bubbles caught in them are magnified; they are all pits and silvery flakes, like the surface of the moon.

* *

Its mountain gone, how small the glass has become!

In the Land of Snows, where the sky, the air, has the absolute dry clarity of a burning-glass, the mind which aspires to attain to that same clarity may, in the vast solitude and stillness, for a time achieve it. The consciousness expands to take in all it sees and knows and has ever known. All time becomes one. In sultry or damp weather it can happen, pilgrims have noted, that the disturbance of the air causes the past briefly to well up and flood into consciousness, only to subside as the air dries, keeping time with the air's drying.

Pack-animals are roped in single file on the bank of a lake at sunset, their bellies afire with the lights thrown up from it; they are a rosary of amber beads. A monastery straddling a low hill is wrapped night and day in a thick fog; the yak-butter lamps burn all day inside; nothing beyond or below the monastery is visible to the pilgrim, for whom it might be afloat in the sky, a ghostly ship with white prayer flags for sails for all he knows (while the monks, having no conception of ships, stay rooted in rock). High on the peaks, the sky is so sombre a blue that to the pilgrim's dazzled eyes the golden incandescent towers of rock that block the sun are themselves light and the source of light.

Winter is upon us. This is the season of rainbows. Gloom, cold, and lamps on inside the whole day long, the old wooden walls shrinking, swelling. Now the bluetongue seldom crawls out from under the house. Frogs are starting to appear, and mushrooms. Crickets creak in the long grass. High among darkening leaves two or three fat yellow quinces dangle, soon to be shed, along with the last bright tomatoes, the four leaves left yellowing on the fig tree. The long sun shafts of the morning and evening catch dead leaves quivering in midair, each folded around the legs of a spider like the shell around a hermit-crab. The red leaves have all fallen from the long-legged grapevine. Gulls soar high overhead without a cry. On some nights a wet white silence descends on this house and on these cliffs and salt marshes — on others the sky becomes black ice — but this never means snow, not here, only a vast fog. Bellowing like cattle, invisible ships on their way out to sea file past the rock shoals from beacon to beacon, lighthouse to lighthouse. The horn of the lighthouse on this shore booms all day, all night. Days, nights; you trace their passage only by the progress of the lamplight; room after room, a rosary of lights. If only snow would fall and this became for a time, for a winter, a land of cold glass and of silence, a land of slow motion then no motion then a slow thawing into new motion. But it will never snow here.

Lamas in those solitudes, those with occult powers, instead of shaving their heads grow their hair and braid it with lengths of black yak-wool. Around their necks they hang a coral-and-bone rosary of one hundred and eight beads, each one carved from a different human skull.

At a great rasp behind him, as of a mountain shifting, the Hermit swings round with a flutter of hems. He is a geranium petal in the sun, a red-golden gnat. Above him rears a glacier-shape of stone lapped with scales of lichen. A great cavern opens in it and lo! it is blue, a blue darkness, ethereal blue, the vault not of any Pure Land of Boundless Light but of his Land alone, of the beloved mountains, of the Land of Snows. A melting tongue of blue extends and thankfully the Hermit of Tsang lets himself be gathered in upon it.

It is so cold on these high passes that if you happen to stand weeping there, the tears will not trickle or splash at your feet as they would anywhere in our land, but will become in their descent beads of ice, hail ringing faintly, hitting the rock floor.

There are dry river beds in the Land of Snows filled with crazed sun and sand only, like those in the hot desert regions of our own land; and they too can suddenly flood, taking unawares the people and cattle camped in them. The glaciers of the Mountains of Snow are old, old, left behind from the last Ice Age of the world, great white lizards clamped in crystal on the crags and peaks. No new snow will arise to take their place. For they are melting.

Every day that the sun shines in their burning glass the surface melts, dilates into drips, and great tongues of water go rolling and ruffling along the ancient paths until at last, far below, as night falls, they come to the dry river beds. With nightfall on the peaks the crystal stiffens. Under the stars no more water flows. By daybreak the absence of the river will have reached down into the gorges and all day the sand will dry its colours in the bare sun. These are the ghosts of rivers, night-flowering vines of water, rivers of dream.

ACKNOWLEDGMENTS

The stories in this collection appear in the order in which they were written.

'Gerontissa', 'Ismini', 'Maria's Girl', 'Inheritance', 'Darling Odile', 'Melpo', 'Sally's Birthday', 'Woman in a Mirror', 'Milk', 'At the Airport', 'Snake', 'Summer on Ice', 'Pumpkin', 'The Captain's House' and 'Saint Kay's Day' were first published in *Milk* (1983); 'Marina', 'The Harem', 'Caffe Veneto', 'Matrimonial Home', 'Our Lady of the Beehives', 'A Man in the Laundrette', 'A Woman with Black Hair', 'Market Day', 'Home Time', 'White Friday', 'Pomegranates', 'Fire and Flood', 'A Girl on the Sand' and 'Place of Birth' were first published in *Home Time* (1985) and are reproduced by permission of Penguin Books Australia Ltd; 'A Drop of Water', 'Among Pigeons', 'Vase with Red Fishes', 'Black Genoa' and 'Land of Snows' were first published in *A Body of Water* (1990).

Five previously uncollected stories were first published in a slightly different form as follows: 'Baptism' in *Westerly*, 'The Albatross' and 'On the Pier' in *The Canberra Times*, 'Snowball' in *Cleo* and 'A Pawpaw All the Way from Queensland' in *Syme Community Newspapers*.

OTHER BOOKS BY
BEVERLEY FARMER

A Body of Water

Like a body of water fed by many sources yet remaining whole and self-contained, this imaginative new work draws on journal, notebook, story, poem, tribute and criticism to produce an astonishingly powerful, many-layered montage. It lays bare the creative process, the connection between text and context, experience and art. As well as presenting five beautifully developed and complete stories in the inimitable style of *Milk* and *Home Time*, Beverley Farmer also incorporates the day-by-day ideas and influences that sustain and nourish her creative output.

"Beverley Farmer is a Recording Angel of the intensities of the emotional life ... she shows how to look at the physical world with fresh eyes, and how things thus seen are refracted by the mind."

Don Anderson

"I know of no other Australia who has even tried to do what Farmer has given us, let alone succeeded in all the ways she has in *A Body of Water*."

David English, *Australian*

"... richly rewarding in its complex counterpoint of themes and voices, its marriage of mind and experience, text and context, its serene and literate prose."

Katharine England, *Advertiser*

"*A Body of Water* resonates with those essential qualities for which the work is to be treasured: depth, humility, sustenance."

Kate Veitch, *Sydney Morning Herald*

ISBN 0 7022 2283 6

The Seal Woman

In mourning for her husband lost at sea, Dagmar leaves the wintry landscapes of the north for the tranquillity of Swanhaven and a healing Australian summer. In the house where she spent her honeymoon twenty years before, she begins another journey, from grief to serenity and unexpected harvest.

Suffused with exquisite aquatic imagery that reflects the currents in Dagmar's own moods, *The Seal Woman* charts the interplay of myth and language between the hemispheres.

"*The Seal Woman* moves and challenges, informs, amuses and stimulates. Above all, it is rich in its imagining and in its human tenderness."

John Hanrahan

"Farmer's prose (plangently beautiful and vivid with seashore and season), like poetry, invites dipping into and savoring again and again."

Katherine England, *Adelaide Advertiser*

"An intense and hauntingly atmospheric novel."

Karen Lamb, *Age*

ISBN 0 7022 2522 3

The House in the Light

An Australian woman returns alone to the Greek village house where she was once welcomed as a bride. Unsure of her reception after a divorce and an absence of many years, she has come to mourn the old man and take part in the age-old traditions of Easter week.

Bell is still bound, by her son and by the past, to this family and its matriarch Kyria Sofia. The old warmth between the two women is quick to surface, but so too are old grievances and misunderstandings. Brimming with dreams and memories, the house reasserts its claim on Bell. As the family gathers for the Resurrection, she is fighting for her soul.

Readers of *Milk* and *Home Time* will welcome the return of Bell to the fold of rural Greece with all its riches and austerities of culture and tradition.

> *The House in the Light* is Farmer at her best ever.
>
> Robin Lucas, *Bulletin*

> Rich with intellectual curiosity, with a fascination with languages and their crystallisation of aspects of culture, and with brilliant, sharp-edged images.
>
> Katharine England, *Adelaide Advertiser*

> There is more to *The House in the Light* than most novels twice its length. It is rich in ruminations on life, spirituality, the family, the past, the future, loyalty, betrayal, and the quest for individual growth.
>
> Matthew Condon, *Weekend Australian*

> Beverley Farmer's new novel is tough, claustrophobic and honest.
>
> Susan Geason, *Sun-Herald*

ISBN 0 7022 2719 6